THE ENIGMA GIRL

Also by Henry Porter

Remembrance Day
A Spy's Life
Empire State
Brandenburg
The Dying Light
Firefly
White Hot Silence
The Old Enemy

THE ENIGMA GIRL

HENRY PORTER

QUERCUS

First published in Great Britain in 2024 by

QUERCUS

Quercus Editions Ltd
Carmelite House
50 Victoria Embankment
London EC4Y 0DZ

An Hachette UK company

The authorised representative in the EEA is Hachette Ireland,
8 Castlecourt Centre, Castleknock Road, Castleknock,
Dublin 15, D15 YF6A, Ireland

A CIP catalogue record for this book is available
from the British Library

HB ISBN 978 1 5294 0 334 3
TPB ISBN 978 1 5294 0 333 6
EB ISBN 978 1 5294 0 337 4

1

Typeset by CC Book Production
Printed and bound in Great Britain by Clays Ltd, Elcograf S.p.A

Papers used by Quercus are from well-managed forests and other responsible sources.

In memory of Dr Annie Elliot
and for Dr Toby Dean
and Dr Mike Elliot

PART ONE

CHAPTER 1

She lets the pickup freewheel to a stop in the driveway, unplugs her phone from the car's audio and gets out, noticing lumps of fen mud in the footwell. It's cold; ice particles glittered in the headlights on the way from the dig. She stands with the door open, deciding whether to check on her mother straight away or ferry the bags of shopping into the house. Her attention goes to the alignment of shrubs in the garden which, in silhouette, look very much like a man watching the house. It can't be anyone because she would have seen them when the headlights swept across the garden as she entered the driveway, but she peers into the thickening light anyway. A thrush starts up with a song that insists spring has arrived. There's no one out there. She shivers and glances at her phone, which has been pinging all the way with messages from the team at the Alder Fen dig, then looks up, catches herself lit by the phone in the wing mirror and rubs the mud from her chin and earlobe. She turns to the back of the Nissan smiling to herself. It's been a good day, spectacular, in fact. The tailgate comes down with a bang and the thrush drops from its perch and disappears into the dark with a few wing beats.

Six bags and the booze. She's tugged two on to the tailgate when she hears a car in the lane, turns and sees an Audi saloon coming into the driveway. It pulls up a few yards behind the pickup, blinding her with a full beam. She doesn't wait to see who's in the car, but reaches into the truck and seizes the mattock, a pickaxe with a curved adze blade, that lies alongside an old jute tool bag, and whirls round, feet planted wide, implement at the ready. She puts a hand up to the glare.

A large man clambers out of the passenger side and hitches his trousers.

'Steady, Slim,' he says. 'We're friends.' He calls to the driver who stands by his open door, 'You want to watch this one, Mr Salt. She'll take your bloody head off with that thing. Won't think twice about it.'

'What do you want?'

'Slim! It's me – Tudor Mills. Remember?' She does. Mills, the ex-Met detective, MI5 fixer, fetcher, tracker, and old-school sexist braggart. He'd pursued her through half a dozen countries in Europe, five months before. But Mills didn't find her; nobody did. She walked into the Madrid Embassy, showed her passport – the one issued to Alice Parsons, which, of course, she shouldn't have had with her on the plane when she was undercover as Sally Latimer – and was eventually repatriated on an easyJet flight.

'I need to see you properly. Turn off the lights and show yourselves.'

The driver leans into the car and dims them. 'See! Just me and Mr Salt here,' he says. 'You haven't met Peter before, because, like you, he's been working out of the office for a considerable length of time. Peter Salt – this is Alice "Slim" Parsons.'

Salt raises a hand. 'Alice or Slim? Which do you prefer?'

'Friends call her Slim,' says Mills. 'And we're friends, aren't we?'

'It's up to you,' she says.

'We're here to take you back.'

'No one said anything.'

'Try answering your phone, reading your text messages. The office hasn't heard a peep out of you for weeks. No response – nothing. You're meant to check in, right? So, that's why me and Mr Salt came all the way back in time to the flatlands where Friday night is fuck-your-sister-night. Now we've found you, we're going to escort you to *la capital* in one lovely piece. Every-one's been concerned for you, honey. I mean *everyone*.'

'I don't use that phone. It's been switched off for weeks. They said I wouldn't be needed until the end of April at the earliest, so I did what I was told, and kept my head down.' She stows the mattock, then rounds on Mills. 'And don't *honey* me, Tudor.'

She hoists two bags and holds them out. 'You can help bring these in – there are two each.' She'll leave the booze until later.

Mills closes his door and approaches. 'What's this – gardening tools?'

'Something like that.'

'Gardening leave doesn't mean you've got to be gardening. You know that, right?'

'I'm not serving my notice, and I'm not on gardening leave.'

'Yet,' says Mills.

'Yet nothing.' She hands him bags and points towards the entrance of the house where she's been living with her mother, Diana, over the winter. But there's something wrong. No lights in the house, no glow spreading from the kitchen across the lawn. She takes two bags and brushes past Mills. 'Bring the rest, will you.'

She drops the bags, goes round switching on lights, calling out. No sound except the click and rumble of the heating system firing up on the timer. Where's the dog? She goes to the study where her mother would normally have come to rest in a stupor with the lights, television, and electric fire all on. The radio, too, on occasions. Her chair is empty; no glass on the table beside the chair, no newspaper folded to the crossword, either. But the rest is as it should be – a book, open and face down, and on the round table by the window with a bunch of wilting daffodils are the photographs of Slim as a small girl, her maternal grand-parents, her dead father Toby, and brother Matthew, the one her mother sometimes holds or props beside her on the sofa. She checks the rooms that are never used on the left-hand side of the house and crosses the wide flagstone passage, which her mother grandly calls 'the hall', to pass through the kitchen and into a pantry where, over the winter, she has sometimes found her sitting with a cigarette in a grim stand-off with one of the litre bottles of gin that are killing her. Her jag, as she calls it. Slim sees a mouse in one of the traps and knows her mother wouldn't linger in the room with that. Where the hell is Loup, the nervous German shepherd–collie stray her mother homed during the first lockdown, and named so inappropriately? Maybe she's taken him for one of those turns round the village that end with a distress call announcing that neither Diana nor Loup can find their way home, or that one of them can't make it for reasons of stamina. But her coat, hat and gloves are piled on the settle and the bootees with sheepskin finish are beneath it, so she hasn't gone out.

Mills and Salt are hesitating just inside the front door with the bags. 'Come in for God's sake. My mother's missing. She may've collapsed somewhere. One of you check the garden, please. There's an outhouse at the back, garage, and greenhouse, too.' *Collapsed* is enough. No need to be explicit. Salt sets down the shopping bags and goes outside.

Mills comes in with no great urgency and drops the bags on the settle. 'Goes missing often, does she, your mother?'

'No, which is why I'm worried.'

'Maybe she's taken the car for a spin.'

'She doesn't drive.' Slim isn't going to explain. Her mother has been banned since an incident in Ely, about which she remains vague. Drink driving was the charge, but there had to be more to explain twenty months off the road. Resisting arrest, giving the officers an earful; that would be her.

'So, it's just the two of you, with your brother being away,' says Mills. 'And out here without a car, that's isolating for the lady.'

He'd read Slim's file before setting off to track her across Europe. In her interviews with the Security Service, she'd had to tell them that twelve years before, Matthew took his charm, talent and addictions to the north of England and, after minimal contact for about a year, was never heard from again. Just bloody vanished.

Mills is moving about looking at the pictures, making a sucking noise with his teeth. She puts a hand up to him. 'Can you stand still? Thank you.' And she dials her mother's phone. They wait, listening to the Victorian-era Steward's House, which is old enough and large enough to produce its own sighs and murmurs. The wind rattles a window at the back, and panels and floorboards in the passage leading to what was once a servant's room occasionally creak.

Their eyes meet. Yes, they both hear a vibration on the floorboards somewhere above them. Slim dashes up the stairs and reaches a short landing six stairs below the top floor where the staircase doubles back on itself. She can't see a damned thing and scrambles up the last stairs to hit the light switch at the top. Her mother is lying with her body dreadfully torqued, her legs wrenched one way; shoulders and head the other. Blood from a head wound has settled in a liverish puddle on the floorboards and runner carpet. Slim kneels beside her and takes her hand. 'Oh, Jesus, Mum! What've you done now? What happened to you?' She bends to puts her ear close to her mother's mouth. She waits, staring up at Mills who is crouching beside her. She thinks she hears, or rather feels a sigh. 'She's alive – just. Get an ambulance.' She dampens two fingers and places them in front of her mother's open mouth – she's sure she can feel breath. Mills waits until she nods then heads downstairs noisily. She shouts after him, 'The house is hard to find. You'll need to help them.'

Salt bounds up the stairs and kneels beside her. 'Can I help?'

'Do you know what to do?' she asks. 'I have some idea, but . . .'

He places two fingers at her mother's carotid artery. Slim shifts so she's not in the way of the light. She sees Salt's expression. 'What?'

'I think her heart's stopped.' He looks her over again. 'And I believe she's hurt her back in the fall, so I'll try this first.' He pinches her mother's nose with thumb and finger and holds her chin with the other hand, then applies his mouth to hers, but quickly recoils. 'Something's obstructing . . .'

Slim takes a tissue from her shirt pocket and wipes the inside of her mother's mouth. 'Sorry.' She knows it's sick.

He applies his mouth again and empties two breaths into her, waits a beat before giving her another two. He alters his position so he can pull her chin back a little more and open the airway better and inflates her lungs a dozen more times. He is worried and shaking his head. 'I need your permission to do chest compressions. If she has a back or neck injury, it might paralyse her. You understand that?'

'Do it. Do whatever you have to.'

'You'll need to support her head.' She works her way round to sit cross-legged and cups her mother's head in her hands. The hair is matted with blood. She feels a wound of two or three centimetres long, yet when she looks down at the face that's still so miraculously unmarked by drink, she sees no suffering. Diana Parsons wears an expression of pained amusement, as though someone has made a feeble joke. Salt lifts her shoulders with great care, arranges her legs and arms.

'You okay?' he asks.

'Yes, go for it.'

He rises above her to give maximum force to the hands crossed at the centre of her chest and starts pumping. The violence of this surprises Slim. She's worried that her mother's ribs will snap like kindling under this pounding but says nothing. After a minute or so, he puts his ear to her breast, shakes his head, then moves the heel of his left hand a few centimetres higher and continues. With the rhythm of the downward thrusts, he intones, 'I'm going to . . . bring you back, lady . . . if it's the last thing . . . I do.'

Slim catches herself processing her mother's death. Does she love her? Certainly not for the last few months during which she's been on ice, based here while an investigation establishes the facts of the incident on a jet over the Balkans and decides what to do with her. What her mother terms Slim's chilly, practical side now kicks in. A few weeks back, her mother muttered into her glass, 'They won't have to look far for the person to switch off my life support, will they, dear?' With a haste that surprises Slim, she now considers what would need to be done with the house, the bills, the bank accounts and the gardener who never showed up. And just for one hopeless second, she wondered how she was going to tell brother Matthew. That was fantasy, of course. Matthew was gone. Years of private investigators and her mother's own erratic searches had found nothing. He'd made sure he'd never be found – that, or he was dead. Diana believed he was alive; Slim doubted it. What hurt was how little of himself he had left them – some photographs, a wardrobe of clothes, drawings from his entry to the Royal College, an arresting self-portrait and, in the case of his younger sister, a nickname given to her during her chubby teen years. Matthew's absence weighed heavily. It was the reason her mother drank, surrendering completely to the bottle during lockdown. They both knew why she drank, but nothing was said. It never bloody was.

'Wait!' whispers Salt. His head is on her mother's bosom, eyes staring, holding his breath. He tears open more of the blouse and presses his ear to the skin just above her bra. 'I've got something. She's coming back.' After a few minutes more of CPR, yet without a cough, jolt, or the least dramatic sign of a return to life, Diana is breathing regularly and her pulse appears quite strong. Salt looks Slim in the eye for the first time. 'She's a tough one.'

For forty-five minutes they wait for the ambulance, packing the wound on her head with a hand towel and holding her, keeping her warm and comfortable. Her breathing grows shallow at one point. Salt does another round of mouth to mouth, and Slim sees her mother's whole chest rise with each blast from his lungs. Eventually she lets out a kind of wail that echoes in the stairwell. They look up. A blue light is flashing in the hall. Paramedics bring oxygen, a scoop stretcher, and a head and neck stabiliser to the landing and are followed by Mills, lugging three large medical kit bags and making a meal of it. A small man with pointed ears and a medical mask too big for his face kneels by her mother and starts addressing her as Diana. 'Or does she prefer Di?' he asks, at which her eyes flutter open and she whispers hopefully, 'Room service?'

'She's back,' Slim says and pats Salt's shoulder. 'Thanks, Mr Salt.'

'Peter,' he says. 'Call me Peter, Slim.'

CHAPTER 2

The pair of MI5 officers are a few seats from Slim in A&E, watching the accumulating wreckage of Friday night. She's heard nothing except that her mother is out of danger. With his legs spread and hands thrust into the pockets of a leather jacket worn awkwardly over his suit, Tudor Mills regards three large twenty-something girls in skirts and tops that are too tight for them, all hopelessly drunk and one sporting a black eye, bloody nose and split lip. 'You see this, and you know we're at the end of things in this country,' he says.

Salt's eyes revolve. He moves to the chair next to Slim. 'We'll go and eat. Be back in an hour or so. We'll crash at the Premier Inn if—'

'That won't be necessary. I can find my own way to London. I'll come as soon as I know she's going to be all right. Surely that's okay?'

'They're worried you'll scoot.'

'Why would I scoot, as you put it? I am literally the only person my mother has on this planet. And, besides, what would be the purpose of scooting when I have done nothing wrong,

I have nowhere to go, and I've been here all damn' winter, waiting for the summons in the spring?'

Mills gets up and joins them. 'We've come to bring you in — that why we're here.'

Slim sees nasal hair, enlarged pores, and a frazzle of broken veins high on his cheeks and nostrils. 'You came to check on me. Fine, you've done that and now you have my assurance that I'll come as soon as I can.' She'd seen the messages, of course, and noted the emails from one of the anonymous accounts run by the Office. She hadn't read them because no one had properly responded to her version of what happened at thirty thousand feet in Bulgarian airspace. Screw them, was her reaction. She wanted to make it work — she was good at her job, the best — but she needed them to agree there was no course of action other than the one she'd taken. The only thing she would accept now was official absolution, *te* bloody *absolvo* from the top. 'You saw the state my mother was in. If she remains out of danger, I'll get there by mid-morning and in my own vehicle. I'll phone in if there's a problem.'

She wasn't having Tudor Mills bringing her in like some teenage runaway, and there were things to do at home: pack for her mother's time in hospital, find someone to feed the dog — indeed, find the dog — and she needed to shower, wash her hair and consider what to wear, because she couldn't very well attend the weekend inquisition in her hi-vis waterproof and boots.

'We'll go get ourselves some sweet and sour and a Tiger beer,' Salt says, interposing himself between Slim and Mills. 'Then we'll see how things stand, eh?' Mills turns without a word and is walking away. 'See you in a jiff,' says Salt. 'Need us to bring you anything? Dim sum, prawn crackers, crispy spring rolls?'

'Thanks, no.'

Her phone is on charge by the vending machines. She goes over, unplugs it, pockets the charger, buys a water bottle and packet of Mini Cheddars at the machine, and gives pound coins to a young woman with dark rings under her eyes and a baby asleep in a pouch, who has no loose change. At the reception, she asks about her mother; someone will be along to talk to her as soon as bloods have been taken and results of an X-ray are in. She returns to her seat and opens her phone with one hand, popping Mini Cheddars with the other, and begins to scroll through the pictures from the dig with jerks of her thumb.

It all kicked off at the Alder Fen dig ten days before, on a raw Monday with an unceasing east wind. Her university friend and sometime lover, Dougal Hass, handed her the trowel, stepped back from Trench Three and announced he was going to the top of the bank for a whizz and a roll-up. The rest of the team were seventy metres away, at the point where a huge excavator, prospecting for brick clay, had disturbed some very old timber. As Dougal never tired of saying, the difference between timber and wood is that timber is worked, in this case by individuals with bronze axes living over three millennia ago. Trench Three seemed unpromising, though Dougal said his nose twitched three weeks before when they first sank their spades in the ground there, after the team's mini digger had cleared the top layers of soil. When Slim saw him gazing down from the bank that day, with his big man's grin, urging her, 'just to keep working at that spot, doll,' she knew he'd given her the find. She began with the trowel, then a stiff brush which could perfectly well handle the clay that had dried in the wind, and in just a few gentle sweeps began to expose a length of timber a metre long and seven centimetres wide. She'd put the brush down and worked with her hands to expose more of the object. It was long and impressively solid. She looked up. 'Come down here, you arse! Come and help me.'

'Got something, have you, Slim?'

'You knew it was here.'

'What?'

'Looks very much like a Bronze Age log boat.'

'A Bronze Age log boat, you say.' He slid down the bank and stood beside her on the scaffolding plank laid along the edge of the trench. 'You're absolutely spot on, Slim – a three-and-a-half-to four-thousand-year-old boat is what you've found, and it's much older than what they've got over there. Got to be! We're three metres down and they're at just two.' He knelt beside her and told her to budge up so he could lean into the trench. 'By God, Slim, get a load of that! The smell of the Bronze Age coming right up at you.' He laid one of his big paws on her shoulder. 'This may be very old indeed, older than we've seen before. Huge find, this! Mega!' She gave him a look that said, 'Don't indulge me, moron.' Yet she was ecstatic. They all were. They covered the boat with a tent that hummed and vibrated in the wind and set about revealing an eight-metre boat, which was broader by half a metre than had ever been seen before in Britain or Scandinavia. They photographed the axe marks where the boat had been shaped at the bow and stern and the incredibly smooth interior, in which two rocks were placed, an indication that, like all the other Fen boats, this one had been intentionally scuttled thousands of years before, probably as an offering.

As the light began to fade on a bitterly cold day, Dougal lined up the team of seven on the planks above the boat for a photograph to commemorate the find, for which Slim, of course, still resolutely declined to take credit. This was the only photograph of her at the dig and she'd made sure she was obscured by the large Scots dendrochronologist Ellie and Jimmy from King's Lynn. She'd taken the additional precaution of throwing her head back and clamping a hand over her mouth in hilarity, which wasn't hard because she was as elated as the others. Dougal attached it in an email to them all later that evening. The subject line read, 'Top Secret. Keep this to yourselves'.

She expands the image again, sees she's unrecognisable, and moves to the message group, feeling renewed irritation at having to leave the dig just as Dougal took the decision to lift the boat and get it into cold storage before the weekend. Everything has been recorded. The first clips show the boat cocooned in a cradle, lifting straps being fed under the hull, the crane taking the strain as the load is inched from the mud. In the last of this series, she sees Ellie gesticulating. Someone is shouting, then whoever is filming – presumably a student called Tustin, for he's sent the clip – lowers the phone and begins to rush forward while still filming. The clip ends. She sees there's an hour and a quarter interval between this message and the next. The boat is now about three metres from the mud. Dougal is kneeling, looking down and with one arm raised. Tustin moves to film what Dougal is gazing at. It is a skeleton that was aligned exactly with the hull of the boat. They believe it is a healthy young man of about seventeen years of age. His wrists are bound by honeysuckle twine. Over his genitals is placed an oblong item about the size of a table mat, made from woven rushes. Near the right shoulder lies a short bronze dagger – a dirk – complete with the remains of a deer-bone handle, but what held the team's attention was the man's skull, forced into profile by the weight of the boat, with the jaw opened wide in a scream, as water and silt from a long-dead river filled his lungs.

Slim expands the skull so that it fills the screen.

'My goodness, what've you got there?' This is an A&E nurse come to speak about her mother. Slim registers a Northern accent, then looks up to absorb the presence of an exceptionally pretty woman in her early forties and with a spiky blond crop and a broad smile. She is waggling a key card on her lanyard and looking down at Slim's phone without embarrassment.

'A murder scene from three thousand five hundred years ago, give or take,' Slim replies, lowering her phone. 'I'm an archaeologist. My mother?'

'Hi, yes, I'm Helen, A&E Nurse Manager, for my pains.' She bobs to her right with a slightly idiotic grin.

'I'm Slim.'

'Yes . . . your mum, Diana Parsons. Well, she's out of danger and conscious. Should we move to somewhere quieter?'

They go to a small room with four chairs and a table and a Covid information poster curling at the bottom. A fluorescent tube flickers, making the room pulsate. Nurse Helen turns it off, and they sit down either side of the table with the only light coming from the corridor. Slim imagines plenty of bad news being delivered in the stark circumstances of this room – the sons and daughters who weren't coming back from the night out in a souped-up hatchback, the heart attack victims beyond saving, the blokes who'd fallen off ladders with a paint brush or aerial in their hand and were incomprehensibly no longer. Yet Nurse Helen irradiates the space with pleasantness.

'Oh,' she says, 'should we be doing this with your companions?'

'No, they're just colleagues.'

Her eyes widen. 'Those men are archaeologists?'

'No, colleagues from my *work* work in London.'

She says a doctor will come to explain about her mother's injuries. 'Your mum – she drinks a little, would that be fair?' She holds Slim's eyes. 'You see, if it's more than a little, we should know because of the medication we may want to use tonight and we may also need to give her Diazepam, or something like it, to control craving. So, I wonder how—?'

'How much she drinks? Nearly a litre a day. That's a litre of gin not Pinot Grigio.' It wasn't her problem, yet it was mortifying to admit to that quantity, which is why she avoided online delivery and instead toured the area to buy from different supermarkets and liquor stores, eventually settling on a distant convenience store attached to a garage where they wanted no explanation and practically handed over the bottles from behind the counter after they've seen the pickup pull in. 'I should say that she never quite finishes the bottle before the end of the day.'

'A lot of drinking to watch.' She jots a note and adds, without looking up, 'If it makes you feel better my husband drinks – I mean *drinks* drinks – and my son is an absolutely useless pothead.'

'It's because she misses my brother who disappeared many years ago.' She'd say only that. Indeed, she now wonders why she mentioned Matthew at all, but knows the image of the skeleton at the dig has stirred dark thoughts: Matthew in a shallow grave; Matthew dead and cold and lost forever. It wasn't impossible because he was a drug user of wildly catholic tastes. Her mother has always half expected to find him in prison, which would have been a relief. Some of this must have shown in Slim's eyes. Nurse Helen gets up and comes round to her side. 'Would you like a hug on the NHS?' Without waiting for an answer, she bends, puts her head next to Slim's and grasps her shoulders. Slim smells shampoo and feels her warmth. She doesn't want to be doing this, yet in the several seconds of an awkward clinch, during which Slim's hands find all the wrong places, including Nurse Helen's left breast, the tension that's been with her for the last five months is released. Nurse Helen detaches herself and straightens, looking rather solemn, as though depositing this amount of energy in another human being is a serious and exhausting business. 'Better?'

'Yes, I guess. Very much so, thanks.'

'It's all part of the service. Now, I'll go find the doctor for you.'

No doctor is available. Nurse Helen returns and reads from her mother's medical notes, which, she says, explain why she will be in the Coronary Care Unit for at least the next thirty-six hours. Diana has a fractured skull, which appears to have been caused by a glancing blow, but the good news is that it's not serious, and the even better news is that her hip isn't broken. However, she has a cracked rib, possibly sustained during CPR. She lowers the notes. 'I wanted to make sure she hasn't any underlying serious conditions.'

'Not that I know of. Is something in particular worrying you?'

She gathers her notes. 'We'll see when the results from her blood tests come back. I'm sure she's absolutely fine. Shall I take you to her now?'

Her mother lies in a cubicle attached to every conceivable monitor, a stand of two IV drips and an oxygen supply that's stuck to her septum. She has a turban bandage, neck stabiliser and dressings where she grazed her arms and legs.

Slim touches her on the arm. 'Hi, Mum, it's me, Slim.'

Her mother's eyes flash open. 'Oh God. What're you doing here?'

'That's quite the welcome. I came to see how you're feeling.'

'Don't be ridiculous.'

Slim sits beside her.

'I can't see you there. Don't you realise I can't move? It's like wearing a helmet. I feel like I'm about to be launched into space. Ten . . . nine . . . eight . . . '

Slim leans forward and smiles her best. 'I wanted to see you before they take you away. It was a very near thing, you know. Lucky my colleagues were there.'

'Your diggers were crawling all over me! Oh God!'

'No, my other colleagues. They are why I need to go to London tomorrow.'

'Ah, your London colleagues! I thought you were in disgrace, but of course you don't tell me anything. Never do! I don't even know what your work is.' She flaps her hand on the coverlet and the oximeter flies off. Slim retrieves it and clips it to her mother's index finger before the machine can protest. 'I've told you what I do. I work in a boring part of the Civil Service that monitors asset purchases and money transfers.' That was true. But her mother has never asked whose assets, income and expenditure this unit monitored, or to wonder if this were not a rather pedestrian way of describing money laundering, which is exactly what Slim investigates.

'Well, I really don't know.' Again, the hand flap. She shuts her eyes then opens them wide. 'Where's my Loup?'

'Doesn't like trouble, Loup. Makes himself scarce. He'll turn up.'

'You mean he's run away.'

'No, probably hiding. Not the bravest is Loup.'

'He was terrified for his life, poor creature. You realise I was attacked in my own house. Beaten, cast down the stairs, trampled on by violent ruffians and left for dead.' Slim must consider this a possibility, but it seems unlikely that anyone looking for her would attack Diana and not wait for her return to Steward's House, and, besides, she has found her mother unconscious in different parts of the house before. From the way she's speaking now, Slim assumes several doubles are sloshing around her mother's system and it briefly saddens her that such a clever, handsome woman, who not long ago was running an international advertising company, has become the caricature of a tipsy Edwardian grande dame.

She lands both palms on her thighs in a simultaneous slap. 'I'd better be going. I'll pack some things for you.'

'Don't bother unless you bring you-know-what in a water bottle, with a squeeze of lemon.' She looks at Slim conspiratorially. 'A big water bottle.'

'I can't do that, Mum!'

'I've got to have something to get me through this.' Her eyes glitter with malevolence, but she's fading, and her voice has become a croak. 'If you can't do your mother this one tiny favour, please don't contemplate a visit.'

Slim gets up and lifts a hand. 'I'll be seeing you, Mum. I know you'll feel better soon.'

Nurse Helen intercepts her on the way to the exit and asks how it went. 'She's probably feeling a bit sorry for herself.'

'Yes,' says Slim, thinking that what she most hates about this situation is being simultaneously her mother's child, as well as her parent. 'I'm leaving for London tomorrow. Who do I call to find out about her?'

The nurse pats down her uniform and produces an aluminium card holder from which she slides a card with her mobile number on it. Slim reads the name Helen Meiklejohn.

'If you can't find the right person to ask, ring me and I'll get all the information or the person you need. Oh, by the way, the two gentlemen returned and were asking for you. We couldn't let them in here, I am afraid.' She frowns apologetically. 'Too much going on.'

'Is there another way out?' Slim asks.

Helen touches her on the arm and says, 'Of course! And do feel you can call me!'

Slim gives her a fleeting appraisal and wonders about Nurse Helen.

CHAPTER 3

A gated farm track lies beyond the entrance to Steward's House. It appears to lead to a dead end in woodland, about fifty yards from the lane, but it takes a sharp turn left before the trees, passes by a hedge of high laurel bushes at the rear of the house, and runs across flat fields to a ford then a settlement of a dozen houses named Hales. The gate is locked against fly tippers that have dumped refrigerators, mattresses, building rubble and, bizarrely for rural Cambridgeshire, a bidet. She puts numbers into the combination lock and eases the vehicle forward using the parking brake, then returns to the gate and leans on it, listening to the night. A squashed moon rises over the fields in the east; an owl screeches in the woods behind her. She's beginning to like it out here, and she can imagine making a life in the country if all goes wrong in London, which it probably will. But, Jesus, she'd need to find a place of her own.

She parks by a hedge of laurel, gets out and goes to the garden fence, grasps the top rail and, despite heavy boots, vaults it with ease. The lights are still on. She waits, watching for movement. It's not that she gives much credence to her mother's story about being attacked, but it triggered old habits of caution. After a few minutes of listening, she unhooks a key from behind a water butt, opens the back door and goes into the house and waits a minute or two more. Nothing moves.

Upstairs, she packs some things for her mother into a suitcase: underwear, nighties, make-up, perfume, dressing gown, shawl and cardigan, together with three books that are in the unread pile. She showers, and washes and trims a little of her hair, which she's still quite pleased with after a visit to Pierre of Ely. Pierre, who surprisingly turned out to be an actual Frenchman from Rouen, suggested frosted tips to her short dark hair, which she'd cut herself when on the run in September. The uneven length and the contrast of bleached blond and almost black hair Pierre declared to be the quintessence of rock chic. She moves closer to the shaving mirror so she can take out the ring from her pierced eyebrow. Her nails and cuticles are filthy from the dig, but she needs sleep more than clean nails, and she'll scrub them in the morning.

Four hours later, the sound of barking wakes her. Loup has found his way home and wants to be let in, but when she turns on the light something else takes her attention. The black-and-white photo of Matthew and her father Toby, from fourteen years ago, is jammed into the left-hand bottom corner of the antique vanity mirror on the dresser. The problem with this is it has been in the bottom right-hand corner of the mirror for as long as she can remember. She throws the duvet back and pads over to the dresser. The slightly curled left-hand edge of the photograph has been forced between the frame and the mirror glass, while the previously hidden right-hand edge is exposed and shows a faint tide mark left by the frame. It's an elementary mistake and she wonders if someone is intentionally letting her know that she's had a visitor. The rest of her room looks undisturbed, but a check of the wardrobe and drawers makes her wonder if they've been searched.

She's a person of few possessions and most of these are in London, stored in a room rented from her friend Bridie Hansen before she entered deep cover as Sally Latimer, in a tidy little Docklands flat. She hadn't been back there, of course. How could she? Sally Latimer is dead, believed to be one of several young tourists missing after a ferry boat disaster off Java before Christmas. There's nothing in her mother's house to connect her to Sally and, when she comes to think of it, very little that belongs to her or identifies her. Certainly, no photographs of herself; she's made sure of that. As to her several phones and laptop, they are in a computer bag, hidden beneath the passenger seat of the pickup and secured with hooked bungee cords.

When she goes to the landing and considers whether her mother did, in fact, hear someone moving upstairs and came up to investigate and was beaten, she finds herself with many doubts. The only conclusion is that her mother was poking about in her room and took the photograph from its normal place and forced it into the other side of the frame.

The barking has stopped. She peers from the large landing window to see if she can spot the dog, a lot of her hoping she doesn't. Dawn has come with a murky turquoise light and birds have started to sing. She sees nothing and turns but does a double take on the shape in the garden that her subconscious suggests is a figure watching the house, a slender man in a long overcoat standing stock still among the conifer shrubs like a piece of topiary or a statue, in roughly the same spot that she briefly imagined she saw a man the evening before. There's not enough light to see more, but she's sure someone's out there. She turns the lights off so she can't be seen and goes into her room to dress, quickly putting on tights, a grey skirt, a polo neck, lightweight fitted leather jacket and trainers. Spare underwear and shirt and a small sponge bag plus ankle boots for the interview in London are placed into a backpack, which she hooks over one shoulder. With her mother's case, she goes downstairs, grabs a banana, a tube of digestive biscuits and a litre of milk from one of the shopping bags and leaves the house by the back door. There's a hidden gap through the laurel bushes which she takes rather than climbing over the fence. Once on the track, she moves quickly towards the pickup, leaving it until the last moment to press the fob key. As she eases the driver's door open to heave the suitcase and backpack over to the passenger seat, she's aware of a rush of air beside her and the smell of wet dog as Loup leaps under her arm and lands in a heap on the passenger seat. The dog gulps, looks anxiously at her and works his chops. 'Right, you're going to London, halfwit dog,' she says, tipping the bag and backpack into the rear seats. She takes the track across the fields to the ford, where she pulls up with the front tyres in a few inches of water and gets out to use her birding binoculars to scan the garden. Sweeping back and forth several times, she sees nothing. She checks the house and moves the glasses over the garden again, still certain she didn't imagine the figure in the long overcoat. Just as she lowers them, she sees a vehicle enter the drive and pull up. The headlights are extinguished. No one gets out. Perhaps it's Mills and Salt come from the hospital. She doesn't wait to see and drives through the ford and up the bank on the other side and makes for the sleeping hamlet of Hales.

CHAPTER 4

She pulls into a motorway service area at 8.30 a.m., buys coffee and a Danish pastry, gets water for Loup and absently feeds him most of the pastry. She's received a text from Nurse Helen, now off duty, telling her that her mother has had a good night and the suitcase she dropped off has been delivered to the Coronary Care Unit, and a group message to the Alder Fen team from Dougal. They will be working through the weekend on the skeleton of a male, now named 'the Boatman'. She goes back to the pickup and dials a number that's answered on the first ring. An arrangement is made for 11.30 am at the Cotton Studios in West London, a large Edwardian red-brick building that contains training facilities, conference rooms, technical and cyber support, and a specialist gym that's used by all the intelligence services, including her section – JEF, the Joint Economic and Financial Intelligence Unit.

Driving south, she works on the transformation of herself to the cooperative, measured being she inhabited as Sally Latimer. Keep it pleasant, keep it cool and rational, she tells herself. She wants two things – her job, or similar work, and the acceptance that she could only have acted in the way she did on Guest's plane. Criticisms around the edges she will accept, but she must have some sort of vindication.

Tall gates open when she shows her face to the camera at the Cotton Studios. She enters a short tunnel and waits at a second pair of gates, which only open when the first close. She parks in a high-sided, cobbled courtyard where there are half a dozen cars. She checks herself in the mirror, gets out, allows Loup a run then returns him to the front seat with an open window. On the far side of the courtyard, she presses the door buzzer and the trim figure of Laurie Tapper, in black workout gear, appears. He runs the gym and trains undercover operatives in basic self-defence and roughs them up a little, so they are not totally surprised when it happens. He taught Slim some moves which she assured him she'd forget as soon as she left the building. She didn't. Like a language learned in childhood, they came back, and she found she was more than fluent. He takes her phones and accompanies her to the seventh floor. 'Keeping out of trouble?' he says on the way up and she grins and shakes her head. 'That's what I thought. Good luck to you, Slim.' He leaves her in a waiting area, where there's a water cooler and cinema posters left over from the time when this part of the building was occupied by a TV production company. The floor is being decorated but has a part-worn feel. Looking to the north, out of a window that shudders in the wind, she channels Sally Latimer and notes, not for the first time, that pretending to be someone else makes things easier. If you screw up, it's not your fault; it's the other one, the dummy speaking independently of the ventriloquist. This makes for an odd sort of confidence.

She is called in and told to take a seat on the far side of a long table by the only person she recognises, Corinna Stone, Head of HR and lately inter agency relations. She introduces Malcolm

Manners, a senior lawyer at the Home Office and MI5, who is suited with an open neck, the only concession to the weekend. There is Mark – just Mark – in pressed jeans, loafers and zip-neck sweater, and a woman identified as Rita who wears a Nike Tennis jacket, sports hair band and trainers. What is odd, and a worrying sign for Slim, is the absence of anyone she knows from the operational level. Her gently sardonic handler Tom Ballard isn't there, nor is anyone else from JEF, which makes her think that, yes, Tom might have been right when he said JEF was a gimmick flourished by politicians to ease fears about corruption of their party.

They all sit with their eyes on the report. Slim waits in silence. Still turning pages, Stone says eventually, 'A pity that you didn't respond to our messages over the last several weeks, and that we had to send people to find you.' Now, she looks up and gives Slim a bleak, official smile.

'I was told to remain out of the office at least until April, possibly May. I hadn't heard anything back in response to the account I wrote, so I assumed, wrongly I realise now, that I wasn't needed.'

'What gave you the idea that we would respond?'

'I inferred it from what Tom Ballard said on my return. Obviously, I was mistaken.'

Stone's eyes return to the report. 'You were.' Silence. She looks up and solicits assent from her side of the table. 'As two of us are unfamiliar with the events of October the thirteenth, I think it best to establish the main facts.

'Softball,' she starts in a dismal voice, 'was an operation to infiltrate Ivan Guest's organisation using the cover of Sally Latimer, an expert in property valuation, with a background in finance and PR. Your assignment was to acquire information on Guest's multiple money-laundering activities, which include large-scale investments in the capital's housing and commercial property markets, as well as enterprises such as hotels, pub chains, night clubs, garden centres, a golf course, gambling concerns and an aviation company. The primary means of gaining this knowledge was the introduction of spyware in as many devices as you could access. You were in this role for a period of . . . ?'

'Just over twenty months.'

'And there were some three months of preparation.'

'Nearer six in all, but Tom Ballard can tell you exactly.'

'And that was spent . . . ?'

'Building a backstory for the cover: parents, school, college, work, a social media presence. I had to learn about property values as well as finance and PR. We needed to establish my cover in a Docklands apartment, at a squash club and gym, provide her with interests and friends, some of whom were our people, and independently to create a social circle for Sally. I needed to get up to speed on the tech. We were using the new programme called Thalli, which was developed in the UK and derives its name from the slow-acting poison thallium. It takes its time and is excellent at camouflaging its presence, unlike Pegasus which is readily detectable. Thalli can put itself to sleep and hide anywhere in a system and stay there for as long as it needs. Hagfish – that's Guest's code name – was always hyper vigilant. All his devices were regularly checked, and homes, planes, yachts and offices were swept. We moved very, very cautiously.' Now she had their respect, or at least their attention, and damned right too. The operation was exemplary.

'Why Hagfish?' asks Rita, slipping off the tennis jacket and letting it fall neatly over the back of her chair.

'A random name,' Slim replies. It wasn't. In their first session, Tom had said, 'Ivan Guest's mother was either Georgian or Armenian – we aren't sure – and we have no idea who his father was. He and his older brother were brought up from an early age as the sons of Charles Guest, and we should regard him as eighty-per-cent British, a product of our society.' Slim fell for it and asked about the remaining twenty per cent. 'Hagfish,' he replied, 'the most disgusting animal on the planet. Look it up.' Which she did right away and found a flat eel, with no spine but a skull and drill-bit mouth, which corkscrews into the bodies of dead and dying fish, and when attacked, produces quantities of slime that congeal in the gills of its predator. 'He's good at the slime part,' said Tom.

Stone continues, 'You took a job in one of his offices and you were spotted by Guest, which is what you were working for, and offered promotion to . . . ?'

'His personal assistant. Yes, we knew that he watched his offices on the CCTV system and that his senior staff *talent* spotted for him. We'd researched his type, what he liked in women and women's clothes. He was brand obsessed – Kiton, Bottega Veneta, Gucci, Ferragamo, et cetera. One of our people has a sister working at *Vogue*. We occasionally borrowed pieces. I dressed Italian because that's what he went for.'

'You were honey-trapping . . . '

'Just complying with his tastes.'

'But he requested you have an intimate medical examination. Is that correct?'

'Yes. I was told to use his doctor, but I got round it by insisting on my own because of what I said were gynaecological issues in the past. A friend of the service was found in Wimpole Street and the report was sent in, so I never had the examination.'

'But that must have given you and Mr Ballard pause. What could the medical examination be for, other than . . . '

'We rode with it. All the women who worked there had it – all the ones he trusted. That didn't mean he was going to attempt to rape them. As it turned out, I became one of the trusted ones and introduced the spyware from within the company, using in-house emails and attachments generated by his own staff, which I intercepted and we doctored. But it could be challenging because he was so paranoid and changed his phones constantly. It required ingenuity from our people.'

Mark raises a finger. 'Can you talk about the intelligence product?'

'Sure. We were mapping his operation, the bank accounts he used, his crypto holdings, and those enabled us to trace the source of funds with great accuracy, plus the hundreds of shell companies involved in buying assets or passing on to beneficiaries the assets he'd seemingly purchased legitimately for himself, for which he then received compensation in many different territories. These crimes don't respect borders. His legitimately operated enterprises in the UK are so big and sprawling, money gets lost in the churn of transactions. This wasn't just about laundering money in the UK. Hagfish was operating a personal SWIFT payment system, pushing dirty cash all over the world from bank to bank, enterprise to enterprise. A lot of it was in his head, which made it very hard. In some way we had to get to know his mind and try to read what he would do in a certain situation.' She stopped. 'This was all very much Tom's operation, as you know, and he was pleased with the model that Softball provided.' She pauses. 'By the way, why isn't he here?'

'He's on paternity leave,' Stone replies. 'Moving on, you

ignored the clear signs of what he intended – the medical checks and the history of abuse of female staff. He had a poor reputation among them, no? You knew him to be an out-and-out sexual predator, someone who could not be trusted in the company of a young woman. And there were stories, weren't there? A lot of these women went to bed with him. Some were compelled, raped in all but name; others did what he wanted for advancement.'

'There were risks but also a big intelligence premium for us. Data analytics, better coordination between us and the police can take you just so far. We were on the inside. I became a trusted aide, sometimes a confidante. He asked my advice and spent a lot of time talking about Kimmie, his wife. We'd got through the golden door. We had undreamed-of access . . .'

Stone says, 'You don't feel responsible for leading Guest on in any way?'

She shakes her head and decides to say nothing to this outrageous allegation because it is the calm and reasonable Sally Latimer in the room, not the occasional hothead Slim Parsons.

Stone plucks at her bra strap through her shirt. 'You found yourself in Guest's car on October the thirteenth going to a meeting in Hampshire, is that right? And on the way, he received a telephone call which resulted in Guest instructing his driver to go to Blackbushe Airport where you boarded his private jet, and you accompanied him, and you knew you were travelling abroad.'

'Yes.'

'And you had your own passport, secreted in the lining of your leather shoulder bag, is that right?'

She nods.

'Was that sensible?'

'It bloody well saved my life,' is what she wants to say but, instead, she gestures to indicate that maybe it wasn't such a clever idea and, to her mild horror, sees that her fingernails are still filthy with Alder Fen clay, and removes her hands to beneath the table. 'I never usually needed it on arrival. I travelled on the plane on many occasions and waited while Guest did business on the plane or nearby. I hardly ever disembarked, and if I did, I remained at the airport.'

'This may be distressing for you, but we need to have a clearer idea of the events on that plane, particularly in relation to the gun you used. I'll read what you wrote and then you can fill in some of the gaps for us.'

CHAPTER 5

Stone begins.

'"We boarded Guest's jet at four thirty p.m. GMT and took off shortly thereafter. I did not then know the destination, but I now believe it to be Hakkari in Eastern Turkey because I overheard one of the pilots mention the city on the radio. We worked for the first hour drafting replies to emails, dealing with legal correspondence, and rearranging his schedule for the next two days. He asked me to handle instructions to his lawyers, which I understood to be a compliment: he was saying that he trusted me to carry out a complicated brief. He was in an expansive mood because during the telephone call in the car he'd received good news about a contract involving Yıo Steel and Cement, his construction company, and he told me we were flying immediately to seal it. There was food laid out in the aft cabin where Guest sometimes rested. Lobster, cold Kobe beef and caviar was on the table. Champagne in an ice bucket."'

'One thing . . .' It's Mark, looking puzzled. 'If, as you say, you left with such little notice – it was less than an hour between phone call and take-off – how is it that such an elaborate meal was made ready in time?'

'I thought about that,' Slim says. 'He knew I was vegetarian. I'm not, but Sally Latimer was, so it was an odd meal if he was trying to impress me.'

'You think he planned a kind of abduction?'

'Yes, I do now.' She needs to be careful here. She mustn't seem naive and therefore unemployable, but neither must she seem nonchalant about the risks that were involved. 'I was focused on the job. Gaining his confidence was a big part of what I was meant to be doing. It was a risk. We knew that.'

'I'll continue,' says Stone. '"He asked me if I would like to get more comfortable and told me to relax. He gave me a glass of champage and made a toast – I cannot remember what he said but I recall that he switched off the main cabin lights with the controls in his armrest, and only the table lights remained on. He drank several glasses more, became loud and somewhat belligerent, and told me that I should lighten up and that I didn't know how to have a good time. He asked me to reach for a brief-case in the locker above him, which required me to get out of my seat. It was then he jumped up, took hold of me by the waist and bent me over a seat. There was nothing I could do. Guest is a big, powerful man, and he was drunk. He attacked me and I resisted with all my strength, which eventually resulted in me hitting him with a bottle."'

The detail was excruciating, and the attack longer than she had implied. Guest forced her down over the back of the seat, ripped her panties down and was gripping the back of her neck so fiercely that she feared he might break her neck or fatally stop the flow of blood in her carotid artery. He had his dick between her legs and was all but raping her when she lurched forward, seized the bottle of champagne from the bucket and, twisting round, smashed it into the side of his face, spraying them both with the remainder. The bottle fell from her hand. He let go, staggered back, then came for her with a murderous look. At that moment the plane hit turbulence. One of the pilots came on the tannoy and said, 'Buckle up please, Mr Guest. This shouldn't be long – just a patch of erratic airflow around Mount Vihren.' Guest held on to the back of a chair with both hands as the plane rose and fell; she did, too. Then, when it levelled off, he launched himself again and she was certain that he would kill her. She stepped back, went forward kicking him in the stomach with a heel and followed this with a kick to his face, which surprised Slim almost as much as it stunned Guest. She was able to collect the bottle and hit him much harder on the same spot as before, breaking the glass, and he went down. 'Buckle up, Mr Guest. Buckle up, you fucking bastard!' she whispered. Evidently, the cockpit put the noise down to the turbulence because the pilot came on the tannoy again. 'Sit this one out, please, sir, we'll be through it in a couple of minutes.'

Mark and Rita wear sympathetic expressions. Mark says, 'How tall are you? About five feet five, six? And weight – about a hundred and thirty-five pounds?' She nods. He picks up a recent photograph of Ivan Guest at a black-tie event. 'And he's six feet, maybe a touch more, and at least two hundred and ten pounds.' She nods. 'You were lucky to prevail, Ms Parsons. Very lucky.'

'Yes,' she says, 'but he was drunk.'

'Tell us about the gun,' says Rita. 'How did you know he kept a gun on the plane? I mean, it's a rare criminal who will fly in and out of airports with a gun. Unheard of, almost.'

'Last summer we flew to Azerbaijan. He normally has a body-guard called Aron, but he wasn't with us on that flight. Before we landed at Baku, Guest used a black teardrop fob on his key ring to open a compartment beneath his seat. He thought I was asleep, but I saw there was a kind of safe under the seat with money and a pistol, which he took out and put inside his jacket. So, I knew it was there and all I needed to do was to find the key ring, which was in his trouser pocket. I opened the compartment, took out the gun and called through to the pilot on the intercom. I told one of them to come through because there was a problem.'

The lawyer is writing furiously and puts up his hand for her to slow down. She waits, and briefly considers telling them about the other item she took, the tablet that she's never looked at because Guest said it was protected by a suicide program, activated if the tablet was tampered with in any way. But she has no adequate explanation for keeping it and dismisses the idea.

'Then what?' says Mark.

'I told him that Guest had attempted to rape me and that he could see it for himself on the CCTV recording. There was a camera in the cabin. Guest recorded everything and I knew it would all be there. Besides his penis was still . . . on show. Then I told them I would kill Guest unless they landed the plane and let me off.'

'In effect, you hijacked the plane.'

'Yes, I admitted that in my account. But what else could I do?' She lowers her voice. 'Ivan Guest was – is – a very violent man and I didn't rate my chances if we continued to Turkey and he came round.'

The door opens. Everyone turns. A tall man in clear-frame spectacles, who is also in tennis kit, enters, carrying sandwiches, an orange and a Diet Coke. He smiles apologetically to the room. 'Don't mind me. I'll just listen in for a bit if there are no objections.' She knows this is Oliver Halfknight, seemingly the vaguest man on the planet, but also one of the most shrewd. It was Tom who suggested that Halfknight, a college contemporary, apply to the Security Service, then watched in awe as Halfknight took the escalator to the top floor and moved into the Deputy Director's office. 'No one sees Oliver coming,' Tom said, 'because he looks like an antiquarian bookseller up from the country.'

Halfknight takes a chair behind the others but then finds he needs somewhere to eat, so moves to the end of the table, opens a sandwich pack, and makes a half-hearted offer to share his lunch. 'Are you sure, Ms Parsons, that you are not a little tempted?'

'Thanks, no.'

He takes a bite and ruminates. 'Please carry on. Oh, I should ask – is that your dog in the Nissan? You should have brought it up here. Probably be happier.'

'It didn't seem appropriate, sir.'

'Well, let's see how we go. Rita and I have a tennis date, after she thrashed someone from the Cabinet Office last weekend. So, we can't be all day.' Slim tips her head, and he looks over his glasses, and for a fraction of a second, she glimpses not the owlish figure he presents, but the eyes of a much more ferocious raptor.

With some impatience Stone says, 'Perhaps we should get back to how Ms Parsons hijacked a jet in European airspace and ordered it to Northern Macedonia.'

That sentence still seems incredible to Slim and she feels something like vertigo when she hears it, but then Sally's cooler assessment takes hold. There was never any report of the 'hijack' in the media, no speculation on plane tracking sites about a billionaire's jet being diverted to Skopje; no reference to Ivan Guest being treated for a fractured jaw and cheekbone; and nothing about the 15,000 euros in hundred-euro denominations that Slim took from the compartment under Guest's chair. It dawns on her then that, as far as the intelligence agencies that oversee JEF and its operations are concerned, it's so much easier if the incident never took place. And this off-the-books meeting, held on a Saturday in a remote precinct of the intelligence community, suggests precisely the same: nothing happened.

'You ordered the pilot to fly to Skopje,' Stone says, 'some forty minutes away, and during that time he said nothing to Northern Macedonian air traffic control? Presumably you threatened them.'

'Not until we landed, when I pointed out I no longer needed them, and I would shoot them without a second thought if they raised the alarm. But they were kind of on my side. They'd seen what had happened to other women, and they were sure I wasn't making any of it up. They knew their boss and they knew me. We were on friendly terms before that.'

Halfknight stirs. 'Did you let them use first aid?'

'Yes. He was still concussed and bleeding and couldn't remember much. I knew I had probably broken his jaw. The left side of his face was badly swollen.'

'You landed at Skopje at what time?'

'At about nine p.m. local, but I can't be accurate.'

'Your account is not clear,' he continues, about to take another bite of his sandwich. 'The plane taxies to a spot on a distant part of the airport, then what? Do they let down the stairway or do you abseil from the plane?'

'They put the stairway down, let me go, then taxied to the apron.'

'And what did you do – simply walk through Immigration and Customs?'

'No, I found a man on a service truck, showed him the gun and a thousand euros, and asked which he would like. He chose the money. He found me an airport employee's hi-vis jacket and gave me his beanie and took me through the perimeter without a problem. Once we were out, I gave him the money.'

'You didn't use your real passport at Skopje at any time?'

Slim shakes her head.

'That's because you knew that Guest's people would go through the names of those arriving at Skopje that night and start looking for a woman called Alice Parsons who had gone through after his jet landed. That was wise. When did you first use your passport?'

'Not until ten days later when I took an overnight bus from Lake Ohrid in Macedonia, to Tirana, Albania, and I don't believe they logged the entry, though I can't be sure.'

They go through Slim's erratic journey through Europe, which included crossing the Pyrenees three times, and ended in Madrid where she presented herself to a puzzled MI6 man in the embassy.

'What was going on in your head?' asks Stone. 'You talked to Tom Ballard once but didn't tell him all of what had happened. Why was that?'

'I had one phone with me, issued by the Guest organisation, and I thought he might have the capability to track it. I bought another and spoke with Tom and told him I'd be away for a few weeks. I knew I'd broken the law and I was waiting to see what happened and where I stood.'

'You broke *international* law – that's the point. And you were waiting to decide if you were going on the run indefinitely. Is that correct?'

'Yes,' says Slim, head lowered. 'I was, you understand,

shocked by what happened and the steps I found myself taking on the airplane and at Skopje airport. I've never held a gun in my life, let alone threatened to kill someone. I knew that if I did anything to reveal my identity it would jeopardise everything we had achieved.'

Rita asks, 'Why didn't you respond to the messages from us?'

'I was keeping out of the way until the spring, as instructed, and I didn't look at that phone. I understand this was wrong.'

'Would you have killed?' asks Mark.

'To defend myself from a rapist, yes, I think I probably would. But not in cold blood. That's not me.'

'Well, I suppose that's something.' Stone closes the report and raps the table with both sets of fingernails, takes a deep breath. 'You endangered life, you broke the law in multiple ways, disregarded procedure, kept your case officer and team in ignorance of the full facts until some three weeks after the incident and, whatever your excuses, failed to respond to our requests to attend meetings and answer for your actions. It's a pattern of irresponsibility' – she searches for a word – 'of delinquency that is unacceptable in a modern intelligence service. We can only be thankful that none of this reached the media.'

The prosecution over, Slim looks around the table for help, doesn't see any and dismisses her prudent alter ego. 'Aren't you forgetting something? Softball was a massive success. The JEF team did a fantastic job, and I was part of the team, and that required me to live undercover for the best part of two years. Being in that deep for that long is seriously alienating. And being with a man like Guest – a repulsive, racist, sexist bully who has almost certainly ordered hits on his enemies – is a big mental challenge. In boarding that plane, I made one bad mistake. I admit that, but I'd flown with him on many occasions

before, twice when he was the only other passenger. I've got
to tell you that there were no objections from our team then
because we were getting so much information.'

'What we need from you—' begins Stone.

Slim raises a hand from the table and speaks softly. 'No, what
I need from you is understanding. I want a complete exoner-
ation because I showed total commitment to this operation.
You know what, a thank you would be great, too. Instead, you
lecture me about procedure. There is no procedure at thirty
thousand feet with a man who is attempting to anally penetrate
you. I was fighting for my survival. Maybe you would all have
preferred if I had submitted.'

'No, of course not,' says Stone.

'Then don't tell me what's appropriate in those circumstances.
I had no option and I want that accepted and on record.'

Mark says, 'We understand the ordeal that you went through,
yet you didn't take advantage of the counselling offered, which
seems unwise, and when we didn't hear from you, we naturally
became concerned.'

'I tired of the counselling. It wasn't for me. I was told by
Tom that I wouldn't be needed for four or five months and that
I should go away, clear my head and keep it down, and this is
what I did. To send Mills and Boon after me was absurd.'

'Mills and Boon?' says Stone. 'His name is Salt.'

'It's a joke, Corinna,' says Halfknight wearily. He looks down
hopelessly at the orange he has been attempting to peel, which
now lies in pieces with most of the skin still on. 'A good moment
to pause, would you say? You can give your dog a run, Ms Parsons, and we'll meet again in, say, thirty minutes. And do bring
the dog up with you if you feel it would be happier.'

CHAPTER 6

Half an hour later, Slim is leaning against the pickup making
a list in her head of everything she needs to do to keep things
going in Steward's House while her mother is in hospital, when
Laurie Tapper opens the door and whistles to catch her attention. Loup is quartering the yard methodically, assumes he's
being summoned and bounds over. There's nothing for it but to
take him up. The moment the lift doors open at the top floor,
the dog shoots out, glances left and right and follows the rumble
of voices to the conference room. When she arrives, he is already
making eyes at Oliver Halfknight.

'Dogs always gravitate to the power in the room,' says Rita
with a squeeze of the eyes.

Corinna Stone and the lawyer are gone, while Mark and Rita
stand at the far end of the table, either side of Halfknight. 'Come
in, Slim,' he says in country house party mode. 'Mind if I call
you that, or would you prefer Alice?'

'Whichever you like.'

'Slim it will be. Right . . . now . . . well . . .' he says, getting
slowly airborne. He coughs a soft bark. But, seriously, does
anyone fall for this act of Halfknight's? 'We've been through

things and broadly concur that you had no options on that aeroplane. And Rita argues that if you'd been a man and your life was threatened in those circumstances, there would be no question that we'd regard the actions you took as unavoidable, indeed heroic. I take her point completely.

'This morning was necessary because form needs to be observed. There is now a record of correct procedure being followed. But the beauty of this incident is that so few know about it.' His eyebrows rise, a hint of a smile. 'And this has very limited circulation. But it does mean there won't be official absolution because a declaration of that kind requires people to be aware of the full facts. If it makes any difference, we all believe you did a splendid piece of work, and you acted the only way you could on the plane, and nothing should be allowed to spoil your record.'

'Corinna Stone agrees with this?'

'It is of academic interest. We have done what was needed and now we move on.'

'What happened to the JEF? Has it been disbanded?'

'Mothballed for reasons that will not interest you.' He moves quickly on despite her look of astonishment. 'Tom Ballard did you a turn by ordering you off the premises and telling everyone that you were burnt out. It saved questions at the time and, what with everything that's going on, people soon find something else to think about. You have Tom and Mark here to thank for the operation to kill off Sally Latimer in the ferry disaster. Mark, I should say, is with SIS, just in case you were wondering. He will tell you about that aspect.'

Mark leans forward and knits his fingers, then splays them. 'Just as we were searching for a plausible *exit*, Tom came across the tragedy in the Bali Sea, and we moved very quickly to place

Sally's name among the list of the missing. It seemed right that she would go travelling after her ordeal at the hands of Guest and end up in one of those hedonistic spots for young people. This meant we had to arrange, in short order, a record of Sally's entry into Indonesia, flights, hotel registration, some social media, a fictional boyfriend, their itinerary through South East Asia, and coverage in Wellington, New Zealand, where, of course, Sally's folks now live. We're still actively helping this narrative along. And the New Zealanders have done a splendid job in conjuring the grieving parents. Someone did call the number they've set up for Mr and Mrs Latimer and this person seemed to be fishing. Guest's people also searched your flat in the Docklands. The good news is we're a hundred per cent sure they found nothing.'

'What about Ivan Guest?'

'We gather he's undergone operations to reconstruct his jaw and cheekbone in Switzerland.' He stops. 'On the other side of the river, those of us that know about this product are hugely impressed by what you and the team achieved. It's textbook stuff.'

'But what you're saying is he's still free and able to move about the world. No sanctions, no charges, no asset-freezing orders – nothing. It's six months since he all but raped me and you've had all the evidence to put him away for a century.'

'We don't put people away,' says Mark evenly. 'But it will happen—'

'In due course,' Rita interrupts.

'What stands is your exceptional service,' Halfknight says. 'That's what we're telling you.'

That's some kind of acknowledgement but she understands she's being softened up and they're going to let her go. Gently maybe, and with a pay-off, but it'll be a defeat all the same. Should she tell them about those twenty months as Sally Latimer, embedded in Guest's empire? The routine and the isolation of it; being in a state of extreme alertness for months on end; the awfulness of Guest's sadistic and suspicious personality; the insufferable people in his inner circle; the absolutely brainless snob of a wife who called her to buy sanitary products, chase down high-end bedding and complain when she was denied a sponsored sun lounger in Antibes. And this is not to forget the adjustments to her own wardrobe and hairstyle to conjure posh wholesomeness with the hint of a filthy mind. 'You're an English rose but you know where the monkey sleeps,' Tom told her when they walked to the White Horse in Berkshire, on the day before she stepped into the world of Sally Latimer. 'I have no idea what that means and I'm sure I don't want to,' she told him, and Tom had said, 'You don't.'

Maybe she should remind them that Guest was the last man standing after Ukraine. Oligarchs lost businesses, yachts, homes, football clubs, jets, and were forced into ruinous fire sales and found all lines of credit suspended. But Guest, the Harrow old boy, avoided all of it, although he was as corrupt as any of them. There was no one smarter or blessed with a more highly tuned survival instinct than Hagfish, plus he'd sprayed money at politicians in ways calculated to confuse if not totally mislead the electoral authorities. The establishment was incapable of thinking of him as anything but a good chap and upstanding patriot.

Halfknight peels the ham from his discarded sandwich and drops it into Loup's mouth. 'You don't mind, do you? He seems peckish.' He looks up. 'How are things at home? We heard about last night's drama. Peter Salt reports that your mother is out of danger. I hope that's true.'

'As of early this morning, yes. Peter probably saved her life. So, I was glad he was there. He knows what he's doing on CPR.'

'Good. That must all be a relief.' He lays a hand on the table in Mark's direction. 'Saturday detention is over for you, dear Mark. Thank you.' Mark departs with a finger salute to the room, and they are left alone. This makes sense if they are going to get rid of her.

Halfknight gives her a look of funereal regret. 'We understand why you acted as you did on that plane, and most would have done the same, but your behaviour after the episode, careering all over Europe, failing to contact us, was questionable. Quite apart from anything else, searching for you was a waste of our resources.'

Rita says, 'Unprofessional, rash, inexcusable.' Slim has been watching Rita. She's attractive, wears her forty-five plus years well, and has some South Asian heritage. She is always very still, is Rita without-a-surname. Slim doesn't trust still because it's only ever about creating an aura of power. Ivan Guest could be very still. The hoods in the Caucasus were waxworks.

She waits before replying, 'Yes. It happened. I made mistakes – too many. I regret them.'

Halfknight glimmers a smile. 'Anyway, I'm glad you've had time to yourself. What did you do over the winter?' Of course, he knows. She told Ballard where she was and what she was doing.

'Archaeology. I was on a dig. It's an interest I've had since college. I have friends who've made their careers in the field. They ask me along sometimes. Unpaid.'

'Discover anything of interest?'

'I can't tell you what, or where it is. Secrecy is all in archaeology.'

'Intriguing.' He glances at Rita. 'Aside from being my tennis partner, Rita is a distinguished member of the Service diaspora, and she has come to us with what seems to be a problem of subversion. The service tends to be sceptical about subversion, but we do keep an eye on certain areas and Rita believes she may have something for you.'

'So, I won't be going back to what I was doing.'

'No, that's out of the question, and given your vanishing act after the Skopje incident, you're lucky to be still employed. In normal circumstances, we would regard you as burned. But this is a far less demanding assignment and relies on your previous career as a journalist.'

'Journalist! I was a grunt on the websites of two newspapers, writing click bait about diets and pets. It was a long time ago. I wouldn't call it journalism.'

'But you did one serious investigation about landlords in Sheffield and Leeds. It's in your file because you must have mentioned or submitted it during your application. Two things strike me about the article: the information is evidently accurate, and the sparseness of your writing style. We propose you now revert to your journalistic career.'

'This is your only option for me.'

'You're not compelled to take it, but we don't see this as an especially difficult assignment, and it will last only as long as it takes you to make sense of what's going on in this organisation.'

Slim looks at them both. 'You're suggesting that I go undercover in a media organisation – isn't that off limits for us? A free press in a free society, and all that.'

'You won't be undercover in the traditional way.'

'I don't expect to be telling whoever these people are that I'm a member of the Security Services, so, yes, I will be undercover, whether I use my name or not.' She is looking unimpressed, and she doesn't care if they see it because she's being pushed into a dead-end assignment that's counter to every possible convention of a liberal democracy. 'Am I being parked? Because if I am, I can go back to my dig, and we can call it time.'

'We want you to accept this assignment. It's important. Everyone wants that. You understand what I'm saying?' Does he mean the Director herself? Is that it? The meeting which they so urgently wanted her to attend might easily have been a disciplinary hearing that resulted in her sacking – after all she'd hijacked a plane and stolen 15,000 euros – but then it came to nothing, and bizarrely for an organisation addicted to protocols and codes of conduct, completely fizzled out. Form had been observed, only to be dismissed along with Stone and the lawyer. And that left her with the thought that not only might she keep her job long term, but she had some leverage, too. Yes, they really wanted her for this.

'I'll do it, but I need two things. The remaining money in Sally Latimer's bank account. I recognise that you had to use some of it to pay for Sally Latimer's last trip, but I earned that money. It's mine.'

'But you were being paid a salary by us,' protests Rita.

'I was doing two jobs and working sixteen hours a day. That's my money.'

'What about the money you took from Guest?'

'Expenses while avoiding capture by a criminal organisation,' she says, looking at Halfknight. 'Have I got it?'

He nods.

'Second, my brother Matthew went missing about twelve years ago.'

'You told us about it when you joined. So, he hasn't been found?'

'No. It's the reason I went to work in Leeds. We've tried everything. My mother's fall made me realise that I must try to get closure for her, but I don't have the means. You do. I will take this job if you do a proper search for Matthew.'

Halfknight says, 'It's unorthodox, but yes. To be arranged next week when you come in to prepare for the job. You'll need to bring all the information you have on your brother and as many photographs as you possess. We will do what we can.'

Rita gets up and says she's going to secure the tennis court.

'Can you give me an idea where I'll be based?' she asks when Rita closes the door.

'Milton Keynes,' says Halfknight.

'Milton Keynes!'

'Fascinating place. Much underrated. Most people have no idea that Milton Keynes contains Bletchley Park, the Government Code and Cypher School during the war. You know about that?'

'Of course.' She wonders where this is going.

'Good. Bletchley is key to this job.'

'Why?'

'That's all for next week. If you could arrive here by ten on Monday, that would be perfect.'

CHAPTER 7

Slim doesn't revisit Sally Latimer's life. Never lets it haunt her. But with the interview at the Cotton Studios, the sensations of that time begin to return. Guest's oppressive and exhausting presence, his cologne, the fleeting look of malevolence, shot from deep beneath his brow while his lips spread in a broad grin. Why people never noticed what was going on in that face was a mystery to her. They just saw that monkey grin and were mesmerised by the hands that played on their own stage, by turns threatening, enticing, dismissing, submitting and seducing in a constant vaudeville of distraction. There wasn't a man alive who used his hands to more devastating effect. One gesture amused her, an impatient twirl of his right hand that ended with it cupped and pointing to his midriff and, if only his interlocutors would look, to the sole beneficiary of the deal being hurried to conclusion.

The reason she survived those two years was that she was able to put him from her mind. Yet she did exactly the opposite for the rest of that weekend in London because, in the view of two doctors and Nurse Helen, her mother was 'too tired for a visit', for which she read, alcoholic withdrawal. She had the time to herself in her friend Bridie Hansen's house in Wye Street, her bolthole for the last three years, to try to answer the question she put to Mark from SIS. Why, when the National Crime Agency was raring to go, had there been not a hint of action? No raids, no prosecutions, no whiff of a sanction or seizure. None of his businesses appeared to have suffered the slightest inconvenience. Having found nothing, late on Sunday, she sent an obliquely worded text to her old boss Tom Ballard asking to see him urgently, but got no response.

On Monday, Slim arrives half an hour early at Cotton and waits in the pickup, making calls to the kennel that has agreed to take Loup for a trial period of ten days; to a security firm in Peterborough, which she contracts to check on her mother's house and install a temporary CCTV system; and to Nurse Helen's mobile. Because of the irregularities in her mother's blood pressure and heart rate, she's still in Cardiac Care and likely to be there for another day or two.

Ten minutes later, Slim is in a former screening room in the basement of the Cotton Studios with Rob Alantree, a crisply dressed Sandhurst type in his thirties. She met him on a training programme four years before where he performed brilliantly in everything but seat-of-your-pants inspiration tests. With no correct answer, Rob was all at sea.

They sit at a table on a raised dais in front of the dozen cinema seats. Rob tucks his tie into his shirt and rolls up his sleeves like a doctor on his rounds. They are joined by a young man called Gerald who carries two laptops and a phone. From Slim's thirty-five years, Gerald looks like a teenager. Rita without-a-surname comes in, wishes her well and underlines her 'good luck', as though a lot depends on the Milton Keynes job. Then as an afterthought, gives her name, Bauer – Rita Bauer.

'So, what we're looking at here,' Alantree begins, 'is a news site called Middle Kingdom.'

Gerald spins a laptop round to Slim with the home page open. He connects the other laptop to a big screen and the same home page appears. 'Obviously, you'll get to know it over time,' he says, 'but you can explore independently on your machine now.'

Gerald works his laptop. Slim looks at the one in front of her. In the menu 'About our work' she reads that Middle Kingdom ranges over the counties of Buckinghamshire, Hertfordshire, Bedfordshire, Northamptonshire and Cambridgeshire.

> *We seek to represent the stories and experiences of the millions who make their lives in the countryside and towns between the north and south and the Midlands and East Anglia. Middle Kingdom is dedicated to quality local journalism, with an emphasis on training journalists.*

She jumps to a section on the site's financing from subscriptions, donations and advertising. She reads,

> *Our ads are vetted to ensure that they come from sustainable, enlightened and socially responsible organisations.*

Given the primness of this statement, it's surprising how many ads there are, and from well-known brands, too. She moves to a final paragraph on authorship and social media which says,

> *Readers will notice that articles on Middle Kingdom are unsigned. Bylines are only placed on certain regular columns. We take collective responsibility for everything published here. It's not who's writing that matters but what is written. Middle Kingdom is represented on most social media platforms, but we don't encourage our*

*writers to engage in social media, unless they are using it to reach
out, or for research, or in a personal capacity that's clearly distinct
from their work at Middle Kingdom.*

'Sounds like a cult,' Slim says.

'They're rigorous and disciplined,' says Alantree. 'Have a look
at this from three weeks ago.' Gerald pulls up an article with
tables of figures, graphs, quotations from emails, screen grabs
and headshots of businesspeople. 'This is an exposé of British
water companies. You may've seen it in the news.'

She shakes her head – she's barely read the news all winter,
but this seems like an old story and she says so.

'The information about the pollution carried out with the
knowledge of the water companies and their boards is a hundred
per cent accurate. But, more important, were the revelations
about expenses and remuneration?' He gestures to the screen.
'Plus, they used official data, the minister's reports, her private correspondence, and memoranda that were only seen by a
handful of senior government officials.'

'Are they hacking into government departments?'

'Yes, plainly, or they have inside sources, people leaking to
them and breaking the Official Secrets Act in the process. But
they are also good with open-source intelligence. They find a lot
on the web that others don't. We're also interested in this person.'

A black-and-white photograph appears of a man in his early
to mid sixties, with a round face, framed by black curls brushed
forward and an unkempt black beard. He wears heavy black spectacles behind which his eyes are closed with pleasure; and he has a
small cigar jammed into the side of his mouth. 'This is Yoni Ross,
one of the world's first hackers. Maybe the very first. Before there
were mainframe terminals in the office or home computers, this

character got into the Pentagon's system and left a masturbating Mickey Mouse for the generals to find on Monday morning. The FBI couldn't prove it was Yoni, but he was advised that if he was ever tempted again, he would face forty years in prison. Mr Ross took the hint and moved to Britain, where he felt at home because his father, Yoni Ross Senior, had spent the last three years of the war at Bletchley Park, working on the first computers with Tommy Flowers and Alan Turing and decrypting Japanese radio traffic. Later he taught at Cambridge. Ross Junior went on to develop several early Internet protocols, then moved into financial trading software in the nineties.'

Alantree gazes at the photograph for a moment. 'He's rich and very smart but he's an oddball. Crazy about rabbits, apparently.' The door opens. Oliver Halfknight enters and settles in the front row of cinema seats. Later, Slim will give him the envelope containing everything she has on Matthew – date of birth, photos, national insurance number, last known address, and the details of two friends – but this isn't the moment. She nods hello and puts the envelope on the table in front of her. Halfknight gestures for Alantree to carry on.

'Middle Kingdom was up and running before Yoni Ross came into the picture. It was founded by a local journalist, a woman named Exton-White, and she was later joined by Yoni and three others, whom we don't know a lot about. They met at an event held by the Bletchley Park Trust, which regularly reaches out to descendants of the people who worked there. We believe they all have parents or grandparents who were a key part of the Ultra operation. That's true of Exton-White and Ross. We think the others live within twenty miles of Milton Keynes, though Ross goes between London and Berkeley, California, and a house in Hertfordshire.'

'To be precise, Mr Alantree,' says Halfknight, 'Ultra was the name given to the intelligence produced by breaking Enigma encryption. Bletchley Park was known as Station X, or more informally BP. You see the difference?'

Alantree nods. 'They originally wanted to call the site Redwood because they met in a rainstorm sheltering under the giant Californian redwood which stands in front of the old house at the park, but they stuck with the name Middle Kingdom, which has a vaguely New Age feel.'

'How come?' Slim asks. 'The Middle Kingdom was a period of Egyptian history lasting two thousand years – roughly, the Bronze Age in Britain. How's that New Age?'

Alantree looks annoyed. 'There are aspects that are New Age-y and they are idealistic. But they are also practical, resourceful and highly motivated. This is not Woke Central, by the way: they are only interested in the facts and reporting what they see as the truth.'

'An exceptional gene pool,' says Halfknight. 'So, what we need to know urgently is where they're getting their information. It's true that this is a small, self-satisfied outfit in Milton Keynes, but the danger to the state looks real to us. Rob is now going to take you through everything you'll need to learn to make a success of this operation.'

She doesn't want to broach the subject of Matthew in front of Alantree and Gerald, but Halfknight seems to have forgotten their arrangement. She jumps up with the envelope in her hand. 'This contains everything I have on my brother. Thank you for doing this.'

He seems surprised but puts the envelope into his inside pocket, and nods to her.

CHAPTER 8

Every evening, she chooses a different route from the Cotton Studios to Bridie Hansen's house in Wye Street, West Kilburn. It takes her over an hour to do the twenty-minute trip but when she lived as Sally Latimer and needed to reclaim her real life and sit gossiping at Bridie's kitchen table, she'd spend much longer on a dry-cleaning routine that started in the Docklands on the Thames Clipper, and included many dive-ins, choke points and sudden stops to use her phone in selfie mode to check the streets behind her.

Bridie is in Amsterdam, supervising a design project. That suits Slim as much as her long absences over the last three years have suited Bridie, a glamorous Nordic loner who lives with a pet rat called Rat. She doesn't bother to disguise her pleasure to be in receipt of Slim's rent without having to share her house and the delicate, needlepoint garden at the rear. Almost certainly, she wonders about Slim's vanishing acts and sudden, unannounced visits, yet shows zero interest in what her ghost tenant does for a living.

Slim cooks for herself, feeds Rat with fresh fruit and a cube of special rodent food and goes to her bedroom where Matthew's self-portrait is hanging and she keeps her clothes on a rail — clothes that reveal her generally undeclared sense of colour and cut, some of which she has had for a dozen years or more. She settles down at her computer to find out as much as she can about Middle Kingdom, its business, journalism, and personnel, and writing it all down in a paper that is already too long and which she is sure no one will read. Alantree and Gerald appear already to have lost interest, but she moves through the three files adding notes and ideas for further research. All of it is committed to one of the disguised thumb drives she used on Softball. This one is a bracelet.

It is the Bletchley gene pool that interests her, and the reason it has gathered at a backwater website, in a town which has lately become a city but is still ridiculed for its roundabouts and un-English grid. She starts with Abigail Exton-White, who founded Middle Kingdom with the aim of covering local news and exploring the mystic and paranormal in Milton Keynes. She's worked in local radio and for a variety of newspapers and is evangelical about the city. Slim learns that the city's grid was adjusted by planners in the sixties to align with the rising sun on the summer solstice and, for Middle Kingdom's emblem, Abigail has chosen the Light Pyramid, the 2012 triangular sculpture by Liliane Lijn at the end of the viewing point known as the Belvedere. It sits on the left-hand side of the home page spreading light over a schematic of the five counties of Middle Kingdom's beat. Once the editor, she is now described as news editor. This demotion is unexplained. However, she retains the only signed column on the site — *Pyramid News* — which deals with ley lines and the like, also dietary matters and homeopathy, and has a large, engaged following. It couldn't be quirkier, or less of a threat to the security of the state.

Abigail and Yoni Ross were the key to establishing the identities of the other three. She finds Abigail in a Facebook photograph of a group at the Whitby Goth Weekend in 2016. Tall with exceptionally white skin, she wears very dark eye shadow and has hair that stands straight up, as though electrified. Sexy. Remote. Strong. Using a face search engine, Slim discovers another photograph, from 2017. She looks much the same but now she's seen at the main entrance to Bletchley Park, which suggests to Slim that Bletchley is where she should be looking for leads. In Alantree's files there's only one photograph, that of Yoni Ross. She finds dozens from Yoni's turbulent days in the States – most of them black-and-white – and just six from the last two decades. Combining Ross and Bletchley Park in a search she comes across Yoni's father who joined Bletchley in early 1942. In an article about Yoni senior, there is a link to the site for the National Museum of Computing, which is in Bletchley, yet not part of Bletchley Park. Yoni donated an undisclosed amount in memory of his pa. A photograph shows him talking animatedly to a woman in her early forties, who is identified as Dr Sara Kiln, formerly a data specialist with Google and more recently an AI engineer with OpenAI. Slim can't find anyone who served at Bletchley with the name Kiln and assumes that the connection must be female, and the name was lost when she or her mother married.

She adds 'Kiln' to 'Exton-White' and 'Ross' in a search and soon finds a photograph of ten people sheltering under a tree in a rainstorm. This is not any tree but the Californian redwood in front of the Bletchley Park mansion. The caption gives her ten names.

Through a process of elimination, she first finds Dr Dan Halladay, 45, lecturer in Modern Politics at New College, Oxford, who was at the centre of an academic dispute and, according to the *Mail Online*, left because of the toxicity of university life. The *Mail* mentions that Dan is the son of Emmanuel 'Manny' Halladay, one of the codebreaking heroes of Hut Six at Bletchley and known in later years as 'The Goat' because of his priapism. He's married to the art dealer and scholar Jen Halladay. They have no children.

Slim goes down the rabbit hole of Hut Six, originally no more than a shed close to the Bletchley Park mansion, which was tasked with unscrambling the radio messages generated by the German army and Luftwaffe Enigma cypher machines from the earliest days of the war. She is surprised to discover the majority of those attached to Hut Six were women working round the clock in cold and cramped conditions. Because the Germans changed the Enigma settings every day, Hut Six was in a race against time to provide the decodes to German signals. The work was punishing and stressful. Cases of burnout were not uncommon among the four hundred and fifty people working in the expanded Hut Six operation by 1943. But there were lucky breaks also. Lax operating procedures on the German side reduced the scale of the task each day, especially the insight that German Enigma operators would opt for the settings on the machine that were the least trouble. Then it was realised that regularly appearing elements in a radio signal, like in the weather reports from U-boats in the Atlantic, or the names of regular senders and receivers on the German side, would provide the codebreakers with the beginnings of a breakthrough, known as a 'crib'. Once they saw the newly encoded version of a familiar name, rank, digit or location they were closer to establishing the setting for the day and deciphering the transcripts that poured in from British radio listening stations.

The hours reading about codebreaking yield another name. One of the young wizards who helped build Colossus, the world's first programmable computer and the successor to Alan Turing's 'bombe' machine, was named Gordon Skelpick, who at twenty-two years of age arrived at Bletchley in 1943. Slim goes back to the group shot and finds J. J. Skelpick, videographer, writer and freelance investigator, who spent most of his career in Africa until he was seriously injured in an explosion, which explains his walking stick and weary, seen-it-all expression. He is the third son of Gordon Skelpick and was born in 1978.

Her study of the site is complete. She sends it to Alantree and Halfknight but hears nothing in response, so goes into the Cotton Studios and finds only Laurie Tapper with three young men, all of them looking rather shocked after Tapper's introductory session on self-defence. The operation, now known as Linesman, seems low on everyone's list of priorities. As she makes for the gate, she phones Tom Ballard, and to her amazement, after a dozen or more unanswered texts and calls that week, he picks up. A baby is crying in the background.

'Sorry, Slim. That's our new arrival, Marcus Aurelius Ballard.'

'Aurelius?'

'The stoic.'

'Doesn't sound it. What happened, Tom? Has Softball been hit into the long grass? And what's this Linesman about?'

'I have no idea.'

'The website in Milton Keynes that someone or other thinks is a grave threat to the state security.'

'You know better than to talk about this on an open line. I'm on paternity leave and hear absolutely nothing.'

'But all that work we did on Softball! The man should be facing twenty years in jail.'

'I can't speak about it now, you know that.'

'What the hell happened when I was away? Why has JEF been mothballed?'

'I'm not going to have this conversation now.'

'When can I see you?'

'You can't and I can't speak about any of it. Is that understood, Slim? I'd love to help but I can't and, as you can hear, I'm needed.'

'Tom, is this for real? You know what I went through, for Christ's sake.'

'Let me just say this. Whatever they have asked you to do, just do it with all the flair and dedication that you always bring to a job. Please just do what they ask. We'll speak at some stage. In the meantime, I must ask you not to call this number again.'

She presses 'off' before he can say goodbye, smarting at the rebuff and angry at Ballard's sudden pompous formality. Not in years of working with him had she ever heard him speak in that way.

CHAPTER 9

Slim was sure Middle Kingdom's story about Japanese knot-weed and the order known as a Community Protection Notice that was issued to an Iranian woman was a kind of test. There were a thousand words about the plant's dire effects. At the end, she found a bullet-pointed note that read:

> *If this story interests you and you would like to try your hand at writing for Middle Kingdom, we are looking for community stringers to work in and around Milton Keynes. Email Abigail Exton-White at aew@middlekingdom.com.*

Slim emailed early Thursday evening and received a reply almost immediately.

Tuesday 10.30 a.m. The Heights Building, Silbury Boulevard. Bring your story ideas. Regards, Abigail Exton-White, Managing Editor (News).

On Friday morning she attaches the first four hundred words of a piece she's working on, with a photograph, and the number of the new cell phone she bought for Operation Linesman. A text arrives: *That looks very promising. See you next week – AE-W.*

Seconds later another phone pings with a message from Bridie: *Dinner 7 p.m. Eagle's Nest. See you there.*

Slim replies, *It's on me.*

She packs and places Matthew's self-portrait by the front door, then phones Alantree to tell him she's leaving over the weekend because the job is starting. She cannot be any more specific and Alantree is similarly constrained, yet she senses irritation. 'To be discussed at eleven o'clock,' he says, 'we'll go through all the issues.' In case Alantree objects, she covers herself with an email to Halfknight with good news about the interview.

She puts on her Yves St Laurent dark grey two-piece suit, made in the eighties, which she bought for next to nothing from the vintage clothing site Lines of London and had altered. It has a narrow trouser stripe in satin and a well-cut, waisted jacket. It's too formal for work but she'll go straight to the Eagle's Nest in the pickup. She looks at herself in the full-length mirror. Despite the beer and pie binges with the Alder Fen crew in the Turk's Head pub, she's lost weight since she last wore it, which was – Jesus! – two and a half years ago, just before she assumed the Italian chic of Sally Latimer's life. The suit works and, hell, she's going into battle.

Alantree has moved the meeting to the screening room. Salt, Alantree and Gerald are sitting around the table, and Rita is in one of the seats in the front row.

'This is a team effort,' says Alantree. 'You can't just green-light an operation when you feel like it. Everything should be in place.'

'What needs to be in place?'

'Your story.'

'It's my life with a padded CV. We've made more of my time in journalism and NGOs and filled out the gaps with looking after my mother. The rest has been sanitised by Gerald, right?'

He doesn't look up from his laptop. 'Yeah, Slim's online presence is non-existent, except for the articles written under the name Alice Parsons for the *Cambridge News* and the *Yorkshire Post*, and I doctored those to remove picture bylines before Softball.'

'What's your recent story?' asks Rita Bauer.

'Archaeology in the north of England and the Fens, which can be verified, but generally we have kept the backstory vague and unverifiable, like the periods looking after my mother.'

Rita tests her for twenty minutes and concludes that the story dangerously lacks depth. 'You may be among the best we have, Slim, but this seems like winging it to me.'

'I'm good at avoiding areas of weakness. I've had a lot of practice.' She wasn't going into the 'scar tissue' strategy that was Ballard's invention. If your backstory includes a tragedy, people tend not to probe too much. 'What's your scar tissue?' he'd asked. She replied that she had lost contact with her brother. It was the only time she used Matthew's disappearance and it worked for her because the emotion that passed through her eyes when anyone came near the subject was real enough. People knew not to ask too much about Sally's history.

Slim hears the gentle sigh of the soundproof door at the back of the screening room opening and closing. Someone has either entered or looked in to see if the room is occupied, but she doesn't turn round. 'Rob thinks you've kicked off Linesman without the green light.'

'What else is there to do?' None of that Latimer tact now. 'I've got the perfect in. They like my story idea. Why don't I just go up there and get what you want? I don't want to seem overconfident, but can this be so very hard?' There's one doubt in her mind which isn't about infiltrating Middle Kingdom, but the off-the-books character of Linesman. However, she's saved her job and there's no point in raising the unorthodox nature of the project. She's in, and that's all there is to it.

Alantree looks peeved and starts shuffling a few papers. 'Tudor Mills and Peter Salt are going to be close at hand,' he says. 'Peter will be your contact and you are going to speak every other day, either face to face or on the phone. Peter will be making a report on a weekly basis. And Tudor will be on hand if you need him.'

She shakes her head. 'I'll make contact when I've got something. I went through two years of Softball without babysitting, and I don't need it now, not for a few left-wing hacks in Milton Keynes.'

'They're more than that,' comes a voice from the rear of the screening room. It's Halfknight. 'These are highly competent and motivated people. Do not underestimate them.'

She peers into the dark. 'I won't, Deputy Director, but I work best when I'm not watched or being crowded.'

'Best to be on the safe side.' Halfknight works his way out of the seat and rises so that she can see him. 'Okay, good luck, Slim, and, Rob, keep me up to date as often as you feel it's necessary.'

Rita rises and follows Halfknight through the sighing door.

'You see – we're a team,' says Salt. 'Your team.'

'Such a boy scout,' she says. 'I'll contact you when I need to. I don't want you or Tudor inside a fifty-mile radius of Milton Keynes or appearing at my mother's house. Twice was enough.'

'Just once,' says Salt, 'and we saved your mother's life. Not such a bad result.'

'And I'm grateful to you, Peter, and so will she be one day, and to Tudor,' she adds. 'You went once?'

'How is she?'

'Doing fine, thank you. You went to the house once?'

'Yes.'

'I assumed you returned to find me that night.'

Salt shakes his head. 'We waited at the hospital until the duty nurse said you'd gone to London. You didn't answer your phone, so we left. Wish you'd told us. Would have saved a lot of hanging about.' The penny drops. 'Something wrong, Slim? Did you have a visitor?'

'Not that I'm aware of.' She smiles.

The vehicle in the driveway at first light on that Saturday morning was perhaps larger than the mid-range Audi saloon used by Salt and Mills and the configuration of the headlights was different. Possibly a Mercedes or BMW. Hard to tell at that distance. Odd no one got out while she was watching through the binoculars. Was the driver checking to see if anyone was in the house, or were they just waiting?

The Eagle's Nest pub is packed by 6.30 p.m. with a young East London crowd that fills the two bars and has spilled on to the pavement. Bridie has booked a booth. The rocky pine table is flanked by two bottle-glass panels and overlooked by a black-and-white portrait of Greta Garbo. Slim orders a bottle of white Burgundy – Bridie's favourite – and bread and olive oil, then people-watches for three quarters of an hour waiting for Bridie to arrive. When she does, she parks her carry-on suitcase and drops her backpack on the floor by Slim and gives her a long heartfelt hug. 'How are you, mystery girl? How's Rat?' She seems taller and more stunning than ever. Practically every head in the bar turned as she entered – male and female.

'We're both doing well last time I checked. Rat misses you and begs to be let out.'

'He needs love. Really you should bring him out to play, Slim,' she says with an admonishing frown.

It's six months since they've seen each other, and they have a lot of catching up to do. Slim tells Bridie about her mother – though not how an MI5 heavy saved her life – and about the dig and Loup. Once they've ordered two unusually meaty dishes – steak and chips for Bridie and liver and bacon for Slim – she shows her the photographs on the Alder Fen message group. 'Is that Dougal?' exclaims Bridie. 'Didn't you—?'

'Yes, a long time ago. How in hell did you know that?'

'People tell me things. At Cambridge, he looked like a Viking warlord. Quite beautiful was Dougal Hass. Is it possible to ask what it was like?' She smiles and lowers her head for the confidence she knows will be surrendered. Bridie expects to be told and no one ever refuses because her beauty is irresistible.

'Like a deep freeze falling on me. He was pissed and I'm not sure how much he remembers.'

Bridie snorts into her wine. 'But he's always been sweet on you. I believe he still holds out hope. He's got a doctorate. He's the big archaeological cheese now. Did he ask you on the dig?'

Slim nods.

'See, I told you. Love among the ruins.'

Slim gives her an exasperated glance and refills her glass.

Bridie looks away. '"When I do come,"' she says, now recalling the quotation, '"she will speak not, she will stand, either hand on my shoulder, give her eyes the first embrace of my face, ere we rush, ere we extinguish sight and speech, each on each."'

Slim shakes her head. 'Your memory is some wonder, Bridie. Where's that from? It's beautiful.'

'"Love Among the Ruins", of course! Robert Browning. A very underrated poet. Let's go back to Dougal. Forgetting the freezer-falling simile for a moment. How is the Viking warlord in bed?'

'Hung like a Norse,' Slim says, deadpan.

Bridie practically chokes.

'What about you?' Slim asks. 'Any romance?'

'Nothing. Just a camel.'

'Camel?'

'One hump in a desert.'

They eat and order a second bottle of wine, though Slim is sure that neither wants more, but it's placed on the table and signals to anyone who has designs on their booth that they're going to be there until the bitter end. But they aren't. A few minutes after the bottle arrives, Slim is aware of an indistinct female shape in front of her, an instantly familiar scent, and her shoulders being gripped, just as in the poem.

'My God, Sally!' says the shape. 'They told us you were dead! Drowned in some fucking boat accident. But you're not dead. You're here. Fuck! God! Fucking hell!'

It's Melissa Bright – Mel, who worked for Ivan Guest until he propositioned her, and she slapped him. She's smiling, crazy-embarrassed and shaking her head in wonder. Slim has stopped breathing and can't speak. Her face is frozen, more from the ferocious calculation going on behind it than panic at being recognised as Sally, although there's a lot of that too.

It is Bridie who speaks, but in Swedish not English. She says something incomprehensible to Slim and lightly touches Mel on the shoulder. 'I am sorry. This is Agnetha from Uppsala. She's just arrived in London for the first time.' Bridie points to the bags beside Slim. 'She doesn't understand what you're saying but

I can tell you this is not your friend. This is Agnetha – Agnetha Ekström. I should know – she is my cousin.'

Bridie's performance is so unassailably reasonable and commanding that Mel lets go of Slim and straightens. She looks from Slim to Bridie to Slim again, jerks her head back in disbelief, runs a hand down her long dark hair and considers the possibility of making such a mistake. Then decides she hasn't. 'No, this is Sally Latimer! I should know – I slept with her.'

Slim manages to maintain a look of polite mystification until Mel takes hold of her left arm and tries to force the jacket sleeve up. Bridie says, 'No, this is going too far. You must stop now. Please leave.' This would normally have earned the woman a decisive slap around the chops from Slim, but she decides to let Mel have her arm and watches patiently as she turns and holds it up to make absolutely sure. She lets it go without a word and walks away to join two women standing near the bar.

'Time to leave,' says Bridie, signalling to the waiter. 'And since you've only just arrived in London, it's better that I pay, don't you think?'

'Thanks,' says Slim under her breath. She couldn't be more annoyed with herself. It was stupid to come to this side of town and by now she should be capable of getting out of a scrape like that without Bridie's help.

'You'd better carry my stuff out, Agnetha,' Bridie says with a tease in her eyes. 'We'll get an Uber outside.'

'I have a car parked a few streets away.'

'Okay, we'll take the Uber to your car. We don't want that woman on our tail.'

'Could you get a couple of glasses,' says Bridie, absorbed in her reunion with Rat, who is snaking round her neck.

Slim shudders and pours the wine. Bridie sits, one hand cradling Rat, the other going through the post. 'Will this be a problem for you?'

'Maybe. Depends on whether she's in touch with people at the office where we worked. She left under a cloud so I'm hoping not. By the way, that was bloody quick thinking. How many languages do you actually speak? You did Russian and Spanish at uni. What others?'

'In all, Norwegian, Swedish, Russian, French, Spanish, German and now Dutch and Danish and I am learning Italian. Eight fluently.'

'Amazing.' Slim takes some wine. 'Look, this is awkward. I can't explain much.'

'Oh, I know that, Mystery Girl! What was Mel looking for on your arm? Tracks, birthmark, medical bracelet?'

'A tattoo. I used a semi-permanent tattoo. It lasted ten days. Before it faded, I overlaid it with the exact same pattern. I had scores of them.'

'Hence on the left arm.'

Slim nods.

'Why?'

'A tattoo is regarded by everyone as a permanent identifier, but also because my then boss loathed tattoos. Although we were giving him the come-on in so many ways, it was thought that a tattoo would ultimately deter him. He was a freak and fearful of every form of disease. He believed that someone who had a tattoo carried hepatitis.'

'"We" . . . "it was thought". Sounds like you were working with a committee.'

'Kind of.'

'And that Mel! I didn't know you were lesbian, Slim. I mean, are you? You didn't used to be.'

'It's complicated.'

She grins. 'How?'

Slim looks away. 'Okay, this is what I'm going to tell you, and it's *all* I'm going to tell you. You probably already guessed my work is secret. Until October, I was undercover with some extremely bad and dangerous people. I needed to escape occasionally, and I used to come here. But then something happened, and I had to disappear. They were led to believe that I was dead, and that's why Mel is such a nightmare.' She drinks. 'It's a strange business being undercover for so long, watching for mistakes, keeping your story straight. It's like permanently holding a stress position. To help, I made the Sally identity a lot of things that I'm not. Sally was vegan; I eat meat. Sally was bi; I tend to like men. Sally smoked weed occasionally; I never touch it. Sally liked sport; I don't. I was being someone else and that was kind of fun, but, importantly, it also helps the demarcation, you understand?'

'*Tend to like men* is a bit vague. But you did sleep with Mel, right?'

'You're sex-obsessed, Bridie! Yes, I let her take me to bed. It was fine, I actually enjoyed it. But that was Sally. Like the obsession with vegan eating.'

'I hope she noticed the undercooked liver you left on your plate.'

Slim shrugs, and Bridie says, 'Isn't this a mental health nightmare, guaranteeing a gibbering wreck at the end? Did they get you any help?'

'I tried it but an emergency winter dig with Dougal was all I needed. I really can't be doing with all that embrace-your-inner-child shit. I've got it all straight in my head. If I could get through the last six months, I can do anything. Really, I'm fine.'

'So, are you a gay?'

'"I'm an equal opportunities lech," to quote Matt's hero, Michael Stipe. I hate the classification business. I do what I feel like with whom I like. Right now, I've got a new job and all my concentration is on that, and my mother, of course.'

'So soon? Undercover again?'

'No, I'll be Alice Parsons.'

Bridie's forehead knots. 'Isn't that more dangerous, now you've been spotted by your lover?'

'Very funny.'

'I'm serious. This shrieks jeopardy. Are you going to tell them about Mel?'

Slim shakes her head and glances at the portrait of Matthew, waiting for her by the door. 'I get something in exchange. They're going to search for Matt in a way that only they can.'

Bridie looks at the portrait, too. 'That's something. He was such a lovely boy. Wild but sweet with it. I know you miss him dreadfully.' Slim nods. Bridie gets up and lowers Rat into his cell and drops a rat cube in with him. She turns. 'Are they using you, Slim? It seems like it to me.' Then she approaches with her hands clasped and she is almost wringing them. She moves a step closer, bends down and lays an arm across Slim's shoulders. 'I haven't a clue what you're about to get involved in but it's too soon. Of that, I'm sure. You aren't free of the risks of the last job, and you haven't flushed Sally whatever-her-name-is out of your system.'

'Sally Latimer was her name.'

'I'm glad you said *her* not *my*. But that woman in the pub knew it was Sally. She wasn't put off by the missing tattoo. She absolutely knew. You admit that's a problem, yet you aren't going to tell your people.' She crouches, holding on to the side of the table with her fingertips. 'I want you to promise me that you are going to be very fucking careful, Slim. You're my absolute best friend – in fact my only real friend, and I don't want you joining Sally Latimer.'

Next morning, she loads the pickup then goes inside to fill her thermos mug with coffee. Bridie is standing in the kitchen in a thin cotton print dressing gown with her hands wrapped round a vintage French coffee bowl. Slim stops in her tracks. 'Don't you realise how depressing it is for us ordinary mortals to see you looking so ridiculously beautiful at seven thirty a.m.?'

Bridie shrugs. 'Maybe I'll come and visit you. Feel like getting out of London and seeing the countryside.'

'You don't know where I'm going to be.'

'I'll find you.' She moves to prepare Rat a salad of crumbled cube, greens, nuts and fruit. 'I always give it to him at the start of a weekend, then he knows I'm going to be around.'

'Raturday,' says Slim.

'That's pathetic. I'm going back to bed.' She comes over, bare feet drumming on the floor, and offers her cheek for a kiss. 'Lock me in when you leave, will you?' She turns towards the stairs. 'And bloody well be careful.'

CHAPTER 10

She clears London by eight and is on the motorway, heading north, when an incoming call illuminates on her dashboard at the exact moment she notices a black SUV behaving oddly in her wake. She answers before the phone can ring, her eyes glued to the wing mirror.

'This is Lola at the kennels. We're looking after Loup for you.'

'Ah, yes! Is he all right?' She moves to the slow lane and notes that the SUV behind her follows suit and drops behind a lorry.

'Not a happy dog. He's off his food and losing weight. His coat's all dry and dusty. We've had the vet look at him, but she couldn't find anything wrong. She says he's healthy, no parasites or anything like that. He's just homesick. Missing you.'

'It's my mother he's missing. As I explained, she's in hospital.' She moves ahead of several cars in the middle lane then crosses over to the right lane and accelerates.

'I'm sorry,' says Lola, 'but we feel you should find a place where Loupy – that's what Martha calls him – would be happier, poor lamb.'

'I can't collect him for a while yet. I just have too much on.'

She pushes on past two lorries in the middle lane and slides left in front of them.

'We'll give you a week to make other arrangements, then we'll insist that you remove him. It's for the dog's sake, you understand.'

'I'll be in touch,' she says, hanging up and wondering if she could pay someone to take the dog for good.

She has lost sight of the car but moves to the left lane to travel in front of another lorry. The two lorries which she's just passed, both from the same logistics company and presumably travelling in convoy, gradually draw level with her and overtake. She is well concealed when a black Ford SUV shoots past in the fast lane heading for a bank of traffic toiling up a hill about a mile away. She reduces her speed to a point where the driver behind her flashes his lights in frustration and almost swerves his wagon into the middle lane to make his point and overtakes her, sounding his horn. She slows to 30, then 20 mph, puts on hazard warning lights and moves to the hard shoulder, on which she coasts for a couple of hundred metres, then stops to watch the bank of traffic ahead of her vanish over the brow of the hill. After a few minutes, she returns to the left-hand lane and continues at a gentle speed. She checks to see if the Ford is waiting for her at any of the junction bridges and then devises a circular route away from the motorway and watches her tail for over an hour. She makes two calls during the diversion: to Dougal to postpone their meetup until the evening – he's relieved because he's managing a half dozen Saturday volunteers at the dig – and to Nurse Helen who is as bright and upbeat as ever, although Slim senses something behind the jollity. 'How'd you feel about an early-ish evening meal?' Helen asks. 'The Salamis Greek Tavern. Vegetarian friendly. Sweet people. No plate-breaking.'

'Well, yes. Is there something wrong?'

'Great, I've got to dash, but we'll see each other after you've visited your mum. Say, at six. We'll talk later.'

She continues north with the elusive character of Bridie Hansen replacing Melissa – who has been in her mind since she woke that morning – and worrying her. Bridie and she were good friends, with an easy relationship, yes, but it was odd that Bridie saw Slim as her best friend, indeed her only real friend. Bridie had never given any hint of that level of affection or shown the slightest need to see Slim regularly. Bridie was a freak, and not only in the language department, but this was odd, even for her. Slim knew she had lovers for, at the same time as being incredibly private and solitary, she was also unwaveringly candid about her love of sex. There was a war photographer – either Spanish or Portuguese – who was killed by a missile. His death had a profound impact on her. Months, maybe years of mourning but she rarely showed it, which led Dougal's sister Rose to say, 'She's part of the polar ice cap, that woman.'

Her mother is in a ward of four beds but with only one other patient, a tiny, misshapen elderly woman, who looks all but dead yet gives Slim a sweet smile when she enters. Which is more than she receives from her mother. Yet it's immediately clear that hostilities are over, and that Diana has returned to her pre-alcoholic self. 'Hello, darling Slim,' she says very quietly and with a rather solemn face. 'It's so nice of you to come. I wasn't expecting you.'

The helmet of bandages has gone. Slim bends down and gives her mother a kiss on the forehead. 'How are you?'

'The bones are mending, and I don't have a lot of pain, except at night. A wonderful nurse brings me library books. She has good taste and keeps up with my rate of consumption.'

'Helen?'

'Yes, Helen. A very pleasant person. I have asked her for a few favours. She says that you are friends – sort of.'

'Yes, she's nice. I wish I'd made it last weekend. But I've had a lot on. Sorry.'

'With your mysterious job.'

Slim doesn't rise. 'Lots of new opportunities. It's great.'

'Did you know that our Polish forebears worked in military intelligence? Military Intelligence – MI.' She says this with a little raise of the eyebrows and, amazingly enough, a smile that Slim meets with a pleasant, noncommittal expression.

'You never talk much about your family, but, yes, I did know.'

Her mother inhales and lets out a long breath. 'I must tell you about them properly sometime, but I'm still very tired. I don't get much sleep here. I must say I could do with a drink. I don't suppose you . . .' Slim is already shaking her head. 'Oh well, I couldn't expect Little Miss Prim to bring the goods, could I?' She stops, maybe to control the nasty side. 'I've been doing a lot of thinking about you know who.'

'Matthew.' Slim said his name because her mother was prone to using 'you know what' and 'you know who' to avoid the awkward reality in a word or a name. 'The people I work for are going to try to find him. If anyone can, they will. I'm not making any promises, but maybe there's hope of some closure.'

'Yes, closure. That's what it's all about these days – a result, a conclusion, satisfaction, an end.' She looks across to her elderly companion who is trying to puncture a juice box with a straw. Slim goes to help her.

'That was kind,' her mother says when she returns to the

chair. 'I've been thinking that Matthew was many things, but he was never unkind. He would not have knowingly caused this level of suffering to us.'

'He was thoughtless,' says Slim, 'and he was an addict, Mum. Addicts can't think of anyone else.' She has said it, and why not?

Her mother nods and studies her before speaking. 'Shame is also a motivator. If he's ashamed of what he has become, he won't get in touch. Every addict feels shame acutely. It's almost the worst part of it.'

There's nothing to say to this. Slim repeats that she is making every effort on Matthew and moves to broach the subject of Loup, but gets nowhere on the idea of finding him a new home. Her mother puts up her hand and says she won't entertain such a thought. Loup saved her, though she does not say how. Soon, Diana's eyes begin to droop, and Slim says she should go, at which they snap open again. 'Have a nice dinner.'

'How do you know I'm having dinner?'

'I asked Helen to take you out. It's on me, so remember to drink as much as you can on my behalf.' She winks.

'I'm driving.'

'Little Miss Prim.' She winks again. 'I'll see you soon, darling.' The use of 'darling' is certainly new and almost puts her off wondering what her mother and Helen have cooked up.

Helen has made an effort, with a full-skirted cotton dress of yellow and red flowers, very 1950s, and a short red cardigan over it. She dazzles the restaurant as she enters, just as Bridie had the Eagle's Nest, and sits down to call for beer, dips and pitta.

She seems on edge, glances at Slim and takes a deep breath. 'Cards on the table,' she says. 'Did your mum tell you she asked me to take you out?' Slim nods. 'Did she tell you why?' Another deep breath, plus a look of limitless sympathy. 'This is very hard. She asked me to tell you that she hasn't very long.'

'How do you mean?'

'She has liver cancer, and she's dying. She may have six months, but no more than that.' A long pause, an awkward look, then, 'It's probably much less. I'm so sorry.'

Slim looks away, profoundly shaken. Helen lays a hand on hers.

'I know it's hard to take in, but she wanted me to tell you because she couldn't face doing it. Not after all you have been through together. Your brother and her drinking. She didn't know how.'

'Thanks. I understand.' Slim doesn't cry because she never does. 'Can you give me more detail?'

'You should talk to the specialist, Mr Stephens. He was trying to reach you but then your mother told him she would handle it in her own way, which is this.' She opens her hands to the restaurant. 'They found a tumour on the first week she was with us. It seems they didn't understand the abnormalities with her blood and took a closer look. Frankly, it's odd they missed it when they were scanning your mother's pelvis. They've told her that it's inoperable. Chemo and radiotherapy may give her some time, then it's palliative care.' She waits for Slim to absorb this. 'I am so sorry, pet.'

'She told me she was killing herself with drink. Turns out she was right.' How did she manage to contemplate her mother's death with such equanimity while she was holding her head and Salt was giving her CPR, but now finds the prospect so shocking?

'It may not be drink that did it, though the doctor says her liver has done a lot of mileage. You need to speak to him to get the full picture.'

Helen leaves Slim to her thoughts. She's good at letting things sink in, a skill she acquired in the room with the faulty lighting and Covid posters – the bad-news room. Helen waits, drinks, loads a stick of celery with tzatziki and flashes an encouraging smile. 'You okay, pet?'

'Yes.'

'She wanted me to tell you that you must arrange everything. She may not be able to go home. She says there are tons of things to organise – bills and that kind of thing. And the dog. She never stops talking about the dog.'

'Yes, I do most of it, anyway. The dog's in a kennel.'

'She says you're super efficient.'

Slim shrugs. Can she do it all with the new work at Middle Kingdom? Of course. She'll make a start this weekend.

They order a bottle of wine but Slim goes easy. Helen doesn't. It's Saturday night: she's had a tough week, her son has gone to London, and her husband is getting drunk with his rugby mates. She shakes her head and her face clouds. 'I can't understand how I married him. I feel such a fool.'

'People change. You'd never guess that my mother was once the smartest woman in advertising, the best dressed and most beautiful, too.'

'I would. She's very sharp and I see the beauty.'

It's easier for them to stay off the subject of their families and, because she wants to avoid talking about her work, she asks Helen about her life. She comes from Middlesbrough, a Catholic family of five children, all of them achievers. University, a job in local government and the birth of her son preceded retraining to become a nurse. Slim is used to listening for what people aren't saying as much as to what they are and, bit by bit, she suspects there's something Helen is avoiding, possibly to do with her last post at a hospital called St Mary's, which was the same job as she has in A&E now. 'Why did you leave?' she asks.

Helen looks up and thinks before she replies. 'We called it Bloody Mary's. A lot of people died who shouldn't have after being treated in A&E. The follow-up care was pathetic. Negligent was the only word for it.'

'Did you say anything – complain?'

'Got nowhere. Couldn't prove anything, but I knew that the patients leaving A&E were already on the road to recovery, then they just died.' She stops and looks up with an intensity that Slim hasn't seen before because Helen's expression is all about making people feel better about themselves. 'We had this lad in a few days ago. Broke his arm and leg falling off a tractor. We noticed he wasn't recovering as he should. The answer was that he was totally dehydrated. And guess what! He had salmonella poisoning. We've seen a lot of that recently.'

'That's interesting.'

'Yes – all from the Ely area.'

'How many died in St Mary's?'

'Oh, a lot. A real lot.'

'And you just left.'

'Had to. I was threatened. I knew they'd use something about my private life, which would damage the other person more than me. I had no proof, so what was I going to do?'

'The media?'

She shakes her head. 'Even the media needs proof.'

Slim picks up her glass, has a thought and puts it down without drinking. 'Maybe they could find that proof. Just saying . . .' Which she isn't.

'How do you mean?'

'Possibly I can help. I have a new job on a website, and they might be interested.'

'Sounds good. Anyway, I absolutely love my job here. It's a good hospital and your mother is in great hands. And I will keep an eye on her. I really like her. She's quite a character.'

Outside, Helen says, 'I'm sorry. I never asked about you all evening! Just wittered about myself, as usual.'

'There's not a lot to say. Very dull.'

'Next time! I'll look forward to it.' She moves closer. 'I'm sorry to be the bearer of bad news. Your mum needed me to do this. I hope you understand.' She hugs Slim. It's closer and longer than the standard Helen Meiklejohn hug – the one she received in the bad-news room – and, with the lingering kiss on the cheek, probably goes beyond a strict definition of pastoral care.

CHAPTER 11

Spooked by the black Ford on the motorway, she waits and watches in farm gates and unlit lay-bys to make sure her route to her mother's house is well and truly rinsed. She's received two pieces of information since leaving Helen that may mean nothing, but she wants to be sure. Earlier, she made a call to Starr Security, the outfit keeping watching on the house. A man named Dave said there was little to report except that the gardener had made a visit for just half an hour, which doesn't surprise her, and a delivery van parked twice at the front door and the driver got out with a package but did not leave it either time.

'The same package and the same man?' she asked. She hasn't ordered anything and knows her mother never shops online.

Dave came back to say it was the same man but he carried two different packages, one was a medium-sized box and the second was more like an envelope and bore an Amazon logo. Amazon rings bells with her. When she was undercover in Ivan Guest's organisation, Ballard used Amazon packaging to deliver thumb drives loaded with spyware updates. Amazon makes for perfect cover.

'The point,' she said crisply, 'is that he didn't return with the box that he wasn't able to deliver. He came back with an envelope. What happened to the box?' She tells him to email her a still of the man from the CCTV footage. He says he'll do better than that – he'll send film clips.

Then, as she was pulling out of a lay-by, Lola from the kennel rang. That afternoon two men turned up and said they were looking for a stolen dog. It belonged to a very rich individual who was anxious for its return, they said. This individual would pay a lot of money for information on the dog and the person who stole it. They mentioned £500.

'It was Martha, my partner, who spoke to them,' said Lola. 'She didn't like the smell of them one bit. Not dog people, if you know what I mean. Very unpleasant air. Big expensive car and expensive shoes, Martha says.'

'Make of car?'

'Mercedes – a big one.'

'An SUV.'

'Yes.'

'What were they wearing, aside from the expensive shoes?'

'Leather jackets. They looked very similar, apart from the fact that one shaved his head and the other had a stubble beard, like a goatee. Foreign, of course.'

'Just to say, Loup wasn't stolen,' says Slim. 'He was a stray. And, if you think about it, who in their right mind would want to steal such a dog?'

Lola presses on. 'Martha let them look at all the dogs, but they didn't recognise Loup. I mean to say, who goes searching for a dog when they don't know what the dog looks like? They asked who brought Loup in but we don't give out personal data, human or dog.'

'I'm sure it's nothing. Can I send you a photo later this evening to see if you recognise the man?'

'Yes, and er . . . we do have an agreement that you will collect Loup at the end of the week, don't we?'

'Absolutely,' says Slim.

She reaches Long Aston village at 9.30 p.m. as fat raindrops begin to splatter the windscreen, goes past the entrance to Steward's House, and sees nothing in the driveway. On the other side of the village, she turns the car and parks by a phone mast, which serves the flat country for miles around, and opens the email from Dave at Starr Security. Everything is as he described. She watches the film until there is a clear image of the delivery man's face, pauses and takes a screenshot, which she sends to Lola by text. Then she phones Dave and asks if there has been any movement at the house. All he can see on the cameras is flashes of lightning in the north. No lights in the house; no sign of movement. 'Keep an eye out, will you? I'll be there in a few minutes.' He asks if there's a problem. She'll let him know.

The storm crashes and flickers for several minutes before the rain starts in earnest and, by the time she's heading back to the house, the lane is near impossible to see. She creeps along at no more than five miles per hour and goes even slower through a flood that has covered the road. Just as she accelerates out of the water, on her right-hand side, she spots a man dressed in some form of cape or hillwalking cagoule. He is turned away from her and motionless and doesn't seem to notice the car or the splash that surely soaks him. She glances in the mirror but can only see the vague shape of him; he is now moving in the opposite direction. She brakes and jumps out. 'You need help?' she yells into the night. 'Can I give you a lift?' No answer comes.

A flash of lightning, and she sees that no one's there; he must have hopped over the stile into the woods for shelter.

'That's the third time I've seen you,' she says out loud as she climbs in.

She drives on towards the house but pulls up short in the middle of the lane to consider what she's going to do. So what if she's being paranoid? Her mother's post and bills are the only reason she's going to the house, and they can wait. She moves the car on to the side of the lane, at the point where there's room for another vehicle to pass, and studies the clips of the delivery man on her phone. In both, she notices he doesn't at first press the doorbell but looks around as if to trying to find somewhere to leave his package. But it is half-hearted on both occasions. He's scoping the place to see if it's occupied, and he's interested in the security. Twice he looks at one of the three cameras the company has installed, which is how Dave got such a clear picture of the man. After a quarter of an hour of the rain pounding on the roof of her pickup, she decides to take a closer look, gets out of the car and shrugs on her heavy waterproof. She's about two hundred metres from the house and there are plenty of bends along this stretch of the lane so there's no danger that her lights will have been seen. She starts off but goes to the back of the pickup and takes out the mattock that she brandished at Mills and Salt. Lugging it over her shoulder, she goes to the gateway. The chain hangs loose. Now she remembers that she didn't return to fasten it the last time she visited her mother's house. She leans on the gate and sweeps her phone flashlight across the ground. The rain has beaten down the grass and cow parsley, but there are new tracks leading towards the trees. The light doesn't go far enough for her to see to the spot where she parked the pickup. She eases the gate open, closes and locks it, then, covering most of the flashlight beam with her fingers, picks her way through the grass.

The worst of the storm has passed, leaving only the sound of water dripping from the trees and the distant crumps of thunder. As she moves, her breath fumes in the rain-cooled air. She nears the trees. Her phone vibrates with a text alert. The message is from Lola at the kennels. Martha recognises the delivery man as one of the two men who visited the kennels. Slim sends a thumbs-up emoji and turns left at the trees. She's unsurprised to see her phone light reflected in the body of a car parked almost precisely in the place she used. It's a Mercedes SUV. She texts Dave. *Intruders in Steward's House. Car concealed on track at rear. Reg – ML24 LXZ. Need police. You call them and keep me out of it. I'm not here.* He replies, *Not a problem. Don't approach!*

She has no intention of doing so. She takes a photo of the registration plate and sends it to Ballard.

Why r u contacting me? he replies.

Need 2 know who owns the car, can u access Police database?

Sorry, no can do.

Give it to Tudor. I'm in a situation here.

No reply.

'Arsehole,' she mutters, stuffing the phone in her pocket. 'Fuck you, Tom.'

She withdraws to the trees, knowing that the Mercedes cannot turn on the track, and that it must either head towards the ford or reverse to the gate. Half an hour goes by. Dave texts to tell her that two police cars are on their way. She puts on a tight-fit black beanie she wore at Alder Fen, smears mud on her face and the backs of her hands, and moves to the field to observe the house, taking care not to be silhouetted by the lightning still pulsing in the north. The house is completely dark. She waits. Then a brief flare of a match or lighter in the kitchen window. Right then she sees one set of blue police lights moving from the north some way off. She retreats to a fallen tree, about forty feet from the car, and sits with the mattock across her knees. She reckons the police are a minute or two away yet – there are many twists and turns in the road, which is certain to be flooded in some parts – but the intruders will soon be aware of them. Suddenly, she hears the back door of the house being thrown open, then the intruders plunging through the laurel bushes to their car. One is using a phone torch. She can make out two shadows. The Mercedes jumps forward but then stops and begins to reverse towards the gate. She slides from the tree trunk and crouches, with her head dipped down. The car executes a clumsy left turn in reverse and arrives at the gate, whereupon the passenger jumps out and realises the gate is locked. She waits to see what the men will do. They could reverse into the gate at speed and hope to force it, but that would need much greater momentum than they can build on the short, slippery length of track. The wheels spin in the wet grass and the car lurches forward to take the track to the hamlet of Hales. Headlights fork through the boughs above her. She phones Dave and tells him to inform the police that the two men in the Mercedes are on a farm track that ends at the old Methodist chapel in a hamlet about a mile away. 'If they're quick, they can cut them off in Hales,' she says. 'Again, keep me out of it. Say you saw something suspicious on one of your cameras.'

She waits for the information to be passed to the police car that has pulled up on the other side of Steward's House, its blue lights reflected in the branches of the beech trees at the front. When it leaves, she enters the house through the back door, which has been jimmied with a crowbar. A smell of men and cigarettes pervades the ground floor.

She collects the mail from beneath the front door, and gives the place a once-over, trying to assess whether the men were lying in wait for her or searching the place again. There are signs of disturbance around her mother's desk. Also the drawers in the kitchen table and those of a Victorian tallboy, which stands in the hall, have been rifled and not properly closed. Were they doing this to kill time while they waited for her to arrive? It's not possible to say. Did they know she was coming? She tramps back to her own car, wondering about the black Ford SUV that followed her out of London.

CHAPTER 12

It's past midnight and the Turk's Head public house next door to Dougal's cottage is dark, but he's waited up and immediately Slim knocks, opens the door, filling the frame like a Roald Dahl giant. '"Come in, I'll give you shelter from the storm",' he says. He's quoting Bob Dylan, an obsession with Dougal. 'You've looked better after a day in the mud at the dig.'

He ushers her into the warm snug of his sitting room. It's tidy, books filed alphabetically, she remembers, a shelf of ancient arte-facts, including the little carved Anubis from the First Dynasty in Egypt and a wall of small oils and drawings he's picked up at country auctions and online. Embers glow in the grate.

'What happened?' he asks. 'You look dreadful.'

'I had some bad news about my mum – it's terminal. And, later, I had a bit of trouble with the car.'

He gives her a doubtful look but nods because he knows from old that she won't elaborate.

She pulls off her boots, goes to wash in the tidy little kitchen and returns dabbing her face with kitchen roll. When she's finished, Dougal takes the damp paper from her and slings it on the fire. Smoke and steam billow up the chimney. She pulls a cardigan out of her backpack and drapes it around her shoulders.

'I'm so sorry about your mum. That's rough. I lost mine to cancer.' He reaches over to a wicker side table. 'Scotch, wine, some of the magic stuff?' He waves a bottle of his sloe gin.

'A massive glass of red would be lovely. Thank you.'

He hands her the wine. 'I've got a problem, Slim. Jimmy from King's Lynn has been chucked out by his wife. Philandering and serial archaeology. He's in the spare room, sleeping off a belter of a night in the Turk's. Only about half of me fits on the sofa horizontally, and even you would be pushed to—'

'I'll sleep with you. But please don't fall on me like a freezer.'

'That's harsh.' He grins.

'Actually, it was more like a collapsing wall.'

'You know how to make a fellow feel wanted. Drink some more of the red infuriater and spill your beans.' He stretches out, all six foot four inches of him, knits his hands behind his head and beams. Few people are happier in their skin than Dougal Hass.

'Well, I'm returning to journalism.' She waits, smiles at him again and says, 'I have a big favour to ask. I want to write about the log boat and what was underneath it for my first story for a site called Middle Kingdom.' She doesn't mention she's already written and submitted most of the story. She drinks some wine and instantly feels flushed and woozy.

He lights a roll-up and looks troubled. 'I'm in charge. I can't authorise a leak, Slim.'

'What if I just do it? You called it *my boat*. Why can't I write about it? At least it'll be accurate.'

He shakes his head.

'Come on. I really need this.'

'Okay, here's the deal. You write the story about your boat and the man under it. And you can date them to about 3,500 years ago, which is what we believed until a few days ago. We do have an exact date now because of the tree ring data, but I'm not going to tell you that. And obviously keep your name away from it.'

'They don't allow bylines. Can I use the photos from WhatsApp of that day? I only need two or three.'

'No, they're traceable. I have some on my phone which no one will recognise. You can have two – that's all I'm giving you – and I will delete them on my phone.'

'Thank you. Thank you. Thank you.' She briefly kisses him on the lips and gets a face full of smoke for her pains. She looks down, marvelling at the big, good-natured beauty of the man, and gives him a much longer kiss. 'Thank you.'

'You're a piece of work, Slim,' he says and crooks one arm behind his head. His face clouds. 'Can I say something?' She nods. 'Whatever has taken you away from the dig and wherever you've been for the last three years is not good for you. And, Slim, you've got to look after your mother now. I cared for my mum in her last weeks. No one else is going to do it for you.'

'I know. I know. Do you mind me writing about the Boatman?'

He frowns. 'You can call him the Boatman, but we don't any longer.'

'Why?'

'We believe he was a sacrifice or ritually punished. There are cut marks in the area of his groin, which *could* indicate that he was castrated before being garrotted.'

'Now I understand the look of that skull.'

'And the thing that looked like a rush mat that was placed

over his genital area was a bag in which there was a very small, coiled bronze ring, possibly belonging to a woman, and a slender palstave axe head, which could be the implement of mutilation. But, Slim, you can't use any of this because only I and Anne at the lab know about it. And these are just theories, which I'm writing up for an interim paper. It's a good story but I want to tell it to the world first.' He stops and grins at her.

They talk and listen to music then go upstairs and prepare for bed to the rumble of Jimmy from King's Lynn's snores. The bedroom is too small for them to move around at the same time, so she sits in a long T-shirt waiting for Dougal to do his thing before taking a shower herself. When she returns, he's lying with his hands together high on his chest, sound asleep. She reaches over him to switch the light off then rests her head below his hands. He's like a ship at anchor, rising and falling with the swell of the ocean.

She wakes at first light, with his arm wrapped around her and his hand lying on her right breast. He stirs, nuzzles her neck then goes back to sleep. Light edges the curtains. Outside, the dawn chorus fills the Norfolk farmscape. She is bathed in warmth and comfort that she hasn't experienced for as long as she can recall. She smiles at the memory of Bridie talking about a deep need she feels even as a confirmed loner and quoting the American writer Roger Angell: 'Everyone in the world wants to be with someone tonight, together in the dark, with the sweet warmth of a hip or a foot or a bare expanse of shoulder within reach.'

She would gladly sleep another couple of hours beside him, but her mind churns with the events of the previous evening. She dismisses the idea that this latest visit by two men to Steward's House had anything to do with that brainless, sexy blabbermouth Melissa Bright recognising her in the pub, though that may eventually reach Guest's ears.

Dougal stretches and opens his eyes. 'You're on spin cycle. What's going on in your head?'

'Not a lot.'

'Rubbish. Go and make us some coffee, woman.' She punches him on the bicep. 'Bloody violent bitch, get out of my bed. Coffee!'

In the kitchen, she finds a tarnished Moka Express pot which she fills with ground coffee and places on a small gas stove. She takes a banana from the fruit bowl and examines the shelf of cookery books, then looks out at her host's vegetable patch, already dug and with runner bean wigwams and lines of seedlings marked by sticks, and beyond it to the great damp flatness of Norfolk; pastel greens lit by thin shafts of sunlight. She calls up to him, 'Have you seen Bridie recently?' She's thinking how they both live in small tidy spaces with incredibly neat gardens.

'Not for six or seven years. How is she? You know what my sister Rose said about her?'

'Yeah. But polar ice caps melt. You should be in touch.'

She takes the mugs upstairs. Dougal has showered and lies under the covers with his damp hair against the headboard. He stretches to take his cup, and she climbs on to him and straddles him. There's an explosion from next door and into Dougal's bedroom comes Jimmy from King's Lynn – dark and feral, with a *Make Archaeology Great Again* baseball hat and glasses held together by insulating tape.

'I heard voices,' says Jimmy.

Dougal says, 'That's exactly why you don't fucking come in, you absolute moron.'

'Oh, sorry!'

'This is not what it seems,' Dougal says.

Looking down, Slim mouths, 'Not yet.'

'No, of course not,' says Jimmy backing out. 'You okay, Slim? Bloody wonderful about the dig, eh?'

'Fine, thanks, Jimmy. Yes, wonderful. There's coffee in the big pot.'

'Ta. Got to be going now. I'm on duty at the site to stop those bastard journalists snooping. Cheers.' He slams the door and rushes downstairs. They hear him crashing about the kitchen then the front door bangs and Jimmy from King's Lynn is gone.

'It's amazing how such a small man makes so much noise,' she says, before draining her cup and taking his and putting them on the side table. 'I hadn't finished,' he says.

She lifts one leg then the other to remove the duvet and looks down at him.

'No collapsing walls,' he says.

'Or freezers,' she says and bends down to kiss him. As their lips meet and begin to play, Dougal groans with the desire that he assumed he was going to have to suppress. The kiss goes on for the longest time and she strokes his face with her fingertips until she wriggles downwards and eases him into her. 'You are better at kissing than I ever imagined,' she says.

'I was pissed last time,' he says.

'Thank you for the boat,' she says pushing up on his shoulders and beginning to work her hips. 'It was very generous of you.'

'Do you always talk while you're having sex?'

'Yes, when I like someone and they're not three sheets to the wind.'

He strains upwards to kiss her breast and she notices there's no spare flesh on him at all. How did she not see this before? He's the Viking warlord of Bridie's memory.

Now, she closes her eyes and is silent as she works for them both to come, which they do one after the other some ten glorious minutes later. She slumps on him, breathing heavily into the side of his face. They give each other myopic looks of gratitude and, in Slim's case, amazement.

He shifts on to his side, one hand under his chin. 'What were you thinking about when you woke me?'

'Everything. What you said last night; my mother's illness; the bills that must be paid; and her dog Loup. You don't want a dog, do you?'

'How would I look after a dog at Alder Fen?'

'He could dig up bones.' She sighs. 'And I was wondering where I'm going to live in Milton Keynes.'

He's silent for a few moments. 'I may have an answer to that. Remember Clive Killick – the Romano-British specialist? He's got a canal boat on the Grand Union, and I know it's in the marina at Milton Keynes. He usually tries to move it to a mooring on a canal near his summer dig, then cycles to the site every day, but he's working at a fort on Hadrian's Wall for the summer and can't get his boat close enough. I'll have a word later. If it's free, I'm sure he will let you have it.'

'How much do you think he'd charge?'

'Got to be at least eight hundred a month and it would only be for the summer. Say to October.'

'Sounds brilliant – thank you.' She kisses him on the cheek and on his fluttering eyelids and briefly wonders at her own mobile sexuality. She likes Helen and Helen was coming on to her, yet now she's in bed with Dougal and loves being with him. Sally has gone and Slim is back, with an interest in good-looking, decent men. Is that it? Does this make any sense? She doesn't pursue the thought because Dougal is saying something and, besides, the question is never answered.

'You were talking in your sleep last night,' he says, crooking his arm behind his head. 'Who's the man in the cape?'

'What do you mean?' she says jerking her head back to look at him.

'That's what you said, "who's the man in the cape?"'

PART TWO

CHAPTER 13

She steps off the narrowboat *Spindle* and calls out to Clive Killick that she'll see him later. She wants instructions on how to fill the boat's tanks with diesel and water, start the motor and move and moor her, which she will need to do periodically because he doesn't have a permanent spot at the marina.

Killick, who, according to Dougal, is the heir to a biscuit fortune, is an unworldly figure in his forties with a beatific grin and wisps of blond hair escaping from an engineer's cap. He talks in bursts of information without caring whether his audience is listening or understands what he's saying. Slim decides it's time to leave when, without warning, he kneels with a rag and wrench and starts adjusting the engine's cooling system. The interview is plainly over. She has agreed to give him a deposit of £500 and will pay £220 a week, which seems steep until Killick says he could let it out to holidaymakers for far more. She will move her possessions on to the *Spindle* in two days' time. He hasn't specified that she can't have a dog, so she didn't mention Loup.

She walks a little way north along the canal, past a pub and a row of maisonettes. It's not exactly Venice. She imagines the architect's drawing of the Milton Keynes waterside idyll – couples walking hand in hand beneath shaped acacia, children playing by the canal, a merry boatman waving from a passing craft. The reality is goose shit everywhere, clapped-out cars and balconies stuffed with rubbish and dead pot plants. She finds a path leading away from the canal and heads in the direction of the central grid of Milton Keynes, which she explored the previous evening. She plans to walk into the city but then receives a text, which reads: *cage.battle.tens@ 9.30.*

She has no doubt this code is from Tom Ballard. They often used the What3Words app to arrange a rendezvous at short notice. She enters https://w3w.co/cage.battle.tens into her phone and is taken to a square in Bletchley Park. She summons an Uber but when they arrive finds the site is closed. Then a man in museum uniform approaches her and says she is expected, and she's shown through the empty reception area and let out into a drive that leads to the Bletchley Park Mansion.

She passes buildings on her right, all evidently constructed during the war but newly painted and well maintained, a lake on her left, then takes the turning to her right and arrives at the three-by-three metres square uniquely named by the app cage.battle.tens. She sees three huts constructed from brick and dark green timber. On her left is the largest, Hut Three, on her right an entirely wooden building labelled Hut One, and ahead of her Hut Six.

Aside from two gardeners working in front of the main house, about a hundred metres away, she sees no one, but she's been given a reference, and until something happens, on that spot she will stay. She looks at her phone, sends texts to the security firm and Helen and thanks Dougal for the introduction to Killick. Dougal and she have already had an exchange of emails about the story, but she wants to say how pleased she is with *Spindle* because it's so clean and uncluttered.

'Ah, there you are!'

She looks up from her phone. Oliver Halfknight stands in the gap between Hut One and Hut Three. He beckons her. 'It's about to rain. Come in.' He goes to an open door, which is concealed by a brick wall, and waits for her. 'You know what this is?' he says patting the bricks with his hand. 'A blast wall. They built these wooden huts and got them into service then put a wall around them to protect the people inside from bomb blasts. They were in that much of a hurry . . . and so are we.'

They enter a narrow passage that goes the length of the building and off which there are several rooms to the left and right. One door is open. It's small with bare wooden floorboards, filing cabinets, two desks and chairs, clipboards and old-fashioned desk lights. Except for one or two memos from the time pinned in a display there is no hint of the work that went on there.

He gestures to two chairs, but she is reading the memo dated 28.10.42 from someone who has only signed A.D.(A).

I told Miss Moore, who is well aware of it, that Hut Six still prefers girls of better social standing even though they may not be quite so intelligent. However, I made it quite clear to Fletcher that it was most unlikely that there would be many Roedean or Wycombe Abbey girls available and that they would have to take what came out of the bag.

'Did you read this? I don't know which is worse – the sexism or the snobbery.'

'I thought it would amuse you,' he says.

'Unbelievable.'

He pulls a chair from one of the desks, turns the other and

they sit down facing each other. 'I thought you'd like to see what people in our profession still regard as a sacred space.' He looks around. 'In this shabby little building they decoded the Enigma radio intercepts sent by Hitler's Wehrmacht and Luftwaffe, the beginning of the work that shortened the war by a couple of years, maybe more.' He studies her. There's no vagueness now. She notices the pronounced downward slant of the lids at the corner of his eyes. 'We have a problem, don't we? Ivan Guest appears to be on to you.'

'The men at my mother's house?'

'Yes. Tom Ballard told us. You should have been in touch with Salt and Mills immediately.'

'I told Peter Salt.'

'Too late. But all was not lost. Using the registration plate you gave Tom, we've traced their movements to a house in Ealing. The car is leased to a company in Barnet, so no joy there. We have eyes on that Ealing property. However, this morning we learned that two individuals of interest left the country on a flight to Istanbul late Sunday. If we can match images from Border Force cameras at Heathrow with material from your security footage at your mother's property, we'll know if the men at the house are gone, and we can refuse entry if they try to return. But that doesn't end the problem because we don't know how they found you. So, the question is – what do we do?'

'They didn't see me and there's nothing in the house to connect Sally with me.' She was recognised by Melissa in the pub, of course, but she can hardly confess to that now.

'The risk is clear.'

'Are you thinking of finding someone else to do the job here?'

He says nothing.

'It would be a waste of all my preparation. I've got the interview with them this morning and they seem to like what I've written.'

'Yes,' he says. He's letting her do the talking. She folds her arms and meets silence with silence.

'Well . . .' he starts after a little time, 'we're keen to get this done, and it should only take a matter of weeks. If it weren't for this Guest problem, it would be the simplest job in the world, although I must tell you that Middle Kingdom is alert to surveillance and is well defended. We've had no success remotely; you'll need to introduce spyware.'

'So, you want me to go ahead.'

'You'll have full protection. Salt and Mills will watch your back. It'll be just a short time and you are *miraculously* suited to this role.' He gets up and looks through a window. 'The rain seems to have held off. Shall we take a stroll? We've still got the place to ourselves for a bit longer.' They leave Hut Six.

As they pass the grass tennis court, he says, 'Bletchley has all been grotesquely mythologised, of course. People think Alan Turing ran absolutely everything. He was important, but an impressive range of brain power was assembled here at the beginning of the war, the classicist Dilly Knox, for example, the chess champion Hugh Alexander, the mathematician Gordon Welchman, as well as the forebears of the people at Middle Kingdom. Most of these individuals are unknown now and never received the credit they deserved.'

'Including thousands of women,' she says.

'Indeed.'

They move up a ramp into a stable yard. He points to a stone memorial of an open book, on their right. 'Speaking of credit due, I thought you should see this.'

Inscribed in the book are the names of three mathematicians of the Polish Intelligence Service who first broke Enigma and contributed to the Allied victory.

She reads the dedication. 'I had no idea,' she says.

'Most people don't. The Poles broke the commercial version of the Enigma machine in the thirties and handed over its secrets two months before the war to the British and French in a special underground facility at a place called Pyry. All very cloak and dagger. The British had got nowhere with Enigma and were astounded at what those three Poles – Marian Rejewski, Jerzy Różycki and Henryk Zygalski – accomplished.' He sweeps the courtyard with one hand. 'So, all this was as much a Polish achievement as British.' He smiles. 'Given your background, I thought it would interest you to see the memorial.'

'My background?'

'Your mother's people! Your great-grandfather Colonel Leon Benski and his remarkable son Jan, your mother's father! Both extraordinarily talented intelligence operatives. That's all in your file. As I said, you are *miraculously* qualified for this job. Your great-grandfather Leon was responsible for destroying evidence of the Enigma breakthrough just after the German invasion of Poland in 'thirty-nine. His name should probably be here, too.'

'Did my mother know I was being vetted?'

'Almost certainly, yes.'

She shakes her head. How typical of her that she had known all along what she did but had played a game of not knowing. 'All I know is that her father was deported to the Soviet Union from Poland.'

'Yes, Jan – Leon's son. He's an entirely different hero. But you should get her to tell you all about that.'

He moves away from the memorial and looks towards the Edwardian stable buildings. 'I'm pleased you're sticking with this, but I want you to know that your safety is uppermost in our minds.'

'Can I ask something? Why did you come all this way to talk to me about the least important operation on the Service's books?'

He nods an acknowledgement that the situation is an odd one, looks around and then his gaze settles on her. For a moment, she wonders if that's a trace of anxiety in his expression. 'On the contrary,' he says at length, 'it may be the most important.'

'Really?'

He looks away and says nothing more.

'Have you any news about my brother Matthew? My mother has terminal cancer and doesn't have long, so this has become rather urgent.'

'I'm sorry to hear that. Very sorry, indeed. It must be a great blow. Can you manage this work, as well?'

'Yes. She's being well cared for. I'll visit as often as I can. And Matthew?'

'They are on the case. Last I heard, they are looking in Ireland. We are doing everything we can.'

CHAPTER 14

She arrives at the Heights Building on Silbury Boulevard fifteen minutes early and looks through the glass door to a deserted lobby and an empty commissionaire's desk. A computer monitor is on and a pencil, attached by a string to a clipboard on the desk, gently pendulums. There's no bell by the door. She knocks and puts her face to the glass with her hand cupped to her right cheek, then steps back to look up at the four storeys and the building's clean, white lines. She can just see a roof terrace with plants at the top. Nothing pretentious about this mid-rise – a good building, she feels. A figure in black overalls, wearing a cap printed with 'Pest Force', a face mask and protective glasses is at the door, waving a gloved hand to indicate that someone is coming. The figure turns away. On her back is a cartoon picture of a rat, the words '24-hr Pest Control' and a web address. A security guard, a middle-aged black man with bunched dreads and glasses on a chain comes to unlock the door. He says his name is Arnold and she's expected. The lift pings. The pest control woman, now without her mask and gloves, is holding the door open and waves to her, but she's also holding it for someone else. A man has just parked a large motorcycle at the rear of the

Heights Building and she can see through the clear glass wall
that he's making his way to a back entrance using a stick. Slim
knows this is J. J. Skelpick, writer, videographer, investigator,
war casualty and son of codebreaker Gordon.

The woman in the uniform says, 'You must be Alice. We're
all excited about your story on the boat and body in the bog. It
was circulated this morning.'

'You work for the site?' says Slim, looking her up and down.

'Hi, Deputy News Editor. Abigail's number two. Shazi
Kalash.'

J. J. Skelpick enters the lift with his arm through the helmet
and pivots awkwardly to face the doors. 'Thank you for that and
good morning.' No hair grows on two square inches at the back
of his head, but longer strands cover the bald patch. He shifts
his weight from one leg to the other. 'You're Alice Parsons?' he
says to the doors.

'Yes, but people called me Slim.'

'Read your story last night. Abigail said we'd all have a
chance to meet you this morning. So, now we've met.'

'And this is J. J. Skelpick,' says Shazi. 'Our star writer and a
very rude man.'

Skelpick turns and offers a crooked smile. 'I try.'

The doors open. He mutters thanks and sets off at a clip
towards a conference room that is surrounded by glass. The
remainder of the floor is open-plan. She is aware of space to her
left and beyond that, a roof terrace. About twenty-five people,
mostly in their twenties, are working at laptops. 'Take no notice
of him,' says Shazi.

'What's with the uniform?' Slim asks.

'Our shitty landlord reneged on a deal he did with Abigail
in lockdown. They were desperate to let the space and now

want our two floors back.' She gives Slim a conspiratorial look. 'Someone just came round – an online gambling company – but they decided against it because of the rodent problem. Now, I'm going to take you over to Abigail.'

Slim has spotted Abigail Exton-White at a desk beneath a sign in giant-size American Typewriter face.

Journalism is printing what someone does not want printed. Everything else is public relations – George Orwell

Below, in much smaller type, are the words: *Fact check – George Orwell never said or wrote this.*

Abigail looks up. A slender white arm rises and gently revolves in the air like a swan's neck.

When they approach, she gets up and the same hand slips in and out of Slim's grasp, as cool as stone. The smile is genuine and warm, however. 'I'm Abigail and I kind of run things with Dan there.' She jerks a ringed thumb over her shoulder. Slim recognises Dan Halladay, the Oxford star turned journalist, bending over a young reporter's screen, reading with his long-distance glasses propped on his forehead. He is tall, lean and has a sharp, animated face. He is speaking quickly and the woman he's talking to is nodding as though it's hard to keep up.

'Please do sit.' Abigail lays a hand on the printout of the Alder Fen story. 'We've all read it and it is obviously incredibly interesting. We have a few issues with the way it's written, but our main worry is how we check the facts.'

'I was at the dig through the winter. I saw everything, except when they lifted the boat and found the man.'

'We appreciate that, but we'd still like to make sure of things. Who can we phone?'

'The only person you can talk to is the man in charge, Dr Dougal Hass, who's based in Cambridge. He can't be seen to be colluding in this. Though he read it last night.'

'I'll leave it to Dan. Maybe those two could speak. Academic to academic kind of thing.'

'Maybe. And the writing? This is a major archaeological discovery, and it's hard to overstate its importance. They've found boats and hut foundations and wooden causeways in the Fens before but never a body with a boat. This is very special.'

'Oh, don't get me wrong. Middle Kingdom readers will be intrigued. But it needs a little more work, and you can cut some of the florid writing.' She shakes her head. The electrified Goth hair, much bigger and more alive than in her photographs, trembles.

Slim's purpose is to get a job at Middle Kingdom, not to defend the story, yet she just can't help reacting with a writer's indignation. 'Florid? How is it florid?'

A hint of a smile. 'Dan suggests you begin with the discovery of old timbers by the company extracting clay, move on to the find of the causeway and finally the boat and the body. You don't need all the tabloid melodrama stuff about the screaming skull. It's fascinating enough without that. And we have those two good photos.'

Even though that seems much less interesting, Slim says, 'I can do that, of course.'

'By this afternoon? Good, we have a space for you.' She points to a desk two away and puts two black fingernails to her chin. 'We're more excited about the other two stories, to tell the truth, the ones about the salmonella outbreak and the post-emergency deaths at St Mary's hospital. Both are very promising. You have a good source?'

'Yes! So, you're giving me work?'

'We like your story ideas, and we're looking for the sort of reporting you did in Leeds all those years ago. But I want to find out more about you. Tell me about the last few years.'

The woman is all Goth on the outside but HR on the inside. And she's a careful listener. As Slim goes through her last five years, all of it rehearsed with Rob Alantree and Peter Salt, Abigail asks some challenging questions. 'Wow! You worked for a rafting company in Canada. Tell me about that. What sort of people go rafting? How much does it cost for a week? Did you ever lose anyone? What are the bugs like?' Slim must think quickly because this obsessive fact-checker in front of her is bound to look something up if it feels off.

Slim expands the time spent with her mother and on the search for her brother. That's the scar tissue right out there, the real stuff she's using, which obviously should be avoided by any normally sensitive person. But Abigail ploughs on regardless, asking about emergency response time for her mother, the treatment she is receiving and wondering whether Middle Kingdom should do something on missing persons. 'You could write about your brother – anonymously, obviously. The experience – what it's like. Maybe a kind of grief is involved?'

Slim firmly says no. Abigail is silent for a short time again, adjusting everything on her desk with her long white fingers. She looks up to speak. 'We could really use someone like you in a general reporter's role rather than as the community stringer we advertised. Would you be prepared to do a trial of three months?'

'That's great, but I need to be paid.'

'Of course, I'll discuss pay with Dan later. Have you got somewhere to live?'

'Some possibilities. And I may have a dog with me, the stray my mother took in. I can't find anyone to take him. Perfectly harmless and well behaved.'

There's a flicker of doubt but she says, 'That's fine.' Slim notices the deep-set grey-blue eyes and the watchfulness in them. It would be foolish to judge Abigail on her Goth looks, the quirky columns and the Tupperware containers of sprouting beans and seaweed, stacked at the far end of her desk. She's all brains and discipline, this girl. 'Do you like our city?' she asks.

'I think so,' Slim says with some doubt in her voice. 'It's weirdly un-English, so confident about the future.' These thoughts have come to her as she speaks.

'I'm so pleased.' Abigail reaches out to touch Slim's hand. 'There's beauty and mystery here. And hope! Real, live, beautiful hope! It's the only city where robots operate without anyone taking the slightest notice.' A silence follows. 'So, if you can start straight away, I've got a couple of things I want you to look at once you've done the rewrite on the *Boatman of the Fens*. You said you have a car. The first story is twenty miles away. It's about the theft of flowers from a charity stand.'

Slim gets up. 'Will you introduce me to everyone?'

'I need you to meet Dan first.' She turns and waves at him. 'There's one thing I wanted to ask,' she says still trying to catch his attention. 'I can't find you anywhere on social media. There's nothing by you or about you. Is there a reason for that?'

'Never been comfortable with it,' Slim replies.

'Unusual,' says Abigail turning to her. 'Most people can't do without it.'

Halladay arrives, shakes her hand and pulls up a chair. 'I assume Abigail wants to try you out. That's good. We're going to start you off on some unchallenging stories and see how things go. I liked the piece you've offered us, and we'll use it this week. Now, money: we'll pay you at a rate of fifteen pounds an hour, which is what most of the others get and, because of your age, review that in three months, but only if we like what you're doing.' He glances at Abigail then smiles at Slim. 'You're not a plant, are you? Not from the water companies or the government? Because if you are, that would be—'

'Extremely disappointing,' says Abigail.

Slim looks at them in turn, conjuring embarrassment and annoyance in her expression. 'No, I'm not a plant. I just want to get back into journalism.'

They exchange looks, then Dan nods to her. 'Good. I'll be seeing you around then.'

The village of Fallow End in Buckinghamshire is forty minutes' drive from Milton Keynes. Once Slim is free of the web of roads and roundabouts that surround the city, she finds herself on a long straight road, with wide verges that support two separate groups of Travellers, with their tethered ponies, chicken coops, tipper trucks and caravans. Top Farm Cottage is at the end of a run of a dozen brown-bread-coloured limestone houses, the last dwelling in the village. It is older and larger than the others and, unlike them, set back from the road with a front garden retained by a wall and raised three feet from the level of the road. To the left is a gated track which leads to some old wood and stone barns, sheds and stables. And there's a mass of haphazardly planted flowers. Slim parks on a gravel patch in front of the house and takes a worn brick pathway up to a front door that is held open by a vintage artillery shell. She knocks. A clatter of pans comes from an interior made darker by the sudden bright sunlight in the garden.

'Hello, I'm from the Middle Kingdom website,' she calls out. 'I believe you were in touch about some flowers being stolen.'

A tiny old lady, very thin, with stiff white hair knotted in a tight bun, darts into the light. She smiles, wipes her hand on a tea towel and offers it to Slim. 'Delphy Buchanan. Delphy with a Y! How nice of you to come all this way!' Slim looks down at the shell. 'Don't worry – it's defused. My father brought it back after Armistice, goodness knows how many years ago. Would you like tea or cordial, or some coffee? And I have a rather nice lemon drizzle cake.'

'Tea and cake would be lovely. Do I call you Dame?' On the card Abigail gave her were the address, telephone number and the name Dame Delphine Buchanan CBE.

'Good Lord no, we're not in a pantomime. I never use it. Do sit anywhere you can find.'

'Do you need any help?'

'I may be decrepit, but I can manage tea and cake.' She disappears into the kitchen and there's more banging.

Slim sits by the window. Shelves either side of a fireplace are filled with books, crammed in vertically and horizontally. She's surprised to see a smartphone and tablet, both on charge. The aerial from an old-fashioned Roberts radio projects over a curved, high-back chair, on which lies a half-completed rectangular tapestry of flowers. Two tables and a mantelpiece are filled with framed photographs and one wall has black-and-white images from the World War II era, all of them fading to grey. 'Do you mind if I look at your photographs?'

She gets up and finds Delphy, petite and pretty, with the same hairstyle, at a dance; with a woman hiking in the mountains and on a beach, and at an awards ceremony. Higher up there are groups of women in uniform, one or two in front of warplanes and another at a concert party with Delphy dressed as a man, with a fake moustache and smoking a pipe.

Delphy returns with a tray. Slim takes it from her and sets it down on a long stool in front of the fireplace. 'Most of the photographs are of Margaret and me. We met before the war. We were companions until 'ninety-nine when I lost her.' She smiles at Slim. 'You're wondering if we were lesbians.'

'Um no . . . well, okay, yes, I was!'

'I was married to George, a sweet man who was drowned in a Scottish loch. That was in the sixties. And then, finding myself alone, I got back in touch with Margaret and eventually she came to live here with me, and one thing led to another, and we became a couple, but neither of us had any thought of that at the outset. At least, I didn't! We were very, very happy together for over thirty years.'

'What was your work?'

'Civil Service, mostly economic planning, hence the gong. Margaret was the truly brilliant one, a pioneering mathematician at Oxford, and of course she worked at BP during the war. I'm surprised Abigail didn't mention that. Abigail's people were there and one of them was close to Margaret.'

'Middle Kingdom has a lot of connections with Bletchley Park.'

'Of course, it does. Four of those brilliant young people working with Abigail are connected in some way. I was at BP but just a dogsbody, whereas Margaret was at the forefront of the codebreaking. She had a jewel of a mind. Quite beautiful, it was.' She reaches over to a side table and picks up a small oval frame, looks at it for a second and hands it to Slim, who is surprised to find no strait-laced boffin in tweeds but a glamorous young woman with a slender figure and 'victory rolls' rising from the centre of her forehead. 'She had brains and beauty, but she was also exceptionally frail,' Delphy says, taking the photo back to polish the glass on the sleeve of her cardigan.

Slim glances through the window at the garden. 'Someone has been stealing your flowers?'

The old lady exhales frustration and dry washes her hands. 'I have a stand outside. You may have noticed. Honey, eggs from my chickens, and half a dozen bunches of flowers that I pick and arrange every morning.' She waves a tiny, closed hand at a bucket inside the door, where there are two bunches of forget-me-nots, narcissi and tulips. 'It takes a lot out of me to do this, but the money is for the church. I give it in memory of Margaret who was a devout Christian.' She is suddenly affected by the loss and has to compose herself, then smiles apologetically. 'It never gets any easier. Anyway, three or four times now, a car drives up and a big fat bugger gets out and takes the flowers without paying, and sometimes the eggs and honey, too. He's cunning because he pulls up so that I can't see him from the window. And then the devil rattles the tin to make it seem as if he has put money in when he has tipped the lot into his fat hand and taken all my flowers and honey. Can you imagine such a person exists?'

Slim makes notes on her phone, for a moment wishing that Tom Ballard could see her in action on Operation Linesman. 'Have you ever seen his face?'

'I have seen a big fat bottom going towards the car but I'm too slow on my pins to race down into the road and, anyway, my eyesight is not good enough to see him clearly, or his licence number.'

'Have you reported this to the police?'

'Yes, but of course they didn't take it seriously. They said they could do nothing unless I had some evidence to show them. They were very condescending: told me they couldn't very well station a patrol car outside my house to catch a man stealing flowers. Of course, I didn't expect that – people treat you like a fool when you're my age.'

'Can I ask – how old are you?'

'Quite right! It's maddening when journalists leave it out. One needs to know! I was born on June twenty-first, 1924.'

'Wow, you're going to soon be a hundred.'

'Extraordinary, isn't it? Margaret was the pure one. I smoked cigarettes – and a pipe! – and drank all my life, but I've outlasted her by a quarter of a century.' She stops. 'She was a dear and I loved her very deeply, you know.' Another pause while she collects herself. 'Everything seems so near the surface these days.'

Slim hears the noise of a door scraping at the rear of the house. A man enters, with damp hair neatly parted and wearing a waxed jacket that is shiny from long service and a well-used backpack over his shoulder. His boots are old but the toecaps glisten in the light. 'Ah, Frank! This is . . . good heavens, I've forgotten your name already.'

'I don't think I gave it to you. Sorry! Slim Parsons.' Slim gets up, but the man is already turning away and heading for the open door.

'Seeing as you've got company,' he says, 'I'll be off. The wood's chopped and stacked, and the light's fixed in the bathroom. I'll do the vegetable patch next time. She needs digging.'

Delphy puts her hands together in a single clap. 'You're a marvel, dear Frank. Thank you so much!'

'And thanks for everything, Miss Delphy. Feel a different man.'

He leaves through the back door, and they hear his boots on a gravel path beside the house.

'If Frank caught the flower thief, I wouldn't fancy the fellow's chances.' Delphy waits for the garden gate to slam then, in a stage whisper, says, 'Funny how everything in Frank's world that is broken or requiring work is "she". *She* wants digging! *She* needs oiling! *She* wants mending! He lives rough, you know. I've no idea where. He comes and goes and uses the shower in our little guest annexe at the back in exchange for a few odd jobs. Perfect manners, but Frank is very much one of those people you wonder about.'

Slim nods, but something already strikes her about Frank. He's ex-army – the habits of spit and polish evident in his clothes despite their wear, and a tattooed wing, possibly part of a regimental badge, is visible through the open neck of his shirt.

'I've had an idea about your flower thief,' she says. 'My mother had trouble with fly tippers, and I think there's a way of getting the evidence the police need.'

'That would be wonderful,' says Delphy. 'More lemon drizzle?'

CHAPTER 15

On the way back to Milton Keynes to meet a lawyer named Annette Raines, who has a story about a missing Romanian national, Slim notices a black Ford hanging back in the traffic behind her. She calls Salt's phone. 'Is that you in the black Ford, Peter?'

'It's me,' says Tudor Mills. 'Mr Salt is at the wheel. But it's us.'

'Was it you on Saturday coming out of London?'

'Yes.'

'Well, can you bloody well back off?'

'We're here to keep you safe. If you hadn't shaken us off, we'd have got those two fellows at your mother's house.'

'You're crowding me. Get lost!'

She is half an hour late for the lawyer, but the woman isn't upset and says she used the time to catch up on paperwork, plus the video call she wants Slim to see has been postponed. She rises from the desk, an elegantly dressed African American, who Slim reckons has an inch on Dougal's six foot four. 'A pleasure to meet you, Ms Parsons.' Slim hazards correctly that she is from the South. Annette Latoya Raines tells her that she graduated from Georgia State College of Law, Atlanta (with the highest distinction, she adds), and came with the Avalon law firm to England where she specialises in insurance cases and does pro bono work one day a week, financed by the firm. She chose the legal advice centre in Milton Keynes, a few minutes' walk from Middle Kingdom, because she wanted a short ride out of London every week to see the English countryside.

'There's not much countryside between London and Milton Keynes,' Slim says.

'Oh, it's just fine, and I really like the people here.' She lowers herself with considerable grace into a swivel chair. 'I feel kind of at home with the city's grid, and the ethnic mix is familiar. Mini America! Did you know forty-five per cent of students enrolling in high school here are Black, Asian and Minority Ethnic? There's a lot going on here. Great arts and I sing in a choir – teaching them Gospel. I'm an admirer of what you people are doing with Middle Kingdom. Hell of a job!'

She puts on reading glasses and finds a file on her laptop screen. 'So, what I want to speak with you about concerns the case of a Romanian national named Andrei Botezatu. This is he with his sister Gabriella at her wedding.' She hands Slim a printout of a photograph of a slight man with the bride. They are unmistakably brother and sister. There's a lot about the rue-fulness of Andrei's smile that reminds her of Matthew, a bad boy yet a charming one. 'Andrei went missing last summer, after texting his sister that he was going away to make something of himself so that she would be proud of him. Seems he messed up pretty much everything in his life, but Gabriella says this is because he's too trusting. She's been in touch with us because she believes that he's being held in England as a slave. She speaks English quite well and contacted several local police depart-ments – God, there are so many! – but got no help. Andrei is an illegal immigrant who likely came to England in the back of a truck, plus he's served time in jail. So, he's seen as undesirable as well as being illegal. Your government would deport him to Africa if they could. The Romanian Embassy made representations to several authorities, but nothing's happened. No one's interested in Andrei Botezatu.'

'Has she used this photograph, made any kind of appeal?'

The lawyer shakes her head. 'Not yet. I believe that could put him in further danger. Andrei made a phone call to her a little over three weeks ago. He left a message to say that *they*, by which I believe he means the people smugglers, stole his phone, passport and money. He said he was near Bedford, but he could be anywhere. Experience tells us he's likely being moved every night and working at a whole bunch of locations. I wanted to bring you in on the start. I notice you're not writing any of this down. Do you need a pen and paper?'

She made notes on her phone at Delphy's but says she needs paper and a pen.

'Right, there's like an international convention that reporters never carry anything like paper and a pen.' She reaches behind her. 'I use American legal pads. I get them on Amazon.' She hands Slim a yellow pad. 'That's on the house but you've got to do the story. That's the deal.'

Gabriella Albescu lets them into her Zoom meeting at 5.30 p.m. It's 7.30 p.m. in Romania. She sits in a deserted office with a fan ruffling her hair. Her English is careful, like a good student's.

Annette explains Slim's presence and asks Gabriella to start from the top.

The story begins with her brother's conviction as the driver for a Bucharest gang. He was implicated by association in two murders, although these charges were dropped, and the police accepted they had no evidence that Andrei handled the drugs or knew what his passengers were carrying in the car he was driving. He was convicted of minor offences, criminal association and given two years. His sister described him as naive and slight of build. She holds up a photograph of him leaning on a sports car, acting the tough guy. He looks absurd in the oversized leather jacket. If it hadn't been for his Roma background, she says, he wouldn't have survived prison. Even that didn't save him beatings and repeated violations – she doesn't used the word 'rape', but that's what she means. Gabriella didn't see him after his release. She asked around and heard that he'd been offered a job in England at £30,000 a year. Only Andrei would believe that offer! She received a text from his new number thanking her for everything she'd done while he was in prison and saying that he would soon make her proud. That was all she heard until three weeks ago when she received two phone messages pleading for her help.

Just after she read the texts, she received another call, but it was a misdial and she heard men shouting at Andrei and threatening him, then Andrei sobbing. He was pleading with them in Romanian. He cried out. She heard the unmistakable sounds of him being beaten and she couldn't stop herself and shouted at them, but they didn't hear. Then the line went dead.

That was not all. About five minutes later, there was another call from Andrei but the moment she heard his voice she knew he was under duress. He was very frightened, but he was being smart, pretending that he was phoning to wish her happy birthday, calling her by the wrong name, referring to her husband as Nikolai, when his name is Stefan; talking about his nieces when she has sons. Then he added in Vlax Romani, 'I am a slave. I love you.'

'I believe he was with a Romanian person – they were

checking he spoke as they wished – but they did not understand the language our people use.'

Slim writes furiously. She looks up. Gabriella is composed but her eyes are full of the anxiety that she knows very well. 'Have you got the phone number they used?'

She gives it and Slim reads it back.

'Did you provide the police with this number?'

'Yes, many times.'

'Did they run any tests on it? You had the exact times of the calls, right? Did they use that information to determine the location of the phone when you received these calls and texts?'

'I don't know this. They do not inform me.'

'Can you send me the call log for that day? That's the times of the calls and texts, the duration of the calls.'

'I have this data, yes. I will send in email to Annette.'

Slim has an idea. 'Did you dial that number after that day?'

'Yes, was that a bad thing?'

'What happened?'

'The first time a man answered. I did not say anything because I did not want to cause a problem for Andrei.'

'Then?'

'He did not answer.'

'But you could hear it ringing – the phone was still in service.'

'Yes.'

'That's important. Have you got the time and date of those calls?'

'Yes, I can find them for you.'

'And don't use that number again. Even if you are very worried for Andrei, you must not call that number. We need the phone to be working. We don't want them throwing it away. You understand me?'

'Yes.'

'I will need your phone number and I want the names of the police officers you spoke with and their numbers, okay? Can you send all that to Annette? I will give you my number and an email address so you can contact me at any time you need.'

'Is there hope to find my brother?'

'I promise I'll try very hard, Gabriella. You have my word. And don't call that phone again.'

'Okay. Thank you.'

After Annette has told Gabriella of the action she's taking, which is talking to an anti-slavery group and one specialist lawyer, the Zoom call ends. Annette sits back and takes off her glasses. 'I notice you didn't ask about her brother. Why was that?'

'I'll get to that later, and I don't think we should write anything yet.'

'You seem more like an investigator than a reporter. Did you work in law enforcement?'

'Nope.'

'Well, you certainly know your shit, that's for sure. Abigail wanted to know what I thought of you.'

Slim smiles. 'Did she now?' No doubt she'd asked Delphy to report back, too.

'I'll tell her that I'm impressed.'

'Thanks. I hope Gabriella understands about the phone.'

'She does. I see where you're going with that, but how are you going to get the location of those calls without the help of the cops?'

'Where there's a will . . . Do you have any tame police officers I can call?'

A slow shake of the head. 'I'm only here on a Monday or

Tuesday and I don't know anyone in the police department.'
She rises. 'We need to find that lady's brother. Have at 'em, girl!'

Which Slim does immediately she's in the street by opening
an email account that Ballard and she used to use to communi-
cate and writing a draft which he can access because they share
the same password. She has little hope that he will reply but she's
going to start with him anyway.

> I need all the data for the last three months from this phone
> ASAP. Please don't ignore this.
> Slim xxx

Then she sends a text to alert him to the draft email.

CHAPTER 16

The promised all-staff meeting for Tuesday morning doesn't materialise, so Slim plunges into the story of the Romanian slave, first reading a summary of the Modern Slavery Act 2015. She speaks with a slavery campaign group, the chambers of a lawyer named Caroline McCarthy KC, who has prosecuted several high-profile slavery cases, then a female detective, who happens to pick up the phone in Milton Keynes Police Station, and who's had experience, while serving in a West Midlands force, of dealing with a Polish gang who enslaved hundreds of people. It was the toughest case of her career and the most traumatising. Before ending the call, she says, 'Those people lived in constant terror. They were told, "we'll dig a hole in the woods, and we'll bury you alive if you misbehave."'

Slim watches the newsroom between calls. The devotion to the work is more obvious than in her last newsroom – the one in Leeds – and the young people working around her are enjoying themselves. Nothing escapes Shazi, though, nor the cameras in the ceiling. Slim's trained eye picked up at least six tiny holes in the cornices on her first visit.

She spots the crime and courts reporter, Craig Whitlock –

older than most of the staff and a seasoned reporter – heading
for the kitchenette, follows him and introduces herself.

'Where's everyone?' she asks.

'They work outside the building on the big stuff, bring it in
on a thumb drive and Skelpick runs it through his laptop here.
He says the vibe is better. That's the only thing Abigail and he
agree on. As far as they're concerned, this is Glastonbury Tor.
Ley lines, magic energy, the summer solstice etcetera, etcetera.
You've met Skelpick, have you?'

She nods.

'Rude bastard but writes like a god. Suffers a lot of pain from
his injuries so, if he barks at you, that's why.'

'Why isn't it all done here? It's such a beautiful space.'

Craig has a solo vape which he sucks on discreetly, letting
out a thin stream of vapour from the side of his mouth. 'That
way we're sure no one's going to get an unofficial preview of
what we're doing. You read the big piece about water company
bosses' pay and what they're pouring into the rivers, right?' He
puts his hands up to his cheeks in mock horror. 'Oops, there's
a million gallons of shit right in that little brook at the end of
your garden! Sorreeeee!' He takes another drag from the vape.
'The companies tried every mean little gimmick to find out
what we were doing.'

'Like what?'

'Spyware, phone interceptions, following people, and they
even tried to bug the office. I mean, they were pathetic.' The
kettle boils. He spoons Nescafé into a cup and mixes in creamer,
then gestures with the cup at a young man wearing a black polo
and headphones 'That, right there, is our secret weapon – Toto
Linna, Finnish-Chinese, genius.' Slim had noted the individual
drifting around the office, occasionally looking at a screen,

and wondered what he was doing. 'Toto monitors the system for viruses and hacks as well as the building for bugs. He saw the water companies coming from a mile off and was ready for them. No one can get past him.' He grins. 'He thinks you're a spy. Are you?'

'Ah, you got me! Hands up, I'm a spy.'

'Seriously, he thinks so.'

'A spy that builds her cover through months on a freezing archaeological site with the guarantee that she's going to find a Bronze Age log boat with a body under it, so she's able to write a story and gain entrance to the inner sanctum of Middle Kingdom. That kind of spy? Or the one that brings in a story about a hospital's negligence and countless unnecessary deaths?'

He raises his hands in surrender. 'Sorry! Don't get me wrong, they're terrific tales.' He gazes at his coffee, sneaks a look at her and says, 'You want a drink sometime? I can show you the better watering holes in the area.'

'You're happy to be seen with a spy?'

'I don't think you're a spy, if that makes any difference.'

'It doesn't.'

'So, you don't want a drink?'

'No, I don't want a bloody drink, Craig. I want help with my story about the missing Romanian Andrei Botezatu and modern slavery.' She's smiling but he knows she means it.

'I'll have a word around,' he says as he leaves the kitchenette.

'I need the data for a phone which is crucial to the story. Do you know anyone who can get it for me?'

'Phone data? Seriously? I can't do that. That would be illegal.'

'We aren't hacking a celebrity. This is organised crime, Craig.'

'Sorry, can't help.' He pockets the vape and goes back to his desk.

She's got much from the encounter with the unlovely Craig Whitlock, however. The idea that she will be able to introduce spyware so MI5 can remotely view what's going on in Middle Kingdom is for the birds. Watching Toto Linna, she reckons Middle Kingdom is probably better defended than Guest's headquarters. Besides, the material likely to interest Oliver Halfknight is plainly kept in quarantine, away from the site's day-to-day journalism.

As Slim returns to her desk, Shazi says, 'You've got two stories.' She peers at the news list. 'Which are you doing now?'

'The one about the Romanian slave, but I wanted to get more before writing anything. We have a photo, but it could be dangerous for him if we used it.'

'What about the flower thief of Fallow End? People love that kind of thing.'

'Wouldn't it be better to catch the man in the act? I've got an idea how to do that.'

'Then research the slave story. But you could help Aziz on the bumblebee investigation, as well. That's Aziz over there – the handsome one. He does all our nature coverage.' She giggles and goes back to her screen.

'A bumblebee investigation?'

'He needs help counting the numbers and species of bumblebees on a farm. They're in decline, but not in this one habitat and Aziz wants to write about that. Plus, you've got a car and people like bumblebees.'

A few minutes after the breezy non sequitur, Shazi jumps up and, with one knee working the swivel chair, bellows, 'Everyone! We've got a meeting in fifteen minutes. Get your shit together and bodies in the conference room. Latecomers will be drowned in acid.'

About thirty-five reporters, editors and designers move to the conference room. A long glass table at the centre is surrounded by a dozen plastic ghost chairs, and around this a set of six functional, low sofas that accommodate three at a squeeze. Along the window is an upholstered bench that will cope with eight people. The sofas fill up first. Slim is beckoned by Shazi to take the seat next to her on one at the far end.

The first of the founders to arrive is Yoni Ross who pads in beaming with hands held together in an Indian greeting. 'Great job everyone – love what I'm seeing. Great job!' His face is no different from the photographs – the hairline and beard describe a perfect circle. His open-toed sandals reveal each of his toenails is painted with a different-coloured varnish, like the keys of a child's musical instrument. He wears chinos, a Stanford college blouson jacket that's seen better days, a magenta polo shirt and a bead necklace from which hangs a photo in a tiny round frame. When he approaches to shake her hand, she sees it's a photo of a woman, most likely his wife.

Shazi introduces them and mentions Slim's story on the Alder Fen dig. Yoni takes her hand in his soft paws and looks down at her. 'Wow, yes, I read it in the car. God, what a thing to be there when something like that's discovered. Unbelievable. Truly, I was impressed. Welcome! Welcome! Welcome!' With this, he heads to the far end of the table, sits, and looks round contentedly, the cult leader benignly surveying his acolytes.

But the peace in the room doesn't last.

J. J. Skelpick, in jeans and a red plaid shirt, comes in followed by Abigail, and they are in the throes of an argument. They sit at the table opposite each other. Abigail places her iPad in front of her and darts Skelpick a look of fury. 'The lawyer needs to see it before tomorrow morning.'

'It's been lawyered,' Skelpick shoots back. 'The rewrite won't affect our liability because I'll be *cutting* material not *adding*, okay?'

'You could easily cut information that's critical to the article. The lawyer needs to check that. Ah, here's Dan.' She waves through the glass to Halladay who has just emerged from the lift with a woman Slim recognises as Dr Sara Kiln, the data analyst and AI specialist. She is taller than she seemed in the photographs and has a more athletic build. She sits beside Yoni. He touches her forearm and smiles at her. They seem close.

Dan Halladay sits and looks around.

'We're glad to see you,' says Ross. 'We have an issue on the timing of the publication of your big story.'

Halladay says, 'How much work is there to be done, JJ?'

'Five to six hours. The top is good, the middle section is mushy and disorganised, and the end is . . . well . . . it doesn't end. It fizzles out. On such a big story you need something that summarises, concludes – they're different, by the way – and calls for action, maybe through one of the voices earlier in the story. It's far too long and my advice is to publish it in two parts.'

Dan shakes his head. 'That's not going to happen. We need to get it all out there at once.'

'I agree,' chimes in Yoni, now with his hands folded across his stomach. 'Have you got reactions from the government?'

'We're not going there until just before publication, because we don't want to release any part of the investigation before-hand, even an outline of the main allegations. By the way, JJ, I think the writing team did a pretty good job, don't you? Callum, Sofi, Mitch – take a bow.' These three are sitting on the same sofa and high-five each other.

Dan pauses, rubs his finger under his nose. 'So, I need to say something about this investigation. I'm not going to tell you what the story is yet, but just that the information comes from deep within government and we are a hundred per cent certain of the facts. It should cause a stir.' He smiles to let the room know that this is understatement.

Slim's phone vibrates with a message. She ignores it, then it moves in her pocket again, this time with the shudder that announces a voicemail. Shazi nods and shrugs as if to say she should look. She pulls it out and sees the number Ballard used throughout her time undercover with Hagfish. His text reads, *Call me now – whatever you're doing.* She looks helplessly at Shazi and whispers, 'My mum,' and gets up to leave. Shazi, who already knows that her mother is terminally ill, explains to the meeting as the glass door closes behind her.

She takes the lift and goes out into the car park. 'Why've you been avoiding me?' she demands when Ballard picks up.

He coughs but doesn't respond to the question. 'You need to know that Hagfish is back in the UK and has been for a month, perhaps much longer.'

She swallows hard.

'He was flown back for a graft on his neck, which took place at the London Clinic, together with some plastic surgery to his ear.'

'Why hasn't he been arrested?' Her eyes travel over Skelpick's motorbike.

'The only relevant point for you, Slim, it that he presents an immediate threat to your safety. You have protection, but you need to be especially alert. Understand?'

'None of this would be a problem if they'd arrested him. Why did we bother, Tom? What was the bloody point of two years with that man?' She stops. 'Who's preventing his arrest and prosecution? Where's that coming from?'

'I cannot say.'

'Why were you avoiding me?'

Ballard ignores this too. 'I do have the records for that phone you asked me about. I'll send them in the usual way. I need to see you soon and will arrange, so please look out for a message. Now, take extra special care, Slim, okay?'

He hangs up before she can say anything more. She phones her mother to make a date at the hospital for the weekend and cannot remember when her mother was last so natural and warm. 'Loup and I will be there,' Slim says. 'It's going to be fine weather, so maybe I can do something exciting like push you round the car park. I'll let you know what time. Love you, Mum.'

'Yes, and me too,' Diana replies, and this does pierce her. She needs to take a moment before returning to the meeting and considers the news that Ivan Guest is back in the UK. It's somehow more shocking than surprising. Shocking that he has been let in without arrest, but given the men at Steward's House, no surprise to her.

As she slips through the door, Dan Halladay looks round and says, 'Ah, good timing! Colleagues, this is Slim Parsons. She'll be with us for a few months.' People nod and say hello. 'Fabulous story on Alder Fen. I talked to your friend Dr Dougal Hass last night and he confirmed everything. He says you've worked on a lot of digs together and he's known you forever.' Slim understands perfectly well that the conversation with Dougal was as much to check her out as her story. Dan continues, waggling a pencil between two fingers, 'And these other two stories about the possible salmonella outbreak and post-operative care at St Mary's hospital are very promising. Do you want to report them, or—?'

'It might be awkward, but I'm sure my source would be willing to help with the St Mary's story. She left after they threatened her, perhaps with something from her personal life. She's angry about the number of people who died because of the after-care failure. And the salmonella outbreak is just anecdotal. She says it seems to be taking off in North Cambridgeshire and the Fens.'

'Who's doing the salmonella story?' Dan asks. 'It feels good to me.'

Abigail consults a list. 'We can make Jethro and Kirsty free. They're out on the tree story, which is promising but a slow burn.'

'Ha! Okay, let's move them to food poisoning. The illegal felling of trees is ongoing; we can keep on it at the same time. We need to think how best to do the St Mary's investigation. And you, Slim, are already well into the slave story. Please keep Abigail informed every step of the way. Right . . .' Skelpick catches his eye. 'Yes, JJ?'

'St Mary's hospital: I'd like to have a look at that. A recce maybe. Need to have a word with the source beforehand, though. See if it's worth the trip.'

Dan glances at Slim. 'As long as the source is happy to talk to you, and Slim is relaxed about that, fine. Please go ahead.'

Slim nods. Everyone gets up to leave and Skelpick stiff-legs it over to her, then grasps hold of the side of the table. An elephant-hair bracelet, with silver knots, slips down on his wrist. 'Your source, is she sound?'

'I trust her. Reliable, not a bullshitter.'

Skelpick scrutinises her for a few moments. 'You're a grown-up, aren't you, Slim Parsons?'

Slim smiles pleasantly. 'I hope so.'

'You know what I'm talking about,' he says quietly. 'You've seen a lot in your life. I can tell. I'm glad you've joined us. If you need help, give me a shout. Slavery is a particular interest of mine. Spent a lot of time writing about it in Africa.'

CHAPTER 17

She never imagined bumblebees could be so interesting, nor hunting for bumblebee nests on her hands and knees in a meadow that hadn't been mowed for years so enjoyable. It was approximately the same pleasure as brushing dirt from an ancient piece of timber at Alder Fen. The day ended less agreeably, back in the city, when she met Peter Salt in the Marlborough Gate car park.

She told him that the Middle Kingdom people were almost certainly on to her because she was being sent on no-hoper stories about stolen flowers and bumblebees, and one member of staff had voiced the opinion, apparently shared by at least one other, that she was a spy. Her plan was to prove herself with the story of a Romanian slave named Andrei and she would concentrate on that from now on.

Salt wasn't listening. He made a half-hearted pass, suggesting they should have a meal when Linesman was over. That was rather bold of him, she had said, and damned inappropriate, too. With his jaw working unpleasantly, he told her to get her act together, so he had something for the office, and she gave him the news that a big story was about to land, one which came from the heart of government and was at that moment being passed through the hands of J. J. Skelpick in Middle Kingdom's headquarters.

When he left, she waited by her car for thirty minutes. She checked the storeys above and below her in the car park, made sure that no part of the pickup was covered by CCTV, then removed the package containing the tablet she stole from Ivan Guest and hid beneath the vehicle's battery, dropped it into a light knapsack used for running and headed for the boat, where she spent most of the evening trying to make the shower work.

Middle Kingdom's big story about huge amounts of taxpayers' money being wasted by profligate government departments is published early Thursday morning, together with Slim's report from Alder Fen. Initially, her piece gets more attention on social media because of the picture of the Boatman, but then, as politicians, journalists and civil servants wake up to the day, the figures on overspends, failed or failing contracts, consultancy fees and outright corruption in seven different departments begin to sink in. Sixty billion pounds is the total calculated by Sara Kiln, and this is just a snapshot of the departments Middle Kingdom had chosen to study. The total waste across government is likely to be far greater. And official explanations about the state of government finances make it look as though everyone involved is either incompetent or lying, especially the hapless spokespersons for the government departments who'd all been trapped into making denials and giving reassurances before they knew exactly what Middle Kingdom was about to publish.

Two hours after publication, Abigail starts answering the phones, permanently on charge on a table beside her desk. One

MP is calling for an investigation into how Middle Kingdom acquired official data and Slim hears her tell the journalist: 'The Member of Parliament can't say our figures are wrong, at the same time as demand a prosecution for the leak of official data. Either she's saying it's inaccurate and all lies, or she agrees the facts are correct.'

Slim returns to the story about the Romanian slave. The data provided by Tom Ballard for the phone number that called Andrei's sister in Romania is revealing. The phone is in constant use from 6.30 a.m. until late at night. The owner moves around a great deal because the log records many different phone masts. Yet when she looks at the telephone numbers of incoming and outgoing calls, only fifteen numbers are involved, and of these only seven appear frequently, often many times over a day. She locates the calls to a number with a Romanian prefix, notes them down and sends a text to Ballard: *Can you give me a location for the two calls made to Romania? Tks Xx.*

On it, comes the reply.

She sees Toto Linna making his way to her desk, removes the thumb drive she's been using and slips it into her pocket.

'Hey there! Enjoying the work? I'm Toto.'

'I know.'

'So, I need to examine your laptop. It's just something we do to protect ourselves, and, with the material we're publishing, those protocols have become super important.' His hair has three kinds of dye, a light brown base with blondish highlights plus streaks of grey. He has pale eyes that are pleasant and friendly at the same time as being implacable.

'You want to go through my laptop?' She sees Abigail, just about to prise the lid from a container of lentils, is looking her way. Her shrug says – why not? Slim wrinkles her nose. The laptop is clean, but she doesn't want to seem too keen to hand it over. 'Seems a bit weird.'

'If you'd rather not,' Toto says, 'we can make other arrangements. But then I'd like you to shut your computer down now.'

Slim turns the laptop towards him. 'Be my guest. How long do you need it? I'll grab lunch.'

'Half an hour, tops. I won't be looking at any of your personal files or search history, just checking for viruses and spyware and other nasty stuff. It's the same for everyone. We do regular checks.'

'Text me when you're done. Abigail has my number.'

She leaves the office and walks a block to Centre:MK, the shopping mall that sits astride Midsummer Boulevard, buys a salad which she eats sitting on a bench reading the follow-ups of the government waste story on her phone.

Someone sits down heavily directly behind her on the bench facing the opposite direction. It is Salt. He is holding a phone to his face. 'We need to talk,' he says into the phone.

Making a private eye-roll at the ridiculous tradecraft, she takes out her phone and brings it to her face. 'Hello! Wouldn't it be a lot simpler to just phone me?'

'I'm sorry we had words last night.'

'How can I help, Peter? You're not going to ask me out again, are you?'

'That story this morning has caused major problems.'

'I'm sure. It's everywhere.'

'They must be hacking government systems. There's no other way they could get those emails and that kind of detail. It's a serious breach of security, yet there's no trace of a break-in. Nothing! And that's really worrying people.'

'Yes,' she says. 'But this is only my first week in the building.

My computer is being examined for spyware and it can't be long before they run a test on my phone. These people are hyper alert, so you're just going to have to be patient and let me do my job in the way I know best.'

'All eyes are on this operation – at the very highest level. Downing Street is watching. The Cabinet Office. Everyone.'

'I'm aware of that but the only way for me to win Middle Kingdom's trust is to put everything I have into my journalism. I'll do whatever's necessary, but there aren't going to be any overnight miracles. It'll take time.'

'You've got to focus. Find out how they're breaking into government systems. Forget the bloody journalism.' He rises, phone still clamped to his ear, and marches off. No one looks less like the average Milton Keynes shopper than Peter Salt.

On the way back to the office, she receives two texts, one from Toto with an *okay* emoji, and another from Tom Ballard with a three-word map reference. Leaning against the wall in an underpass, she finds the location where the calls to Romania were made, about forty miles north-east of Milton Keynes. Flipping to satellite imagery, she sees a large group of farm buildings and a row of mobile homes.

Five minutes later, she's at her desk with the satellite imagery on her laptop. She counts fourteen mobile homes, notes a large hay barn with a curved corrugated roof and many sheds. A lot of equipment is parked haphazardly around the barn and beyond there is a large junkyard. She identifies crane parts, tankers, silos and mounds of scrap and tyres. She places the pointer on the lane which the drive leads to and goes to Street View and finds the entrance – a high, wire mesh gate on which is a notice of four lines in red: 'Manor Farm. No Visitors. Deliveries by Appointment Only. CCTV in Operation.' Either side of the gateway is a fence topped with barbed wire that runs in both directions into tall hedges. She moves the Street View arrow so she can see up and down the road and concludes from the spine of dirt in the middle that it's seldom used. This is certainly where Andrei made those two calls. The isolated compound, the amount of accommodation available in the caravans and the unusual levels of security are right for a large-scale slave operation.

Abigail rises from her desk, catches Slim's eye, and comes over. 'Laptop okay?'

'Yep.'

'Great. I wanted to check how things are going before what looks like a very long meeting.'

'Sure! I'm working on the slave story,' says Slim, looking down at a message alert on her phone. 'I've just got a text from a Romanian number. Probably Andrei Botezatu's sister.' She turns towards the conference room. Dan Halladay, J. J. Skelpick, Sara Kiln and Yoni Ross are all there. A man and woman have just come from the lift. They're carrying laptops and briefcases. 'Something up?' Slim asks.

'A nasty email from the Treasury Solicitor, head of the Government Legal Service,' replies Abigail. 'Our lawyers are here to advise. The government is demanding we take down the lead story and threatening an injunction to prevent us publishing more material. They say they will refer us to the police and CPS with a view to prosecution under the Official Secrets Act.'

'Can they do that? Doesn't public interest count?'

'We're going to hear about that now.' Abigail moves away. 'You're not in tomorrow, so I'll see you next week. Oh, I forgot. Aziz had the idea of setting up his trail cameras outside Delphy Buchanan's place. Should be fun if he gets a result.'

Slim opens the message from Gabriella who explains she's

just found a text from Andrei with a photograph of him sitting at a table smoking and holding a bottle of beer. He said he was having the time of his life but that was plainly untrue. He was half the size she remembers him, and she adds, 'Look at the hand! This is symbol of prisoner, no?'

Slim peers at the photograph attached. The right hand is thrust forward with the thumb trapped by four fingers in the international sign for someone being held against their will. It's surprising that whoever choreographed this scene hadn't noticed. Apart from the pathetic sight of Andrei doing his best to act cheerful, what interests Slim is the circumstances of the photograph in which the side of a caravan can be seen in the foreground, the barn in the immediate background and, way in the distance, a church spire and a white silo.

She's got the time and date of the text and a new number – unsurprisingly, the number that the first phone calls most often. That's crucial information but not as important as the location of the photograph, which she's sure is Manor Farm.

CHAPTER 18

Early next morning, she attempts her first one-hundred-and-eighty-degree turn in *Spindle* on a stretch of the Grand Union Canal that seems slightly wider, and where there happens to be a man on the towpath who stops to watch, which she could certainly do without. When it looks as if she is going to wedge the boat across the canal, he makes a few gentle suggestions and she manages to complete the manoeuvre. But, being Slim, she must repeat it twice to get it down pat. Finally, she's facing the direction of her mooring and the man helps her to bang fore and aft pegs into the bank and tie up. She gives him coffee and gets his story. He is Lambert Bantock and he's lived most of his life on the water since being born on the Leeds to Manchester Canal forty-three years ago. His card with his mobile number summarises the ten-minute life story she heard: 'Barge Boy, Wrestler, Fiddler, Engineer, Painter, Dog Whisperer and Walker'.

'Can you whisper to my mother's stray, which is coming to live with me for a while?'

'A stray, you say. Probably damaged.'

'Yeah, but not crazy.'

'Will you be moving far?'

'Just enough to keep one step ahead of the authorities,' she says with a grin.

He rubs the curls on top of his head with the flat of his hand. She sees several rings and tattoos on all his fingers. 'Then you'll be needing Clive's collection of alternative names and serial numbers for the boat,' he says.

'Why didn't you say you knew Clive?'

'Thought you'd be wanting your privacy.'

'I do.'

'Somewhere on the boat he's got a whole bunch of name plates and fake serial numbers. They Velcro on to the side. He's a canny fellow.'

'What's he need them for?'

'Doesn't like to pay council tax. Hard on a penny, is Clive.'

Text messages regularly announce themselves on her phone, but she keeps listening to him. There's something majestically unhurried about Lambert Bantock, as if he's the only individual in England who is free from the demands of time and society. At length, when she indicates that she ought to attend to her phone, he gets up and steps on to the towpath saying he looks forward to the pleasure of Loup.

The four texts are in fact one message which combine to make *Jumpy Owner Decoded @4.00*, the coordinates and the time of a rendezvous. She finds the spot on What3Words though she has no clue whether Halfknight or Ballard will be there because she doesn't recognise the number. The rendezvous is a small church named All Saints, in Norfolk.

Long ago, the people and their tiny settlement of Ecksfield were wiped out by the Black Death, marooning All Saints in quiet, unvisited countryside, where it's possible to go round in circles before finding the church. Wind tears at the trees and upturns the new leaves as she walks down a grass path towards a wooden gate. Beyond is a small flint-and-brick church without a tower and an overgrown churchyard, where four white chickens and a cockerel peck among a few gravestones. It is a lonely place and hasn't changed in seven centuries.

She goes to the porch at the far end of the building and opens an ancient door, catches herself wondering if there's enough tree-ring data in the timber to date the door, and enters an echoing, simple white nave, with an old brick floor and box pews either side. At the far end stands a plain altar with two candles and an altar cloth covered in a plastic protector. A head appears from a box pew at the front. Tom Ballard rises with a book in his hand. 'Welcome to All Saints,' he says in his best churchy voice. 'Take a pew.'

There's a bar of chocolate beside him on top of an envelope. 'I was preparing for a long wait.' He stops and reads the words on a plaque above them on the chancel wall: '"Lo, I am with you Alway". That might apply to Hagfish.'

'What's going on, Tom? Why didn't you respond to my calls?' She doesn't bother to hide her anger.

He shrugs. He has no intention of answering. He turns over a printout and slides it along the bench. 'Posted on Instagram by someone called Gaia, a friend of yours, apparently.'

She looks at the photograph. It is a summer's evening at Steward's House. Slim is nearest to the camera. Matthew is to her left. They are standing on the ha-ha wall looking out over the fields in the sun. Around them is a group consisting of Bridie, Dougal, his sister Rose and three of Matthew's friends from art college. Bridie, in a big straw hat, glances down as one of Matthew's friends tips a bottle over her glass. Dougal, in shorts

and sleeveless T-shirt, towers above them all. Matthew holds a
reefer between thumb and forefinger. She dimly remembers a
woman getting on top of the straw bales in the field to take the
photograph but is sure she has never seen it before. That must
have been Gaia, although she has no memory of her.

'August 2009,' says Ballard. 'Someone picked it up yesterday. It
was posted six weeks ago. So, just before the time Guest's people
started showing an interest in your mother's house. Problem is
that Matthew's full name is provided, and you are ID'd as his
sister, Alice. In the post, Gaia wonders where you have all got
to, particularly Matthew, "the most gifted artist of her year".
And that's not all, Slim.' Ballard has his phone in his hand. 'This
comes from someone called Melissa Bright. She recognised you
in a pub. Were you aware of that?'

'What's that silly bitch said?'

'That either Sally Latimer had a twin or double, or she didn't
die in the ferry disaster with her *boyfriend*, because she is certain
that she saw her *Baby Spinach* with her own flaming eyes in the
Eagle's Nest pub with her new *girlfriend*, and she'll never forget a
lover like Sally for as long as she lives.' He looks up, his tongue
moving along his upper gum. 'Baby Spinach,' he says slowly. 'I
have never thought of you as someone with a baby prefix. Did
she spot you in the Eagle's Nest?'

'I was with a friend – not a *girlfriend*. We thought we put her
off . . .'

'Evidently not . . . Baby Spinach?'

'Don't ask!'

'But you had a fling with this Melissa. That's strictly against—'

'You wonder how I loaded so much spyware on to the system
at the beginning? I sent emojis to Mel's phone. Worked like a
dream. So, no, don't ask.'

'You truly are something, Slim.'

'Why hasn't he pulled me out? I'm burned, aren't I?'

'*Crème brûlée.*'

'Why then?'

'Because Halfknight believes you're equal to the challenge.'

'What challenge?'

His hand falls on the used brown envelope. 'I've been asked to make sure you see and photograph these.'

'Halfknight asked you?'

He shrugs again and looks away.

'None of this makes sense. What's going on? You were my friend, Tom. We worked together. You can tell me.'

'Yes, we worked together, Slim, but then you misbehaved, hijacking a plane and failing to own up about the thing you stole.' He raises a finger. 'No, don't bloody deny it. Just look at these papers and photograph them.'

'Why?'

'Because I believe you are an essential part of an operation that I don't fully understand and, well, the service is looking for your brother and sparing no expense in the process and . . . just do what you're told.'

She opens the envelope. There are five encrypted pages. 'What do they mean?'

'We don't know and because we cannot currently ask Cheltenham to apply their massive resources to the problem, we will have to find someone else. Or rather you will.'

'Sorry, why can't you use GCHQ?'

He looks at her with his hangdog expression. 'Things are difficult. Let's just say that.'

'Is that why JEF disbanded?'

He says nothing.

'Who am I meant to ask to decrypt this material?'

'The people you're working with, naturally.' He looks up at the rafters of the little church. 'There are two things you need to know. This material comes from Mayfield-Turner in Boston.'

'The firm Ivan Guest used.'

'That's correct, and second, there are almost certainly encrypted pages like them on the item you took from him and kept.'

She looks at her feet.

'I think we're being watched. A barn owl. Do you see?' He points to a far beam in the nave. Slim takes a second or two to make out the surprisingly large bird perched at the end, utterly still, its plumage merging with the whitewash of the walls. 'Must have found another way into the church.'

'Forget the bird, Tom. Just tell me what's going on. Currently I'm undercover in Middle Kingdom, tasked with trying to find out the source of their story about government waste, and yet . . .'

'Cracking good journalism if you ask me. High time government waste was exposed. That's what hacks are for, for Christ's sake! Maggots cleaning the wound.'

'And yet,' she continues, 'at the same time as spying on them, you're asking me to get their help on the decryption of these documents. How do I explain that? How do I explain where the documents come from?'

'Early days, Slim. Things will become clear. You'll find a way. Now, I'm going to have a look at that bird – so rare to see one close to.' He squeezes by and pushes the pew door open. She takes out a phone, turns it on, puts it in flight mode and starts photographing each of the encoded papers. By the time he is standing beneath the owl, she's taken the photos, put away the phone and arranged the sheets as they were. No one takes needle-sharp document photos quicker than Slim. She could pass Ivan Guest's desk and take pictures of every piece of paper on it in seconds, and by the time he returned to the room the photos had been sent and erased from her phone.

Ballard talks to the owl. It opens its eyes and considers him for a second then glides from its perch through a gap in the eaves. He comes back to her and gathers the papers. 'Right, I'd better go and relieve Jules.'

She leaves the pew, and they walk to the door together.

'Beautiful place, isn't it?' He lays a hand on her forearm. 'These are tough times, and we have to get through them as best we can. You may be a fourth-generation spy and the most aggressive young woman I've ever come across, but you're not invincible. You need to be very, very careful.'

'I've got Peter Salt and Tudor Mills protecting me.'

'No worries then.' A broad and utterly insincere smile.

'The phone data. I need more numbers checked. Can you do that for me?'

He looks exasperated. 'I will try but remember I'm on paternity leave. It's not always going to be easy.'

CHAPTER 19

Slim watches the hospital entrance for Helen to push Diana to the shady part of the car park where she is waiting with the surprise guest – Loup, who is trembling with excitement and doing the thing with his chops. His day has vastly improved since the handover in the disabled bays at a service station near Spalding, the furthest Slim could persuade Lola and Martha to travel from the kennels. The couple were taken with the covert aspect of putting Loup into the back of their old Land Cruiser rather than the kennel's van and driving cross-country to the service station. They arrived twenty minutes late at the rendezvous in front of the supermarket, where in the past Slim purchased cut-price gin for her mother and that morning had bought a lemon, a small bottle of Gordon's, two tonic waters and a paring knife to cut the lemon.

As Helen and her mother hove into view, Slim clips the lead on to the red harness the kennels preferred to his old collar. She gets out and points to a bench beneath a tree. But Loup is having none of it and tears from her hands to meet Diana and introduce himself to Helen. They arrive at the bench with the dog dancing in circles round them, the lead whiplashing in the air. Helen turns the wheelchair, locks the wheels and gives Slim a brief hug.

Her mother puts out a hand – thin and frail – and grabs Slim above the wrist.

Helen winks at Slim and says, 'Okay, I need to be getting back. Call when you want to go back inside.' She gently kneads Diana's shoulder and leaves with a fleeting smile to Slim.

'That woman is an angel, quite the kindest person I've ever met,' says Diana.

Slim sits down, inhales deeply. 'Brought sandwiches from the Greenspace store at the service station, if you don't have to go back for lunch or roll call, or whatever . . .'

Her mother smiles. 'I tend to do what I want nowadays.'

'You always did, Mum. How's the head?'

'Better. It may heal before I die.'

Slim inwardly recoils. 'Sandwich? Chicken, prawn, egg mayo?' A tiny shake of the head. 'You must eat something, then you can have a drink.'

'A proper drink?'

'I thought it should be your choice.'

'Thank you, darling. Thank you for not being judgemental. I mean, I know that you've hated my drinking, but I'm also keenly aware that you never criticised me to my face and I'm grateful for that.'

'Take a sandwich and I'll get the drink organised.' She stops. 'Will it make you feel ill?'

'Probably, but I want to talk, and I need a drink. I haven't had one for weeks, so it won't be a question of topping up, will it?'

Slim makes the drink in a paper coffee cup she took from the store and unscrews water for herself. She hands her mother a triangle of prawn sandwich then the gin and tonic and chugs her water watching her mother take her first sip and nod to herself.

'Thank you,' she says and looks across the car park. 'Tell me, Slim, are you gay? Are you a lesbian, darling?'

'Jesus, Mum! For heaven's sake don't beat about the bush.'

'Are you?'

'Why's it important?' She looks away, takes a decision then meets her mother's gaze. 'If you really want to know – kind of part time.'

The skin twitches beneath her mother's cheekbones, a grin spreads and her eyes dance. 'Same as me when I was your age.'

Slim's head jerks back, like someone overplaying astonishment, but it's entirely genuine. 'What!' She looks away. 'My goodness, I never dreamed . . . never dreamed I'd be having this conversation with you.'

'Well, I thought a bit of candour might go down well to get things rolling, eh?' Diana takes a sip of her drink. 'I had a girlfriend before I met your father. Her name was Sally Kershaw.'

'Sally! That's so funny. I know a Sally and she's totally gay.'

'I have no time left. You understand, don't you? So, I want to hear about your life, Slim. No lies, no dissembling in that clever way of yours. I want to know about my daughter and the risks she takes, because please do not think for one minute that I believe any of your tales.' She has more of her drink and eyes Slim with amusement and a fondness that Slim hasn't seen for years. 'So, tell me all about it.'

'I can't.'

'Of course you can!'

'The Official Secrets Act is one reason I can't.'

'Bugger the Official Secrets Act. There were men in my house! They were looking for you, poking about among your things . . .'

'You saw them?'

'Yes. One of them pushed me and the other thug hit me. Of course, I was sloshed, but I remember what happened. So, I have a right to know what's going on. And before you go telling me a lot of lies, please understand that I know there were men at the house the other night. And apparently you have a security firm watching the place. Nancy Scott told me.' She leans forward in the wheel-chair. Her skin is pale and there's a yellow tinge to the whites of her eyes, but she's no less beautiful and much more animated than Slim has seen for a long time. 'I love you very much and I'm sorry for all that has passed between us, even if most of it was unsaid.'

'No need to apologise, Mum. I know you've suffered. Dad and then Matthew.' Loup has placed his muzzle on her mother's knee. She strokes his nose and the top of his head with her free hand, looking down and nodding to him. 'I know they were mortal blows. Dad dying out of the blue and Matt just vanishing like that! Devastating. And never an end to it.'

'For you also, Slim. You miss him as much as I do.' She waits for Slim to react, but there's nothing Slim wants to say. 'This thing I have, this deadly thing that's crept into me, has made me think clearly about the situation. Matthew has gone. I don't want my other child to put herself in danger to find out what happened to him, if indeed it were possible.'

'What makes you think I am?'

'The only way you would have tolerated me over the winter was because you had to. I knew you needed to hide. I also understood that you had been through something shocking, something that terrified you. I'm your mother, for God's sake. I saw what I saw and yet I said nothing. Gave you no comfort, no love! You were traumatised, and I failed you because I was drunk. I apologise for that, too.'

'Don't, Mum. You'll have me crying and you know I don't do that ever.'

'It's true, I cannot remember when I last saw you crying. Matthew, yes. But you, never. Maybe you should. You're too demanding of yourself, too disciplined. Anyway, I worked out that the only thing that would persuade you to go back to whatever you were doing would be to find Matthew. And how do I deduce that? Well, I know you work for MI-something-or-other because a long time ago a man and a woman came to ask me about you. They said it was a regular background check for those who applied to work for the government, but this was no routine check, and I knew that my Alice was following the family tradition. I was very proud of you, by the way.'

'Tell me about that tradition. My boss mentioned it to me because, astonishingly, it is in my file.'

'So, you do admit it!'

'Get on with it, Mum.'

Diana smiles and looks down at the coffee cup. 'I've told you a little about it.'

'Not much.'

'Let's not get off the subject. I want to know – are you placing yourself at risk to find out about Matthew for me?'

Slim says nothing.

'I want you to stop. I accept that Matthew has gone. I loved him like I love you, but he went and there's nothing either of us can do about that. So, be a sensible girl and stop whatever you're doing. When I'm gone, you'll have money, a house that you can sell. You can take your time and find what you really want to do.'

Slim shakes her head, aware of an emotion racing through her at the same time as trying to identify it. Is this sorrow? Love? Panic?

'I'm really doing something that I enjoy – journalism,' she says. 'My story was published and caused a bit of a stir.'

Diana couldn't be less interested. 'This is not a time for avoiding things. I won't have you taking risks on my behalf.'

'Won't? What's with *won't*? Maybe *I* want to know what happened to Matt, too. Maybe I'll decide.'

'So, you have done some sort of deal to find him!'

Being outflanked by her mother, reduced to the status of hopeless teenager, is what she'd come to resent most during the long months of winter, and she wasn't having it now. 'I cannot talk about this and you're just going to have to accept that. I'm working as a journalist. I'm living on a boat and, to tell you the truth, I'm really enjoying it all. I even like Milton Keynes.'

Anger flashes in her mother's eyes. That's usually as far as it goes, but now she snaps, 'I haven't got the time for this BS. Grow up and tell me about it.'

Slim silently shakes her head. Her mother turns away and chucks the last of the gin to the back of her throat.

'How much time do you have?' Slims asks, then adds softly, 'Do *we* have?'

'A month or two. Maybe just weeks. It's a question of whether the cancer or my dodgy heart gets me first. It's going to be quick.' She stops and sighs, then pleads, 'Let's not row. Let's just speak the truth.'

'Are you in pain?'

'Almost none, though I feel lousy most of the time. Today is a good day, however.' Her hand swings out with the cup. 'I'd like the rest of that drink.'

'You need to eat a little more.'

Diana surveys the sandwiches with resentment, chooses chicken and begins to take wee bites while dropping scraps of white breast meat into Loup's mouth. She manages one triangle before returning the packet with a nod to the little bottle of gin, and Slim pours a second drink.

'So, I'm going to tell you as much of the story of my family as I can recall. It may explain things to you. They were called Benski, having changed their name from Bernstein as part of the Jewish assimilation into Polish bourgeoise society that took place a century or more ago. The Benskis converted to Catholicism, but their true religion was always the Polish army, which my grandfather Leon joined when he was in his twenties. He was a good organiser, a strategic man with an eye for detail and an exceptional ability with people. So, you see where you get that from, Slim.'

Slim gives her a pained look. 'Was that necessary, Mum?'

Her mother smiles. 'Oh, don't be so bloody serious. Just a tease. Anyway, Leon entered Polish Military Intelligence. He was chief of an intelligence station on the German border before World War Two. He was married to a wonderful woman named Rosa. In 1924, they had a son – their only child – and called him Jan. This was my father. After Hitler invaded Poland in 1939, Leon took his family to a property they owned in the east of the country.'

'After he'd destroyed all evidence that the Polish had cracked the Enigma machine.'

Diana looks surprised. 'How did you know about that?'

'My boss mentioned it. Seems like an important part of the story.'

Not to Diana. She dismisses it with a flick of the hand. 'You see, he was worried that his and Rosa's Jewish ancestry would be problematic – they were aware of what was happening to Jews in Germany. But it was a case of out of the frying pan and into the fire because they ran slap into Stalin's army, which invaded two weeks later and seized eastern Poland. They were arrested. Rosa and Jan, now fifteen years old, were forcibly separated from Leon. He was sent to the Russian Gulag with many thousands of Polish soldiers, and Rosa and Jan were put on a train, without food or water, and eventually dumped at the other end of Russia in a place called Nikolaevka, southwestern Siberia. That's what Russia does. It takes people and loses them in its vast lands, stealing and transporting families and dropping them in some godforsaken place and forgetting them. Rosa and Jan had nothing; they didn't know where Leon was, or even if he was alive. They just had to get on with it and try to survive the Siberian winters. Rosa made clothes and taught in a makeshift school and Jan put his flair for construction and engineering to work, repairing roads and bridges in the summer and repairing and insulating buildings in winter. They survived and Jan grew into a strong and capable young man.' Diana's eyes are fierce and distant, and she doesn't seem to see Slim as she talks, just the people in her story. 'Then the miracles happened. Not one but several. The first was Hitler's invasion of Russia, which meant that Stalin allowed Polish deportees and some Polish military personnel out of Russia. There were heroic long marches. Many died on the way. Without money or food, Rosa and Jan travelled over five thousand kilometres by train from Siberia to Krasnovodsk on the Caspian Sea. God knows how they managed without food or money. Yet the greatest miracle of them all occurred right on the dockside in Krasnovodsk. They turned round and found themselves looking straight at Leon, who was organising a company of soldiers boarding a ship to Pahlavi in Iran. Of course, they hardly recognised each other, but there he was, an officer in the army that left Russia under General Wladyslaw Anders.

'But imagine that! Imagine the chance of that happening, after all that time, after all the chaos and peril and starvation they'd faced. The vast distances involved! Millions were lost but their family became whole again on that quayside.'

'Unbelievable!' says Slim. She has heard a little of this before, mostly about the encounter on the quayside.

'You know why I'm telling you this? It's to explain about my father, Jan, whom you resemble in many ways. He became a soldier and joined the army. But instead of remaining in Palestine with those young Jews that came out of Russia and marched across the Middle East, he went on to fight all the way up Italy and was decorated on his twentieth birthday.'

'I've seen the medal, Mum. I wish I'd known him.'

'So do I, Slim.' She reaches for Slim's hand.

Slim feels she ought to be taking her inside. 'Can I get you a rug or something? You look cold.'

'Listen, this is about you! It's about what's inside *you*. And what was once inside me.' She's still got hold of Slim's hand. This, and the look of urgency in her eyes are so very unlike the distant, sarcastic mother of the winter.

Diana continues, 'Jan trained as a construction engineer after the war and then went into selling heavy plant, which he did all over Eastern Europe. He was a charming man: marvellous company and very, very clever. He was already fluent in Polish, Russian and English, and during the fifties made it his mission to learn German. So, you know what's next, don't you? A man with his talents very soon came to the notice of British Intelligence, and not just them – the East German Stasi wanted him also. So, he served both, but all along he was working for the

British and against Communism. He'd seen the brutality of
Stalin's Russia, you see – the mass murders, slavery, starvation, people eating each other – and he loathed Communism
viscerally. Utterly! My father, your grandfather, became one
of the most successful double agents of the Cold War. He operated in Berlin, Dresden and Leipzig, where he helped run and
protect networks. He fed the Communists false information
and led them a merry dance and they never had an inkling. He
took enormous risks, recruiting agents and, when they got into
trouble, saving them, arranging their escape. A true Scarlet
Pimpernel.'

'And you never thought to tell me this before now?'

'No, I'm not sure why. Maybe there wasn't the opportunity.'
She lets go of Slim's hand and gives a pathetic shrug. 'I had
things to deal with, not just Matthew and your dad. Emotional
things.'

Slim isn't going there. 'Those people who came to check me
out, did you mention any of this to them?'

'Yes, I probably did.'

'So, you told these nameless civil servants but not me.'

'I mentioned it only because I wanted them to understand
you came from reliable and resourceful stock.' Slim cannot help
smiling. She remembers the other product of this reliable and
resourceful stock, Matthew standing on the garden ha-ha, reefer
in hand, stoned out of his head.

'Did Matthew come up in that conversation?' Slim asks.

'I think you must've told them. They were interested but
only up to a point. Maybe they wanted to know if he'd become
a Jihadist.'

'Something like that,' says Slim. Had they already checked
out Matthew? Did the Service know what had happened to

him? She holds her mother's gaze. 'Do you think they knew where he went?'

A look of irritation. 'No, of course not! Why would they ask if they knew? Look, I'm tired. I will just say this: I lost one child; I don't want to lose another. I'm begging you to be careful, whatever you're bloody well doing.'

'I will.'

'Will you come tomorrow, darling? I'd like to see you again.'

'Of course. Now I'm going to wheel you back to Helen. I see her by the entrance.'

'And bring you-know-what when you come,' says her mother. 'And, of course, dear Loup.'

As she hands Diana over to Helen by a line of dedicated smokers, some with legs missing, others who do not have the breath to walk and are in wheelchairs, her mother asks, 'Where are you staying tonight? Not the house, I hope.'

'No. I'll go to my new residence. I hope to show it to you soon. It's only an hour and a bit away.'

'Your boat! I'd like that very much.'

'A boat! How romantic. Can I come?' asks Helen, pushing it a bit, in Slim's opinion.

CHAPTER 20

The Romanian petty criminal Andrei Botezatu is always at the front of Slim's mind, maybe because she identifies with a sister searching for her brother, but she doesn't go too deeply into that. What matters is that using geolocation techniques, Toto has confirmed that the photograph of Andrei sent to his sister to reassure her that all was well was taken at the isolated compound called Manor Farm, thirty-five miles from Milton Keynes where the counties of Bedfordshire and Cambridgeshire meet. And it was sent from the phone she has named Phone B, the one that phone A is always calling. She feels certain that A is checking in with his boss on phone B.

She chooses a Wednesday and leaves in the pickup with Loup around midday, having set up an email account in the name of Bob and Barbara Kemp, and written an email to a second fake account in the name of Georgina May. This email is on her phone screen when she climbs out of the pickup in the gateway of Manor Farm with Loup on a lead. There's no bell, but she's sure she will be seen on the CCTV and mimes puzzlement straight to the camera, as though she's lost. And sure enough, she hears a door bang in the distance and a man appears from inside the open barn. At the same moment a stout middle-aged woman issues from the nearest mobile home, drying her hands on her apron. Slim notices a lot of tyre marks, some deep ruts leading to the junkyard, a line of twenty or so two-tone green mobile homes, a JCB digger working in the distance, and a large blond man standing looking on. She switches to the camera and videos the man and the woman as they walk towards the gate.

The man calls out to her, 'No visitors without appointment. Can't you fucking read?' He's large – 17 st, at least. His head looks like a cork stuffed into a bottle. He has a chafing, fat-thighed walk and his hand is wrapped round a phone. She switches back to the email as he reaches her, smiles pleasantly, and proffers the phone so he can read the message. 'Is this the right address for Mr and Mrs Kemp with the collie?' He doesn't bother to read the email and says nothing. 'I'm looking for the Kemps. I have an appointment. My dog's going to mate with their bitch Molly. Do you know the Kemps?' She glances at Loup who likes the man no more than she does and, for the first time ever, sees him bare his teeth.

'That dog needs putting down,' he says.

The woman is standing back, hands thrust into the purple cardigan worn over the apron, eyes moving between Slim and the pickup. Now the man peers through the wire mesh at the email and grunts. 'Wrong postcode. You're miles out.'

'Oh, I'm so sorry for troubling you. I'm going to be late. I do hope my dog isn't going to miss his date.' This is calculated to elicit a smile, but their expressions don't alter. 'So, I'll be on my way,' she says, ushering Loup into the pickup. She places the phone she's been using in the holder on the dash, and with her nimble hands at the same time presses 'call' on Phone B's number, which she entered before pulling up at Manor Farm.

The pair are still there on the other side of the gates, waiting for her to leave. She hesitates for a beat then lowers the window. 'Really sorry to have disturbed your afternoon.'

It is then that the man's phone rings but as he answers the unidentified incoming call, she presses 'end', and it stops.

'Cheerio,' she says and, as she moves off, adds under her breath, 'Gotcha, bloody turnip head.' This is the man who's running things, the owner of phone B, the one that phone A is always calling.

She circles the property, occasionally stopping to look through hedges with her birding binoculars, but Manor Farm is truly isolated in these flatlands, and it is hard to get any better idea of the place than is available in the satellite imagery. At dusk she backs the pickup into a spinney on the main road, about a mile away, then walks to a spot behind a bush to watch the end of the narrow road that leads to Manor Farm. She hides at the intersection for an hour. She ignores several calls from Peter Salt before the first of four vehicles takes the road to the farm. A white van is followed by two minibuses and then a smaller Ford Transit minibus. She sees only silhouettes in the back of the vehicles and can't count the number of passengers, but she notes down on her phone all licence plate numbers except that of the white van, which is too dirty to read. A quarter of an hour later, the vehicles return separately and join the main drag towards the south.

Slim returns to the pickup and calls Salt.

'Where are you?' he says.

'I thought you'd know.' They must be watching her phone or have a tracker on her car, which would explain how the black Ford picked her up coming out of London. But so long as they keep their distance it doesn't bother her now.

'We're outside the Feathers pub at Graston village,' he says.

She pulls up in the car park half an hour later and finds Salt and Rob Alantree in a Lexus. She gets into the back of the car. 'Can't be long. I've got the dog.'

'What's up?' says Salt pleasantly. Alantree gives her his usual know-all smirk in the mirror.

'Hewing at the rockface of journalism,' she replies.

Alantree turns in the passenger seat to face her. He's wearing a neckerchief and a fancy motorcycle jacket. 'Slim, we need you to concentrate on the business in hand. The Prime Minister and Home Secretary are concerned about the material appearing on that site. Identify the sources they're using, then we've got something to tell them.'

'Do we work directly for politicians? I don't think so, Rob. But you can tell our people that there's a full staff meeting tomorrow, and it looks like Middle Kingdom will announce Part Two of the government waste story, or something similar. I have no way of knowing because they keep me totally isolated from anything sensitive. You'll just have to wait until they start to trust me.'

'Why don't you follow them?' asks Salt. 'The key players must be meeting somewhere else. They're never in the office.'

'If I'm going to follow them, I don't want you two in tow. I'll do it in my own time. Where's Tudor?'

'Tudor's busy,' says Salt, 'but Rob's here instead. We're never going to be far away.'

'Well, that's reassuring, Rob up here in the wilds to protect me. Look, I've got to go and feed the dog. And I have a ton of work. You'll be hearing from me.'

She gets out. Salt leaves the driving seat and closes his door behind him. 'Had any more trouble?'

She shakes her head then jerks it towards the car and opens her hands. 'Rob? I mean bloody Rob!'

'I know he's a bit of a dick but . . .'

'You're a dick as well, Salt.'

'A dick that saved your mum's life. How is she?'

'Not good. I see her all I can. That's where I go every weekend.'

'We know.'

'Thanks for staying back.' She looks at Alantree through the window. He's on the phone, fiddling with his jacket zipper. 'Imagine thinking that an undercover operation in Milton Keynes is best carried out in coral trousers, a Belstaff jacket and a cravat.'

Salt says, 'He's not undercover – you are.' He scuffs the gravel with the sole of his boot. 'Look, we've been told that Guest is back in the UK, and we know what that means for you. I just wanted to let you know we're here for you.'

'That's not the point. Forget my safety: Guest isn't in jail. He's free to do exactly what he wants, corrupt whoever he chooses, murder, steal and rape.' She stops, looks at Alantree, now scrolling through his phone. 'Guest's not the problem, it's us.'

Salt looks blank and moves on. 'This job isn't going to last beyond a week or two. All we need is the name or names of those breaking the Official Secrets Act, then you can properly go into hiding for as long as you need.'

'When that happens, I need to be within reach of the hospital, so it's not going to be easy and obviously I can't live at the house since she was attacked there.'

'Yeah, at the time I didn't believe those injuries were consistent with a fall.' He stops, looks at her, not unsympathetically, and buttons his jacket. 'The boat seems a good solution for the present, but it must be chilly even at this time of year.'

'You found it.'

'Yes, but we'll keep our distance, of course.'

She moves off and he says, 'We must do that drink sometime.'

'No chance,' she says. 'You're way too much of a dick.'

'Have a lovely evening, Slim!'

That's exactly what she does. Lambert Bantock thumps on the cabin roof at 9.30 p.m. and hands down a bottle of Scotch, a four-pack and an old aluminium canteen filled with stew and dumplings, which they set about consuming, beer alternating with slugs of Glenfiddich. He has a gift as a storyteller and his eyes glitter, inviting Slim to relish the absurdity of the fraught romantic entanglements along the canal, or the 'cut', as he refers to it — the bare-knuckle fighting in dewy meadows, skulduggery in sunflower contests and pepper eating championships. She hasn't laughed like this in years. He departs at midnight, leaving her to ponder printouts of the encrypted documents Ballard laid out in the church for her and the photograph of that evening long ago with Matt's and her friends at Steward's House. She struggles to remember much about that weekend, except her father Toby's fury at finding the evidence of weed in the ashtrays. Always so understanding and supportive of his children, he lost it just that once and broke a vase.

God that was a blow, Dad's death. Catastrophic stroke at the airport. Out of nowhere. Dead on arrival. She misses him badly. Being his daughter. The jokes. The craic. The listener who really seemed to want to know what she was thinking. 'Speak up, Slim! Ideas are born on the lips, not in silence.' With Toby's death, Matthew went completely off the rails. Drugs. Bad people. First vanishing act. She folds the photograph and tucks it into the paper at the back of the frame of Matthew's picture, so it can't be seen, and picks up her glass and jiggles it so the liquid whirlpools.

An idea was indeed born on the lips when she was berating Salt about the failure to prosecute or sanction Ivan Guest. 'Guest's not the problem,' she'd said, 'it's us.' Salt didn't pick up on it but that was right, wasn't it? Who was us? The security and law enforcement establishment? Politicians? The decrepit state of the country? Or just MI5? Something was profoundly wrong when a man like Guest could continue his business untroubled by the law, when all his corruption and crimes were plain to see for anyone who cared to look.

CHAPTER 21

Bantock appeared on *Spindle* at 6.30 a.m., no worse for the Scotch, and started making coffee before she was up. As she dressed, he went to sit at the stern and, with his arms hanging over the tiller, to smoke a cigarette, inhaling deeply as though his life depended on it. The changes he would make to *Spindle*'s appearance, he told her, once he'd moved her to a quiet spot a few miles away, would seem radical but could be reversed within an hour or so. Nothing permanent. He asked which name she wanted – *Jupiter*, *Meadow Song* or *Razor's Edge*? She chose the most forgettable – *Meadow Song* – then left Bantock with Loup, who showed no sign of regret.

By ten she had parked the pickup in the usual spot, hired a little black hatchback and left it a couple of blocks from the office before walking up the hill to the shopping mall to buy several new phones.

At the office, Yoni Ross is pacing up and down in the empty conference room on his phone. There's no sign of Abigail, Dan Halladay, Skelpick or Sara Kiln. The young writers who worked on the government waste story aren't there, nor is Toto Linna. She sends a new number to Shazi and Abigail and writes them an email, cc-ed to the lawyer Annette Raines, with details of everything that she's found out about Manor Farm, and attaches a photo of the owner of Phone B who she has named 'Turnip Head'.

Shazi gets up and passes Slim with barely a glance. Slim follows her to the loo and using the basin to remove a non-existent stain from her shirt asks what's happening.

'They're trying to shut us down.'

'How?'

'An injunction to stop us publishing anything more.' The noise of the hand dryer stops her in mid-sentence. Her hair blows upwards in the draught, and she smiles artlessly. 'But we're going ahead. There's a meeting in a few minutes.'

'But no one's here.'

'They will be.' The door bangs behind her.

Slim texts Salt, but not on one of her new phones, which are reserved for when she doesn't want to be tracked by her MI5 colleagues. She writes: *Second bite of article imminent despite injunction threat.* Salt replies with an *okay* emoji. She deletes the exchange and returns to her desk. Skelpick has appeared in the conference room and is sitting with his fingers laced behind his head, listening to Yoni Ross, who is still on the phone.

Shazi glances around the floor several times. Still, no one has come. Then she calls out suddenly, 'Okay, they're here. Meeting in five.'

There's a rush from the lift and the stairway and suddenly over thirty people are in the conference room.

Halladay signals to Abigail who goes through with the news list and corrections that need to be made that day, then Yoni takes over. He blows out his cheeks and folds his hands over his stomach. 'We've got a problem with the government which says that we don't have the right to publish the story about the waste of public money because the material is stolen. How can that be in a democracy, where folk have a right to know how their money is spent?' A pause follows during which he sweeps the young faces in the conference room. '"The press should serve the governed, not the governors." That's a quotation from the US Supreme Court which backed the *Washington Post*'s decision to publish the Pentagon Papers, which exposed the Vietnam policy. That same principle guides our little site here and, you know what, our readers tell us they love those principles. But that means nothing to the government and the UK Official Secrets Act doesn't provide for a public interest defence. So, if you're in possession of what they define as an official secret, that's enough to send you to jail. And this is what they have threatened today. We're up against an injunction and mass prosecutions.'

'Are we going to publish more?' comes a woman's voice from behind Slim. She turns to see Sofi, one of the team who worked on the waste story.

Dan Halladay says, 'We're not saying what we've got or what we might publish.'

'And we're going to keep them guessing,' says Ross.

'Which is why,' says Halladay, 'it's very important that none of you speculates in conversation or email or social media what we're planning.' He stops. Abigail is signalling at him.

'I have a message from Arnold downstairs,' she says. 'It's swarming with police outside.' She raises her voice. 'Now, everyone, you know what to do. Take your devices and have your IDs ready. The door code is 6661. Go!'

The room rapidly empties. Abigail comes over to Slim. 'I'm afraid you need an ID to say you're employed by Goth Travel on the floor below. They can't touch the employees of another company.' Slim had noticed the sign on the third floor for Goth Travel and assumed it to be a defunct enterprise set up by Abigail.

'So, what do I do?'

'You stay here, or try to leave the building by the back, but they've probably got that covered. Yoni, Dan, Skelpick, Shazi and Toto will be here and a couple of others who don't have their Goth ID. Okay, I need to go. Sorry about this.' She touches Slim on the arm. 'You'll be fine.'

CHAPTER 22

Slim grabs a bin liner from the kitchenette, wraps her laptop and places it at the bottom of a food waste bin beneath discarded wraps and unidentifiable mush. She washes her hands and returns to the newsroom. Dan Halladay is making calls; Shazi is busy shutting down two desktops and Toto aims a remote at the ceiling, turning on spyhole cameras hidden in the cornices. He says, 'We're live-streaming from . . . now.' Slim turns away and, as far as possible, moves out of the cameras' fields. Skelpick has positioned himself to face the door to the stairwell, cane held in both hands. In the conference room, Yoni is sitting with his eyes shut and, from his long slow breaths, Slim suspects that he's meditating.

The floor falls quiet. Halladay has finished his calls and joins Skelpick by the entrance. He turns and says to the group of seven, 'Be polite. Don't obstruct them. I doubt they're here to arrest anyone but if they do, say nothing. Legal help will be on hand.' He smiles. 'Whatever happens, never doubt you are on the side of justice.' He turns to face the lift. 'Without truth, democracy dies.'

'Hear, hear!' says Skelpick softly. At this, Shazi tears up but quickly regains control and sets her face to the entrance.

They wait thirty seconds more. Slim is now certain that her single-line text tipping off Salt that Middle Kingdom was going to publish more on the waste story is responsible for the raid.

The lift bell pings and three men in uniform and one in plain clothes appear. They ask Skelpick to step aside.

'Who's in charge?' says the plain-clothes officer. Halladay raises a finger and says he is the editor.

The uniformed officer says, 'I am Superintendent Staples. We have powers, under the Official Secrets and National Security acts, to search and seize material if it is believed an offence has been or is about to be committed, which, in this case, is the obtaining and disclosing of protected information. If you all return to your desks, my officers will carry out the search and remove such items and material as we believe will help in our investigation. Obstructing my officers or concealing information are offences, and we will have no hesitation in arresting individuals if they do not comply with the law.' He looks around. 'Where is everyone?'

'Out on stories, days off, annual leave, sick,' says Halladay. 'We have a challenge to fill the site sometimes. It's a small operation.'

Officers, many wearing pale blue vests stamped with 'Police', pour on to the floor with big transparent evidence bags and empty crates. Slim counts seventeen men and women. The remaining staff drift back to their stations to watch as desktops, three Dell servers and the few laptops in evidence are unplugged and gathered at the centre of the floor for labelling and crating. All the box files behind Halladay's desk and stacked by Abigail's are removed. Desk drawers are opened and emptied of paper, notebooks, and various means of backup. The cavities behind desk drawers are searched, hands are run

underneath the surface of the desks. They go into the lavator-
ies, lift the carpet, knock on the walls, and prod the ceiling to
see if any of the tiles move. But they do not disturb the food
waste bin.

Ross remains in the conference room, apparently unaware of
what's going on. He stirs and Slim hears one of the constables
ask, 'Who're you – the cleaner?' Ross looks down at what he's
wearing, which is admittedly shabby, replies he's the chairman
of the company and reminds the constable that journalistic
material is privileged under the definition of 'confidential material'. He clambers up and comes out of the conference room to
make the point again to the superintendent.

'In the case of emergency,' intones Staples as though reading
from a script, 'I'm authorised to order the seizure of journalistic
material, and to retain that material once a warrant has been
granted. In the unlikely circumstance that the judge doesn't see
fit to grant that warrant, the property will be returned to you.
In certain circumstances it may be destroyed. As the new legislation requires, the Home Secretary has been informed of this
action.' He returns his gaze to the pile of machines and papers
being labelled and bagged. Ross makes a glum face then sticks
out his tongue. Because Slim is keeping out of the way of Toto's
cameras, she sees this and smiles.

'What's funny?' asks a plain-clothes officer, a young version
of Tudor Mills.

'A private thought,' she says.

'What do you write about then?'

'Bumblebees and stolen flowers,' she replies. Halladay gives
her an imperceptible shake of the head to tell her not be pro-
vocative.

'What's in that backpack?'

'This?' says Slim, picking it up. 'A new phone that I use to call my mother who is seriously ill in hospital, make-up, sanitary products, tissues, a sandwich, a dog lead.'

'Give me the phone.'

'You want my phone. How do I call my mum?'

'Give me the phone.'

She looks inside the bag, selects the new phone used to text Salt and, covering the one she is protecting, hands it over. 'You want everything else?' she asks.

'Of course not. Name?' he demands with a Sharpie poised over a label.

She tells him. He mishears, writes Parton instead of Parsons on the label and takes her phone to the centre of the room.

A woman police officer approaches the superintendent. 'Sir, they're filming this. It's all going out live on their site. It's everywhere on social media.'

'Is this true?' Superintendent Staples demands of Halladay.

Ross interposes himself between the officer and Halladay, and says, 'I don't believe there's a law prohibiting the filming of police officers carrying out their work.'

'There is if you are obstructing my officers in the course of their duties. Arrest this man.'

Two officers take hold of Ross's arm. 'If you think about it for one second,' says Ross calmly, 'the evidence that I am not obstructing you in any way is now being livestreamed to hundreds, maybe thousands of people, with you in shot. You have no case against me and no right to arrest me. But go ahead, look like the knuckleheads you are.'

'Where are the cameras?' demands the superintendent, looking round furiously. 'Who's in charge of the filming?'

Toto, who has been lounging with his feet up on the

windowsill, uncoils and raises a limp arm. 'They're security cameras,' he says, 'designed to catch unwanted intruders.'

'Shut them down now.'

Toto shakes his head. 'Not possible.'

'Then turn off the streaming.'

Toto has his chin cupped in his hands with fingers splayed like Betty Boop. 'Well, you know what they say, officer – if you've nothing to hide you've got nothing to fear from surveillance.'

'Arrest that man and see the filming stops immediately.' Toto is grabbed and an officer ineptly stabs at the remote. 'Aim it at the ceiling!' fumes Staples. 'There, where the holes are in the cornice.'

Within a quarter of an hour, the police have removed everything and taken Ross and Toto away. As the last of them leaves the floor, Skelpick mutters something to the officer who took Slim's phone and is promptly arrested. He's led to the lift waving his stick and shouting, 'Free the Milton Keynes Three!'

'Was that absolutely necessary?' says Halladay to Slim. 'He just can't resist. I need him here to write.'

'So, you are going to publish,' she says.

'That's for me to know. We haven't made up our minds, whatever you've heard. But the public is watching, and we can't be seen to cower in the face of this.'

'But all the equipment they took—'

'Means nothing. Replaced by tomorrow. We won't be intimidated, and we won't be shut down and we won't be hurried. Now, you'd better go and get that package you hid in the kitchen. I'm going to talk to the lawyers and spring the Milton Keynes Three.'

CHAPTER 23

Slim waits at a distance in the hire car with binoculars occasionally lifted to the main entrance of Middle Kingdom. An hour into her vigil, Salt calls. 'Where are you?'

'Having a sandwich outside the office.' She knows he knows where she is. As soon as she moves, she'll turn off the phone he's monitoring.

'There's nothing on the computers and servers that were seized,' he says. 'So far, there's no trace of a second story.'

'Of course there isn't. By the way, that was such a stupid thing to do. The whole country is now rooting for the little website being terrorised by the authorities.'

'We had no option. Once you'd told me they were going to publish Part Two, it was inevitable. Are they?'

'I have no idea. These people aren't stupid. They'll keep everyone guessing. They're strategic, they weigh outcomes, unlike our halfwit government.'

'Right, but all you have to do is focus on finding out where these stories are being worked up and the data stored.'

'Then you'll raid that location and close them down.'

'We're talking about grave breaches of the country's secrecy laws.'

She says nothing.

'You there?' says Salt.

'Yeah. I am wondering if the penny has dropped with you that they were still streaming on the Middle Kingdom site after the police disconnected all the servers in the office. That means they are several steps ahead.'

He absorbs this. 'Stay in touch.'

'You need to be careful of the data dump.'

'What do you mean?'

'Or a killer revelation they've held back.'

Now she has his attention.

'It would make sense to keep something back. It's a favourite newspaper trick to publish something even more devastating when all the denials have been issued and the fuss is dying down.'

'I see.' He stops. She guesses he's writing this down. 'What do you mean by a data dump?'

'Well, if they're all charged with OSA offences, Middle Kingdom could easily publish everything they've got. I mean everything – all the embarrassing emails, secret figures, and official reports they've had access to. Then every journalist in the country will be trawling through the raw material looking for stories. And the process will go on for weeks and there will be nothing anyone can do about it.'

'Do you think this is what they plan?'

'I'm second-in-command in the bumblebee investigation unit, remember! They tell me nothing. But it stands to reason. I keep on telling you these people aren't stupid. Do you want me to put all this in an email or are you—?'

'I'll write it up,' he says.

She'll write it up too, just to cover herself.

It's past five when she sees Sara Kiln and Halladay leave the office. Sara waits with him under an umbrella until a Tesla pulls up and he gets in. A woman is driving, no doubt Halladay's wife, the art dealer Jen. Sara Kiln sets off towards the shopping mall, umbrella bent to the wind. Slim starts her car and turns left, having calculated that she will have a much better chance of tailing the Tesla if she meets it at a right angle at the traffic lights on Silbury Boulevard. When her light turns green, she accelerates and slots into a file of traffic two cars behind the Halladays, which allows her to watch the direction they take at the first of several roundabouts. She follows them across three and, on the last, goes right the way round to ensure she isn't the car directly behind them. They travel for a further nine miles until they reach a cluster of houses, turn down a country lane and soon afterwards enter a driveway. Slim accelerates and stops in a muddy gateway about fifty yards on, gets out and walks into a field so she can look through her binoculars. The house is modern, the sort that hides in the landscape. There's turf on the roof, a bank of solar panels at the rear and reed beds in the garden to deal with the sewage and grey water. Lights come on downstairs. She sees a well-laid-out sitting room and a kitchen, abstract canvasses, a wall of big-format books. The Halladays are standing close to each other. Jen moves towards Dan and touches him on the cheek. They seem so near to her that Slim feels if she coughed, they'd jump.

That's enough snooping. This house is no secret, and moreover it wasn't at all difficult to find. Salt and Mills could have found it. Why didn't they? She returns to Milton Keynes, switches on her usual phone and calls Bantock to say she's twenty minutes away. When she arrives at the new berth, it's dark but she can see the narrowboat has been transformed. The name *Meadow Song* is on both sides of the cabin. There's a funnel for a non-existent wood-burning stove, strips of tape that alter the outside of the cabin's appearance, curtains where there were once blinds, a red tiller handle, flashes on the rudder, and a satellite dish, which Clive Killick would never have entertained on the roof of his beloved *Spindle*. Bantock is with Loup at the stern, illuminated by a paraffin lamp. He's pleased with the work, and he has whisky with him to celebrate the transformation.

'And you may want to keep this safe, whatever it is.' He hands her the package containing the tablet and printouts of the photographs she took of the encrypted documents. 'It was behind the batteries.'

'Huh! Right, I'll send it on to Clive. I've got a forwarding address.'

'Good! I guessed it must be important for one of you.' He knows its hers and gives her the dazzling grin of the Grand Union Romeo. 'Looks like you need a dram.'

God knows she does.

Dawn has just broken when the boat is rocked gently by the wash from a wide beam going south. She wakes with a start and immediately texts Bantock: *Can you take Loup this morning? Back later.* Then she showers under a miserable trickle – the water heater is still playing up – makes coffee and breakfasts on two boiled eggs and toast while looking at the Middle Kingdom home page on her phone. Nothing's changed on the site overnight, which is unusual. She leaves Loup with a bowl of food and the remains of her buttered toast and drives out to the Halladays' house.

She approaches from the opposite direction this time, passes the driveway, and sees the Tesla and a smaller EV on charge.

Further down the road, she noses into a recessed gateway to a field of wheat and walks to a corner where there is a burnt-out Massey Ferguson combine harvester that looks like it has been hit by a missile. She will watch the house from behind the wreckage. The blinds are up but there are no lights on and no sign of activity in the open-plan kitchen and sitting room. No movement from upstairs, either.

An hour goes by before she sees someone in the kitchen. She brings up her binoculars. It's Halladay moving around in haste, grabbing breakfast, she thinks. He leaves by the main entrance at the side of the building and stands, drinking coffee from the insulated red cup he brings to the office. He's waiting for someone and, unusually for Halladay, he seems anxious, looking at his watch several times and pacing. He starts forward as a vehicle pulls up at the entrance to the driveway. A moment later the car moves off in the direction of the main road. She sees a dark brown SUV but nothing else. She races along the firm ground on the side of the field and reaches her car about a minute later then, after a few seconds of wheelspin, she shoots back on to the road and is in pursuit. The SUV has vanished.

She reaches the main road and is faced with the choice of two directions, three if she includes the minor road that branches to the south a hundred metres away. She chooses the route west, towards the Cotswolds and away from Milton Keynes. Three or four miles on, she spots the SUV and gets close enough to see that it is a new Porsche and is, in fact, dark red. She pushes the hire car and runs a couple of lights to catch the Porsche behind a tractor towing a crop sprayer. The Porsche gets past the tractor and takes a minor road to the left, just outside the village of Aynho, but it is another two minutes before Slim can overtake. The roads are clear and Slim presses the accelerator to the floor to reach ninety miles per hour on two clear stretches. She has just one sighting of her quarry before it disappears for good. This doesn't make sense to her. The Porsche wasn't travelling at anything like her speed, and she should have caught up by now, or at least spotted it in the distance. She pulls up and consults the Maps app to look for possible turnings in the last five miles then flips to satellite view. About half a mile back, there is a group of thirty buildings laid out along a central spine, almost like a ribcage. Around this formation, other long structures of the same design and size have congregated. The site is bordered by woodland on two sides and fields to the north and south. Nearby is a country house, identified in the app as Tender Wick Park. She remembers passing a sign for Tender Wick Residential Care on her right. The other signs were a blur.

She goes back to the turning and finds dozens of signs of all sizes announcing specialist garages, furniture makers, tyre fitters, cobblers, video studios and reclamation companies, all with premises at the Tender Wick Business Park. Middle Kingdom has a cover operation in Milton Keynes – Goth Travel – so, why not here, among the garages and reclamation yards? She follows a van through an old gateway, passes a gravel driveway that goes to the care home, and continues through an open security barrier on to a poorly maintained metalled road. There's a narrow one-way system that circles the park, which is much larger than she expected and with many more businesses than advertised at the entrance. Around the body shops, garages and small engineering companies are accumulations of junk, but the upholsterers, furniture hire companies and interior decorators have potted bay trees and newly painted walls and doors. The sheds and Nissen huts might have been lifted whole from Bletchley Park and dropped here. They're the same design and size, and date from World War II when what was a prison camp, she reads in a business directory beside the road, was built in a hurry on the requisitioned grounds of Tender Wick House. But, unlike the pampered buildings at Bletchley, the camp shows signs of its age with broken windowpanes and occasional holes in the roofs. Along the covered walkway – the spine of the camp – roof panels have fallen, and briars are taking over.

In a couple of laps, she doesn't spot the Porsche, so she pulls up on the deserted side of the park, in the shadow of a Nissen hut. Her hunch about the place is probably wrong. She gets out to stretch her legs and walks to a pair of apple trees in blossom about fifty metres away.

'Can I help you, young lady?' A man in his seventies, spry and in a blue-checked shirt with the sleeves rolled up, has emerged from a kind of grotto that is made of rough Cotswold stone and surrounded by privet. He carries a trowel and a bin liner. He has been weeding the gravel inside the grotto.

'No thanks. I was just marvelling at the smell of the blossom. Is it always so strong?'

'These are special trees. The sweetest apples you've tasted in all your life. They were planted by my father – oh – sixty-two years ago, but they still provide a very good crop each year. If I didn't come with buckets and baskets, they'd rot.'

'They are rightfully your apples, I guess.'

He shows her the grotto, which is a memorial to the Polish families who were accommodated at Tender Wick after it was decommissioned as a prisoner-of-war camp in 1945. There are tea-light holders, three Madonna figurines, some plastic dahlias, and a few small photographs.

'I lived in this place for the first ten years of my life,' says the man, who has introduced himself as Piotr. After reading about the camp and the displaced Polish servicemen, she is astonished to see the inscription on the memorial.

Their ordeal started after deportation from Poland to Siberia in 1940. On their release by Stalin following the invasion of the Soviet Union by Hitler, the Polish Army in Russia was formed under General Wladyslaw Anders, and they undertook a heroic march across Russia to freedom. Following retraining in the Middle East, they contributed greatly to the Allied victory in World War II.

'Why are you smiling?' he asks.

'Things seem to be coming full circle in my life just now. My grandfather and his parents were deported to Siberia from Eastern Poland and were miraculously reunited on the Caspian Sea. My grandfather and great-grandfather served with Anders.'

He is pleased and smiling broadly. 'My father, too. Maybe they knew each other.' They are silent for a few moments. 'General Anders stood where you are now in July 1952 and opened this memorial.'

She hears a motorbike revving and looks over the curved stone wall of the memorial. It's Skelpick. He's on a concrete ramp that leads from a long shed two buildings away. His foot is on the ground, and he's looking down at his machine as he works the throttle. Smoke is coming from the exhaust, but he decides it's all right and moves down the ramp to take the road that passes the memorial. She ducks down, pretending to take a photograph of the memorial plaque, although there's little chance of him spotting her. A minute later, the Porsche comes down the ramp, followed by a Honda EV, which Slim knows to be Abigail's. As the Porsche passes, she sees Sara Kiln at the wheel, Yoni Ross in the front seat and Dan Halladay in the back, winding the window up. With Abigail is Toto Linna and Callum, one of the writers on the government waste story.

'The American Jew,' says Piotr with a note of contempt. 'He's here always. Big car, big money. Every time I am here, the American Jew is here.' He's looking at her hard, wanting a reaction or maybe testing her. Then, after some thought, he says, 'I knew that building. It was our concert hall, the place for special occasions, where we celebrated weddings, Easter, and Christmas. There were parties for us kids, concerts for the grown-ups, and dances, oh so many dances. But now it is like a fortress. You can't see in.'

'It's probably all legitimate,' she says and makes to leave.

'No, the Jew is up to no good, I'm telling you.' Again, he looks at her hard, wanting something.

She leaves him, walks until she's out of his sight, then passes between two buildings to reach the covered walkway which was originally the main approach. A double-door entrance that linked the old concert hall to the main thoroughfare of the covered walkways is bricked up, as are all the windows. She scrambles on to the walkway roof, and shimmies up on to the concert hall roof, which is flat, not pitched like the other buildings. It has a couple of large satellite dishes – not visible from the ground – several turbine ventilators, solar panels and, dead in the middle, a raised square turret with four windows. Moving round this structure, she peers through each of the windows. One or two lights are on below and there's a long white desk on one side, though she sees no one working at it. Through the final window, she sees the bottom edge of two very large servers and masses of cabling. LEDS flicker and the ventilation system hums. A glance around tells her that three other huts, all finished to the same high standard, may be connected in some way to the old concert hall. She moves to the front of the building and looks over a false gable end down to the garage door, which is probably operated with a fob carried by each driver who wishes to enter. The parking bay consumes about a quarter of the space in the building, which leaves plenty of room for the activities that interest her MI5 colleagues.

She's seen all she needs, takes photographs through the windows of the turret, of the roof and the surrounding buildings, then drops a pin on a map to record the exact location of Middle Kingdom's secret facility. She climbs down the way she went up and circles to get back to the car, where she finds Piotr.

'Those people I was telling you about,' she calls out to him, 'my people who came out of the Soviet Union.'

'Yes.' He sways slightly and lets his bag of weeds drop to the ground.

'Those people who crossed Russia without food and dragged themselves to a port on the Caspian Sea, then marched through deserts under General Anders, fought their way up Italy, like the heroes who are remembered here.'

'Yes, brave Polish people,' he says.

'And were decorated on the battlefield and went on to serve the cause of freedom right through the Cold War, risking a bullet in the back of the head.'

He nods. 'Good people.'

'Those people – my people – they were Jews. Just thought I'd make that clear. Have a terrific day and I hope your apples are every bit as sweet as the blossom.'

His mouth drops open, and he begins to say something.

'No, that's okay, Piotr. Please don't say anything more.' She smiles, turns and gets into the little hire car she will return before heading north for a weekend with her mother. 'My people,' she mutters as she drives away.

CHAPTER 24

She waits for them at a gentle bend of the canal, near an old brick bridge. On one side, there are trees, branches arching down over the water, and on the towpath side, pastures with Friesian cows, old water courses and ditches that are filled with yellow iris. The hawthorn is still in flower. Small white clouds are evenly spaced across the sky in diminishing bands towards the horizon. In this stretch, little has changed since the canal was carved through the landscape to link London with Birmingham over two hundred years ago.

She spots Helen manoeuvring her mother into a wheelchair on the lane that leads from the bridge down to the canal and lets Loup off his lead. She jogs after him, reaches her mother, kisses her, links an arm with Helen and mouths 'thank you'. They wheel Diana down to the boat together but at the water's edge, they realise it's going to be difficult to transfer her aboard. Bantock is summoned from the galley, where he's been making lunch. He steps on to the path, introducing himself with a courtly bow and his full name – Lambert Charles Bantock – and before Diana has time to object, picks her up, carries her on to *Spindle* and sets her down on a seat on the port side. A gin and tonic is produced with miraculous speed and handed up to her. Diana is appallingly thin, half the size she was when she was taken to hospital. Now, as Loup lays his muzzle on her knee and she smiles, Slim sees five or six lines in each cheek where there were just one or two.

They cast off and go north, gliding through the spring countryside, her mother glorying in the landscape as though experiencing spring for the first time. Occasionally, she turns and nods to Slim. This was such a good idea; everything's so new and beautiful; she's so happy to be there with Slim and Loup. Very happy. A hand is placed on the tiller next to Slim's. The rings are loose. 'Know that you are loved, my daughter. Know you are loved.'

'Thanks, and you too, Mum. You too! You want to steer?'

'If I don't have to stand, but I think we need less noise, don't you?' She reaches down and pulls the throttle back. Slim looks surprised. 'I've been on a bloody boat before.' They sit in silence, Bantock and Helen talking up a storm below. 'I'm at peace about Matthew,' her mother says suddenly. 'I know he's gone.' A tear rolls down her cheek. 'We have to get on with life, or, in my case, death.'

'Why are you so certain?'

'I knew a few weeks ago. It's why I was drinking so much. I was more certain of it than anything in my life. About three weeks before I was attacked.' She studies the effect of this on Slim, then asks abruptly. 'What's going on with you? Something's up, something more than the usual drama of your life.'

'Nothing, Mum. We've got some problems at work. That's all.'

'Which work? Your work as a spy or as a journalist?'

Slim gives her an eye-roll and bends down to check that Bantock and Helen haven't heard.

Mother continues, with, 'Well, by the look of you, it's serious and my guess is that you don't know where you stand.' Daughter looks ahead, determined not to give anything up. 'Live your truth, my darling. If you believe in something, live it whatever the consequences. I know you will because you're a product of tough-minded people who did the right thing.' She blows a kiss.

'Thank you. You look cold, Mum. I'll get you something.' She finds an old fleece and woolly hat below, then has an idea. She jams the opened bottle of white under her arm and picks up Matthew's portrait and climbs the three steps. 'Oh, my goodness!' says Diana. 'I haven't seen this for years.'

'I thought you should,' Slim says. She takes the tiller and leans over it to pour wine into her mother's empty glass.

'He was so gifted,' says Diana.

They raise their glasses.

'To Matt,' Slim says.

'To my son, darling Matthew.'

They chuck back the full tumblers of wine. Diana has tears in her eyes and is shaking her head.

'Put that fleece on, you're white with cold.'

They tie up and eat Bantock's lunch of cold salmon, cucumber and mayonnaise, but Diana tires quickly and needs to go back to the hospital, and – no offence to Helen – she would like Slim to drive her with Loup. For most of the way, she sleeps. She's run out of road, thinks Slim, doesn't want to live a day longer and looks half dead curled up in the front seat with Loup. But thirty minutes from the hospital, she wakes, sips gin and tonic from a plastic bottle supplied by Bantock and talks animatedly about her will, her lover Sally, Steward's House, which both agree is drenched with sadness, and the cash in two accounts that Slim should transfer now to her own account so that it's not caught up in probate.

She begins to talk about her funeral and reaches out to touch Slim, first her arm then her shoulder, where her hand remains. 'I need someone to recall my family's history. Tell them how they saved the Enigma secret from the Germans, tell them how they fought for democracy wherever they landed, how my father came to this country with nothing and served that cause of freedom under the noses of the Stasi. I'm proud of that service, and you are the best person to do that, Slim.' She looks at her, then gives a slow wink. 'Tell them about the Benskis, those assimilated Jews who became brilliant soldiers and intelligence officers. I have written it all down for you in a note. And, darling, I want you to say that I did my best, failed often, and that I was lucky to have known love and to have met the sweetest of men to have children with. Talk about my heartbreak over Matthew. It's my greatest failure and the only source of pain in my life. And I want you to acknowledge Sally, even if she can't face being there. Can you do all that, darling Slim? Her name is Sally Kershaw; she never married. Her address and phone number are in my desk.' She pauses, looks at Slim with limitless affection. 'I'm setting the record straight, darling. The plain facts, nothing fake, nothing twee. Death is death and it's bloody grim.'

Her hand drops from Slim's shoulder, she rests her head against Loup and closes her eyes.

CHAPTER 25

A text from Abigail that's addressed to all the Middle Kingdom staff arrives early next morning. It is headed 'Update'.

Yoni Ross, J. J. Skelpick and Toto Linna have been charged with obstruction. All three were held for questioning on the Official Secrets Act (OSA) late into Friday. There are no OSA charges, and they've been released.

This is a blatant attempt to silence us and prevent legitimate scrutiny of the government. We will not give in. But please do not talk about this or offer comment on any issue in social media. Thanks, Abigail.

Is this living Slim's truth? Hardly.

When undercover in Ivan Guest's organisation, every deceit, subterfuge, lie, theft and manipulation was justified but now she couldn't feel more conflicted. Yes, the founders are up to something out at Tender Wick Park — that massive computing power isn't innocent — but she hasn't told Salt and Alantree about it because the plain truth is that she's on the side of the maggots cleaning the wound. And the only reason she's holding the stress position in Operation Linesman is her brother. She'll stay so long as there's hope that he's alive, whatever her mother's convictions.

The phone that has just brought her the message from Abigail lights up and the name Delphy appears. The old lady doesn't waste time. 'You need to come as soon as possible and don't delay,' then without any explanation she hangs up. Slim checks in with the office and drives out to Top Farm Cottage.

She finds Delphy waiting at the front door in a long cardigan that's several sizes too big for her and a flat cap, which is also too large and covers her ears. The look makes Slim smile. Delphy says, 'I think they call it a bad hair day, but I have been up since six. Come in, come in, and you'll see why.' She moves from the door to the kitchen.

At the table is the odd-job man Frank, who was there the first time she visited Delphy. Opposite him is a small woman of south-east Asian origin, who rises and lowers her gaze. Delphy touches her hand. 'Sit, dear! We don't stand on ceremony in this house.' She turns to Slim. 'This is Tam. She's from Vietnam. And you remember Frank Shap? Frank has quite a tale to tell you, but before he starts, I want you to know that he is a hero, because he won't tell you himself.' She admonishes him with a tap on the shoulder. 'He risked his life to save Tam.'

Tam nods. She understands English. But she keeps her head bowed.

'Neither Tam nor Frank want to involve the police at this stage, but they need you to act as an intermediary and find the help that Tam needs, then Frank will vanish, though it is my opinion that he should be awarded a medal.'

Slim takes out one of her phones to record the interview and a notebook and pen from her backpack. 'What's this about?'

'Tam here was a slave,' Frank says, 'and her sister is still with the gang who brought them into the country. That's why she can't go to the police. It's a big operation with maybe hundreds of people.'

'Start from the beginning,' says Slim. 'Then maybe Tam would like to speak about her experiences.'

Delphy nods and revolves her hand impatiently.

'I sleep rough, see,' Frank says. 'Had a bit of trouble and made mesself scarce these past few years. Last Saturday, was making tea – late, like – around ten in the evening coz I switched off the news on my radio. No call for news in my life. Weather forecast, yes; news, nah! Then I heard these noises, a crash, like a metal door being dragged across concrete, a lot of bangs, then nothing. So, I go around the small hill, where I've got my camp, to the road and soon enough I find a big hole in the hedge, but I can't see nothing coz there's a steep hill. There's a bloke in the road yakking on the phone, right little Betsy shitting himself and saying everyone was dead. Then I notice a glow at the bottom of the hill. But I wait, see, and hear what he says. He's talking to a bloke called Kegs, and I hear what this Kegs says because our Betsy has got the phone on speaker. Kegs is asking how many are in the minibus and Betsy says there were four, including him. Then he asks what their status is. He used that word – status. Then Betsy says they're all dead. Ozzie, the Arab and the Chink woman.' He gives the Vietnamese woman an apologetic look.

'So, I sneak past him and go down and I find a minibus on its side – driver's side up – and there's a fire in the engine, but it's not bad. I climb in and look about. The front seat passenger, a male, has his head stoved in by the side stanchion and he's properly dead. I go through to the back. There's another man in the second row. His neck is broken. No seat belt, see. Feel his pulse.

Nothing. And then I look around and see there's someone near the back row and this is Tam here. But she's in the far left-hand seat and because the minibus is on its side it means the seat is hard to get at. I reach down and feel the pulse on her neck. Alive but out. She's got her seat belt on. The tongue and the buckle of the belt were wrenched through the gap between the seats, and I can't reach it to release her, see. I'm there for five minutes yanking and pulling. Then the vehicle shifts and there's a hell of a creaking noise and I think we're all done for because I know it's only halfway down the slope, but the movement frees something behind her seat, and I'm able to unclip the belt. Then comes the problem of lifting her out of the row of three seats and I struggle with that. Too many smokes, see. But she comes round, and she helps with her arms and then I get her out of the window where I came in. There's a fire taking hold in the engine and quite a bit of smoke, and I think she's going to blow, and I get Tam to safety.'

'What happened then?' says Slim.

'I'm coming to that. We're out of the minibus and in the field when a vehicle arrives in the road and two blokes get out. They've got extinguishers and they run down and put out the fire. You'd think they'd check inside the vehicle, right. But, no, they don't bother with that. They just get busy in the engine and at the front and rear of the vehicle.'

'Doing what?'

'Removing the reg plates, chipping the engine number off.'

'They don't look inside?'

He shakes his head. 'Then they threw a can of petrol in the minibus. And whoosh! No more minibus. No more bodies.'

Tam is shaking. He steadies her with a hand to her shoulder. Slim notices the bond.

'Can you tell me where the crash took place?'

Delphy, who has perched on the edge of a chair at the end of the table, has already been through this with Frank and produces her iPad with a map of the crash site. The old lady never ceases to amaze.

Slim asks Frank, 'Do you have a phone?'

He says no.

Slim says, 'I am going to see if I can get some info on that phone Betsy used. See if we can trace the number he was using and the one he was speaking to.'

She sends the coordinates of the accident site to Tom Ballard with the message,

Need phone data for late Saturday evening from this spot. V. Important. I am hoping that two phones we've already covered were being used there.

She adds the numbers for phones A and B.

Frank is looking worried. 'We want your assurance. No names. No police.'

Slim considers this for a second. 'I'll need to know your names and there will come a time when we'll want to use them.'

'Then you'll ask our permission. Is that agreed?'

She thinks for a moment. 'Yes, you have my word.'

Tam has still not said anything. Slim reaches out across the table, but she withdraws her hand. 'Are you able to tell me your story?'

Tam looks down, eyes brimming.

'Can you speak English?'

'She can,' says Frank, 'but she's shy and anxious about her sister. I spent all yesterday persuading her to come to Miss Delphy's.'

'Where she will stay as long as she wishes,' says Delphy.

Slim opens her hands and says, 'We will get advice, but I'm certain that you have a legal obligation to report the accident. Leaving the scene of an accident is also against the law. But then no one knows you were there and as far as the gang is concerned, you're dead, Tam.'

Tam nods.

'Tell me your story.'

Delphy nods encouragingly and says, 'Yes, dear, tell us what happened to you.' No one could mistake the tenderness in the old lady's expression.

Her English is good but halting and she pauses often to compose herself, which she does with a small, demure smile. It was Tam – full name Le Thi Tam, Le being the family name – whose idea it was to travel to Europe to work in nail bars and hairdressing salons so she could send money to her widowed mother. Her younger sister Lan begged to join her and together they borrowed money from a man in Saigon to fly to Romania. It turned out he was a member of a people-smuggling gang. They were taken across Europe in a truck with thirteen other Vietnamese. They entered Britain in a container, their passports, money and phones were taken, and they were told they owed £20,000 each. All the people in that container developed Covid and a teenage boy died in transit. After two years working in nail bars, cannabis farms and vegetable and herb packing stations, the gang told her that the debt had risen to £33,000 because of interest. It was the same for her sister. The two sisters only saw each other fleetingly at a variety of jobs, especially at a particular nail bar, where the owner liked their work, but they were never allowed to exchange more than a few words. Of course, no money was ever sent home to their mother and in those two years they never managed to call her. She didn't know whether they were dead or alive. This caused Tam the most distress. She used Delphy's phone to talk to her that morning. She is very happy that her mother is alive and well. Tam is silent for a minute or two, as she relives the pain of the last two years.

'On Saturday night, where were you coming from?' Slim asks, after a long pause.

Tam replies robotically. They'd been at a cannabis farm. She was suffering from a headache. The driver, Gethin, and the guard whose name was Ozzie were making jokes about having sex with her. They were drinking from a bottle and were both drunk. She'd closed her eyes, tried to rest and the next thing she knows is the minibus is rolling down the hill. That was all she remembers. She blacked out.

'So, we have two more names – Ozzie, the man who died and Gethin who called for help, right? Who was the third man?'

'A Kurdish man, name Hozan. He worked at the cannabis farm always. He was a farmer back home. That is all I know.'

Slim sits back in her chair, suddenly struck by the horror of the Kurdish man's end – someone's son, someone's brother, someone loved – killed and burnt beyond recognition in the English countryside.

Tam rests her forehead on her hands on the table and sobs.

Slim reaches across the table and touches her head. 'It's going to be all right. We'll find your sister, I promise.'

Delphy has risen and is filling a kettle.

'There's more,' says Frank. 'She hasn't said as much but it's obvious that . . . you know . . . those bastards took advantage of her.'

Slim shakes her head, appalled.

Delphy makes tea and places a sponge cake in the middle

of the table. Tam accepts a little. Slim stops the recording and pulls up the photograph of Andrei Botezatu, sent by his sister, and holds the phone out to Tam. Her face lights up – she even touches the screen – then her eyes cloud, and she looks at Slim properly for the first time 'They hurt him. They place him in the Tank. That is a very, very bad place.'

'Where is the Tank?'

'At farm.'

Slim shows her the film of the man and the woman walking towards her at Manor Farm. 'At this place?'

She nods, amazed that Slim has the film.

'Do you know these individuals, this woman and the man?'

She nods. 'Kegs. Kegs is boss. Woman's name I don't know.'

'Kegs!' says Frank. 'That's the name of the man the driver was phoning from the crash.'

'So Gethin was calling Kegs,' says Slim. 'That's important.'

She shows Frank the film. 'This is him. Did you see him at the crash site?'

'Too dark to tell.'

'Did anyone use his name while you were at the crash site?'

He shakes his head.

She again shows the film of Kegs approaching the gates to Tam. 'You stayed here in those mobile homes?'

She nods.

'How many people in the mobile homes at one time?'

'Maybe fifteen. Sometimes many, many – twenty-five, thirty.'

'Do you know how many slaves there are?'

'Many, many – maybe hundred, two hundred. I see many different people.'

'And they lock people up in the Tank as a punishment, like a prison?'

Tam replies that it is well known that people have died in the Tank. They threaten people who cause trouble with the Tank. Andrei was beaten and thrown into it for stealing a phone. She hasn't laid eyes on him since that day, but she believes he was let out because others have seen him.

Slim nods. She knows about the phone. Phone B was the one he used to call his sister.

'Where is the Tank? Can you see it in the film?'

Her hand pushes the air to say it is far away from the gates. Then she squints at the screen and makes a nipping motion with her hands to enlarge the picture. In the far distance a huge man stands in outline against a grey silo that lies on its side. He wears a jacket with a sheepskin collar. His hair is a froth of blond-white curls. Tam tells her that this is Milky, the young man who guards the Tank. He has a reputation as a killer. He is very stupid and very violent, and he likes hurting people.

Frank gets up and says he needs to smoke outside. Slim joins him while Tam goes to wash her face and is fussed over by Delphy, who insists she needs to eat more and put on more clothes.

'You think she was sexually abused?' Slim asks Frank.

'Definitely. Yeah, a lot. You saw her for yourself. That is one damaged young lady.'

'Could she identify anyone at the crash site? Did she recognise Kegs?'

'She was in shock, maybe concussed. I was going to take her to the hospital, but she just fell asleep in my tent and the only thing I could do was keep her warm.'

'We have to tell the police about this,' she says. 'Even if it's just an anonymous tip-off. It's a major crime and leaving the scene of accident, even if you weren't involved, is also a crime. But I'll get advice on all that tomorrow.'

'I wasn't there,' he says.

Slim leaves him smoking and walks out of earshot to phone Abigail. She listens carefully to the summary of the accident rescue and Tam's life as a slave, and occasionally asks her to pause so she can make a note. 'You're right,' she says. 'This is big – huge. But you're going to have to do it on your own. Dan wanted Skelpick to do this slave story with you, but Dan and Skelpick have been arrested and are being interviewed in connection with offences against the Official Secrets Act, together with Sara and Yoni.' It's typical of Abigail that she coolly left this until after Slim had given her five minutes on Tam's story.

'I thought they were let out.'

'Rearrested this morning at ten.'

'How can they do this?'

'We'll speak later. But your story looks promising. Well done.' Abigail stops, audibly draws a breath. 'We must keep going. We can't let them shut us down.'

Inside, Tam is sitting in an easy chair by the fireplace, now wrapped in a shawl. She looks up shyly as Slim comes in and sits down on a long, tapestried stool in front of the fireplace.

Slim says quietly, 'Seven months ago, a man tried to rape me. It was the most terrifying and humiliating experience of my life. I want you to know that if that is what happened to you, I have some idea of what you feel.'

Tam says nothing.

'You understand what I'm saying?'

She nods. Slim takes hold of her hand. 'I'm here for you, Tam.'

Tam looks away, then nods. 'Three times,' she says.

'Three times! Sweet Jesus! By the same man?'

She shakes her head and holds up three fingers.

Slim says, 'I'm so very sorry.' And hugs her, the first time she has ever sought to give a stranger comfort in that way, and maybe it's something she has learned from Helen. 'I'm going to help, I promise. But now I should go back to my office and speak to the people I work with. I have a lot to do.'

CHAPTER 26

Her mother is dying. She must get that into her head and dismiss from her mind all thoughts about slavery – the connections to be made between Andrei the Romanian, Manor Farm and the minibus crash. Also, there's her beloved brother, the threat from Ivan Guest, and the weird, contradictory behaviour of MI5. On the one hand, they're insisting she does everything she can to help close down Middle Kingdom, but on the other, requesting that the site's founders decode Ivan Guest's documents. She pulls into a lay-by on the way to Milton Keynes to give herself a pause and walks about, murmuring, 'Mum is dying. Mum is dying.'

With this grim focus she arrives on the fourth floor of Middle Kingdom just as Abigail's briefing to the staff ends. She waits for the journalists to file out, leaving Abigail and Toto alone at the glass table, and asks Abigail about the arrests.

'We don't expect charges today, or in the immediate future. They're playing with us, trying to silence us by intimidation.' She stops, takes in Slim. 'You look dreadful.' Toto nods.

'I've got a lot going on.'

'Can you say more of what you've heard this morning? I've brought Toto up to speed with what you've already told me.'

At the end of Slim's account Abigail says, 'If this gang is smuggling people to use as slave labour and picking off the women as sex slaves, that is a vast national scandal. Ideas about how we should proceed, Toto?'

'One issue is solved for us,' he says. 'The police have discovered the wreckage.' He searches his phone then reads a headline and report: '"Bodies recovered from crash site. Police say an undisclosed number of bodies have been recovered from the wreckage of a Ford minibus that crashed through a hedge and plunged a hundred feet down a steep embankment on an isolated road at Legion's Hill, in Northamptonshire, sometime during the weekend. They are appealing for witnesses."'

He lowers his phone. 'So, the gang doesn't know Tam is alive.'

'But that doesn't get us round the problem of whether we should tell the police,' says Abigail. 'That's the issue here. She's the only witness to the crash and is the victim of multiple rapes. Many other women may be subjected to the same treatment. Plus, there's a murder allegation. She said that people had died in the Tank, right? We can't sit on that.'

'I gave my word that I wouldn't use her name,' Slim says, 'nor that of her rescuer, Frank, without their permission. That includes talking to the police. She thinks they will harm her sister. I don't know why Frank is so nervous, but I agreed to their conditions.'

Abigail thinks for a few seconds with a pen pressed to her lips. 'Okay, write up your notes. I need them by this evening so that Dan and Skelpick can read them when they're released, which we expect will be in the early evening. I'll go and see Tam this afternoon. Tell Delphy I'm coming. We should give them and ourselves a time limit – say thirty-six hours – then take a decision about telling the police.'

★

By 8.30 p.m., Slim has sent her notes to Abigail and is about to leave the office when Helen calls. 'Is this a good moment?' she asks.

'Of course. How's Mum?'

'To be honest, not at all good. She's fading fast. She wants to go, pet, and I don't think she has a lot of time. I talked to the ward sister. They were planning to move her to the hospice, but she's just too poorly and . . .' She stops and waits for Slim's reaction.

'And?'

'She's in quite a lot of pain. They are managing it well, but if you want to see her, you should come as soon as you can. Tomorrow, or Wednesday, at the very latest. You understand what I'm saying, Slim? I don't think she will be here by the weekend.'

Slim is silent, then says, 'She said she didn't want me to come.'

'People say that to save their loved ones. I'm just telling you the situation.'

'Are you saying Wednesday will be too late?'

'Yes.'

'Should I come now?'

'No, she's asleep. I'm on duty tonight. I can pop in to see her tomorrow morning early, and I'll let you know.'

'I'll come first thing.'

Later, she sits at the galley table, with Loup's head on her knee, trying to connect her phone to her laptop to use the Internet. Bantock has left her a half bottle of whisky and food from Sunday's lunch. She eats, feeding Loup bits of salmon, and wrestles with thoughts about her mother, none of them very clear. She tries to imagine what it will be like without love and guilt tugging at her, then, being alone.

She reaches for the bottle but sets it down again when Loup's muzzle jumps from her knee. He is trembling and lets out a steady low growl. She slides from the bench, at the same time as grasping the largest knife from the block of three and backs away from the cockpit towards the bow doors. Loup holds his ground for a few seconds more, then darts in front of her and, as she noiselessly pushes the doors outwards, rushes on to the forward deck. She follows and peers into the night. Someone is waving a phone torch over *Spindle*'s stern. Loup jumps on to the bank and starts barking.

A man's voice comes. 'Is that you, Slim? It's Tudor.'

'What the hell are you doing here?'

'I need a word. Is that dog dangerous?'

'Very. Don't move! I'll come and let you in.'

She goes to the stern and Tudor comes aboard, wheezing in the damp night air.

'That chest doesn't sound too good, Tudor. How did you find me?'

'You were using your phone for a long spell, so I knew where you'd be.'

'What's so urgent?'

'Can I sit or will that dog bite?' He looks washed-up and sick.

'Sure, do you want a drink? What's this about?'

He waits until she's poured the whisky and added the same again in mineral water before saying, 'Your brother Matthew.'

'You've found him!'

He takes a hit, a big one. 'This isn't easy.'

She knows what's coming. That's why he looks terrible.

'Matthew is dead.'

She's been with living the idea of Matthew's death for a very long time, but that sentence, 'Matthew is dead,' the absolute, categorical truth of it hits her in the stomach and she slumps against the cabinet behind her, shaking her head. 'I can't . . . I don't know what . . .'

'I'm sorry to break it to you like it this, but I believed you had to be told in person.' He looks down at the whisky then checks her eyes. 'I hear your mother hasn't got long. You said she needed closure. The agreement was that we would try to bring you news before the end. I'm keeping to that.'

'Thank you,' she says quietly. Does he expect her to break down? She has no idea what to do, sitting there with Tudor bloody Mills. How to react. How to function without that slight hope that her mother was wrong, and that Matthew was alive. God, she wishes she'd never asked Halfknight to find him.

Tudor says he's sorry several times, and she sees genuine feeling in his eyes.

'When?'

He looks away, takes more Scotch. 'This is the hard part, Slim. About two months ago. Sometime around the beginning of March.'

'Two months ago!' Just when her mother sensed something was wrong.

'Between March the second and the fifth, we think.'

'Where?'

'Outside Dublin. He was living under the name Matt Donnelly. Married to a woman named Norah Kinneal. He was clean; she's struggling to get off heroin. They had a boy named Liam. He's four years old. Your brother kept the show on the road, freelance designer and artist.' He looks down at the self-portrait. 'That's his work. He obviously had talent. He'd made something of himself. You should know that.'

She rubs her face, pulls her fingers through her hair. 'This is

a very big shock. I mean . . . a son. My mother has a grandson!'
She stops. 'How did he die?'

He shakes his head, searching for the words.

'Come on, Tudor. Tell me! How?'

'He was killed sometime between those dates I gave you. He
disappeared. Norah reported him missing and he was found
on some rough ground outside the city on March the twenty-
second.'

'Killed how?'

Tudor is now holding her gaze. 'Shot in the head.'

'Matthew shot! Murdered! Why, for God's sake?'

He is silent.

'Tell me!'

'I don't know for sure, but it's my belief that he was protecting
you and your mother.'

That silences her. Then she says, 'Jesus, are you saying he was
murdered to protect us? Are you saying that?'

He nods. 'And he didn't give anything away.'

'Who did this?'

'We're working with the Irish authorities, but by the look of
things it was the two men who came to your house, then fled
the country a few weeks back. But we're by no means sure.'

'The Georgians.'

'They're probably Chechens. Georgian passports.'

'Killers hired by Ivan Guest.'

'Got to be. You're aware of the group photograph of you
and Matthew and your friends taken at your mother's house. I
believe they traced Matthew through that photograph. He did
some publicity in Ireland, won a design award and was photographed. They made a match using facial recognition. He'd
changed very little.' He glances at the portrait.

She gets up, casts around, has to steady herself with fingers splayed on the roof, then sits down again.

'I spoke with Norah. She's on methadone now, trying to get off the junk for the boy's sake. If it's any consolation to you, he wanted to be in touch with his family and resolved on several occasions to do so. She doesn't know why he didn't, but it upset her, and they rowed about it. She's not a bad sort.'

'Was Matthew tortured!'

He says nothing.

'Was he fucking tortured, Tudor? No, I don't want to know.' Her head is in her hands. 'He was tortured because of me. God, poor Matt. Guest tortured my brother.'

'We can't be certain that it's Guest. When we have a record of those two men in Ireland, we'll know. Still an outside possibility it was drug related. A debt from his past maybe, something like that.'

'But the photograph, why did it lead them to him not me?'

'There's nothing of you on the web, remember. That photograph was the only thing. They simply found Matthew more quickly than you. I believe they worked out the house from geolocation techniques. There's a lot of information in that photograph – layout of the garden, appearance of the house, etcetera – to lead you to the location. I'm certain that Matthew didn't tell them you and your mother's whereabouts.'

'Why?'

'Because of the time between his death and their appearance at the house. If he had given them anything, they would have gone straight there. As it is, they had to wait twenty-five days before they found the house and, even then, they weren't sure they'd got the right one.'

'So, the office knows. Halfknight, Salt, Rita Bauer, they know.'

'Yes.'

'But you're doing this now off your own bat.'

He stops, looks down at his near-empty glass with his mouth hanging open. 'An undertaking was given to you. I knew your mother was seriously ill. So, I hurried things along. They would have told you tomorrow.'

He takes hold of the bottle. 'Can I?'

'Of course, go ahead.'

He looks appalling when he moves into the light. She's suddenly aware of the sounds of the canal, the water slapping against *Spindle*'s hull, a duck quacking, the faint rustle and whisper of reeds on the other side of the water. She swears softly over and over. He asks if he can smoke, lights up with a Zippo and is convulsed by a coughing fit. 'I'm sorry about your brother,' he says between coughs. 'I was hoping to bring good news.'

'How did you find him?'

'The same way they did – the photograph.'

He's still coughing, asks for kitchen roll, blows his nose. 'Damp air. Always gets me.' He's about to say something, then thinks better of it.

'Go on,' she says.

'Another time.'

'Come on, Tudor.'

'Keep your powder dry is what I'm saying. The best thing for you now is to pack your bags and disappear. If I found you here on this disguised boat, so can they.'

'I'm stuck. My mother's dying.'

'Then go as soon as you can. In the meantime, I'll hang around to see you're okay. You have my number. I'll be nearby. Peter Salt will be here for the time being. I'd better leave you in peace. Are you going to be all right?'

She wishes he would go but at the same time doesn't want to be alone. 'I'll be fine. It's rough, knowing about Matthew, that's all. Very rough. Not sure how to process it, get it into my head.' She gives him a weak smile.

He swings his legs from the bench and stands. 'Thanks for the drink. You and I have had our issues in the past, but I'm sorry for your loss and the time you're going through with your mother. Really sorry for you, Slim. Thought I'd make that clear.'

'Yes, Tudor. Thank you.'

He inhales and she hears the wheeze. 'That doesn't sound good.'

'A few problems, which means I'll be taking early retirement end of August. Oh, I nearly forgot.' He delves into an inside pocket and hands her an envelope. 'You'll need these.'

The envelope contains a folded sheet of paper with Norah Kinneal's phone number and address on the outside. In the fold is a photograph of a small boy holding a dinosaur up to the camera. 'That's your nephew, Liam. Judging by that portrait there, he takes after his father.'

'He does,' says Slim and tears spring to her eyes. Tudor is already clambering up to the aft deck and does not see. She manages to say, 'Thank you, Tudor. You go easy now.'

CHAPTER 27

Diana is in a single room with a view over the car park. She is asleep with an ironic smile on her lips, and she seems even smaller than she did forty-eight hours before. Her left hand is bruised from a canula, which is attached to a drip of liquid in a blue bag. Her right arm lies on the covers, white and incredibly thin, with the bracelets and rings on her fingers loose. She stirs occasionally but is never conscious for more than a few seconds, during which her eyes rove in bewilderment before closing again. Slim sits with her back to the window, holding her mother's hand but occasionally letting go to check her emails from Middle Kingdom to keep up with Abigail's thoughts on the slave gang story.

She has with her the backpack and an overnight case of green canvas and tan leather, which belonged to her father and which she rediscovered at Steward's House. She has no idea how long she will need to be at the hospital, but after the news about Matthew, she's decided to stay with her mother until the end. In the overnight bag, she has a water bottle filled with gin and tonic, and the folded note containing the photograph of the little boy. She considers stepping out of the room and calling Norah

Kinneal, but decides against it on the grounds that neither of them is probably up to the conversation that she wants to have.

At five, her mother wakes. 'Hello, darling,' she says in a whisper. 'I thought I told you not to come.'

'I didn't have much else on,' Slim says.

Her mother smiles. 'That's my girl. Bolshie as ever.'

Slim helps her sit up.

'I brought you some you-know-what.'

'Splendid. But you will need to help me. My hands don't seem to be doing what I tell them.' She lies back on the pillow and smiles. 'Thanks for coming. I hoped you would.'

Slim removes the cellophane from a sanitised hospital tumbler, fills it to the brim and holds it to her mother's lips. 'Reminds me of when I used to feed you,' her mother says after several tiny sips.

A nurse named Iain comes in. Slim has already decided on her mother's behalf that Iain with the stud earring, undercut and topknot is annoying. He closes the door and stands with his arms folded in matronly displeasure. 'What are you doing?'

'Giving my mother a drink.'

'We don't advise water at this time,' he says.

'It's not water, it's a bloody strong gin and tonic.'

He begins shaking his head.

'I'll tell you what,' says Slim before he has time to react, 'please fuck off and leave my mother and me in peace.'

'I won't be talked to like that, whatever the circumstances.'

'I apologise,' says Slim unconvincingly. 'But I want to speak to my mother privately, and I don't need you here. Please go.'

'The hospital policy about aggression—'

'Take a running jump, friend,' she says with much more menace than she intended.

Helen's face appears round the door. 'What's going on here?'

Slim glances at Diana who has fallen asleep with a look of amusement on her face. She turns. 'I'm trying to tell my mother something of great importance, and Iain here is fussing about what sort of drink I'm giving her.'

Helen frowns and ushers Iain from the room, telling him that she'll deal with Slim. 'He's such a pain,' she says, closing the door behind him. 'How is she?'

'Quite happy until Iain arrived.'

'You look done in, love. Take a break, I'll stay with her until my shift at eight. I'll phone if there's any change. Now go!'

Slim goes to a hotel with vending machines in the lobby and a scrum of rowdy young conference delegates, who eye her up as she checks in.

At six, Abigail texts a video conference link. Dan and Skelpick are on the call, sitting in what looks very much like Dan's house. He says, 'Are you okay to talk?'

Abigail says, 'We can leave it until tomorrow, if this is a difficult time for you.'

She says it's been a rough day with her mother, although that's just half of it, of course.

'I'm sorry,' says Dan, 'but I felt we had to discuss this story you've brought us. We've had legal advice that we can't sit on it because of the implications for the people who are still at risk. There are allegations of rape and murder, and God knows what happened in that crash. I mean, are we even sure the people in that minibus were all dead? Crimes are still being committed.'

'I gave my word to Tam and Frank. That may have been wrong, but I wanted them to talk. I should be the one to tell them and in person.'

'You've done remarkable work. Abigail confirms everything

in your notes. But, Slim, delay means we are placing people's lives at risk.'

'I can't go back on my word.'

Skelpick murmurs that she has a point.

Dan looks exasperated. 'Right, decision late Thursday. Sorry. It's too big to keep to ourselves. Abigail will distribute her notes this evening. You will work with JJ on this, and he will start thinking of an approach and structure.'

Slim returns to the hospital and says she'll take over from Helen who needs to eat before her night shift. They look down at her mother together. Helen smiles, squeezes her hand, and kisses her on the cheek. 'Call me when you need.'

She reads on her phone until one, then stretches out on the floor, using two chair cushions as bedding and her knapsack as a pillow. Listening to her mother's breathing and the occasional garbled sentence murmured in her sleep, she dozes then finally falls into a deep sleep.

Helen arrives after her shift. She's brought coffee from the canteen. Slim takes the cup, and they put one arm round each other in a semi hug. A peck on the cheek. Slim smells sanitiser or something medical.

'How are you bearing up?' Helen asks.

'Okay, thanks. You look exhausted.'

'One of those nights. Look, I'm making no sense. I need to go home and get some rest.'

Slim drinks her coffee.

Diana's eyes open. 'What're you doing down there, darling?'

'Noodling things.'

'Your father used that word. Is that coffee you have? Can I have some?'

'Of course.' She gets up and holds the cup to her mother's

lips. Diana's eyes never leave hers. When she nods to say she's had enough, Slim sits down in the chair and drains the cup. Her mother says, 'I can't talk very much, but I can listen.' Her smile is warm, the intelligence all there, but her voice is weak.

'I've got something I want to show you,' says Slim, hand diving into the bag again.

'All in good time. I'm not going anywhere. Tell me what's eating you.'

'It's too complicated. I'm not sure where to begin. There's a lot I can't say.'

'I'll take it to my grave with me.' A twinkle but no smile. 'But that's not why you're holding back. This is about Matthew, isn't it?'

She nods and gets up, goes to the window, looks out.

'If it were good news, you'd have told me by now.'

She turns. 'Mum, Matt died. I learned the night before last. I prayed I wouldn't have to tell you.' She shrugs at the hopelessness of her situation, looks down, shakes her head and goes to take her mother's hand.

Diana is silent. Her eyes water but no tears flow. 'I knew.'

'How?'

'Just did. Felt it. I told you! Up until that moment in March, I knew he was alive.'

'Mum, he lived in Dublin. He had a partner called Norah and they had a son. He's called Liam. I have a photograph of him here.'

'He kept that from us!' Diana's eyes are wide and uncomprehending. 'Why? What did we do to him?' Slim can't answer this. 'I don't think I want to see the photo. What's the point?' She turns away, devastated.

'I think you should.' She finds her mother's reading glasses, glances at the photograph herself – the likeness seems even more remarkable – and helps her put on the glasses. She holds the photograph in front of her. Diana takes it in stiff, erect fingers and moves it in and out of focus. At length, she looks up. 'It's Matthew.'

Slim nods. 'It's him all right.'

Her mother hasn't asked about Matthew's death yet, but she will and Slim has a prepared story of his getting clean, turning things round, his success as a designer, his relationship and a car crash that ends it all. It is unthinkable to add to her suffering with the truth – her son was murdered protecting her daughter. But for the moment, she's saved by a nurse arriving to check her mother, take readings and change the bag on the drip stand. Slim goes out while her mother is washed and when she comes back, finds her asleep with her mouth open as though she is about to say something. The photograph is still in her hands.

Through the day, Diana becomes more restless, moves her head from side to side, lifts her hands from the bed, holds them dramatically in the air for a few seconds then lets them fall back on the blanket. Her lips move as if she's saying something, but no words come. A nurse suggests music. Slim plays show tunes on her phone, which she places on the bed, 'Masquerade' from *Phantom*, and the original *West Side Story* recording of 'I Feel Pretty'. She hit the spot with that one. Her mother's lips move with the words, 'She thinks she's in love, she thinks she's in Spain. She isn't in love, she's merely insane.' And Slim says the words too, because after hearing them so often as a teenager, she knows them by heart. The last is Sondheim's 'Send in the Clowns', sung by Sinatra. She murmurs, 'Isn't it rich? Are we a pair?' then abruptly makes an irritated motion and shakes her head. She wants no more.

Slim reads Abigail's notes of her interviews with Tam and Frank. They confirm everything in her account, but Abigail has more detail on the women's journey from Vietnam, the conditions the slaves endured: moving from house to house with nowhere to keep their belongings; the back-breaking work; the ever-increasing 'debt' – now standing at £66,000 for the pair of them – and the casual, routine sexual abuse and rapes. The only time Tam sees her sister Lan is at the Jasmine Nail Bar in Northampton on Fridays, when demand for manicures is high ahead of the weekend. Slim looks up the nail bar and finds a shopfront in a dismal strip mall: photos of south-east Asian women bent over customers' hands in a space that is cluttered with exotic fishbowls, plants and a device that spews scented steam. She locates it on the map and drops a pin on the spot.

Helen comes in on her way to the third night shift in a row. She's tired, says almost nothing and lays a hand on Slim's shoulder from behind. It remains there. 'You need a break? I've fifteen minutes to spare.'

Slim leans forward and whispers to her mother. 'I'm going to the loo. Won't be long. Promise!' Her mother's eyes crack open, she nods and smiles. The eyes close and she sighs.

Helen says, 'Go! She doesn't want you sitting there bursting.'

When she returns, Helen is standing outside the room.

Slim knows.

'I'm very sorry, pet,' she says moving towards her, hands clasped. 'She's gone.'

'I should have stayed.' Slim hesitates at the door, opens it, looks in, then immediately closes it. 'That's not my mother.'

'No,' says Helen, 'she's left us. I am so sorry for you, Slim. She was wonderful. Magnificent!'

'Yes,' says Slim, too distraught to take in the words.

CHAPTER 28

It was a bad idea, but she reckoned the pain couldn't be worse. Yet it could. With a bottle of Italian red in the hotel room, she searches for and finds the newspaper reports on Matt's murder. There's a paragraph on the identification of his body after he was discovered in woodland, close to a minor road in County Meath, then a longer piece by a crime reporter named Michael Lodge, beneath the headline, 'Was Murder Victim in Debt to City Drug Gangs?'

Officers investigating the death of graphic designer Matthew Donnelly (37), whose body was found on 22 March in woodland between Mount Calm Alpine Nursery and the Fox Hill Golf Club, in Country Meath, ten miles from Dublin city centre, believe the victim may have been killed over a long-standing debt to drug dealers that operate in the Loftus Lane area of Dublin.

Mr Donnelly's partner, Norah Kinneal, reported him missing on 2 March. Gardai forensic teams place the time of death two to three days after that date and are appealing for witnesses who saw anything suspicious in the area where the body was found or have knowledge of the victim's movements between 2 and 4 March.

Ms Kinneal told officers that in the last year Mr Donnelly had got off heroin and was becoming a success as a freelance designer, recently winning an award for his work as an animator.

She expressed doubt that Mr Donnelly was in debt because, whatever the pressures in his life, including addiction, he managed his money well. She dismissed the idea that he was dealing in drugs and that he incurred the debt as a dealer rather than a user. 'That is never Matt,' she said. 'He was an artist. He wanted nothing more to do with drugs because of our son.'

The couple had a four-year-old boy named Liam. Ms Kinneal says she herself is undergoing drug rehabilitation for the sake of the child.

The Gardai admit that the brutal circumstances of Mr Donnelly's death do not tally with the life he was leading in the months before he disappeared. His hands were bound behind his back; he had been tortured before his death and he was shot in the head at close range. Failing other explanations, they are leaning to the theory that his death was the legacy of his drug-using years. 'We have little to go on,' said a spokesperson. 'He had conquered his addiction and now lived a blameless, law-abiding life. We need help solving the mystery of Mr Donnelly's last days.'

The date for an inquest has not been set.

Slim slumps on the bed shaking, more shocked even than when she left the hospital with the image of her dead mother in her head – the terrible nakedness of death, so undignified, so very un-Mum. She finishes the bottle and eventually falls into a fitful sleep. At five, she wakes. Light edges the blinds. She makes a cup of instant coffee and tears with her teeth one of the packets of shortbreads lined up on the tray next to the impossible-to-open milk sachets.

She is no less shaken, but is at least able to reason. Mum died because she drank. Matthew hid in Ireland because he was an addict. Yes, he'd be alive if she hadn't stolen the tablet from Ivan Guest – she has to live with that – but she did not kill him. Ivan Guest had him tortured and murdered and dumped. And Guest is still free. That's what matters to her now.

She takes a shower and sends the same message by email and text informing people of Diana's death. The activity helps. She sends more texts. To Abigail, she writes:

My mother died. Can I have leeway on Dan's deadline tonight? I need to be able to tell Tam in person what's happening. Hope you understand.

To Tudor Mills, she writes:

Read coverage around my brother's murder. Have you got any more? My mother died last night, and I was able to tell her that she had a grandson and show her the photo. It meant everything to her in her last hours. Thank you for that, Tudor.

It is still early, and she doesn't expect replies, but Helen, who has a couple of hours of her night shift to go, calls in response to her note thanking her for everything she did for her mother.

Slim says, 'I just wanted to say I was glad I was out of the room when it happened. I didn't want you to feel that you got that wrong.'

'I've seen it dozens of times. They hang on until their loved one leaves the room, then they pass. That's what she wanted.' Slim hears people talking, a trolley with a squeaky wheel, the beeps and commotion of the A&E department. 'It would be great to see you, Slim. I know you're going to be awful busy, but I'm here when you want, and you are in my thoughts.'

'I'll call when things quieten down. Thank you, Helen.'

'I hope you do call, pet.' She hangs up without saying goodbye.

Slim goes through her mother's list, talking to her solicitor, the bank, her financial adviser, and examines the contents of a padded envelope in which there's a twist of tissue paper plus two notes from her mother, one to be read out at her funeral and the other addressed to Slim. Inside the tissue paper is a ring of gold and blue enamel, with a crest formed of a heraldic eagle inside the Star of David. The ring belonged to her great-great grandfather Jakub Benski. Diana calls it 'the spy ring' because it was worn by Leon and his son Jan and carried by Leon in the lining of his jacket when he was deported to the Soviet Union. Even in the harshest of times, it was never bartered for food. It passed to Jan when Leon died in 1965 and was worn by him throughout his time operating in Eastern Europe. 'It came to me on my mother's death,' writes Diana. 'It blessed its wearer with good luck, though it was always too big for me. Let's hope it fits one of your sausage fingers, darling.' Slim smiles and pushes it on to the middle finger of her right hand.

By late afternoon, she's completed everything on the list and plans what she will say to Matt's partner, Norah Kinneal. At first, the woman is reticent, but when Slim tells her of Diana's death and adds that she doesn't blame Norah for Matthew's disappearance, she begins to talk. She is far from the clueless junkie Slim expected, just young and lost. 'How old are you?' asks Slim.

'Twenty-seven last week.'

'And you have family?'

'A sister, but the rest I don't bother with. It's awkward, my mother's okay but my father's a right bastard.'

She will listen to Norah all she needs when she goes to Dublin to see the boy and to give her some of her mother's money, that is if Norah gets her act together and stays off drugs. But now she needs information. 'You met my friend Tudor Mills, is that right? And you told him all you could remember at the time. He said you were coming off heroin, so maybe there are things that have come back to you. Can you tell me what happened, Norah?'

'Matt was seeing a client at five. He was, like, due back at the flat at six thirty but he just never came. He never missed Liam's bath time. Never. And always he read him a story, or they watched cartoons together. After he got clean, Matt did everything for the boy. And that's what I'm doing now because he has no one else.' Then she breaks down and drops the phone and Slim hears her sob.

After a long pause, she picks it up and apologises.

Slim says, 'Sorry to push you, but it's important. I need to know everything.'

'I was crazy with worry. I thought he might have gone back to see his mother. He was talking about it always, you know, wondering how to explain himself, how to reach out, like. He wrote a letter. I can find it now, read it to you.'

'I really want to hear what's in that letter, but let's do that later, okay?' says Slim. She didn't need to hear that now. 'Tudor says you don't think he was dealing, or that he was in any kind of trouble with a drug gang.'

'I told the Gardai and your friend – that wasn't Matthew at all. They want to blame it on drugs, but—' She stops. The boy is making a noise and she tells him to be quiet.

There are so many things Slim wants to know about her brother's life but doesn't ask. 'Anything odd happen before my brother went missing? Did he seem worried? Had he been in any kind of trouble?'

'No.'

'Nothing comes to mind about the last weeks of his life?'

'No . . . oh yes, there was this time about a week before he was . . .' She can't say 'murdered'.

'Go on.'

'It was nothing. It was like some man took a photo of him when he was in the pub. Matt didn't drink but you know the social and business life of this city is in the pub. And this character gets into his face and keeps taking photos of him, and Matt hated his picture being taken, for obvious reasons, so he was right pissed off about the man doing that.'

That was it. They'd found him by matching the Instagram group photo with photographs taken for his awards ceremony, but they needed to be sure, hence the snatched pictures in the pub. 'When did this happen?'

'Maybe a week before . . .'

'Did you tell the police?'

'No.'

'Did he describe the man?'

'Men! I think he said there were two men, and they were pretending to make a joke of it. Two men, maybe two foreigners. I can't be certain. They gave him some story about Matt having a double in Germany, but Matt knew it was bull.'

'Norah, you need to tell the police about this and try to remember anything he said about them. Clothes, age, accent – everything he told you about the incident.'

'You think they had something to do with it?'

'Maybe.'

'But they hurt him. Why did they do that?'

'They wanted to know something that he knew. Maybe where I was.'

'Why?'

'It's complicated. I'll tell you when I visit. We'll talk properly then, Norah. In the meantime, I—'

'He'd never tell people about you. He loved you very much.'

Slim inhales and pinches the flesh at the side of her stomach so hard that she cannot think of anything except the pain. 'Then why didn't I hear from him for twelve years? And my mother, that was unforgivably cruel, Norah.'

Norah sniffs and blows her nose. 'I don't know. I really don't know why. Maybe it was something before my time with him.'

Slim can't take any more of this and ends the conversation by repeating that Norah needs to go to the police.

When her father Toby died, the shock and grief were immense, but then she had family to fall back on. Now she has no one. She's the last of her people, those assimilated Polish Jews who changed their name from Bernstein to Benski, and the sense of being alone is somehow as raw as her grief.

Yet one thing is familiar to her. Obsession. The way she dealt with Toby's death was to throw herself into her final exams with the aim of winning a First, which she achieved, greatly to the surprise of her tutors and mother. Now the obsession that is taking over in her mind is about someone else's brother – Gabriella Albescu's brother, Andrei, the Romanian slave who fell for a promise of honest work, was robbed of everything and held by his captors in a punishment cell called the Tank. She can't do anything about Matt, but maybe she can about Andrei.

She's waiting in her usual spot in the car park in Milton Keynes, expecting Tudor Mills or Peter Salt to show up, but there's no sign of them so she calls Abigail. 'Have I got any flexibility on Dan's deadline?' she asks without saying hello.

Abigail is taken aback and hesitates. 'We're all very sorry to hear of your loss, Slim. Truly, it must be a blow for you. Shouldn't you be going easier on yourself while you grieve? I mean, work is out of the question, right?'

'Thanks. Can you give me until midday tomorrow to get Tam on the record before you release the names to the police? I did give my word to them.' She stops. 'Or have you already told the police?'

'We've made overtures through an intermediary.'

'Annette Raines?'

'Yes, and another lawyer.'

'Caroline McCarthy KC, the slavery expert?'

'Yes, but the police haven't followed up the information, as far as we know.'

'So, in effect, our undertaking is still in place.'

'I wouldn't say that. We believe we have greater obligation to the people still held by the gang than the one individual who miraculously escaped.'

'But it would be good if I got Tam on the record.' What Slim isn't saying is that the only way to do that is to spring Tam's sister, Lan. 'Give me until tomorrow before you have any more conversations with the police, and I'll see if I can get you the story you want and the witness they need.'

'Okay, but you should take time for yourself, Slim. This is good advice. Please don't ignore it.'

Slim sees Salt in her wing mirror. 'Sorry, got to go. I'll be in touch soonest.'

Salt leans into her open window. 'I'm sorry about your mum, and after the news about . . .'

She stares ahead of her. 'About Matt. Yes, it's very, very hard, but you saved my mother's life back in March and that gave us time together. So, I'm grateful to you.' She turns to him. 'Thanks, Peter.'

He glances away and runs an index finger across his forehead. He's uncomfortable. 'Are you getting out or shall I climb in? We need to talk.'

She gets out and leans against the closed door with her arms folded. He looks around. Some kids are skateboarding the ramp a couple of floors below but that's the only sound in the car park. There are just a couple of dusty vehicles on their floor. 'Linesman is over. They've canned it.'

'Who says?'

'The director has canned it because the objective has been achieved. The government is effectively about to shut down Middle Kingdom and those people will be prosecuted.' He gives her a defensive look. 'They knew the seriousness of what they were doing.'

She pushes herself off the car door. 'Tell them I'll leave this operation when I have confirmation from Halfknight. Until then, I'm staying on the job. He's the deputy director and this is his operation. Just an email or a call.' She thrusts her hands in her jacket pockets and studies him for a few seconds, wondering how much he knows about what's going on.

'You've been through a lot, Slim, so yeah, you do it the way you want. A few days can't do any harm. Say Monday or Tuesday next, and we'll see you in town for a debrief and tie a bow around it all.'

'I'd better be going,' she says.

It's nearly 8 p.m. She's late to pick up the dog and she has several calls to make and a lot of planning to do if she's going to free Tam's little sister.

CHAPTER 29

The Jasmine Nail Bar lies halfway along a strip of eleven shops on Swann's Way, a cracked concrete road that runs parallel to the main drag into town. At one end of the parade, there are two EV charging pillars and four spaces, which is where Bantock parks his old Defender. At the other end, about fifty metres away, Slim has backed the pickup, carrying Tam, Frank and Loup, into a space that gives her a clear view of the nail bar. Graffiti covers the boarded-up premises of Swann's Way and waste bins are overflowing, yet there's brisk trade at an Indian greengrocer, a pet supplies shop, a café, and a minimart that has buckets of tulips outside.

Slim puts Loup on a lead and walks to the nail bar, where she studies the charges for waxing, eyebrow threading and nail extensions on two collapsible pavement boards. From a mesh basket by the door, she picks up a complete price list printed in blue type. They seem low – most are under £20. She folds it and puts in her back pocket, and peers into the shop for long enough to count three raised pedicure chairs and a dozen manicure stations, six either side, complete with dryers and beverage holders. Beyond this is the back room, with a door open and a couple of massage beds visible. To the left of the door is a young man lounging across two chairs, legs spread, reading his phone. He's no more than eighteen but he's big and strong and could pose a threat. In the front of the shop, there are just three customers, two having manicures and the third a hair extension fitted. A dumpy receptionist of south-east Asian heritage, with large spectacles on a chain, works a calculator.

It is just 10 a.m. Tam has told her that the minibus is unlikely to arrive until just before noon when business picks up at the beginning of the lunch period. Slim walks into the café and buys takeaway coffee for Frank and Tam and a sausage roll for Loup and carries it all back to the pickup. She sees Bantock watching her in his mirror. He lifts a finger to her.

They drink the coffee in silence. Tam wrings a handkerchief and Frank gently works her shoulders with one big hand. By midday, Slim is concerned that the minibus won't come, but Tam points to the number of customers arriving in the Jasmine – six in the last ten minutes. A few moments later, a dark blue Ford Transit minibus pulls up close to the front door, narrowly missing the pavement boards. Three women exit from the side passenger door and hurry into the nail bar. Tam fails to spot her sister with Slim's binoculars, but the women are bundled up and wearing face masks.

Tam says the minibus is the same model as the one she was rescued from. It parks opposite the nail bar. Two men get out. Tam puts her hand to her mouth and identifies them as Gethin, the driver of the minibus when it crashed, and Milky, the huge blond man, the enforcer and possible killer that she identified in Slim's film of Manor Farm. The pair go to the café, then emerge with cups and the advertised speciality of bacon and sausage baps, which they consume outside. Slim photographs them, then checks that Tam has her new phone ready and is receiving her livestream through the messaging app.

She climbs out and makes for the nail bar. The receptionist is on the landline and indicates that she should take a seat in the waiting area by the window, but Slim casts around seemingly looking for something. The receptionist understands that she wants the lavatory and lifts her chin towards the back of the shop. Slim holds the phone clasped to her chest and films as she moves through the nail bar. A minute or two later, when she exits the lavatory, she holds it a little lower, pauses by the youth scrolling through his phone and then takes her time with the nail technicians, angling the phone discreetly and making sure that Tam can see each one clearly. The receptionist is now showing interest in what she's doing but hasn't yet cottoned on. Slim smiles at her, taps her head and says she's left her money in the car; she'll be back in a second.

In the pickup, Tam is overcome with joy, but also fear. Lan is the one nearest to the back of the shop. She hasn't seen her face clearly because she's still wearing a mask and her head is bent low over her client's hands, but she recognises a barrette clip on the top of her sister's head. She bought it for Lan's birthday in Saigon a little over two years ago.

Slim calls Bantock. 'We're on. Lan is in a pink shirt and is wearing glasses. You know what to do.'

'Yes, but those two fellows have just gone inside now,' he replies.

'Shouldn't be a problem,' murmurs Frank.

To Frank she says, 'You need to arrive at the door with Tam just after I go in.' He nods. 'And Bantock, you'll take over from Frank and protect Tam if there's any trouble inside. Got it?' Despite his impressive height and life as a wrestler, in her estimation, Bantock isn't a fighter. Frank is different.

She gets out and walks quickly to the door, flourishing her wallet at the receptionist. Milky and Gethin are standing in the waiting area. She smiles at them and says good morning, but, oh gosh, she realises it must be afternoon, so corrects herself with a ditzy smile. They say nothing. Gethin gives her the once-over, and Milky regards her with steady, bovine indifference. He has seven or eight inches on her, is powerfully built and has lifeless grey eyes. She is assigned a station two away from Lan, glances outside as she sits down and is relieved to see Frank and Tam standing ten feet from the front door. Gethin and Milky move to the back of the shop to speak with the youth. He shifts to let Gethin sit down. Milky stands with his back to the shop.

Now is the moment.

Slim gets up and apologises to the woman who is about to do her manicure and moves quickly to the end of the line of stations, touches Lan on the shoulder and says, 'Lan, your sister is here, and we are going to take you to her.' Lan doesn't understand. Slim gestures to the door. Tam gives a little wave. Lan nods, rises from her seat but is uncertain what to do. Slim takes her by the arm. 'Come, I am with Tam. It's okay. We're going to take you to safety.' Lan pulls down her mask and takes off her glasses. Tears of disbelief are showing. Slim puts an arm round her. 'I'm going to get you out of here. Just walk with me, and it'll be fine.'

They start towards the door. Gethin is up and shouting for Slim to let her go, but short of climbing over the row of manicure tables as well as several large women, there is little he can do to stop her. A general commotion erupts. The receptionist is on her feet yelling in what Slim guesses is Vietnamese. The customer with hair extensions, now having her nails painted, lets out a scream while others withdraw their hands, stand up and fan wet nails in front of their faces. The young man, who was lounging at the back, has shot to the front of the store to bar Slim's exit. But then he meets Frank, who is coming in with a smile on his face and is softly punching his palm. Frank does two things very quickly. He pushes the dumpy receptionist back into her chair and tells her to stay there if she knows what's good for her, then takes hold of the youth's left arm, ducks under it, as in a dance move, locks it behind his back and wraps his own arm around a slender, tattooed neck. The youth's legs are kicked from under him, and he is lowered to the floor, struggling to breathe. One movement could snap his neck, but Frank releases him and says, 'Stay down or I'll put you down for good.'

At some point, either when Frank pushed the receptionist into her chair or took hold of the youth, an aroma diffuser was knocked from its base and is now belching steam across the floor. A tall vase with bamboos rooted in water and gravel has crashed and broken, and the music system's relaxing, almost subsonic tinkling sound has been turned up to maximum.

This is all that Slim absorbs because Milky has come from the back of the store and has seized her from behind. He lifts her and is forcing her to let go of Lan, who drops to the floor like a wounded bird. Slim writhes from one side to the other, and as he lifts her higher, presumably to throw her against a table or the floor, twists and smashes the back of her upper arm into the side of his head, gets a better angle, and aims her elbow into his eye socket for a second blow. He swears, staggers and loosens his hold. She struggles free, goes back on her left foot, springs forward – the move that always seems to come to her – and aims her boot at his groin. This doesn't disable him, yet it does provide her with an opportunity to kick him again as a head of creamy blond hair, like a Charolais bull's tuft, comes into range. He wobbles, plainly astonished that such a thing should happen to him and not knowing whether to clutch his eye or his balls. Slim grabs Lan and rushes her to the door, where Tam and Bantock are waiting. Lan runs to her sister's arms. 'Get them into the pickup,' Slim shouts to Bantock, 'and stay with them.'

She turns and goes inside where now there is a stand-off between Milky and Frank. 'Don't bother with him,' she calls out but Milky has taken one wild swing, like a punch-drunk prize fighter, and is winding up for another. Frank opens his hands as if to say, 'You really don't want to do this,' ducks and takes hold of Milky's arms, yanks him close and smashes his forehead into Milky's face. Milky falls and the blood that instantly gushes from his nose flies up into the froth of hair. 'That, son,' says Frank, 'is the Liverpool kiss.' He whips round, searching for Gethin who has retreated to the rear of the premises and is fumbling with his phone. Slim says, 'No, don't bother with him, Frank.'

'If I'm not mistaken, that's the murdering cry baby Betsy Bloomingfuck. He would have burned Tam with the others.' He steps over the prone youth, marches to the rear, grabs Gethin by the throat and propels him to the wall where he forces him up so that for a few seconds Gethin is suspended and cannot breathe. Slim yells, 'No, Frank, let him go.'

Frank says, 'I'd like to do you now, you little fuck, but you aren't worth it.' He relaxes his grip and Gethin falls to the floor, choking.

On the way out, Slim sees the receptionist with a phone. She grabs it and smashes it against the desk, then Frank and she jog to the pickup. Tam and Lan are in the back seat with Loup. As she approaches, Bantock says, 'You might want to look behind you.' Two Vietnamese women are standing in the doorway

imploring them. 'Why the hell not?' says Slim and beckons to
them. 'You take them, and I'll see you in Milton Keynes with
Tam and Lan, okay?' He puts his arms round the two women,
very gently says, 'Welcome to a free life, please come with me,
ladies, and I will see you to safety.' They look at each other and
nod, with the incredulous expression of game-show winners.

On the road, Slim calls Abigail and tells her that Tam will
now be on the record because her sister is free. In addition, they
have rescued two other nail bar slaves from Northampton. Abigail doesn't skip a beat. 'Bring them all here. I'll talk to Yoni
because this is obviously going to be expensive, but it will all
be in hand by the time you get here. Looking forward to seeing
you, Slim. Sounds like a cracking little story.'

'You really think so?'

A whisper of a laugh, then Abigail hangs up.

Slim phones Delphy Buchanan to tell her that it all went
well, and that they had, in fact, rescued three women in total,
including Tam's sister. 'Oh, that's wonderful news,' enthuses the
old lady. 'I've been sitting on the edge of my chair all morning
praying that it would be all right.'

At Middle Kingdom, Dan Halladay has moved the meeting
from the conference room to the newsroom. The four Vietnamese women are seated in the centre. Frank stands behind
Tam with a hand on the back of her chair. Three lawyers from
a Birmingham firm, Finch, Merritt & Willis, specialising in
human rights and slavery, brought in by Caroline McCarthy
KC, sit with her and Annette Raines around one desk. Skelpick
and Yoni Ross are at another, all the young writers and editors
are perched around the room. Abigail is speaking about the
arrangements for the weekend. All the women will stay at Yoni

Ross's house near Harpenden, where there's plenty of room. Security will be arranged, and each woman will be given a phone to contact their loved ones and online credit for clothes and personal items. Tam has been elected their spokesperson. Although each speaks English, she is easily the most fluent and makes sure they understand everything. They are in various states of anxiety and exhaustion, but they are supporting each other and are buoyed by their sudden freedom. The dignity and immediate cohesion of this group of abused women is very moving to Slim and everyone in Middle Kingdom is affected.

Dan takes over from Abigail. Instead of standing, he turns in his chair and leans forward with his hands clasped and engages the women in turn with a grave but kindly expression. He speaks slowly so Tam can translate when it's necessary. 'First, I want to welcome you all here. I'm profoundly sorry that your treatment in our country has been so inhumane. It is a source of deep shame for us all that you were abused in this way and that our police did so little to protect you. You bring us a story of enormous importance and we are grateful for your help.' He waits while Tam translates this part. The women nod and smile.

'There is the question of sexual abuse. It will be our policy to write up this shocking aspect of the story if an individual wants to speak about it, and her friends are happy with what she says. I believe there should be a degree of unanimity on this subject because, of course, one person's revelation may be read as applying to all, and not everyone will find that desirable.' Tam summarises quickly and they all nod.

Dan looks around the newsroom. 'Okay, so we are all working through the weekend. Anyone who hasn't got a significant family occasion or better excuse should be here. We will aim to pub-lish the first part of this, with other material that we have been waiting to use, early Sunday morning. Each of our friends will be given a chance to make a short video to tell as much or as little of her story as she wishes. But we do need the accompanying written material to cover all the basics, such as when and how they came to the United Kingdom, who recruited them and took money for the journey, where they were housed, the mistreatment and abuse they suffered and witnessed, and the sorts of work they were forced to do. It is important that in everything we publish we convey the scale of what is going on in modern Britain. In passing, I have already heard that our friends have been made to work in private homes, hotels, nail salons, fruit and vegetable packing operations and cannabis farms. We need to get that detail.' He looks around the room as people nod.

'Now this is where the first problem occurs,' he says, addressing the women. 'I understand all of you were forced to work on cannabis farms run by the syndicate that brought you here. That's illegal. You also all came here illegally. How much you want to admit to these crimes is up to you. We will have lawyers look at everything you say and have written, so you will be advised on your liability. We hope to have an interpreter here by tomorrow morning to relieve Tam and to make sure absolutely everything is understood. But look, I do not expect you to suffer the penalties of the law when the enormous scale and cruelty of the operation that we are uncovering is revealed. This is a catastrophic, systemic crash of policing and the fact that they have moved so slowly since we alerted them to Tam's eyewitness account of the crash at Legion's Hill, and much else besides, underlines this depressing pattern.'

Slim doesn't take in much more, though she is aware that Skelpick is going to write up the minibus crash and Abigail has decided on reporting teams for the Vietnamese women, the names of whom are sent round in a text so that everyone has the spelling correct: Le Thi Tam, Le Thi Lan, Vo Thi Phuoc and Nguyen Thi Diep.

Eventually, she puts up a hand and raises the only thing that now interests her. 'Can I mention Andrei Botezatu, the Romanian national who we know is held by the same group? Tam identified him from the photograph we have. I just want to know if Lan, Phuoc or Diep have seen him recently.'

Dan frowns and looks down at his notepad. 'When the police eventually act on this,' he says, 'we must hope that he is among those released.'

'Can I just show his photograph and see if anyone has seen him recently?'

'It's one case among what seems to be hundreds.'

'It'll just take a minute.'

He looks irritated and glances at Abigail then shrugs. 'Sure, go ahead.'

Slim passes her phone to Tam. The others gather round to look and immediately start speaking and gesticulating.

'What?' says Slim.

'He is in Tank.'

'Yes, we know he *was* in the Tank for stealing a phone and making a call to his sister.'

Tam consults with the others then turns to look at Slim. 'He is in Tank now. They saw him this morning when they leave the farm. They say he stole motorhome from the Big Boss, and they catch him, and they hurt him bad. This is what Milky and Gethin say, too. He is in Tank now. Much blood. A lot of pain.'

'This happened today?'

Lan and the two other women nod vigorously.

'And he was beaten up?'

Phuoc places her fingers beneath her eye and pulls down the flesh, then taps her arm and gestures that it is broken. Diep mimes a tugging motion to say he was being dragged. Slim looks over to Annette Raines. 'This is a man who has been beaten and imprisoned. Aren't those crimes which require immediate police intervention?' Annette nods and the other lawyers concur. Slim opens her hands. 'I mean, shouldn't we be doing something? Shouldn't the police be made to act?'

'We've made every effort to inform the police. I understand there will be no action until after the weekend.' Dan gives a resigned look. 'We've done our best. Now we need to concentrate on publishing what we've got and gaining the attention this appalling situation deserves.'

By six, the Vietnamese women are flagging, and arrangements are made for them to be driven to Yoni Ross's house in two cars provided by Yoni. Before they leave, each comes over to Slim and shakes her hand or hugs her. Tam gives her an especially long hug, with Frank looking on.

Slim returns to trying to identify the owner of Manor Farm and, eventually, she finds a company, AMG Holdings, that owns the land. Half the buildings at the site are owned by individuals identified as D. & D. Tavern, while the rest belong to a scrap metal business, West Vale Recycling and Reclamation, which is, in turn, owned by Ridgeway Containers and Shipping. The information isn't going to help free Andrei, but it may be important when they come to write about the gang running the slave operation. She is beginning to see a pattern to the obfuscation that is reminiscent of Ivan Guest.

She happens to look up and sees Abigail beckoning from the conference-room door. She goes over to her.

'Have a seat,' says Dan. He doesn't smile. Skelpick looks on from the far end of the room. 'We just wanted to go through with you what happened this morning.'

'Okay, we had a good result, no?'

'Well, yes and no,' Dan says. 'There was a degree of violence offered to the three men guarding those women by Frank Shap and you. We understand from the women you rescued that all three men were injured and that you yourself were involved in at least one brawl.'

'It was hardly a brawl. The man picked me up and was trying to crush me before throwing me. I was defending myself. None of us would have left that place without Frank eventually neutralising all three men.'

'But what were you doing there in the first place?'

'It was your deadline, remember! You were going to the police, but I had agreed with Tam and Frank that that could only happen once Lan was free, and Tam would go on the record. I gave them my word, so when you pressed me with the deadline, I had to act to get Lan out.' She stops and looks at them. 'What's the problem? Now, we have the whole story about the minibus crash with two witnesses prepared to go on the record, and three other compelling individual stories into the bargain.'

'There are several problems,' says Abigail. 'One, you were representing Middle Kingdom. Two, you didn't tell us what you planned. Three, instead of calling the police with your suspicions about the nail bar, you stormed in like vigilantes and engaged in a bloody fist fight.'

Slim throws herself back in the chair. 'The police! Give me a break. You yourself say they are showing little to no interest, and that was my experience working on the story about Andrei

Botezatu. Okay, maybe I should have told you. I'm sorry I didn't, but you would have stopped me, and those women would be spending another night in shitty accommodation in fear of being raped. I think we did a good job.'

'What are you?' asks Dan.

'What do you mean?'

'Where did you learn to take the risk that you did this morning and to fight like that? All the women attest to the extraordinary aggression you showed those men and, also, the command you exercised over the whole operation.'

'It's natural, I guess. Anyway, Frank did most of the fighting. He's the hero of our story. Without Frank, we wouldn't have a story.'

'Frank was in the military,' says Dan. 'We know where he learned his combat skills, but you, Slim, are a mystery. Who taught you all that?'

Skelpick saves her. 'But we did get the story, Dan, and there haven't been any complaints from the Jasmine outfit. They were using slave labour to compete with other nail bars and drive down prices. Fuck 'em, Dan. They're bad people.'

Abigail turns to him. 'But she was acting on behalf of Middle Kingdom. Imagine that coming out in open court.'

'Abigail, love, we're already in court, charged with obstruction, and there's plenty more to come our way, no doubt. Fuck Jasmine up the jacksy. With due respect to both of you, let's get on with reporting the story. There's a lot to do.'

Dan shakes his head wearily. 'What about this man Frank Shap? Where does he come from? I know he was in the Paras but why was he sleeping rough?'

'He hit someone in a pub in Liverpool,' says Slim. 'He thought he might have hurt them badly, maybe even killed them, so he decided to vanish. This was before the pandemic and he's stayed hidden for all that time, doing odd jobs for Delphy and a few of her neighbours. He's going to turn himself in because he's fallen for Tam, apparently. And she seems pretty keen on him. Says he will call the Merseyside Police tomorrow.'

'Hell of a story,' says Skelpick.

Dan shakes his head. 'That's not the point. You must see it's hardly ideal, if this man has killed someone in a bar room fight and is beating up people in a salon under Slim's command. He overpowered three men in as many minutes. That's a frightening level of violence.'

Skelpick says, 'It doesn't matter, Dan. I'll say it again, we got the story and that's what counts, and it couldn't come at a better time for us. You know that.'

Dan turns to her. 'If you do anything like this again, Slim, you're out. You're a promising reporter and a fair writer but one more incident . . .'

'Understood,' she says and gets up and nods to Abigail.

CHAPTER 30

Three hours later, Slim's still at her desk, doing her best to delay returning to the boat. A few young reporters are around but most of the senior staff have gone home. Skelpick comes over, wearing his scarred leather jacket, an arm through his helmet. He rests the helmet on her desk and asks what's cooking.

'I hit a wall with the ownership of Manor Farm and now I'm looking into pub killings in Liverpool.'

'And?'

'I don't think Frank killed anyone. Can't find any incidents for three months either side of the time I estimate he left Liverpool, and certainly not in the White Hart pub, near Lime Street Station, which was his usual boozer and where he says the man came at him with a broken bottle one Friday night. Checked the *Liverpool Echo* – nothing. Called the Merseyside Police. They were mystified. I even phoned the pub. The manager said there'd been plenty of fights, but no one could remember a GBH or murder. Even in Liverpool, that sticks in the mind.' She stops. 'Frank was awarded the Military Medal for something in Afghanistan. Saved his commanding officer. It was on one of the websites for ex-Paras.'

She looks up and waits a beat before saying, 'Shouldn't they be called Parasites?'

Skelpick salutes the joke but doesn't smile. 'Are you all right, kiddo? You look strung out, and a bit demented, if I'm honest. You should rest.'

'I'm fine. Got any ideas how I investigate that farm where he's being held? Right now, he's in the Tank, beaten up and alone. Probably thinks he's going to die. Shouldn't we try everything to get him out?'

Skelpick sits down on the desk and folds his arms. 'Tell me you're not planning a raid on that farm. The police will find him on Monday.'

'What makes you so sure? After the thing at the nail bar, this gang is going to be on high alert, hiding people, destroying evidence, eliminating witnesses. They burnt some people in a minibus, remember! They would've killed Tam. What's to stop them killing him and disposing of his body? If they've beaten him so bad that he can't work, what use is he to them? He's an inconvenient witness, held on property which they rightly guess will be raided.'

'You think this because the Vietnamese women you freed were at the farm this morning, saw him and can identify the location.'

'Well done – I knew you'd get there in the end.'

'There's no need for that, we're on the same side.'

'Apologies.'

'Don't worry. You're going through a rough time.' He gets up, wobbles, and seems to be heading for the door, but then he does a pirouette on his good leg and sits down on a chair beside her in one awkward movement. 'What've you got?'

She plays him the film she shot from the gates of Manor Farm to the scrapyard, Skelpick pauses and expands the image and sees the big blond man now identified as Milky. 'Who's that?'

'Frank took him out today. Gave him the Liverpool Kiss. The three women we rescued say the Tank is in the middle of all that junk.'

He's unimpressed. 'You aren't going to find him. It's far too big an area. Let the police do a proper search on Monday.' He asks to see a map of the farm and nods as she expands it to show the surrounding settlements of Oxbourne, Annbury and South Bridge. She watches his face, illuminated by the phone light as he peers at the map. For a man in his late forties, he is extraordinarily lined. Another kind of map – of experience and pain.

He looks up from the screen. 'Whoever owns this set-up probably runs the show, agreed?'

'Not a single individual, apparently. There's a maze of companies that own the buildings, the scrapyard, the land, which is all tenanted, as far as I can tell, and the agricultural recycling business here.' She points to a spot to the right of the farm buildings. 'And that's linked to an incinerator two miles from the farm.'

He scrolls through her notes, then takes out his phone, dials a number and turns away to speak. 'Have you got today's access code?' He writes a number on the back of his hand. 'Need to input some data. Won't be more than ten minutes. Thanks, Callum.'

He doesn't answer her questioning look but moves his chair to the end of her desk, asks if he can borrow her laptop, then begins to work the keyboard and, finally, enters the code he's just received. 'Right, let's see now.' He looks at some of her notes, copies and pastes them into a search field and types a few words, and begins a series of prompts. Then he sits back with fingers interlaced and two index fingers pointed at the screen. She cranes to see what's on the screen and moves her chair as an area below the search field fills with blue type. He says, 'Dominic Dekker mean anything to you, also known as Dominic Davidyan?'

She shakes her head in astonishment.

'That's your man, I guess.'

'What did you use just then?'

'A private search facility.'

'AI,' she says.

'It's *private*, Slim. Goes the extra mile. It's new, and bloody well keep it to yourself, okay?' He stands. 'You won't join me for a drink?'

'I'd really like to another time.'

He shifts his weight, looks down at her. 'What you did at the nail bar was crazy.' He jerks his head at the newsroom. 'I supported you in there because you've reeled in a big story, but I'm telling you now, do not go to that farm. Leave it to the police.' He waits for a reaction, but gets none, shakes his head and turns towards the exit. 'Don't!' he says over his shoulder.

She turns the laptop towards her. The blue text has been joined by an image of a man in an open floral shirt with medallions nestling in his chest, and a hat on the back of his head that supports sunglasses on its brim and a backstage pass in the band. His arms are around two musicians, one slung with a guitar, the other with a saxophone on a neck strap. This was Dominic Davidyan, promoter of rock concerts in former Soviet bloc states, Czech Republic, Hungary, Romania and Bulgaria, manager of heavy metal bands, one of which, named Bed Rock, had success in the East in the mid-nineties. Davidyan, known latterly as Dekker, owns businesses with names that include – in purposefully vague deployment – the words logistics, services,

distribution and storage. But there is one more obvious enterprise with which he is associated, an outfit based in Lincoln
called Hit-the-Road-Jack, a car and camper van hire company.

Access to the AI helper is frozen. She looks in the search
history of her machine to see if she can get back to it, but the
link doesn't work, so she goes to a standard search of images of
Dominic Dekker. There are just two, one of him in front of the
then new vehicle hire business in 2011 and another from 2022 –
from a news site specialising in monitoring the activities of the
Far Right in Bulgaria, Romania, Hungary and Czech Republic.
Dekker is connected to Romanian and Bulgarian extremist
political parties, but the site doesn't say in what capacity, except
as a 'facilitator'.

She takes extensive notes and screen grabs. She copies the photos
and clips such text as she can find on the businesses he owns as well
as his house – a ranch-style, single-storey spread near Boston with
lions on the main entrance gateposts. Dekker makes no appearance in the local news media or electoral roll, but one final search
for images turns up – improbably – a photograph from a village
fete, hosted at his home, showing Dekker presenting a prize. She
knows she's got her man, for the smile is all there but his eyes
look steadily at the camera with unconcealed menace. Dekker
does not like having his picture taken, even in the circumstances
of rewarding a pensioner for his giant marrow in the company of
his buxom partner, identified as Cynthia Petito.

But there's something else about the photograph which makes
her rack her memory. After a few minutes, she texts Tom Ballard: *Was Hagfish's mother called Davidyan? What happened to his
brother?*

It's past midnight but she gets a reply. *Yes, but we knew nothing
about his brother. He vanished.*

She replies, *I've found him up here.*

Leave well alone. Please just do what I asked ASAP.

She has all but forgotten about the tablet and Ballard's encrypted sheets but now wonders if the AI chat that Skelpick was so nervy about could help her.

Three pulsing dots appear on her phone screen. Ballard is typing. A text follows. *So sorry about your mum. Huge sadness on top of everything else. My sympathy X.* The X is a first over two years of messaging.

Tudor tell you?

Yes.

Where is he?

With you.

Thanks.

Goodnight.

She messages Tudor with, *I may need you later. Will call if I do.* She notices he has alerts switched off. Yet a few minutes later, Tudor sends her a question mark.

Do you have any contacts with Bedfordshire/Northants police forces?

Can find one. Why?

I'll be here. Will let you know if I need them. Having added the coordinates of Manor Farm she shuts off the phone so Tudor can't call her not to go.

CHAPTER 31

It's 4.30 a.m., an hour before sunrise. She hoists the mattock over her shoulder and leaves the pickup in the spinney, where she parked to watch the comings and goings at Manor Farm, and heads down a gentle hill to flat farmland, at the centre of which lies the Manor Farm compound. She has about a mile to walk and is just able to navigate in the available light, although there's not yet enough for her to use binoculars. Half an hour later, she's two hundred metres from the last in the line of static caravans and two fifty from the scrapyard. To her right, farm floodlights are on at the entrance gates and nearby, in the Dutch barn. In the first wash of dawn light, the scrapyard remains a place of shadows and fantastic silhouettes. Something's going on in the barn. She lifts the binoculars and sees a skip attached by chains to a loader truck ready to be lifted. Two men are urging an object from a forward-tipping dumper, by turns dragging it and pushing it with a shovel towards the skip. She moves closer and sees they are wearing face masks and protective suits. They manage to shift the object into the skip before departing on the dumper, but she can't see in which direction they go, and the noise of the engine soon fades and dies.

She waits then, holding the mattock in both hands, runs across the open ground to the scrapyard, and delays a minute more before feeling her way along a line of old agricultural plant – bailers, ploughs, an incline conveyor and tangles of hydraulic equipment. There's no way through to the centre of the yard, so she must retrace her steps towards the caravans to take one of two aisles she remembers from the satellite imagery. She watches for any activity in the barn before rounding a collapsed crop sprayer to take the first aisle, which consists of towers of tractor tyres and capsized silos. Her breath smokes in the first light. She drags a hand along the cold metal of a hopper bin, feeling the condensation and causing tears to flow down the surface, looks up and down but sees nothing that could be used to imprison Andrei.

She goes back again and finds the second aisle, which is at an angle to the first. With cranes overhead and drums and tanks resembling columns on either side of her, it's almost as if she's entered a cathedral space. It's lighter now, and she's able to move quickly, but after about seventy metres, she freezes at the sound of an engine starting up ahead of her. It's joined by the familiar noise of the dumper. Diesel exhaust from both machines fills the clear morning air. A man is shouting instructions. Two bright lamps are turned on and there's more shouting. She moves closer, finds a gap in the mounds of scrap and sees a mini digger depositing soil on to the dumper. There's one man on the dumper; another stands by with a shovel. Their faces are in shadow, but she believes the individual operating the digger is the overseer Kegs, the one she christened Turnip Head. He has the same bulk, and he's doing all the shouting.

She becomes aware that underlying the smell of the diesel there's a stench of decay, which is probably being released by the digger as it disturbs the earth. Her first thought is that they are tackling a drain. But at this hour? And out here, where there are no buildings? She retreats behind a tank and takes out her phone, thinks for a moment then dials Tudor Mills. He doesn't answer. She texts. *Send police to coordinates I gave you. Call me.*

She pockets the phone, swings the mattock to her shoulder and looks back the way she came, but it's several minutes before she realises that in the half-light, she missed a gap between two containers. The door of one is open. It moves just a few centimetres in a breeze that she can barely feel on her face, but it's enough to make the door squeak. She passes between the containers to an area surrounded by old lorry tankers, most of them detached from the vehicle chassis. The air in this space is still and much colder. The grass is starched by a late ground frost and her trainers make a soft crunch and leave a trail. She spots a faded white milk tanker resting on a metal frame with the slogan 'Is Your Man Getting Enough?' visible in the roundel at the back. It must be the Tank. Midway along the tanker's flank is an opening with a crudely fitted door which is made from a heavier metal than the rest of the tanker. It's secured by a bar with a padlock at one end.

As she approaches the door, her phone vibrates. Before she hears Tudor's voice, she says, 'You need to get the police to those coordinates right now.'

Tudor wants to take things slowly and starts asking questions.

She interrupts him. 'Trust me. I have every reason to believe they're removing human remains. They're cleaning the place before the police make a search on Monday.'

'That's your supposition. I can't make that request – and it is only a request – on your word.'

'But you can if I tell you I'm in grave danger. I am, and so is the person I've come to free, if he's still alive. Tudor, I need you to do this. I've got to go now. Just do it.'

She hangs up to his protests, climbs the two steps up to the hatch and puts her ear to the gap. 'Andrei!' she whispers several times. There's no response. She drums with her fist softly on the tank, making it reverberate, then adds to the noise by knocking the end of the adze blade against the door. 'Andrei, are you in there?' she says softly. 'Andrei, please speak! I'm here to help.' There's a slight hum from the wind pushing through the gaps around the hatch. She places her ear to the void again and this time thinks she hears a movement.

'Andrei, is that you?'

This is answered by a groan, then the murmur of a man's voice, followed by movement. He's working his way towards her along the curved interior of the Tank.

'Andrei! You're there! Great!' She's not sure how much he understands so she doesn't say more, but rises to her feet, examines the staple and hasp arrangement that holds the bar in place. There's no hope of breaking the heavy padlock, but the staple looks weak, and she takes a swing at it. She connects first time but doesn't dislodge it. Crouching, she finds there's some give and delivers several blows in quick succession. She stops. The noise of the engines has died. She looks down. The hasp is almost detached, and she's able to lever it free with the pick end of the mattock then slide the bar to her left. Because of its weight, the door clanks open of its own accord, and the Tank exhales a breath of foul air. A man's face appears in the gloom. He is filthy, bloodied, gaunt with two black eyes and a cut in his left eye socket. He holds his left arm with his right. His face is racked with pain and his eyes plead with her, as if to say, tell me this is really happening. He looks to her to be on the edge of insanity. Quite instinctively, she reaches to touch his face with the back of her hand. 'It's all right, Andrei. Come with me. We need to walk. Can you walk?' He nods, but he's weak and is unable to climb over the lip of the opening without her help. She props the mattock next to her on the steps and puts her hands under his arms to lift him, but he cries out. 'Lean on me with this hand,' she says, pointing to his right. He grips her shoulder and gets his legs free of the tank and rises, his right hand shaking as he puts all his weight on to her. She rises with him, wraps an arm round him and guides his feet down the two steps to the ground. He leans back exhausted as she lets him go in order to reach for the mattock.

'Come,' she says, holding on to his right side so she doesn't knock his left arm. They go a few paces with him leaning on her heavily. He says, 'Thank you!' several times but walking makes him breathless, and it's all he can do to stumble along with her. They reach the pair of containers at the entrance to this part of the yard. He needs to rest and slumps against the one with closed doors. He smiles at her, almost sweetly. He's still having difficulty believing this is real. She pokes her head out into the wide pathway to see the best way to leave. The sun has risen but the only hint of this is a yellow underlay to the blanket of cloud. A mass of birds plummets to a field in the distance – iron filings drawn by a magnet. She turns to him, and smiles because she wants to reassure him and make him feel he can pull this off. 'I think we should go,' she says touching his shoulder. He tries to smile but grimaces with the effort then pushes himself off the container and staggers a little.

'Wait!' she says, raising her hand.

They hear two male voices approaching from the area where the digger was working. They're getting closer. Andrei's eyes widen and he shakes his head violently. Slim puts a finger to his lips and takes him by the hand and leads him into the container with the open door. 'Stay there,' she whispers as she pushes the door almost shut. She retreats to a space between the back of one of the tankers and a radiator grill of an old lorry where she squats. The side of her face touches the ice-cold and long-dead vehicle marque of Leyland.

The men have passed the container where Andrei is hidden and are almost level with her when she sees they are the pair from the nail bar, Milky and the little runt Gethin. Milky wears a bandage on his nose. Gethin carries a coil of wire and is laughing. They still haven't noticed that the door of the Tank is open, when Slim moves from her hiding place and, as Gethin flicks his cigarette away, aims a blow with the adze blade to the side of Milky's leg. It's a precision strike and there's a sharp crack as the man's leg or possibly knee splinters, and he drops, unaware of what has hit him.

Gethin dances back as Slim moves to swing at him. Now she sees he has a knife in his hand, but her worry is that he will turn and run for help. She saw only three men but there may be others. Of equal concern is that if she misses with the mattock, he will be on to her with the knife before she can recover. So, she doesn't take aim but just moves towards him, watching his eyes, searching for the best option. This seems to go on for minutes, but it is, in fact, just a few seconds before Slim is saved from having to decide by the man she came to rescue. Andrei has lurched from the container, picked up the nearest piece of scrap – a short, twisted length of girder iron – and landed it clumsily on Gethin's shoulder and head. Gethin falls forward and the blade drops from his hand into the mud. She doesn't think he's dead. He's still clutching a coil of brass picture wire and she reckons that he planned to strangle or garrotte Andrei, probably once they'd got him at the barn and could tip his body into the skip to join the other human remains. Andrei begins to shuffle, without her help, in the direction of the caravans because he knows they must reach them before heading across the fields, the only route out if they are not to go through the gates. She stops him and takes out her phone to dial Tudor.

'I've got the man I came for,' she says. 'Have you phoned the police?'

'Yes, and I'm on my way and so should Peter Salt be by now. You stay hidden.'

'We can't. We have to go north over the fields and the man I'm with is in a desperate state and can't walk far. I have disabled two of their men, so they'll soon know we're here.'

'I can hear one of them.' It's true, Milky is bellowing like a wounded animal. 'Keep the line open! We'll be there in around twenty minutes.' She hears a car revving, Tudor swearing, a door being slammed.

She takes Andrei by the elbow and leads him. He wants to go quickly but he must stop every few seconds to bend with a hand on one knee and get his breath. At the point where the scrapyard ends in a crochet of vehicle tracks, she says to the phone, 'I can see a large motorhome which wasn't here before and a skip waiting to be lifted on to a lorry. Shit! The gates are open. They must be about to leave.'

'Got it,' he says.

Andrei tugs at her arm and points to the motorhome. 'Big boss.'

'Dominic? Dominic Dekker?'

He shrugs. He doesn't know the name. He mutters 'Big boss' again and makes a slashing gesture across his throat, then points to the caravans. He's right. They can reach the gates by going behind the line of caravans, and they'll be hidden from the barn except when they cross the gaps between. They cover a lot of ground, even with Andrei taking frequent rests. 'You're doing great,' she says. 'Gabriella would be proud of you.' She regrets saying this because at the mention of his sister he lets out a sob of joy that also expresses terror and desperation. The man is absolutely at the end of his tether. Working his shoulder, she whispers, 'We're going to make it. I promise.'

Five caravans from the end and just a hundred metres from the open gates, they hear a voice behind them, and she whips round. Kegs has crept up on them from behind. He has a double-barrelled shotgun levelled at them. 'What the fuck,' he keeps repeating until he eventually says, 'What the fuck have you done with my men?'

'Man named Kegs has a gun on us,' she says loudly so that Tudor can hear on the phone. 'I hope you don't intend to use that shotgun. That would be stupid. The police are on their way. They were called thirty minutes ago.'

'You're just saying that. What're you doing here with the pikey?'

'I'm taking him to a hospital. An ambulance is coming. Don't do anything to stop me!'

He comes closer. 'I recognise you. The lesbo with the dog. Fancy that – the dikey and the pikey.' He is amused by his joke and gestures towards the barn with the barrel. 'Move! Let go of the pickaxe.' The handle drops softly into the grass. He hasn't noticed the phone in her hand. It's tucked up her sleeve with the microphone just exposed.

'You want us to walk to the barn,' she says for the benefit of Tudor. 'Maybe we get to meet your boss, Dominic. That's his motorhome, right?'

'Shut the fuck up.'

She takes hold of Andrei, who is muttering in his own language, trembling and shaking his head crazily.

'Let go of the cunt. Make him walk. You'll catch something off of him, else. Look, he's pissing hisself now.' There's steam coming from his trousers.

'Leave him be,' she says.

'Fucking pikey needs putting down.'

They are prodded to the barn sixty metres away. 'What you done with Gethin and Milky?' Kegs says from behind them.

'Nothing. Let us go.'

As they reach the barn, the door on the passenger side of the motorhome swings open. A man climbs down and rounds the back of the vehicle into the light. He's big and ungainly. His hands are thrust into the pockets of a belted overcoat, and he wears a dark brown pork-pie hat. No shades, no medallions, but this is certainly Dominic Dekker, with his broad face and unforgiving eyes. 'Where are they?' he says quietly. 'We need to leave now.' He coughs and brings out one gloved hand and holds a finger under his nose. The stench arising from the plastic bags in the skip is appalling.

'What about these two?' Kegs says.

He studies her. 'That's the woman from the Jasmine that caused all the trouble. Put them in the skip then leave. Forget about Milky and Gethin. They'll find their way. I'll see you at the plant. Everything is ready.'

Slim begins to reel off everything she has learnt about Dekker, the company and directors' names, his home address, the address of Hit-the-Road-Jack, the managing director's name and the company secretary, Cynthia Petito, the big blonde standing beside him at the village fete. She holds her phone in the air and shouts, 'Dominic Dekker or is it Davidyan today? Either way, you are the brother of Ivan Guest. And by the way, everything you've just said has been heard by my colleagues.' She puts it on speaker and prays the connection hasn't dropped. 'That's right, Tudor?'

'Yes, we heard.' His voice rings clear in the barn. 'We'll be with you in a minute. The police are just behind.'

Dekker cuts the air with his hand. 'Get that phone off her. Finish the job and move that load out of here.' He returns to the motorhome, on the back of which Slim notices in a moment of disassociation a sticker that proclaims, 'One life, Live it'. The vehicle has been gently idling all this time, and before he's shut his door, begins to reverse. Then it moves cautiously to find the ramp over a shallow concrete watercourse that runs along the open side of the barn.

Kegs shouts, 'Give me the fucking phone then come over here.' He gestures to the skip.

'Come and get it,' she shouts back, then to Tudor, 'He's going to kill us.'

There's one thing she knows. Kegs hasn't got time to shift two bodies into the skip from where they stand. He needs to get them both beside it, then execute them and this must be done quickly. Andrei seems to have come to the same conclusion and is shuffling backwards. She moves with him, speaking to Tudor all the time, giving him the registration number of the motor-home, and a hurried description of the blue skip lorry, which has the words 'Workhorse of the waste management industry' on the door.

'Give me the fucking phone,' Kegs shouts again.

'Come and get it,' she repeats.

He aims the gun at her then swings upwards and fires a

warning shot into the corrugated iron rafters. He's got just one shell in the breech, and he breaks the gun to reload. She throws the phone at him and runs towards him, but he's too fast for her. He snaps the gun together and brings it up and fires over her head. She freezes. Andrei can take no more and collapses in a dead faint; there's so little of him that it looks like someone has dropped a heap of old clothes on the ground. 'Right, Dikey, put him in the skip,' Kegs says, quickly reloading. 'That'll keep you out of trouble until it's your turn.'

'No,' she says, her voice trembling. 'I won't do that, not with what you've got in there, the bodies of the people you murdered.'

He marches up to her and aims the gun at her head. His face is covered in filth and there are lines in his skin left by the respirator mask that now hangs around his neck. She bends down and takes hold of Andrei's jacket and gives one feeble tug. But then several things appear to happen all at once. The sound of hysterical screams reaches the barn. She glances towards the open gateway to see a middle-aged woman in a nightie, housecoat and rubber boots hugging the radiator grill of the motorhome. The lights of the vehicle make her face grotesque. Kegs says, 'Jesus fucking Christ.' The vehicle reverses, revs and goes forward but she clings on, wailing and screaming for them to take her with them. It's the woman who stood at the gate when she filmed Kegs. At that moment, she sees a light in the sky appear over the trees along the main road, just about where the pickup is parked, a mile away. A powerful beam is travelling towards them in the dawn, picking out snapshots of lone trees, hedges and an old brick cattle shelter. They can't hear the helicopter yet, but Kegs knows that he's out of time and casts round, wondering whether he should run for it or get into the lorry.

He doesn't seem to notice Gethin, who has walked unsteadily into the light of the barn holding his head with one hand and the knife in the other. Kegs lowers the gun then runs to unhook the chains attaching the lorry to the skip. He needs two hands to undo the clips and his progress is hampered by the gun under his arm. Gethin stops and gawps at the scene, unable to process what he's seeing.

The motorhome has managed to shake off the woman, but now she lies in its way, and it reverses once more to avoid her. As it moves forward, she scrambles through the mud screaming and blocks its path again. The driver steers at her but just misses her legs. It can't go any further because an SUV with a single blue light clamped on its roof has parked across the gateway. Streaking down the lane to Manor Farm are the flashing lights of two police vehicles and a third and fourth have sprung from the treeline along the main road. Presumably they're using their sirens, but these are drowned out by the regular thump of the helicopter's engine.

It is now hovering over the caravans, the searchlight flicking from the scene at the gateway to probe inside the barn. Kegs has abandoned the idea of escaping in the lorry and vanished into the shadows at the back of the barn. Moving like a zombie, Gethin staggers after him. Slim squats by Andrei and feels his pulse. He's still out cold but breathing steadily. He's safe, she tells him, and doing well and very soon he will see Gabriella and, hell, they made it, didn't they? She crosses the barn floor, searches for and finds the phone she flung at Kegs and runs back to Andrei, calling Tudor's number at the same time.

Tudor answers. 'Where are you?'

'In the barn and I need an ambulance now.' She kneels beside Andrei and puts the phone on speaker. She takes his hand – it's ice cold – then removes her jacket and lays it across his shoulder. She looks around and barks at her phone. 'Where's the fucking ambulance?'

'Five minutes away.'

Police are now chaotically fanning out across the compound. Dekker is wrestled from the motorhome and handcuffed, followed by the driver, who turns out to be his co-director and pneumatic companion at the village fete, Cynthia Petito. Two officers come over and crouch beside Slim. She tells them that Kegs has a shotgun and is likely to use it; that his associate Gethin is hiding out in the back with a knife but is plainly suffering from the effects of concussion; that the individual known as Milky, who has a reputation as the killer of the gang, lies injured in the scrapyard and, finally, that the skip just thirty feet away is likely to contain the remains of people who were buried in graves that lay somewhere beyond the scrapyard. With the stench that now fills the barn, they don't argue with this. They begin to stretch crime scene tape around the skip and the lorry, clamping hands over their faces as they go.

Tudor arrives and waves the ambulance to the spot where Slim is tending Andrei. In short order, he is diagnosed as hypothermic, probably suffering from pneumonia and certainly from multiple fractures to his left arm and ribs. The crew exchange looks. They are worried about his heart, and he is promptly lifted into the ambulance, hooked up to monitors and to a drip. They leave within ten minutes of their arrival.

'Right,' says Tudor. 'We need to get you out of here.' He leads her to the Audi – it was his car that blocked Dekker's escape – and they drive to where she parked the pickup. He gives her the address of the northern headquarters of the Bedfordshire, Cambridge and Hertfordshire major crime unit, which is in

Huntingdon, and the number of Detective Chief Inspector Nick Price. 'We had to tell them about you – wouldn't have got them moving so quickly otherwise. There will be problems down the line when you come to give evidence in all the slavery cases and what just happened, but people more senior than me will sort that out when the time comes. Just Price and two senior officers know who you are. No one else.'

'Was London aware that Dekker is Ivan Guest's brother and operating up here?'

'No, my guess is that they weren't. All the focus is on Middle Kingdom.'

He's giving her an intense look as if to say, concentrate, but something is tripping in Slim's brain about his appearance. He coughs repeatedly and he doesn't just look tired; his face has the cast of someone who is sick and knows it. She says nothing though, and hops into the pickup. He revolves his hand and she lowers the window. 'Nobody else is going to tell you because you're a bloody pain in the neck, Slim, but you did a fine thing tonight.'

'Thank you.'

He's shaking his head with frustration. 'How can we protect you when you go off and tangle with some of the most violent men in the country?'

'The job comes to an end soon, Tudor. Salt told me Linesman is over and I'm to report to Thames House next week. I guess your duties are over, too.'

He gives her that look again, sniffs and pulls out a packet of cigarettes but thinks better of lighting up. 'The job is far from over, whatever anyone tells you. I think you know that, so you need to find a place to hide, rest up and deal with the losses in your life. London still needs you.'

'Who needs me? Halfknight has gone silent. What's going on, Tudor?'

He shrugs a 'no comment'. 'Keep your head down and keep out of trouble. You were minutes away from being killed in that hell hole. I was listening – remember!' He stops. 'Why did you do it?'

She doesn't answer and starts the engine.

He looks away and now takes out a cigarette and lights up, but then is convulsed with a coughing fit. He blows his nose, leans on the roof of the pickup with one hand, holding the cigarette away.

'You should give them up. They're killing you.'

He smiles bitterly. 'You're worse for my health than the cigarettes. I almost had a heart attack trying to get to you down there.' He takes a drag. 'I know you did it because of Matthew, but I can't decide whether you were trying to get yourself killed out of guilt, or you were bent on saving his proxy.'

'Gabriella will see her brother if he lives. I will never see mine.' She thinks for a second. 'I may have some guilt about Matt, but I didn't kill him. Ivan Guest did.'

He nods and bangs the roof of the car. 'Be nice to Nick Price. He saved your bacon today by moving so quickly.'

CHAPTER 32

She wakes up in a police station cell with the door open and cannot remember how she came to be there. Yes, she was being interviewed by Nick Price and his deputy, Inspector Christine Waite, and she'd begun to nod, and her head fell forwards on to her hands on the table. They'd found her the only place in the station where she could sleep – in the cells. An officer in the Custody Suite was keeping an eye on the CCTV inside the cell and spotted she was awake.

Then Nick Price himself brings her tea and a BLT sandwich, and they talk.

They clashed a few times in their first encounter that morning, although she had tried to say she was grateful for what he did. Why had she gone to Manor Farm, he demanded? Why did she take such a stupid risk? What possible relevance did a slavery network have for MI5's work? She replied that she couldn't answer because these were all operational matters. He was prickly and self-important and fuming about the extent of the criminal activity she had exposed going on under the noses of his major crime unit. Ambition leaked from Nick Price's every pore, but he was bright and quick, and she knew that despite his

Saturday roll neck and groomed, wet-look hair he had a subtle grasp of where his interests lay. So, now, she decides to make the pitch that began to form in her mind on the drive from Manor Farm and properly came into focus just after she woke in the prison cell.

'What if I wasn't there?' she asks after her first sip of tea.

'Go on,' he says, then leans out of the cell and shouts for a chair.

'I haven't made a statement, so you've got nothing in the official record that says I was at Manor Farm. What if this was a raid put together at the last minute because you received a tip-off and you needed to act quickly to prevent the remains of four people being removed? You also had information that one of the slaves, a Romanian national who had been reported missing, was there, and you searched for him and found him. Basically, you tell a story about the police responding to good intelligence.'

A police constable steps into the cell and hands him a chair. He sits and unbuttons his jacket.

'Continue.'

'Andrei Botezatu knows I was at the farm but he's out of it right now and will have difficulty remembering what happened. Even if he does remember, I'll explain things to him and his sister, so he sticks to the story. And the man known as Milky—'

'Malcolm Roy Beanie.'

'Didn't know what hit him and never saw me. And Gethin—'

'Gethin David Jones.'

'Was knocked out by Andrei and, in any case, won't want to testify that he was anywhere near the Tank where they held Andrei and presumably the other people they murdered. So, he's not going to say anything, even if he remembers. And Kegs—'

'Yes, Mr Bob Lyttle, who blew a hole in his side when his

shotgun went off as he was climbing a fence. He'll be lucky to live.'

'Wow! Can't say I'm sorry.'

'And what about Mr Dekker?' asks Price.

She thinks for a moment. 'He's not going to want to remind anyone of my presence in the barn because he admitted to me that he knew what was in the skip and then ordered Kegs to kill me and Andrei.' She takes up the sandwich packet. 'You have enough evidence without me saying he knew about the four people in the skip.'

'In actual fact there were five bodies, but, yes, we do have enough evidence. They're bang to rights. Gethin Jones will talk to save his skin and we'll get all the testimony against Dekker we need. The organisation will unravel, and people will talk. There's evidence at the site – fingerprints on the digger, shovel, skip and lorry, their own CCTV footage.'

She unwraps the sandwich and takes a bite. 'And Dekker and Cynthia Petito can't explain why they were there at that time of day, unless Dekker was supervising the removal of human remains to an incinerator ahead of a raid that they expected. They suspected you would follow up our release of the Vietnamese women from the nail bar with a raid on Monday, right? They were cleaning up.' He nods. 'Plus, you have the woman they tried to run over. She'll sing like a nightingale.'

'Zofia Belka.'

'So, you don't need me. I wasn't there.'

He nods. 'And that will presumably suit your managers at MI5.'

'The less I'm involved the better. And the beauty of it is that your team gets all the credit for stopping a dangerous criminal enterprise that was responsible for human trafficking and modern slavery on a vast scale, five murders, rapes, sexual abuse, mass production of cannabis on poultry farms, and the burning of the three people at the crash site on Legion's Hill.'

His expression doesn't alter. It's as though he's doing her the favour, but she knows he couldn't be happier. 'What do you need in exchange, Ms Parsons?'

'No charges on this or the nail bar until after we publish the story on Middle Kingdom. We don't want to be hampered by sub judice laws at this stage. And no media briefings, even if the press get wind of events at Manor Farm. No confirmation. Nothing!'

'You're talking like a journalist.'

'You agree?'

He nods. 'Anything else?'

'There's a man named Frank Shap who was the witness of the events at Legion's Hill. Tough. Ex-Para. He rescued Tam from the minibus then watched them set fire to it with the dead inside. Without him, she wouldn't be alive, and we wouldn't be where we are now, but he won't come forward as a witness because he believes he's wanted after a fight in a pub, two or three years ago. He thought he'd killed the man, but I couldn't find anything in the local media, and I checked with the pub and Merseyside Police. Neither knew anything.'

'I'll find out.' He requests the spelling and the name of the pub and sends a text. 'Is that it?'

She takes another bite. 'I need you to inform a lawyer named Annette Raines that Andrei has been rescued so she can tell his sister. She will also be immediately in touch with me, which then means I'll be legitimately in possession of the knowledge that Andrei is safe and I can write up his story for the site this evening.'

She sips her tea between bites of the sandwich, watching him
go through it all. In his mid-forties, he wouldn't have climbed as
far without the discipline to look at an offer such as she's making
coldly and without hurry. While he does, she pulls up Annette
Raines's number and shares it with him by text.

'That's all agreed,' he says eventually. 'If you weren't at Manor
Farm, there's no reason for you to be here, so . . .'

'I'd better leave now. Your officers will be okay about this?
Won't talk?'

'Of course.'

She rises from the cell bed and offers her hand. 'We have a
deal?'

'We do, indeed, Ms Parsons.' He gets up from his chair to
take her hand and smiles. 'I wish I had an officer like you in my
team, but there again, maybe not.'

Just past six o'clock that Saturday evening, she enters the Middle
Kingdom office. Every desk is occupied, and the place is filled
with the almost luminous energy of young people working to
one purpose. Slim, feeling better after a shower to wash the
stink of the barn from her hair and a change of clothes to make
a clear contrast with what she wore the day before, knows that
in another life she would do a lot to stay at Middle Kingdom.

The four Vietnamese are chattering and showing each other
photos on their new phones of people and children they were
denied contact with for years. They've all made statements
at the police headquarters a few blocks away, and these, Slim
knows, will be fed into the understanding that Nick Price will
build of Dekker's operation. The women are waiting for their
story to go live, helping with the last-minute fact-checking
and adding details. Tam tells Slim that they are all amazed

how much they've buried their experiences and are only now beginning to remember what they've been through. They'll all need counselling – years of it, she thinks – but, of course, they probably won't get it.

The three teams of reporters are poring over their contributions, the videos, the fact boxes, summaries, and interviews that accompany each woman's story. Dan and Abigail stand either side of a large computer screen, a replacement for the design desktop taken by the police in the raid. On the far side of the newsroom, Yoni Ross, Sara Kiln and Toto Linna chew the fat in the evening light that touches that side of the building, and slants into the newsroom. Yoni surveys the scene with his usual beatific satisfaction; Sara occasionally checks a laptop. They are the tech side of Middle Kingdom, which she now understands has little to do with the day-to-day journalism. Slim remembers the AI tool that Skelpick consulted the night before – God, less than twenty-four hours ago! – and knows now that it must have been used to acquire all the data on government expenditure and waste.

Dan tells everyone to listen up and takes them through the presentation of the story. The main headline reads, 'Huge Slavery Network Uncovered', and the strapline, 'Trafficked survivors tell of years of violence, sexual abuse and exploitation'. Below are three photographs of the four women – the sisters Tam and Lan are seen together – and each one has a 'play' arrow in the middle for the videoed interview. He checks with reporting teams that all the material has been checked by lawyers and the four women understand the jeopardy they may face after admitting entering the country illegally and working on cannabis farms. He says that there are fifteen elements to the coverage and that they are now waiting for a reaction from the

Home Office on three issues — the ease with which the women and others were brought into the country; the failure of several police authorities to spot what was going on; and the Home Office's attitude to illegal immigrants who were forced to work in criminal enterprises, like the cannabis farms. 'We want an assurance that these good people won't be prosecuted because of the failure of so many authorities to do their job,' he says.

As the three team leaders each confirm they have closed their stories after final edits, a text arrives on Slim's phone. It's from Annette Raines and she is excitedly informing her that a police raid has rescued Andrei Botezatu and that Andrei is now in an ICU in Peterborough. She expresses amazement that, after so many months of being stonewalled, they got back to her. Abigail is looking at her own phone. She has the same message and shows it to Dan who looks up and calls out, 'We have good news. Today, the police rescued Andrei Botezatu, who is now in hospital in Peterborough being treated for bone fractures, numerous lesions, double pneumonia and malnutrition.' He looks up, finds Slim, and says, 'This is your man, isn't it? Did you know this?'

'Just got the same text from Annette.'

'Can you write it up for eight?'

'Sure.' She looks at the phone. 'But there's not a lot of information from the police. It looks like Annette has been told unofficially so she can inform Andrei's sister in Romania.'

'Yes, yes,' says Dan impatiently. 'But we had information from our friends here,' he sweeps the Vietnamese women, 'that this man Andrei was being held in the Tank at Manor Farm, and you've got a photo of Mr Botezatu, satellite imagery of the farm and the film you shot outside the gates. That's all very good material. What about ownership of the farm?'

'I was up last night trying to establish that but didn't get far — just some shell companies, and a name.'

Thus far, she hasn't said anything that's untrue, and she plans to keep it that way, but she notices Skelpick is looking her way, and then his eyebrows rise interrogatively, which she chooses to ignore, but it's obvious he suspects she had a hand in Andrei's release. This will be her last story for Middle Kingdom. She'll write it quickly and get the hell out of there before she is forced to explain herself to Skelpick or anyone else.

Dan asks her to coordinate with Craig Whitlock, the courts and crime reporter, now tasked with tracking down any police contacts who might have knowledge of a raid at Manor Farm. Whitlock looks doubtful and says there's probably an operational reason to explain why there's been no briefing; maybe they are planning raids on other premises. He's covering his rear in the expectation of getting nowhere on a Saturday evening. Dan tells him to have something ready to add to Slim's story once it's published, even if that's in the middle of the night.

She goes to the only desk available, on the far side of the conference room, and writes an article that tells of Andrei's rescue, his condition and treatment in Peterborough and then builds on everything his sister told her: the trusting nature of her brother and how he left prison in Romania after serving a short sentence, determined to make good and pay her back all the money he owed her.

That was his downfall. Like the Vietnamese women, he was conveyed to Rotterdam, trafficked into the UK, stripped of his phone, wallet and identity papers, and put to work in gruelling jobs without pay. She tells of the rumour that he stole a motorhome and tried to escape, but was caught and beaten, and thrown into the Tank, a punishment cell located at Manor

Farm, where according to the Vietnamese, other slaves were rumoured to have died. It is easy to imagine the cruelty of this confinement, the deathly cold, the filth, isolation and not knowing whether he would ever again see the light of day, let alone his family in Romania.

Andrei was determined to gain his freedom and had already been punished once for using a mobile phone belonging to one of the gang members to phone his sister. Investigation by Middle Kingdom showed that this phone was also used at the crash site on Legion's Hill where Le Thi Tam was rescued. The number most frequently called belonged to a man known as Kegs, whom Middle Kingdom had tied to Manor Farm where Andrei was held. Research at Companies House and Land Registry indicated that the compound might belong to a man named Dominic Dekker – formerly, Davidyan. It was thought significant, given the rumoured theft of a motorhome, that Dekker owned a camper van and motorhome hire business in Boston, Lincolnshire. She didn't, of course, mention Skelpick's use of a mysterious AI entity to gain Dekker's names but assumed that somewhere in the records she would have eventually found them on her own.

She checks the story for any detail that might give away her presence at Manor Farm that morning, attaches the photos of Andrei and his sister, the records for phones A and B, and the film she made of Kegs at the gates of the compound and sends it all to Abigail at 7.30 p.m.

Slim wanders over to the newsroom and sees that Dan and Abigail are reading from one screen. She assumes they're looking at her story for, apart from the Home Office reactions, this is the last element to be put to bed. She sees that on the home page, displayed on the big desktop, a space has been created on the right-hand side, and imagines this is for a photo of Andrei and a headline. She goes to the kitchenette, makes coffee and turns to find that Skelpick has snuck up on her.

'Are you going to make me some tea?' he asks.

'No, make it yourself,' she says, smiling, and hands him a mug and a teabag on a string.

'Quite the charmer,' he says and pours the water, just boiled by Slim, over the teabag, which he proceeds to jerk up and down in the cup. 'Whitlock has got something from one of his contacts that might interest you. Apparently, the police were called to Manor Farm and discovered a young woman with your friend Andrei and at least two men down. One was found with a badly shattered knee having been hit by a pickaxe or mattock – also found at the scene – and the other was wandering around with head wounds.' He looks at her. 'But luckily for you, Slim, the police comms team have denied any such thing took place. Thought you'd like to know that.'

'Thanks. Sounds crazy,' she says without the slightest flicker of embarrassment. 'Oh, by the way, what was the thing you showed me, the powerful AI tool that produced Dekker's name?'

'Nothing that you need worry your murderous little head about, my dear. And, anyway, you're getting off the subject.'

'Since we're on the subject, I won't tell about your super bright AI entity if you don't tell of your suspicions.'

He sniffs an okay. 'Good piece of yours. It was almost as if you were there,' he says, as Shazi bounds into the kitchenette.

'They're very, very pleased with that. Dan's making a few edits but we're all good to go. I've got a surprise for you downstairs. I'll meet you down there in five.'

'Great,' says Slim, catching Skelpick's crooked smile as he leaves for the Conference Room, where his laptop is set up.

CHAPTER 33

Bantock has moved *Spindle* to a stretch about a mile from the marina and it's now moored next to his own narrowboat, *Regina*. She wakes to intense birdsong coming from the trees on the other side of the canal, and 'Danny Boy' being played slowly on Bantock's fiddle. She looks around and is quickly aware of the hangover gripping her neck and the back of her head.

Yes, the evening before. What happened? She gathered her things together, lifted a hand to say goodbye to everyone in the newsroom and went downstairs with Shazi. They sat on the steps of the entrance to wait for a six-wheeled delivery robot to show. Shazi puffed at her vape and conjured wine from her shoulder bag and Slim complimented Shazi on the new look; her black hair was now streaked with dark indigo. 'The best colour job I've ever seen, literally the best,' said Slim and meant it. They clinked plastic glasses and Shazi aimed a cloud of sweet-scented vapour away from Slim with a toss of the head. 'Triple Mango,' she explained unnecessarily, then moved to the subject of Abigail, whose self-control and discipline amaze her. 'You know I think she's taken a shine to your friend Mr Bantock.'

'You serious? I can't think of two people less suited. I mean . . .
Bantock and Abigail. That'll never work.'

'You should have seen her when he came in with those two
Vietnamese ladies. I've never seen her smile like that. Looked
like a different person.'

'Bantock! No!'

The headlights of a white robot vehicle came into view a
hundred metres away. It juddered to a halt to let a car cross its
path before trundling towards them at little more than walking
speed. 'It's clever – cameras all around,' said Shazi. The robot
stopped directly in front of them. Shazi pressed 'Unlock' on
her app, the lid opened, and the robot sang 'Happy Birthday'
with its lights and the burgee on top of its aerial flashing. 'I just
love the way it does that, so I always say it's my birthday on the
order.'

They took their pizza and wine to a bench between two lines
of trees in the centre of Silbury Boulevard. No one was about
and there was little traffic. Surges of blossom scent came to them
on the breeze. Shazi continued to talk. 'So, Abigail says you're
going to take some time off. I want to know you're coming
back, right. She seems a bit doubtful.' A trail of cheese hung
from her lips to the pizza box, which ended up stuck across her
T-shirt. Slim smiled and replied that she had a lot of personal
stuff to get through. She loved the job and she hoped she'd be
back some day, but who knew?

They finished the wine and Shazi laid her head on Slim's
shoulder then kissed her on the cheek. Slim smelt shampoo
mixed in with triple mango and pizza. Another kiss, this time
just missing her lips, and there was no longer any doubt what
Shazi intended. 'No?' she whispered into Slim's ear. Would
she sleep with this artless but sly chatterbox? Another time she

might. Now, all she needed was her own bed. She said some-thing lame about mixing business and pleasure. Shazi kissed her ear and then her neck. Slim moved away. 'What about that handsome nature correspondent Aziz?' she had asked. 'What happened to all that swooning?'

'Ha, a most conceited young man is Aziz,' said Shazi, pulling back with disdain. 'He's well and truly up himself like no one I ever met.' Then she kissed Slim passionately and Slim gently pushed her away, even though she felt something move in her.

'I'm sorry. I'm really, really tired,' she said.

Back on *Spindle*, she showered for the second time and began to regret not taking Shazi up on her offer, because she certainly didn't want to be alone. The lights were on in *Regina*, and she went over to Bantock and they made a night of it with more wine, whisky and Bantock's bizarre stories. She got to bed just before three, after Bantock walked her back to *Spindle*.

Now, she lies listening to the canal, trying to remember where the painkillers are, then reaches for her backpack, which is wedged between the bed and the hull, and locates a packet of Nurofen in the front pocket. She drinks a lot of water, swallows two pills and pulls the phones towards her by tugging the multipoint adapter across the galley table. Three out of four phones have been active. There were calls during the night and several that morning, but the phones were all on 'silent', and the vibrations didn't rouse her. She dials Peter Salt, the most persistent caller.

'What the hell have you been doing?' he demands.

'You know where I am. You could come and find me.'

'Were you aware of what they planned?'

She knows better than to ask what's happened and scrambles to open and turn on her laptop.

'Were you aware of what they were doing last night? Did you have any knowledge at all?'

'Peter, how was I meant to know anything?' She's buying time. 'I had to write a story, then I went home. Remember that I'd been working for forty-eight hours, and I'm dealing with personal stuff that you know about.'

Now she's in the Middle Kingdom website. The space that had been left blank on the right of the home page has been enlarged and now carries the heading: 'Government Budget and Waste, a Statement by the Editorial Board of Middle Kingdom'.

Salt is going on about how embarrassing it is to be blindsided by a poxy provincial website, so she has time to skim the statement.

> *The government has decided that the public won't see the extent of the waste, inefficiency and, sometimes, dishonesty that has left the UK's public finances in a state of chaos. Ministers have taken steps to suppress legitimate scrutiny of the waste scandal by threatening Middle Kingdom and its journalists with prosecution under the Official Secrets Act. After consultation with our legal team and an exhaustive internal debate, the board has taken the decision to publish, in unedited and unmediated form, all the evidence that Middle Kingdom has gathered on this story. Our decision is based on the self-evident fact that the information belongs to the people who pay the government's bills and, indeed, the salaries of politicians – the British public. We would have liked to have presented it in a more digestible form. It is the job of journalists to make sense of complex material, but our hand has been forced, and we now take the unusual step of publishing everything we have so that people can draw conclusions about the record of this administration and the behaviour of those in power.*

'Are you there?' says Salt.

'Should we be having this conversation on an open line?'

'Did you know about this?'

'No. I would have told you immediately.'

'Why didn't you know?'

She doesn't reply though the answer is clear to her. Everything is clear. Middle Kingdom suspected she was a government spy all along, which is why they had given her a succession of no-hope stories and kept her at a distance. Then, when the flower thief story produced an extraordinary lead, which developed into a nationally important story about people trafficking and modern slavery, they used its publication as cover to defy the government and dump a vast trove of secret data into the public domain. Shazi's role last night was to get her out of the office during the final preparations to publish the data beside the more dramatic interviews and revelations of the slave story. Bloody Shazi, the phony pest control operative and Mata Hari of Milton Keynes.

'Have you got anything to say?'

'Not here, not now.'

'There's a meeting tomorrow at ten down here. Usual place. I'd be on time if I were you.'

'I thought you were meant to be protecting me up here. You weren't there yesterday with Tudor.'

'Got there afterwards. It's over, as I said.' He hangs up.

Slim feels like slamming the phone down on the galley table but doesn't because she notices one of the other phones illuminate with an incoming call, the second from the same number.

'Is that Matt's sister Slim? Hi! Sorry! It's Norah Kinneal.'

'Hi, good to hear from you.' It isn't. She needs coffee.

'The Gardai told me Matt's body is released for burial and I was thinking about a funeral. I have no idea how to arrange a thing like that.' Nor have the money, thinks Slim. 'I'm asking what you want for your brother.'

'To be honest I haven't had time to think it through. I'm sorry, I should've been in touch about it.' She's on the towpath in bare feet heading towards *Regina*'s stern, where Bantock and the dog are seated gazing into space. She reaches the boat, scowls at the faithless Loup, and almost spits the word, 'Coffee!' stirring them both from their transcendental funk. Bantock goes below. She climbs aboard and pushes Loup along the bench so she can sit.

'Well,' says Norah. 'I was wondering if, like, it would be possible to reunite Matt and your mam, like.'

'How do you mean?'

'Having a joint funeral over there, with you.' She waits for Slim's reaction, gets none and hurries on. 'You see, he's still got friends over there. Matt's roots were in England. So, I just think it's right that he comes back to you.'

Slim's gaze has settled on the trembling poplars on the other side of the canal. Bantock passes coffee up to her, which she places on the bench, then hooks an arm around Loup's neck. 'Okay,' she says at length. 'I'll think about it. There'd be a lot to arrange. The first thing you need to do is to find an undertaker to collect Matt from the police morgue.' These words catch in her throat. Then, after several seconds, 'This will cost money, I'll cover it.'

'Oh, that won't be necessary, Slim. Matt had a tidy sum put away in our account. You'll let me know, then?'

'Within a few days,' she says. Matt never had money, thinks Slim. Never! He was terrible with money.

CHAPTER 34

A label on the pot plant informs Slim that the *Calathea Sander-iana* was purchased from the Garden Museum shop, just across Lambeth Bridge from MI5's headquarters at Thames House. She's had nothing else to look at for a quarter of an hour because, as everyone is required to do on entering the building, she deposited her phone at the security gate before being escorted past the memorials to Security Service personnel and up to the sixth floor. Five minutes later, a suited Rob Alantree pops his head out of a pair of doors and beckons her into a room that she's never been in before.

Alantree is looking extraordinarily solemn at the same time as pleased with himself. He shows her to a place in the middle of a long table on the other side of which are ranged Rita Bauer, Oliver Halfknight, the head of personnel and inter agency relations, Corinna Stone, a man she recognises as Erskine Mack, a section head, though she doesn't remember which section, and a large, bluff type with a shiny chin and small square glasses, to whom, it is quickly evident, everyone defers. Rob is fussing over the man's coffee and Stone aims a sickly look of pleasure at him. Halfknight introduces Slim and says, 'This is Victor

Warren, Permanent Secretary to the Ministry of Defence and Director General designate of MI5. I know I can rely on you to keep this to yourself until the announcement is made.' He sits back, nods to Erskine Mack, then almost visibly shrinks his presence in the room, which indicates to Slim that Halfknight, technically the most senior person present, is washed-up.

Erskine Mack, thin with an air of ascetic superiority, begins. 'I'm going to read the Home Secretary's statement of this morning. "We have suffered a catastrophic breach of government data, which must be regarded as an unprecedented blow to national security. The information so irresponsibly published by the Middle Kingdom site at the weekend lays out private emails, personnel assessments, strategic plans, secret consultations and budgetary information from four government departments, and presents myriad opportunities for the enemies of the United Kingdom. I have instructed the Security Services and the police to take urgent action to identify those responsible and bring them to justice."' He lets the piece of paper drop to the table. 'The point of this meeting is to establish firstly how the publication of the material took place over the weekend, and how Operation Linesman failed to anticipate this development. You, Ms Parsons, have been undercover in the site known as Middle Kingdom since April, is that right?'

'Yes.'

'Why did this happen?'

'Ten days ago, I predicted to Peter Salt in an email that they would dump all the data they possessed. My report will be in the record.'

'Why did you write that?'

'It was bound to happen because they were being pressurised. Immediately after I informed Peter by text that Middle Kingdom was considering a Part Two of the story on government budgets, the headquarters were raided, the site's equipment was seized and three people were arrested for obstruction. Later, members of the founding board were arrested and questioned under the Official Secrets Act. I made the fair assumption that this pressure would encourage Middle Kingdom to publish all they had, because they were determined to get it into the public domain before they were prevented from doing so by the law. I warned of this risk because, as you are seeing today, the media is trawling through the material looking for stories. I suggested that the slow release of information, the drip-drip effect, as I called it, would be harder for the government to deal with.'

'What were the authorities meant to do?' demands Warren.

She looks at him, remembering that the MoD was one of the ministries exposed. 'I cannot answer that, sir. I was undercover at Middle Kingdom and had no input into any of the response.'

'Exactly,' says Mack, 'you were undercover, monitoring the situation. Yet at the point when they decided to carry out this "data dump" you were otherwise engaged,' he looks at another sheet of paper, 'pursuing your own campaign against a gang involved in slavery, which necessitated a rescue of you by the officers of two police forces who attended the scene.'

She is silent.

'At the precise moment Middle Kingdom was preparing to drive a train through the secrecy laws you were absent. Can you explain why?'

'Yes, I can.' She guesses he has Peter Salt's account of what happened at Manor Farm in front him. Salt didn't get to the farm to help her, as Tudor had, but he must have found out all he needed from the police and reported back about the deal she made with Price. 'I was trying to establish my credentials as a journalist by reporting on a real story. I had to prove myself before they trusted me. Working your way into a position of trust is a key part of an undercover role, as we found in Softball. It takes time and patience. I've been at Middle Kingdom just a matter of weeks.'

'They suckered you. They used the story about slavery as cover to publish the information they had stolen from government.'

'I cannot deny that, and I take full responsibility for what happened.'

Corinna Stone raises a finger. Mack gives way and sits back. 'We understand that you agreed a deal with the head of the local serious crime unit to delay charges so that Middle Kingdom could publish the story,' her finger rises in the air, 'and so provide the cover Middle Kingdom needed.'

'Yes, but—'

'The point,' says Mack, 'is that you took it upon yourself to negotiate – on behalf of the Security Service – a deal with the local police so that you appeared nowhere in the record of the investigation. I mean, it's unbelievable. You were acting totally without authorisation.'

'I thought it would be less embarrassing for the service.'

'What's embarrassing is that you were at that farm, armed, we understand, with a pickaxe and prepared to mete out violence to anyone you encountered. You smashed a man's leg and brained another.'

There seems little point in correcting the record on Gethin's injury. 'I went equipped to break a lock not a leg, because we knew the man was being held in a makeshift prison,' she murmurs. 'By the way, I probably saved his life.'

'Maybe you did, maybe you didn't.'

'I believe I did,' she says firmly. She considers adding, 'And while I was about it, exposed the failings of the police and border force.'

'Do you imagine you're exempt from the rules, protocols and procedures developed by the Security Service over a very long time, Ms Parsons? Are you alone permitted to roam the country with a pickaxe, like some sort of vigilante?' She notes this is the same word Dan Halladay used after the nail bar raid.

'No, of course not, but it wasn't a wasted effort. Dominic Dekker, older brother of our previous target Ivan Guest, will now go to prison for a very long time. That's some kind of result, surely?'

At this, Halfknight stirs from his torpor and pulses a look at her, but too late.

Mack says, 'So, a personal vendetta explains why you all but ignored the purpose of Operation Linesman?'

'I had absolutely no idea the two men were related until the end of last week. I wondered if that was the hidden agenda of Linesman, but of course that idea makes no sense. I accept it for the coincidence that it is.'

'You expect us to believe there was no element of revenge,' says Corinna Stone, who has been busy making notes.

'Yes, because it's true,' she says.

Victor Warren has been drumming the table impatiently. Now he suddenly slaps his hand down so that his coffee cup jumps. 'We're getting off the subject. The Cabinet Office needs to know if you can salvage anything from this affair. How are these lefty journalists getting their information? Who are their spies in the Civil Service? Where is the information being processed? What is their agenda? Are they working for hostile actors outside the country?' This is directed at Erskine Mack, who nods with each point and is eagerly mirrored by Alantree. Warren ends by glaring at Slim. 'Well?'

Will she speak about the facility out at Tender Wick Business

Park, the enormous computing power spread through four or five buildings that once housed displaced Poles? Is she going to tell them about her encounter with what appeared to be Middle Kingdom's private AI helper? It wasn't so much the speed of the response, although that was impressive, but rather the fact that Middle Kingdom had exclusive access to a very powerful investigative tool, which would explain why the authorities hadn't the first clue how a mass of detailed government secrets came to be in the site's possession. She'd kept the tablet she stole from Ivan Guest and now finds that she's decided to withhold information that could be vital to the case against Middle Kingdom. Living her truth? No, it's because, at some basic level, she doesn't trust her employers, didn't trust them to support her after she'd hijacked Guest's jet and now, as she looks across the table at Victor Warren, Corinna Stone and Erskine Mack, doesn't trust them to put the principle of a free media before their own interests. Journalists may be maggots, but at least they're cleaning the wound. These people are the wound.

'Well?' repeats Warren.

'I'm sure they aren't working for hostile foreign interests, and they don't appear to have a subversive agenda beyond wanting to publish the truth, as they see it. How they are getting the information and where they are holding and processing it are unknowns. In my last operation, it was twelve months before we achieved good insights.'

He's been shaking his head through the last two sentences. 'Publish the truth! Who says it's the truth?'

She studies him long enough for it to be regarded as dumb insolence, the phrase her mother used when she was a teenager. 'The government says it's the truth, sir, by insisting that state secrets have been stolen.'

'You're talking as if you share their aims, young lady.'

'It's a while since I've been called *young lady*, sir, but thanks.' This has Erskine Mack and Rob Alantree clutching their pearls. Corinna Stone makes a furious note. 'For the record, I don't share their aims, but my job is to understand the target and to that extent I need to empathise with the target's aims. As to salvaging the operation, it's hard to say. I've made clear in all my reports since April that Middle Kingdom suspected I was a plant, and I was openly accused of being a spy on two or three occasions. The success of my story on the slaves may change that.'

'Have they plans to publish anything more?' asks Warren.

'I don't know, but we're not dealing with run-of-the-mill journalists. The top team are very bright, strategic, and cool under fire.'

'You sound like an admirer. These people should be charged and incarcerated for a very long time.'

This is too much even for the career MI5 man and Erskine demurs. 'That's not actually our job. We can only provide the intelligence and then leave it to the police.'

Slim says to Warren, 'I'd move carefully if I were you, sir. It may look like they've published everything, but it would make a lot of sense to hold back something really eye-catching. That's what I would do.'

'I'm sure you would. I think I've heard quite enough of this.'

Slim shrugs indifference. Warren is a bully and thick with it. She catches Rita Bauer gazing at her. Rita blinks, her eyes slide left, towards the door, and she blinks again with a slight nod that is aimed to Slim's right. Slim considers the signal, and after a few moments, says, 'I wonder if a comfort break would be in order? The morning has been a rush.'

Warren looks irritated. Halfknight moves forward. 'Perhaps

another cup of coffee, Permanent Secretary. Rob, you're neglecting your duties.'

'Do you know where the washroom is, Ms Parsons?' asks Rita Bauer, already out of her chair. 'Follow me. It's not terribly easy to find.'

Rita walks a few paces ahead in the corridor, turns left, indicates a door on the right and says, while looking back the way they came, 'Leave the meeting as soon as possible. Do not wait for them to institute dismissal proceedings, which is what they have planned. Just get out of there. We need you in Milton Keynes.' She turns without waiting for a reaction and heads back to the meeting room.

A couple of minutes later, Slim enters the room, which now seems rather hot and stuffy. Warren gives her a dismissive glance and continues to murmur to Erskine Mack. She sees red cheeks and bushy eyebrows that rise and fall as he speaks and reflects on the thoroughly unappealing entitlement made flesh in the Permanent Secretary who is about to take over MI5. 'Right,' Warren says decisively, 'we need now to think how best to stop Middle Kingdom over the next twenty-four hours.'

Slim moves forward. 'Excuse me, sir. I've told you all I know. I'm an undercover specialist and have no experience of planning and decision making. It's not my training. I mention this because I did put in a formal request for compassionate leave starting yesterday because of the loss of my mother and news that my brother was murdered in Ireland. I'm sorry, but I'm the only member of my family left, and I'm dealing with my brother's grieving partner and having to arrange both funerals. Unless there's anything else, I need to go and attend to all of that.'

'These matters couldn't be more urgent,' says Warren.

Halfknight says, 'Ms Parsons's email reached me yesterday

and as instigator of Linesman, I agreed to a period of compassionate leave.' This is untrue because Slim's request left her
phone five minutes before she entered Thames House. 'There's
another consideration which made me grant her request without
a second thought. Whatever the rights and wrongs of her presence at that farm, she was witness to the excavation of five sets
of human remains in a state of advanced decomposition and,
moreover, believed she would be killed by the gang members
present.' He smiles regretfully. 'Corinna and Erskine will tell
you better than I can that the service has a duty of care to
officers who place themselves in harm's way every day. We are
particularly concerned with those who may be subject to PTSD,
Permanent Secretary. As Corinna will confirm, it's something
we have learned to take very seriously in this building.'

'This will take just a few minutes,' Mack protests.

'A few minutes . . . yes. That's what Ms Parsons was given
before she faced execution by a brute named Bob Lyttle a little over
seventy-two hours ago.' He stops there and looks at Warren and
Mack in turn. 'The horror of that situation is easy to imagine – the
filth, the fear, the seeming inevitability of a violent death. I won't
go on. But Ms Parsons has appeared here without complaint, nor
the slightest sign of impairment or self-pity, and offered the best
account she can, and I believe we should salute that, despite our
views on the failure of Linesman. With your permission, Erskine,
I believe we should thank Ms Parsons for her service and let her
recover from her ordeal and mourn her loved ones.'

Mack opens his hands and looks at Corinna Stone, who reluctantly gives her assent. As head of personnel, she couldn't do
otherwise.

CHAPTER 35

Slim collects her phone, steps from the building into a bright early summer's day, and walks slowly towards Horseferry Road, considering what she's just witnessed. Halfknight saved her, but that was due to the card she handed him about compassionate leave, which he turned into a trump, not because of any residual power of his. It's clear that he and Rita Bauer are out, and Warren will take over as DG, almost certainly with Mack, the seasoned professional, as his deputy. Peter Salt and Rob Alantree, though hardly players in the great game, are already signed up and doing the new team's bidding, hence Salt's report of the events at Manor Farm and on the deal she did with the head of the serious crime unit to keep her presence secret.

She buys coffee and an egg mayonnaise sandwich at Gianni's café on Horseferry Road, rarely used by her colleagues because of its proximity to Thames House, and walks to the steps of St John's, Smith Square, the baroque church that is now a concert venue, and finds a place with the office workers eating their lunch in the sunshine. She sits and sips her coffee but decides to leave the sandwich until after she's called Norah.

'Have you got a moment?' she asks her.

'Sure, Slim. Anytime!' Norah sounds up, less tentative. 'Guess what? I've been for an interview, and I think they're going to give me the job. Course it's not much – helping out at a little nursery school. That's what I was at before me and Matt hooked up.'

'Norah, you mentioned that he'd left you with a tidy sum. I wondered how that was. I mean, he was so bad with money.'

'Are we talking about the same man? To be honest, Matt could peel an orange in his pocket. To put it in plain English, he was tighter than a nun's snatch.'

'Surely not.'

'Yes, he scrimped and saved.'

'Saved!' she says, astonished. 'He never had money. He was a spendthrift.'

'Well, he changed. That's all there is to it. There's like thirty-six grand in our account right now. There's the fifteen grand he won for the prize, which he never spent, then all the commissions of the last two years. Even when he was using, he was never a dosser. You know the Samsung ad they're running all over. That was Matt. His concept, like. Have you had any more thoughts about the funeral for the both of them?'

'I like the idea. I need to work on it though.'

'Grand. It'll be good to meet you and you can get to know the little man.'

'Norah, I forgot to ask about the business of those two men in the pub taking photos of Matt. Did you tell the Gardai?'

'I did that. It was in the Celt Pub. His friend Morris Noonan was with him, so he's a witness to what happened, and they have the CCTV. Morris gave them a description of the two men.'

'Okay, I'll be in touch soon.'

She ends the call and leans back on the step, turning her face to the sun. A few seconds later a woman starts speaking to her. 'I wonder if you could hold my baby for a second. I need to feed him and arrange things.'

Slim shields her eyes. A tall blonde, of about her age, in sunglasses, jeans and loafers, is standing a few feet away with a baby in a pouch. A pushchair has been dragged up to the platform between the two sets of steps, and the woman is searching in the back pocket while trying to keep the baby upright.

'Sure,' says Slim. 'What can I do?

'If you could take him out of the pouch while I find the nursing cloth, that would be very kind.' She straightens so that Slim can lift the baby free. It isn't easy and she bumps its head against her chin. The baby looks astonished and immediately starts crying.

She holds it almost at arm's length and finds something distinctly familiar in the unhappy, scrunched-up face. 'Is this baby called Marcus Aurelius Ballard?'

'How very clever of you. Hello, I'm Jules Ballard. If you feel inside his little jacket, there's a folded note for you with a SIM card. Don't look now, obviously! My lovely, ridiculous husband says it's urgent.' Slim finds the folded paper, palms it and hands the baby back. 'Thank you so much,' says Jules. 'Could we sit together for a moment while I feed him and do the baby talk thing that I find so very tiresome?'

'Of course.'

They sit and Jules attaches the baby to her breast and covers her shoulder and the baby's head with muslin. 'Tom says he's being watched. He says they will start watching you too, but you've got a few days' grace.'

Slim touches the baby's tiny bootee and pretends to find it cute. 'Who's watching?'

She jerks a head as though putting a ball in the back of the net in the direction of Thames House. 'This cloak and dagger stuff is really very tiresome.' Slim imagines a lot of things in Jules's life are tiresome.

'Tom says you are the best in the business at what you do, whatever that is. Funny, you don't look it at all.' Supercilious eyes peer over the sunglasses to make certain that Slim is, indeed, unimpressive-looking.

'Maybe that's the whole point,' says Slim.

'I think he's a bit in love with you.'

'We worked very closely together for over two years. But please have no fear on that score.'

'Yet he couldn't wait to see you at our church. Mind you, he'd do anything to get out of the house. He and Mother have never seen the point of each other.'

'All Saints is your local church?'

'Yes, my family keeps it going. Mother runs concerts there, not like this place, of course,' she says looking up at St John's. 'Cello and harp recitals. Father pays a lot of the bills. Romantic, isn't it?'

'Beautiful place,' says Slim, suddenly wishing she were there. 'Do they do funerals at All Saints?'

'I'm sure they do. You'll need to book the vicar, the Reverend Joanna Wilbury, who covers six parishes and is known as the Travelling Wilbury. Nothing like a funeral to breathe life into an old church.'

Slim smiles. 'I'd better go and read this note.'

'He asked me to tell that you still have protection, but that it's limited, and you must be ultra careful.'

'Thank you.'

'You have to wait to be contacted.' She pauses, flashes a bleak,

Norfolk cocktail party smile. 'Tom is a dear. I desperately want him to survive this. He and others of his view have joined an order of extreme obedience, which means they aren't going to put a foot wrong. They are not giving those bastards an excuse to fire them and that, I imagine, includes talking to you.'

'Who's the mother superior of the order of extreme obedience? Oliver Halfknight? Rita Bauer?'

'The names mean nothing to me, I'm afraid.'

'And you can't tell me what's going on.'

'No.'

'Give Tom my best and thanks for doing this. It must have been extremely tiresome for you.'

Jules looks down at Marcus Aurelius Ballard as though he were an alien life form. 'No, what's tiresome is having babies. Avoid at all costs.'

'I will,' says Slim.

She dumps the sandwich and walks to St James's Park, where she sits on a bench and unfolds the note. There's a SIM card with handwritten instructions.

Use on a virgin phone and text me when you're set up. You have protection but not as much as we would like, so please keep your head down. Will be in touch soonest.

She slips Ballard's SIM card into her wallet and shreds the note, puts the pieces into her pockets and heads to the West End, an area she knows well for its dive-ins, choke points, and pubs and restaurants with two exits, which she'd used when picking up instructions or needing to consult with Ballard face to face. On the way, she distributes some of the pieces in waste bins and flushes the rest in a pub loo. She heads into Mayfair and to the

Catholic Church of the Immaculate Conception in Farm Street. It's no accident that she's chosen the church. It is an excellent choke point on any route in the West End, but she also wants to check on something in Mount Street, which she knows happens two or three times a week, sometimes every working day. She leaves by the side entrance to take the path through Mount Street Gardens, then emerges opposite the Connaught Hotel. Here, she turns left into one of the more expensive streets in the capital, passes a cigar shop, handbag store, a jeweller, two expensive cafés, and reaches a run of gentleman's boutiques. In the first, she catches sight of a gun-metal blue silk scarf. She peers at it then goes into the store to take a closer look. She considers the cotton shirts in the window display and lets her eyes drift across the street to the window of the Rock Seafood Restaurant & Caviar Bar. Somehow, she knew Ivan Guest would be there but recoils when she sees him and moves behind a display of cashmere jerseys. He's at his usual table by the window, on the right-hand side of the restaurant, with his back to the wall, so he has a clear view of the street, the people coming into the establishment and the line of bar stools, on which, most often, women are perched for caviar, blinis and vodka. She's been at the Rock a dozen times, delivering documents for signature, sitting with him while he waited for a late lunch guest. Nothing has changed. He's with three other men, one of whom she can see, and recognises. He is a hedge-fund manager named Carline and he specialises in oil and gas. Guest is doing all the talking, using his hands to bludgeon the air and intimidate his companions into submission. He holds them high, like an evangelist conjuring the promised land, fingers splayed to catch and bring everything into his orbit. His smile and the whitened teeth are visible from where she is, but there's no sign of the damage she inflicted to the left side of his face with the champagne bottle. He is wearing one of his checked linen and silk sports jackets and his shirt is unbuttoned to his chest, which is the norm. The great manipulator and murderer is back in his usual spot and doing business, and does not appear to be remotely concerned about his brother Dominic who is in police custody and likely to go away for two or three decades.

She brings out her phone and shoots a dozen frames before an assistant approaches and asks what she's doing.

She manages a smile and says she'll take the scarf and asks about shirt sizes. The woman – pretty with a freckled face and auburn hair – persists with the question.

Slims looks at her squarely. 'If you really want to know, I'm taking photographs of the man who attempted to rape me eight months ago. He's in the restaurant over there. His name is—'

The woman looks out of the window. 'Oh, I see – Mr Guest,' she says quietly. 'He's a customer. Buys plenty here.' She glances into the back of the store where another good-looking assistant is hefting bolts of material, while a third is with a customer in the changing room. 'I'm not surprised. I delivered some shirts to his office in Culross Mews. Groped me and said he'd got a job for me.'

'Culross? His office is in Knightsbridge?'

'No, it's Park Lane, but the delivery address is Culross Mews.' She looks Slim up and down and frowns. 'I don't think we're going to have a size that'll be right for you in the shirt. You can have it made to measure but that's going to be a lot of money and it'll be a few weeks.'

'Measure me, anyway. And I'll take the scarf.'

'I'll fetch the tape measure.'

Slim turns to look at the restaurant. Guest often held court at his regular table long after the lunch period had ended, inviting people to join him for coffee and brandy. She assumes some members of the group have recently arrived and now sees a man hovering to the left of the table. Guest gesticulates impatiently and a chair is brought. He sits back and places his hands on his chest, miming pleasure at the man's arrival.

The assistant comes back with the scarf and a card machine and hands Slim a scribbled address. 'It overlooks Park Lane. The one with curved windows, if you know what I mean.'

'Bay windows.'

'Right, bay windows. But the entrance is on Culross Mews, which is off Culross Street.'

Slim pays with cash and gives her name as Alice Benski for the shirt order. The assistant is called Rhona. Rhona measures her neck, shoulders, chest and back, filling in a printed card as she goes, then says, 'Arms out, please.' Slim has the phone in her right hand and takes more photos in landscape. At this point, a little magic happens. Two attractive women sway past the restaurant. Guest points and all four men at his table turn their heads to face the street. Her phone makes the noise of a camera shutter four times and she's sure she's got the group shot. The newcomer she recognises but cannot think where she's seen him before. The other two mean nothing to her. Guest's eyes linger on the street then drift to the clothes store and seem to be focusing on the window. She turns to face Rhona. 'Is he looking this way? Can he see inside?'

Rhona checks. 'He may be perving after me or Sam.' Her eyes flick to the woman arranging the cloth at the back. 'He often does that.' Slim says she'll be in touch about the shirt, places the scarf over the back of her head, crosses the ends and throws them backwards in the way she's seen Middle Eastern tourists wear a scarf loosely as a hijab. She waits by the door for a few seconds and leaves when a van pulls up and double-parks in front of the store. She turns left along Mount Street, then crosses to the other side, so she can't be seen from the restaurant. She is shaking, not from fear but outrage that Ivan Guest is free to lounge with his cronies in one of the most expensive restaurants in central London, untroubled by shame or justice. This only stops when she reaches Marble Arch tube station, by which time she's decided exactly what she's going to do.

Now she has a plan.

CHAPTER 36

Slim boards a train at Euston and spends much of the journey to Milton Keynes catching up with the Middle Kingdom site and the fallout from the slavery and government waste stories. The site has been through several cycles in the last thirty-six hours, and it is struggling to keep up with developments on the investigation of Dominic Dekker's sprawling criminal enterprise.

Police have raided eighteen addresses across six counties. Over a hundred and seventy exhausted and bewildered slaves, representing twenty different nationalities, have been rescued from the network's clutches. Two cannabis farms, in Bedfordshire and Northamptonshire, were stormed that morning by specialist drugs teams, and millions of pounds worth of drugs seized. Police entered the headquarters of Hit-the-Road-Jack, the camper van and motorhome hire company in Lincolnshire, on Sunday at the same time as Dominic Dekker's home, a large single-storey, ranch-style residence. Scores of phones and computers were seized from the house and the vehicle hire garage. Operations at the haulage company were frozen until police had examined every vehicle travelling to continental Europe. Serious charges have not yet been laid against Dekker, his partner

Cynthia Petito, the overseer Bob Lyttle, aka Kegs, who is still
not out of danger from self-inflicted gunshot wounds, Gethin
Jones and Malcolm Roy Beanie, aka Milky. The delay reflects
the scale of the investigations. Five separate police forces are
involved, with hundreds of officers now interviewing victims,
collecting evidence of multiple crimes, including murder, rape
and other sexual abuse, people trafficking, slavery, false impris-
onment, and habitual and extreme violence. The spokesman
added that inquiries were at an early stage and over twenty
arrests had been made, including the owners of businesses that
used slave labour and paid the Dekker crime organisation. One
of those held was the Vietnamese proprietor of the Jasmine Nail
Bar in Northampton.

She clicks on the editorial leading the home page, which she
guesses Dan Halladay wrote.

Behind the mindboggling statistics of this story there is a land-
scape of suffering and tragedy that existed alongside us all – at the
end of our street and in the fields, farms, and workplaces we pass
every day – stories of isolation, despair, helplessness, separation
and the deliberate crushing of the individual spirit. The pain
inflicted by the organisation first exposed by Middle Kingdom
is incalculable.

She sits back and watches the fields of barley and yellow rape
slide by and thinks about clearing up the boat and returning it
to its original look, finding somewhere to hide where she can
work – she has an idea about that – and how to keep her lines
open to the founders of Middle Kingdom, essential if she is to
get those encrypted documents deciphered.

Near Milton Keynes, the screen of her phone lights up with

a call. 'This is Shazi. I've been trying you all afternoon. So's Abigail. Where are you?'

'On the train,' she murmurs to the window. 'I told Abigail I wouldn't be in for several days.'

'We need you here. We have a surprise.'

'Okay, I'll be there in twenty-five minutes.'

She walks from the station up Silbury Boulevard to Middle Kingdom's building and, as she nears, wonders if the staff have any idea of the surveillance immediately around the building. She spots six watchers in parked cars and at different points in the street, which means there are plenty more. At the reception, Arnold looks up from his puzzle magazine and says, 'A lot of them police out there, Slim. They even in the building yonder with cameras and suchlike.'

'Do they know upstairs?'

'I told them, but they know already.'

She arranges her face at the top of the stairs before going through the doors and hanging right to the newsroom, teeming with young journalists, evidently still surfing on the energy of the weekend. She sees a huddle of people around Abigail's desk: two women with their backs to her, one of whom is Annette Raines, and Shazi leaning in from the desk in front of Abigail's to catch what is being said. She seems excited, whereas Abigail is at her most solemn. She catches sight of Slim first and lifts her head so that Annette and the other woman turn. Slim understands in a flash what's happened. This is Gabriella Albescu, Andrei's sister, and she has visited her brother in hospital, probably with Annette, and he's improved enough for her to leave his bedside and travel from Peterborough to Milton Keynes. But how much has Andrei remembered of Saturday morning at

Manor Farm? What has he told his sister and the lawyer about his rescue? Have they relayed the full story to Abigail and Shazi and unwittingly compromised her? Judging by Shazi's expression, which is filled with the urge to tell, they know everything.

Gabriella hesitates, smiles and then is out of her seat and navigating her way through the desks towards Slim. She is well dressed, not expensively, but nicely turned out, with care taken over her make-up and hair. She looks older than her thirty-six years. Though Slim has only ever seen the emaciated wreck of her brother, he looks like he's from the rough end of Romanian society, while Gabriella plainly aspires to or has already entered a respectable middle-class existence. She reaches her and stands with her hands clasped, tears filling her eyes and head shaking in wonder and gratitude. She's pretty; strong eyebrows and very dark eyes. She comes closer and tentatively takes Slim's hands. 'You saved Andrei's life. He tells me everything.' She shakes her head in disbelief. 'You risked your life to give back my brother to me.' Her hands move to Slim's shoulders, and she wraps her in a hug and whispers into her hair, 'Thank you. Thank you. Thank you.' She squeezes Slim as if her own life depended on this stranger who has ended the torment of her brother's disappearance, then draws back to gaze at her, takes hold of her hands again, sniffs, and blinks rapidly to stop the tears and finally releases Slim to dab her eyes. 'Thank you.'

Annette has moved to their side. 'Come on, girl. I want a piece of this,' she says, drawing Slim into her magnificent gravitational field and giving her light hug. 'I knew you had rocket fuel in your veins, but that was a wild, wild thing you did out at the farm. Audacious, brave, and totally and utterly crazy.'

Slim releases her and Annette immediately catches her expression. 'Oh my God. You didn't tell them about everything you did. That's why Abigail is so pissed.' Her hands go to her mouth. 'What should we do?'

'Nothing.'

'And now you're in trouble?'

'I believe so,' she says, seeing Abigail having a word with Dan and Yoni, who has just drifted from the conference room where Skelpick has set up with his laptop.

Annette says, 'I'm so sorry. I should've called you.'

'Can't be helped,' says Slim.

'I think we should go.'

There are more hugs and thanks for Slim to endure before they leave, and Slim wonders if she can escape too, but she needs to face whatever music is waiting for her. The orchestra, in the shape of Abigail, Dan and Yoni, has moved to the conference room. Skelpick listens to Dan, leaning back in his chair with hands locked behind his head.

She is summoned. Dan points to a chair facing the newsroom and begins, 'I must ask you if you were at Manor Farm with Andrei. We heard rumours from police officers on the ground that a mysterious young woman got there before they arrived, released Andrei Botezatu and was herself nearly killed, and now Annette and Andrei's sister confirm everything that we had dismissed.'

Slim glances at Skelpick.

Dan persists, 'Were you there and did you act in the way that's being talked about?'

'Yes.'

'And you broke a man's leg with a pickaxe.'

'Yes. I knew I might need something to smash a lock. I didn't intend to use it as a weapon. But, yes, I did hit him with it. I'm glad I disabled him. He's a stone-cold killer.'

Dan shakes his head. 'I told you – didn't I? – that one more incident like the nail bar and you'd be out. I mean, we can't employ someone who behaves in this way. You must—'

'Milky – the man I hit – and Gethin were about to garrotte Andrei with picture wire. He'd have been thrown into the skip and burned in an incinerator with the others. What would you have had me do?'

Dan doesn't attempt to answer this.

Yoni has been stroking his beard and now lets his hand drop to the table. 'You saved a man's life, but you're like a . . . a . . . Hell's Angel, Slim. We're journalists. We don't do this kind of thing. That was an unbelievable level of violence.'

'I accept what you're saying,' she says and pushes her chair back to go.

'I'm not finished,' says Dan. 'Firstly, you deceived us and wrote a story which was dishonest in the many omissions you made.'

'What else could I do?'

'Tell the truth. But what I want to know now is how you persuaded the police to cover up your involvement.'

'I told them they could have all the credit for the intervention if they waited before charging those men. They intended to bring charges on Saturday evening, and you wouldn't have been able to publish anything.' This is all true, although, of course, the only reason she could make the deal was because she was a serving MI5 officer, and Nick Price took her seriously.

'And that was your idea?'

'I could see that the chief inspector was annoyed that I had got there before them, both at Manor Farm and the Jasmine Nail Bar. It seemed a good idea to defuse things by saying they could have all the credit. Also, how was I going to write this up for you? The site doesn't do first-person derring-do, and I sure as hell would have been embarrassed to write it.'

'How did you alert them?'

'I phoned and gave them precise details of what was going on at the farm, a map reference, and told them that I and Andrei were in extreme danger. They sent a police helicopter, which was already airborne, returning from an incident, and that's what saved us.'

Dan shakes his head. 'I wonder about your sanity. This is not the action of a person in their right mind. Why did you do it?'

'I told Skelpick that I knew Andrei wouldn't last the weekend. I was certain they'd clean up and that meant there was a chance they'd dispose of Andrei. That was my only motive.'

'By the way,' says Skelpick, turning to Yoni and Dan, 'I told her not to even think about going.'

'That's right,' says Slim, 'he did.'

'Well, she did go, and we have deceived our readers.'

'She didn't lie,' says Skelpick. 'Nothing in the story is untrue.'

Dan looks exasperated. 'Oh, come on! Don't be an idiot, JJ!'

Skelpick is unintimidated by his old friend. He leans forward, briefly kneading his back before both forearms come to rest on his thighs. 'I've got to say it. Andrei is alive because of Slim. He's been reunited with his sister. You saw her face not half an hour ago. It was a complete joy to behold. What a gift that is to those two people. There are a hundred and seventy plus individuals who stand blinking in the sunlight today and who may now get to see their loved ones again, because of Slim.'

'Frank Shap, too,' she murmurs.

'And our Vietnamese friends? Have you noticed something in the last forty-eight hours? They look totally different. They smile and stand tall and don't jump when someone approaches them. They've begun to live and to trust again. That's what I'm seeing, anyway.'

'I'm sorry, JJ, while I'm editor, this behaviour, whatever the circumstances and outcomes, is simply unacceptable.' He swivels on his chair to face her. 'Slim, we won't expect to see you in the office for three weeks. When we know how we stand with the Official Secrets Act investigation and the story of the Dekker gang has run its course, we'll see what, if anything, you might be able to do for Middle Kingdom. But I have to say that it's hard to see how we reconcile our differences on this issue.'

It seems like she's lined herself up for dismissal by both MI5 and the organisation that she's infiltrated on the same day, a feat probably never achieved before in the history of the Security Service. She moves her chair back and rises. Only Skelpick gives her a nod; the rest would rather look elsewhere. She could say a few things about the insufferable piety of Dan's position after she's done much for the site, for while listening to him, she noticed a whiteboard on the other side of the newsroom which records that Middle Kingdom has had 2.7 million hits in the last thirty-six hours; that social media activity has gained 25 million impressions; and the site has signed up 14,700 annual donor/subscribers. She's done them a turn, but what the hell! She always knew she was leaving, so no surprise there. Before too long, she'll need these people and their rare set of skills, so she looks pleasantly around the four of them. 'I was doing my best for you and those people. That's all.'

'You did,' says Yoni Ross, 'but Dan's right. We will talk about this and get back to you.'

PART THREE

CHAPTER 37

With one of the cheap phones she bought in London for the sole purpose of using Ballard's SIM card, she texts him on the number she finds in the SIM's contacts under the name Aurelius. *What now?* she writes and immediately receives the reply, *Keep the phone with this SIM switched off but check 3x a day. Stay hidden and use that material I gave you.*

She responds, *Will do, if I can do Mum and Matt's funerals at All Saints.*

She walks from Silbury to Midsummer Boulevard and then to the Milton Keynes Rose, an enclosed, circular space containing a hundred or so granite pillars, sixty of which are dedicated to special days in the calendar. She pauses by the pillar commemorating the day of the manufacture of the world's first teabag – oddly enough, in Bletchley village – and reads a second message from Ballard: *Fine will make arrangements with Vicar now.*

She moves towards the Light Pyramid at the end of the viewing point known as the Belvedere and stops just short of it to admire the panorama. The sun is setting behind her and the countryside is bathed in a gentle orange light. Half a mile away, to the north-east, a ribbon of mist traces the course of the

Grand Union Canal, the warm airflow from the south having met the cool, inert waters of the canal. She moves back a little and considers taking a photograph, as so many do, of the glacial twenty-foot white concrete spike. However, her action is designed to draw out whoever is following her, because for quite some time now she's been aware of something in her wake plucking at her subconscious. An incoming call makes her jump. It's from Helen Meiklejohn's number. She doesn't answer because she needs to concentrate, but there are few things she wants more than to speak to her. She slips behind the Pyramid and into a recess made by the join of two of the five steel wedges of the sculpture. Leaning against one, she replaces her shoes with the light trainers in her backpack. Her suit jacket is folded into a neat square and placed with her shoes in the pack. She tightens the pack's shoulder straps and hip belt and checks her phone for the pin dropped on the map that afternoon by Bantock to indicate *Spindle*'s new mooring. It's at a place called Blackhorse Wood, just before the canal veers north, away from Milton Keynes towards open countryside.

It shouldn't take her more than half an hour and there are several housing estates on her route where she can easily lose a tail. She moves forward in the shadow of the monument, drops down over the lip of the platform on to the grass and jogs down the slope. When she reaches level ground, she makes for some trees and looks back. Five people are on the path, two heading towards the Pyramid, three returning to the town centre. Nothing conclusive in their behaviour. She watches a few minutes longer but sees nothing. Whoever's out there is very good. A minute or two later, she moves off with an easy, flowing rhythm towards the housing estates and the thickening mist she saw from the Belvedere, which is now smothering the canal.

After some twenty minutes' running, she reaches Marsh Drive Bridge over the canal. She lingers on the bridge and looks up to see stars beginning to show through the fog. Four cars pass through the bridge's traffic lights from the city side; there are no pedestrians. She descends to the north-side towpath and, with the sensation of being swallowed up by the fog, gropes her way along the path to where she hopes there's a line of a half-dozen moorings.

She comes to a lone boat, a wide beam named *Talk on Water*, which she knows is owned by the Grand Union's very own pastor. She thinks it would be a lot easier if Bantock found her, or, better, he told Loup to come to her. She texts him and moments later, she hears the dog tearing along the path towards her, yelping with excitement. He reaches her and does such a frantic dance that his back half drops into the canal, which cools his ardour. She sees an orange light, one of Bantock's paraffin lanterns, being swung in the fog ahead of her. It feels like she's stumbled into a film of *Treasure Island*.

'You're a good man,' she calls out as she nears the light. 'Thank you for everything.'

'The least I could do,' he replies. 'But wait until you get here.'

She's only ten paces away when she sees a shadow move against *Spindle*'s cabin lights, then a voice calls out, 'Don't be cross, doll. I felt you needed me, so I came.'

It's Bridie. She hops on to the towpath, and gives her a brief hug, while explaining that Dougal rang to tell her about Diana's death. He mentioned Slim was on the canal in a boat named *Spindle* with Loup. She drove to Milton Keynes Marina and made enquiries but failed to locate the boat. She walked up and down the marina and happened on a man and a dog. She called out Loup's name. 'And guess what,' says Bridie, 'dopey old Loup gave the game away.'

'How long did she take to wear you down?' Slim demands of Bantock. He looks sheepish. Like many before him, he's helpless in the face of Bridie's beauty and brisk authority.

'Five minutes tops,' says Bridie. 'No one can resist. Come! We have drink, food and all our love to share.'

They all go aboard. A Bantock pie is being heated. There are baked beans and greens, cheese, and sourdough. Slim changes her shirt in front of them. 'Jesus, you've lost weight,' says Bridie.

'Great figure,' says Bantock with a frank look of appraisal.

'Fuck off,' says Slim. She sits down at the galley table, not entirely pleased about Bridie's visit, for she was intending to start work writing down everything she could recall about the Guest organisation. But Bridie glows with pleasure and keeps reaching across the table to touch her hands. 'You're not cross, are you, doll? Say you're not angry with me, Slim. Say it!'

'A little cross,' says Slim, measuring an inch between her finger and thumb, as Bantock pours wine into her tumbler.

'You've been a busy girl. The moment I read the story about the women in the nail bar, I knew it was my friend. I mean who else raids a nail bar in broad daylight? And then Mr Bantock was kind enough to confirm that it was you who broke open the slavery investigation and half of England's police forces are now struggling to catch up. I'm in awe, darling, but in truth I'm not surprised.'

Slim opens her hands at Bantock. 'You told her everything!'

He shrugs. 'She seemed to know and, besides, she doesn't take no for an answer.'

'She always *seems to know* but the rule with Bridie is that she knows fuck all and she's just pretending.'

They eat and then Bantock packs up the remainder of the pie and tells her he's moved *Regina* to around the bend, near the

Jehovah's Witnesses' hall. Slim gets up and kisses him on the cheek. 'I owe you money and all the gratitude in the world.'

'Tomorrow or the next day will be fine, but I'll take the gratitude now.' He hesitates. 'I wanted to mention that Abigail called me . . .'

'She called you! Amazing!'

'Wants to look at the boat, go on a trip, like.'

'You going to ask her?'

'Already have.'

'Wow! Fast work.'

'What a dish,' murmurs Bridie when they are alone. 'I mean Bantock not the pie. Have you done it with him?'

Slim shakes her head wearily.

'I would.'

'Join the queue! He's sleeping with women up and down the canal and now he's about to make off with another.'

'Too bad. Anyway, I'm saving myself for Dougal. I asked if I could go up for a few days. I feel like having a baby and it seems to me that Dougal would make lovely babies and he'd be a terrific, Viking warlord dad, don't you think?' She smiles. 'Oh, by the way, he told me that you two had a Memory Lane fuck a few weeks back, but that's fine with me.'

'What man ever keeps his mouth shut?'

'He was just being loyal to you, sweetie. Told me he loved you, but you were too much for him. Spitfire was the word he used.'

'Does he get a say about the baby idea?'

'Haven't broached the subject as yet. Only came up with the notion this morning. But it's genius, no? We'd be so good together.'

'But you're wedded to a rat. No man wants to live with a woman who has a rat on her shoulder.'

'Deceased.'

'The rat's dead? I'm so sorry.' She sees her friend's blank expression and shakes her head. 'And you've got to tell Dougal about the other little problem, Bridie.'

'Which is that?'

'You're a psycho.'

'I'll save that for later. But his sister Rose must've filled him in. You remember her. Never my greatest fan.'

'She *has* filled him in, but I did mention to him that you might be good together.'

'Has she? Bitch! I'll bury her with love. But thanks for planting the suggestion.' Her hands reach out across the table and settle on Slim's. 'Sorry, I've been babbling. You turned Matt's picture around when you came in. I didn't want to say anything while your friend was here. But why?'

'Deceased.'

Bridie's face registers horror.

'I can't talk about it. He was killed in Ireland at the beginning of March.' Slim shakes her head, horrified and speechless for a moment. 'They may have been looking for me,' she says eventually. 'That's all you need to know.' Her eyes come to rest on the dog. 'What am I bloody well going to do with Loup?'

'Give him to Bantock or pay him to take him.'

'My mother would kill me.'

'If someone else doesn't first.'

Slim doesn't react. She pours wine. 'Two men took photos of him in a pub. Then he disappeared. They hurt him but he didn't tell.'

'And they didn't find you, but they came near to it. What about the chick in the Eagle's Nest? Did she post anything?'

'I believe so.'

'I don't get it. Why haven't they pulled you out?'

'They have. The operation is done. And . . . well . . . things are going to happen at the site. That part I can't speak about.'

'Where's the support, the fit young men with guns conveying you to an Orkney hideaway? Where's the bleeding succour, honey?'

'I have some protection.'

'Bollocks you do. I found your boat in under two hours, and no one stopped me. This is all so bloody sketchy.' Slim can't remember seeing Bridie so angry. 'Tell me what's going on. I can help.'

'I doubt it.'

'What about Matthew?'

She shakes her head, but then says, 'He was clean. Got off heroin. Seems he was making a fist of his life. Doing well in advertising. He had a little boy. I have a photo. His name is Liam. I showed it to my mother before she died. That's all you need to know.' She stops. They are silent. Bridie reaches for Slim's hand but doesn't find it because it has been suddenly tucked into her armpit. 'Not really a psycho, are you?' says Slim. Bridie mouths no. 'Do you ever smoke?' Slim asks.

'Hardly ever. I don't carry cigarettes if that's what you mean – who does? But Mr Bantock left his tobacco and papers up on that shelf, and I do a mean rollie.'

'Let's get some air.'

Loup leads the ways to the stern deck and sniffs the night. Slim closes the hatch door behind them and leans against it to keep the heat in the cabin. She drinks, sipping at first but then quickly downing all the wine. Bridie rolls the tobacco, filter expertly held at the side of her mouth, drinks, then lights up and smokes, lolling over the tiller. They both look up into the night. The cigarette is passed between them. They say nothing. Slim's attention goes to Loup because he's trembling. 'You can't be cold already,' she says and strokes the top of his head with her fingertips. His gaze is aimed along the towpath; his hackles are up and he's emitting a steady growl. She peers down the towpath. There's something in the fog. She's seen it before and on two of those occasions it was always so still she imagined she was looking at a bush, yet both those times the shape resolved into the wisp of a man. This time it remains ambiguous, nothing more than a dense patch in the mist that might or might not settle into human form, and because the shadow is so still and the outline indefinite, she decides that maybe she is just imagining something. However, Loup is convinced, and Bridie spins round and stares into the fog, then glances back at Slim. 'What?' she whispers. 'What's out there?'

Slim chucks the cigarette away and says, 'Quick! Go to the bow, take the mallet, and loosen the mooring peg. Throw the rope on to the boat.' She bends to start the engine, jumps off, undoes the stern line, works to free the mooring peg with both hands, and steps back on to the boat, coiling the line. She lays the line across the tiller and jams the mooring peg into the back of her waistband. Bridie runs back to her and gives her the mallet. Before she can jump back on, Slim hisses, 'Take the boat hook from the roof then push the bow out. Don't get on.' When the bow is a few feet from the side of the canal, Slim lashes the tiller to keep *Spindle* aiming straight, engages the engine and leaps off. Loup follows.

Without a word, they merge into the dripping undergrowth and watch *Spindle* move slowly away from them. Slim is aware of damp blossom petals falling on her. She can't see Bridie's expression very well, so doesn't know how she's reacting, but she's

thankful she hasn't questioned any of this, which, on the face
of it, is lunacy. She takes hold of Loup by the collar and peers
down the towpath. There's no sign of the figure she saw, and
she again wonders if, with the help of the fog, her overwrought
mind conjured the shape of the man. Then they hear something
in the fog: three separate noises, a report of some sort, maybe
something being banged twice, then a muffled crump.

They wait. Slim's breathing has returned to normal, while
Bridie is so still and quiet, she can hardly believe that her friend
is just a couple of feet away.

They wait some more, listening to the trees dripping and
the sounds of the canal – water licking the sides, a coot calling
out, the complaint of ducks. Then they hear men's voices, rapid
exchanges in a foreign language. Slim can't make out which
language, but the rhythm and intonation certainly aren't English. A faint glow shows along the footpath. They're using the
light of phones and moving as quickly as the fog allows. Not
running but hurrying and not minding about the noise they
make. Slim lets Loup go and readies the mallet. Bridie moves a
little to her right. She hopes she's going to plunge into the dense
undergrowth behind them. The men jog to a stop a few feet
beyond where *Spindle*'s stern line had been pegged and consult.
It is a little lighter on the towpath, and she can see the contours
of each man and the paleness of their skin in the night.

Any hope she has that the men will move on in pursuit of
the boat vanishes when Loup springs forward snarling and
barking. There's nothing for it but to follow, and with three
rapid strides Slim has landed the mallet on the side of the head
of the man closest to her. He drops. She is aware of a whirling
shape to her right as Bridie assails the second man with the boat
hook, assisted by Loup, who has, she thinks, taken hold of the

man's leg. She beats him twice on either side of his face with the book hook, like a skilled martial arts fighter using a baton, then simply aims at the centre of his chest with the end and pushes him into the canal. Slim crouches and runs her hands over the gravel of the path where she finds the object she heard thud to the ground – a gun with a silencer.

'Jesus, where did you learn all that?' she calls out to Bridie.

'Same place as you, no doubt. The Cotton Studios dance class with Laurie Tapper.' She's breathing heavily, but her voice is exultant.

She kicks the man for good measure, but he's out cold.

'You don't work—'

'The other lot. Laurie does for both MI5 *and* SIS. Efficiencies!'

'You're in SIS!'

'Yes, but I'm here strictly as your friend. No spookery, just love. What shall we do with this idiot?' she says, looking down at the man who has struggled to the bank and is coughing out canal water.

'Get him out, take his gun and push him back in the water.'

'Ever the charitable one.'

They haul him out and lay him on the ground. Bridie pats him down. 'Goodness, that water stinks, or maybe it's our little Chechen buttercup. Aha! Very nasty!' She twirls a pistol fitted with a silencer above her head. 'Men like these don't deserve to leave the scene totally unharmed.' She places the gun at the back of his leg. 'Kneecap them or tie them up with rope and leave them for the authorities, which do we do?'

'Waste of a good bowline,' says Slim, looking up the canal and wondering where *Spindle* is. 'But don't shoot them. Maybe just shove this one back in the water. And we'll put the other one in, so he'll have to hold his friend up to keep him alive.'

'Good thinking.' Bridie lets off a silenced round, which fizzes in the water beside him.

'How do you know they're Chechen?' asks Slim.

'I'm a linguist, remember? They were speaking one of the Nakh languages of the northern Caucasus. Could be Ingush, in which case they may well be from Ingushetia, or possibly even Georgia. My bet is Chechnya, however.'

Slim is patting herself down for her phone and finds it in her left hip pocket. She calls Tudor Mills. No answer. Then texts him. She is searching for Salt's number when Mills calls back.

'Where are you? We're looking for the boat.'

'You're here!'

'Yeah, we were keeping track of you until we lost you in the park.'

'That was you!'

'We've got a man down. I'll stay on the bridge with him and wait for the ambulance. Police are coming. Are you okay?'

'Yep – we have two men in the canal. One needs an ambulance. We have their gun.'

Mills wheezes a chuckle that becomes a hacking cough.

'Your man, will he be okay?'

'They shot him in the leg. Flesh wound. He'll be fine. The police are coming. You stay there and shoot them if you have any problem. We're covered legally.'

He's coughing again but stays on the line to say, 'Where are you? Where's your boat?'

'It was moved by my friend. I'll send our location.'

She hangs up and messages the location. Then, having removed the second man's phone and wallet, they roll him into the canal. He's barely conscious and it is all his companion can do to keep his head above water. 'They would have killed us just like that,' says Slim clicking her fingers twice. 'So don't feel sorry for the bastards.' They stand back with the guns lowered. Loup patrols the bank growling.

'Who was that?' asks Bridie, taking her eyes off the floundering assassins.

'A colleague. He's on the bridge.'

'Yeah, I know. But the other person, the one you and Loup saw.'

She doesn't respond.

'Slim, I'm not an idiot. You and Loup saw something, and it wasn't these two because they were too far away.'

Slim turns. 'Did you see anyone, Bridie?'

'No.'

'Then there can't have been anyone there.'

Bridie chews this over in silence. Then she says, 'I know you saw something, and the interesting thing is you don't appear to be shocked.' A pause. 'Not shocked, nor even surprised. Why?' She waits for an answer. None comes. 'I get it. You saw it before.' A pause. 'Jesus, was it Matt?'

Slim waits, then replies wearily. 'This is private stuff, Bridie – my stuff. But I'll say this – yes, I've seen him before. Four times now and on every occasion these bastards have shown up.'

'Is it Matt?'

Again, she considers what she's going to say. 'Maybe a kind of distillation of Matt. That's the best I can do.' She shivers despite the fleece she put on when they went for a smoke.

'So, he's warned you before. Jeez . . . When?'

'A few times over the last six or seven weeks. Always near home. This is the first time away from the house.' She stops. 'If I'd admitted to myself that what I was seeing had something to do with Matt I'd be acknowledging that he was dead.'

'Brother and sister, both spooks,' says Bridie, and immediately puts her hand to her mouth in horror. 'Oh God, Slim, I'm so sorry. It just came out.'

Slim darts her a look of alarm. 'Is there something wrong with you, Bridie? I mean . . . '

'A bit spectrumy, or neurodiverse, as it is these days. That was a truly awful thing to say. Won't happen again. God, I'm an idiot. Sorry.'

After a moment, Slim turns and says, 'Actually, it was a good joke.'

'Thank you, honey. I feel ashamed. I wasn't being disrespectful. It's a miracle that he protects his little sister. Beautiful! I'm lost for words.'

'Never,' says Slim.

They hear a siren and see a blue flashing light come to a halt on the bridge and pulse weakly in the fog. There are voices on the towpath, feet pounding towards them. Two men appear out of the night. They are in ski masks, beanies and black clothing, and are carrying guns. 'I'm Ambrose and this is Andrews,' says the one who arrives first. 'So, what've we got here?'

'Two wet assassins,' says Slim. 'Who are you?'

'The Mills Irregulars,' he says crouching to look at the men in the canal. 'We help out occasionally. We'd better have them out of the water. Don't want these fellas catching their death of cold, do we now? Andrews, give me a hand here.' They take hold of the man that Slim hit with the mallet and haul him out and lay him on the ground. 'Looks bad to me,' says Ambrose. 'We'll need another ambulance. Andrews, call in for help and give the location.' Ambrose and Bridie lift the second assassin over the edge of the canal and drag him on to the path, where he rises on his hands and knees to cough the canal water out.

Andrews is on the call giving an assessment of what happened and details of the head injury, then he hands the phone to Slim. 'Mr Mills would like a word.'

Tudor says, 'I don't want you there when the police come. We'll handle things from now on. Make yourself scarce. I'll find the boat.'

'It's on the way to Birmingham, *Marie Celeste* style.'

'Can't have gone far. I'll see you in the next hour or so. Don't go to sleep. And do not speak of this. Understood?'

She hangs up without giving a response.

CHAPTER 38

Spindle has come to rest half a mile beyond Blackhorse Wood, having passed under a footbridge without damage. She is wedged between the stern of an unoccupied wide beam and the side of the canal. The stern line of the larger boat is stretched across her bow and caught on *Spindle*'s forward cleat. Slim jumps on board, puts the engine in neutral and loosens the wide beam's mooring line to free *Spindle*. They moor a few hundred metres to the north, where a breeze coming across the fields has dispersed most of the fog. Slim sends her location to Tudor. They slump in the cabin, exhausted, wordless. Bridie rolls another cigarette and sits on the steps up to the aft deck, puffing the smoke out of the cabin door, then Slim takes over and Bridie rolls again, and they both begin to feel better but also a little woozy, as though they'd used the weed that also lies in Bantock's bag of Manitou Gold.

The silence is broken by Bridie. 'You ever been in love, Slim? I mean proper, high altitude, zero gravity love.'

'That's a fantastically random question for this particular moment. Are you smashed?'

'This is a fantastically random situation.'

'No.'

'That's because you're an Amazon. Know about the Amazons, do you, Slimbo?'

'No.' She wishes that Bridie would shut up. 'But you're going to tell me.'

'We've got to wait for your colleague, right? So, we're going to talk about Amazons. The Victorians said the warrior women that roamed the Pontic Steppe were myth, but what did they know? The archaeological record – and this will interest you, Slim – proves they existed. Women, scarred and mortally wounded in battle were interred in some of the biggest burial mounds of the Steppe with their weapons, horses and a young man to keep them company in the afterlife. Nice touch, that!'

Slim groans and says, 'I'm going to need another drink.'

'I brought some, the bag on the floor over there.'

Slim opens the bottle and pours.

'This was all about three thousand years ago,' continues Bridie, 'not far from where those two thugs came from. Those women ruled and rode and fought and died like men. Herodotus, who is, as you know, the father of history, gathered stories about them during his travels. He says they could choose any mate they liked, but not until "they'd slain a man of the enemy". If that thug you hit with the mallet dies, you're free to fall in love.' Then she adds with a smirk, 'These days, I guess that's with a man or a woman.'

'You're a lunatic,' Slim says into her drink, then looks up. 'Don't destroy my friendship with Dougal. It's special. You can go to bed with him, but he's mine on the dig. Is that clear? No archaeology!'

'You mean that?'

'Yes, and if you're going to get pregnant, you've got to tell him. He has his life well set up and he needs to know that you're going to upend it.'

'Agreed.'

'Don't mess up his life, Bridie.'

'I won't. Promise.' She drinks. 'So, what the hell's going on, Slim? Who were those men with guns? Not the assassins but the Irregulars! What's that mean?'

'No more questions. Bridie, you're going to tell me about your work.'

'I'm in the Fabrics and Wallpaper Section,' Bridie says. 'In fact, it is fair to say, and boasting a little, that I *am* the Fabrics and Wallpaper section of SIS.' Then, after an eye-roll from Slim, she adds, more seriously, 'I'm the security officer for European embassies and sometimes beyond. I go in usually under cover as the clueless interior designer, swatches and a copy of *House and Garden* to hand, and check on things – general security, the personnel, the suppliers, the protocols of our people at the embassy, the little Russian weevils that get into the woodwork. I plug holes, look at communications breaches. With the help of your people, I catch the odd bogey like the security officer we nabbed the other day in Basel who was selling addresses and telephone numbers of embassy staff to the Russians. Right little cunt. British, too. And if you tell anyone any of this, I will have to kill you.'

'I should have guessed. My mother said that when I was being vetted, they wanted to know about you, too.'

Bridie raises her glass. 'Here's to your mum and Matt.' She drinks. 'And to my imminent window of fertility.'

Slim drinks but says nothing.

'I'm sorry about the joke. It was unforgivable.'

'You've got off the subject. Tell me more.'

'I literally can't. I have ambitions. I want to go all the way and I'm not going to make silly mistakes like telling state secrets to my best pal.' She rests her chin on her folded hands and levels her grey eyes to tranquillise Slim with her beauty. 'So, tell me what's going on?'

'I literally can't. It's way too complicated, moreover I'd have to kill *you* if I did.' Bridie nods acceptance.

Loup growls and jumps up. Slim goes to the cabin door and the dog bolts past her up the steps. She hears Tudor Mills telling him to shut it before he climbs on board and comes down into the cabin, wheezing. 'Hello, Miss Hansen. I didn't expect to find you here.'

Slim whips round. 'What the heck, Bridie!'

Bridie shrugs. 'Mr Mills came looking for you at Wye Street last year. That's all. I gave him coffee once when we were trying to work out where on earth you were. Isn't that right, Mr Mills?'

Tudor leans forward on the table with white knuckles. He's still wheezing. 'I need to talk to Slim alone. Could you give us a moment? One of my people is out there. You'll be quite safe.' Bridie exits with her glass, wrapping a thick cashmere scarf around her with one hand.

'Sit, Tudor. You look beat.' She reaches for a tumbler and pushes the bottle to him. He squints at the label and says, 'Lynch-Bages 2018! Have you any idea how much this goes for? A hundred and fifty minimum.'

She shrugs. 'Bridie brought it. I'm pretty sure she meant it for someone else.'

He waves the wine under his nose and drinks. 'Excellent.' He lowers the glass and shakes his head. 'Smart to send the boat off like that, but risky to attack them unarmed.'

'We had no option. The dog gave us away.'

'But to disarm those two killers like that, well . . .' He stops. 'You were very, very lucky.' He snorts a laugh. 'And they'll never get over it. We know who they are. Adam Gorgiev, thirty-eight, and Aleksandr Lyanox, forty-three. They're Tbilisi-based but originally from Ingushetia.' Slim mentally salutes Bridie's linguistic triangulation. 'Ex-military, no doubt. European arrest warrants out for them both under other names. Six kills we believe. Probably more.'

'Including Matthew?'

He looks down at the wine. 'Excluding your brother, but we are near certain they were his killers. The Irish authorities are checking all the imagery from the pub and Irish ports now. We know they were filmed at Heathrow and believe they returned one week later in a container from Rotterdam to Grimsby. They were watched by the Dutch port police, who lost them, then recorded a day later in Grimsby town centre. These two dangerous men were sent to kill you and, well, here you are, Slim, very much alive and kicking, and they are going away for a long, long time. It really looks as though you apprehended your brother's killers, but I'll confirm that as soon as I can.'

'Wish I'd shot them.'

'I'm glad you didn't. By the way, the police wanted to know if there was a second weapon.'

'In the canal,' she says although she can feel the handle of the silenced pistol under the cushion she's sitting on. 'So, where does this all leave me?'

'The threat is clearly over for the time being.'

'But Guest is swanning about London without a care in the world.'

'That's why you've been told to disappear, which, given your history, shouldn't be too difficult.' He winks at her. 'I've been told a communications channel has been set up and that you'll be contacted. That's all I know.'

'Come on, Tudor, something is going on. Really big. I mean this is all so abnormal and weird. For a start, who are the Mills Irregulars? Why not the police, or SAS, for Christ's sake? Why the private army?'

'They are Mr Halfknight's people, but they are known as the Mills Irregulars because I put them together and Mr Halfknight would not want his name attached to that kind of outfit, although it's entirely legal and above board.' He finishes the drink, shoves his hands in his pockets and gives her the dead-eyed look with his lips slightly parted, which, if Tudor is considering a dating app, is the expression he should avoid. 'But from now on, you are on your own. Even if I wanted to protect you unofficially, I can't because I'm having an operation at the end of the week, and I'm due to retire in September. So, that's me done.'

'Nothing serious, I hope.'

'Lung cancer. Small tumour. Size of a grape, they tell me.'

'I'm so sorry, Tudor. That's appalling.'

'Thanks, but I expect to live to grow roses. It was caught early.'

Slim shakes her head at the idea. 'Well, I'm very sorry.' She waits a less than respectful beat before saying, 'You can't tell me anything?'

'No, because I don't know anything. I'm basically the help. I fix things for Mr Halfknight. However, I do know that you are in this because you're tough and he knows you'll go the distance. That's why you were chosen.'

'To infiltrate a do-gooding website?' She feels herself doing a teenager's mime of incredulity and stops herself.

He grins and gets up. 'Even I can see that's not the job. Take your dog and get lost somewhere. Don't go ignoring your bloody phone like you did last time. And don't tell your beautiful friend anything. She's far too sharp for her own good.' He pauses to think. 'We're keeping you out of this, although the man you clobbered – Lyanox – is in a bad way. We do not think his companion Gogiev, however, will want to admit that they were whopped by two unarmed women half their size.' He laughs and turns to leave.

Slim jumps up and snatches at his sleeve. 'I need to thank you for everything. That picture of Liam was hugely important for my mother.' She gives him a peck on the cheek. 'And good luck under the knife.'

'No knife,' he says. 'They cut it out through a hole.'

She shudders.

He studies her with a smile. He has one foot on the first step and is searching for something on which to haul himself up. He says, 'You didn't like me at first, did you?'

'No, but I do now.'

'Thank you.' He seems relieved and looks down. 'I have one thought for you. It's just an opinion, of course but . . .'

'What is it?'

'Softball equals Linesman. They're the same operation. It stands to reason, if you think it through.'

'What makes you say that?'

He grimaces his worry about saying as much as he has and searches her face. She thinks he may add something, so she waits in silence but then he exhales, and she hears a rattle in his chest, and he mutters that it's just a hunch, but he's glad he's mentioned it because it's been on his mind and, hell, what's he got to lose now?

'Cheerio,' he says as he leaves.

'Good luck,' she says again.

'Keep it for yourself, Slim Parsons. You're going to need it.'

In the few minutes she is left alone while Bridie and Tudor talk on the towpath, she considers the Mills equation, Softball equals Linesman. Something like this has been in her mind for a few weeks, but never as stark as this, never as absolute, and it does stand to reason.

She rises before Bridie in the morning and takes Loup for a run through the crescent of lakes that surround the Great Ouse to the north of the city. At the furthest point from the boat, she switches on the Ballard phone and finds nothing. No texts, no emails, nothing. 'Two men killed my brother,' she mutters to herself, 'then come looking for me with silenced pistols, and Ballard can't be arsed to get in touch.' Again, she'll fight silence with silence. She has the other phones with her. She uses one to text kisses to Helen Meiklejohn, switches it off and returns it to the knapsack with the others, which she'll leave on charge on *Spindle* when she goes that afternoon.

On the boat, she peers into Bridie's cabin and sees she's still asleep. She puts the kettle on, spoons coffee grounds into the cafetière and goes on deck to loosen the lines and start the engine. By the time she's turned *Spindle* round, the kettle is whistling, and Bridie is complaining about a visit from Loup. A few minutes later she appears, wrapped in a sleeping bag, with coffee for them both and lands heavily on the bench, like the wan subject of a fashion shoot.

'Okay?' Slim asks.

She shrugs. 'Yep, have you got anything to eat?'

'Ryvita, butter, apples and blackened bananas. Maybe baked beans.'

Bride sniffs and doesn't move. 'What's the plan?'

'Going to lie low and plan my mum and Matt's funeral. Then I'll see.'

Bridie looks along the canal. It is not yet 8 a.m. A few joggers and cyclists are about, but no boats are moving yet. Everything looks pristine. Slim thinks of her mother inhaling the beauty of spring.

'That was really fucking frightening last night,' Bridie says and shivers. 'It didn't hit me until this morning. I'm not used to men coming to kill me with silenced pistols but you, Slim, you just let it wash over you.'

Slim slows the boat to allow a mallard with ducklings to cross the canal. 'I was as terrified as you were, believe me. I was shaking.'

'Yes, but you bury stuff and get on with it. The thing that happened to you on the plane, you just let it go and you don't obsess about it.'

Slim looks down at her and shrugs. She hasn't let it go. She thinks about it all the time, but doesn't say.

'Can I give you some advice?' says Bridie.

'People say that when they are going to give an opinion. If it's advice and not an opinion, sure.'

'This is advice. Don't bury the grief for your mother and Matt. Take it from me, it's the short way to madness.'

For several minutes they are silent, then Slim says, 'What was your boyfriend's name? You never told me.'

Bridie lets the sleeping bag fall away and lifts her sweater and shirt. Beneath her left breast is tattooed, *Gus Gustavo 1980-2019*. 'I hate tattoos, but he has no gravestone that I can visit so this is where he rests, buried in my heart.' She tucks in the shirt and pulls the sleeping bag around her shoulders.

Slim says, 'Gustavo, the famous war photographer. I had no idea.'

'The *photographer* – he didn't like the "war" prefix. He was a huge talent – best of his generation – and a tall glass of water, if ever there was one, and my deep, deep love. Will never love like that again because it's impossible. But I really could love our friend Dougal and give him the rest of me.'

'Let's see how that goes. Dougal will have his own view. He may seem big and cuddly, but he's no pushover. And he'll have that tattoo to contend with.' After an awkward silence, Slim says, 'I knew you were grieving.' She sees Bridie standing in her kitchen ashen-faced, frozen to the spot, a broken coffee pot on the floor. 'I should have reached out, done something, helped you.'

'You tried, dearest Slim. You tried.'

That same Saturday, Slim remembers them sitting in her garden, and Bridie quoting King Lear speaking over the body of Cordelia, as though she had only just understood the finality of it. '"No, no, no life? Why should a dog, a horse, a rat, have life and thou no breath at all? Thou'lt come no more. Never, never, never, never, never!"'

Bridie says, 'It's five years. Atomised by an RPG or something else. We don't know. Nothing left, except in my head and here.' She places a hand on her chest, then shakes her head violently to free herself of the emotion. 'Sorry. Get a grip, girl.' She takes two deep breaths and says, 'You want more coffee?'

'No, I'm fine.'

She gets up, slings an arm round Slim and kisses her. 'We did pretty good, didn't we?'

'We did,' she says.

★

Bridie leaves and, by the afternoon, Slim has cleaned and tidied the boat, returned it to its former appearance, packed the things she'll need, and paid Bantock generously, as well as dodged all his questions about the previous night's events, which he's only just hearing about on the canal message group.

'When shall I expect to see you?' he asks.

'I don't know but I'll need to check the phones. I may call you. By the way, you don't want to keep Loup permanently, do you?'

'No, he's your dog, and he knows it. I'm the entertainments officer, you're the owner.' Loup is looking worriedly from Bantock to her.

'Come on,' she says to him moving towards the pickup.

'What about the picture of your brother?'

'I'm leaving it with some other stuff and some phones on charge.'

'You want people to think you're there?'

'It's important you don't unplug them. They're out of sight. Leave them be if you move the boat. I'll call you when I have a new number.'

Hours later, having bought yet another phone, she heads north-west to the village of Fallow End and, as instructed by Delphy Buchanan, instead of parking in front of Top Farm Cottage, goes on fifty yards to a gated, overgrown track, which leads behind the barn that once served the long-defunct Top Farm. She goes to the back door with Loup and knocks loudly. Delphy has already spotted her through the window, and immediately wrenches open the door with remarkable force for someone about to enter her second century. She looks down at Loup and says, 'He seems nervous.'

'He has reason to be. As I explained on the phone, we're

hardly ideal guests. I just need somewhere I can keep my head down and work.'

Delphy looks up. 'Of course, my dear. Anything for you, Slim. And what do I have to fear at my age? Nothing! Besides, Frank will soon be returned from Liverpool, and nobody in their right mind wants to upset Frank.' Her eyes glitter. 'He telephoned to say that everything was fine, and he wants to marry Tam.'

'That's wonderful.'

'Life is extraordinary. If Frank hadn't thought he'd killed that man, he wouldn't have been out there in the woods when the accident happened, and he'd never have known of the existence of the love of his life. And Tam would, in all probability, be dead, and her mother and her sister would never have known what befell her. Makes you think, doesn't it?'

Delphy accompanies her across the old farmyard, where holes in the concrete are plugged with flowering shrubs and standard roses, to one of two converted cowsheds that were let out to ramblers when Delphy's partner, Margaret, was alive. Cow One, as the suite is called, has an unmistakable eighties imprint: floral curtains, matching skirts around the bed and dressing table, a wastebasket celebrating the Queen's Silver Jubilee of 1977, cord-pull switches that twang. But it is light and comfortable and is in direct line of sight with the broadband router in Delphy's kitchen. Having ensured that the gas water heater fires up, and the old Hobbs kettle is working, Delphy prepares to depart to hear the BBC six o'clock news. 'Come in whenever you feel hungry,' she says. 'I'll be glad of the company. But if you're too busy with your top-secret work, I will understand. We Bletchley girls are used to it.'

Slim removes the material from around the dressing table to

make room for her legs, puts the vanity mirror to one side and rubs the surface with her sleeve. All her writing will be done on a flash drive that she'll take out when she is away from the laptop or connected to the Internet. She opens the laptop and runs a program to seek out and destroy spyware, which she has on another flash drive that is disguised as a lighter. The computer is clean. She downloads a VPN – a virtual private network – that will hide her IP address and web.

She sits on the side of the bed, suddenly exhausted and depressed, and listens to the silence of the countryside around her, which is broken only by a blackbird singing from the rooftop across the yard. She swings her legs on to the bed, kicks off her trainers and shuts her eyes to plan the next few days. But the only thing she's aware of is the extraordinary beauty of the blackbird's song and soon she is asleep.

CHAPTER 39

This is how it is for several days: she sleeps and grieves, and gradually begins to recall everything she can from Operation Softball, which she writes down in a red A4 school exercise book. Each item contains the basic details of an enterprise – name, sector, rough date of purchase by Ivan Guest, estimated turnover, associated bank accounts and likely manner of money laundering. These entries are connected by dotted and unbroken lines that indicate shared directorships and countries of registration, most often the British Virgin Islands, Cyprus, Belize, or Luxembourg. The last was Guest's favourite since the European Court of Justice overturned EU anti money-laundering laws requiring beneficial owners of businesses to be identified. He owned plenty in Cyprus, too.

Much remains imprinted on her mind and, as she progresses, more comes back to her, like Guest's dependence on Mayfield-Turner – the financial outfit in Boston – as well as the law firms that silenced journalists and investigators with strategic lawsuits, the security outfits employed to spy on competitors and disrupt their operations, and the PR companies that burnished his reputation. Everything a sophisticated money launderer like Guest needs is found in London and after the invasion of Ukraine, when the Russian oligarchs were banned and sanctioned, he had the run of the place and the pick of services. At the time of Slim's escape in Skopje, his wealth was increasing exponentially and that was for one reason only: Guest was essentially an oligarch and the last one standing.

The work is hard but exhilarating. Around the middle of the afternoon, she takes herself on a cross-country run with Loup keeping pace beside her and never veering off, even when they disturb hares and muntjac deer. She runs for six or seven miles at a time, going through the lush, wet countryside, returning soaked from the rain, splattered in mud, with heart pounding and a clearer mind. A long bath follows. And each evening the blackbird performs from the same rooftop until all the birds around suddenly stop singing, as if someone had flipped a switch, and finally the blackbird calls it a day.

She eats with Delphy at eight, meals from a fifties menu – Welsh rarebit, bubble and squeak and bangers and mash, always with frozen peas – and listens to the old lady's stories. Slim says a little about her mother's addiction and death and Matt's disappearance and death but doesn't burden the old lady with too much tragedy. The most she says is, 'I never thought I'd see him again and now I can't believe I'll never see him again.' Delphy nods. She knows all about that finality, the one expressed by King Lear and quoted by Bridie.

After Slim has filled two dozen pages in the exercise book and drawn all the connections she can, she has the skeleton for a story that she sets about writing, reaching the five-thousand-word mark by Friday, fast even by Skelpick's standards. The sun is out and Loup, who has taken to lying by Delphy's Rayburn cooker when Slim is working, has wandered over to Cow One and is asking for exercise. Instead of a run, she walks a route around Fallow End, along hedgerows of may blossom and field margins brimming with cow parsley. At a far point from the village, sitting on the exposed roots of an ash tree, with her back against the tree trunk, she checks in with Bantock and gives him the passcodes to the phone sets on *Spindle*. He tells her there are six missed calls from Peter Salt, a text from Tudor Mills saying that he's been through his procedure and a message from Helen that she's free from Saturday midday.

She catches a troubled note in his voice. 'Something the matter?'

'I think the boat's been searched. You'd be better able to tell, but things feel like they've been moved.'

The gun, tablet, and sheets of encrypted text are all in the knapsack beside her, so she is unconcerned.

'Did you see anyone suspicious?'

'One of my mates saw a bloke in a fancy bike jacket and his friend. Said they were looking to buy a boat.'

'Yeah, I know them. Did you speak to Abigail?'

'We're taking things slowly, like.'

She thanks him and calls Tudor. 'Okay to speak? How're you feeling?'

He clears his throat. 'They had a slot in the schedule so called me in on Thursday. Feeling okay, considering.'

'Good. I won't trouble you now then.'

'Those two men killed your brother. No doubt about it. They're on the pub CCTV taking pictures of him, just as you suspected. Then, on March the second security-camera footage from outside a furniture store shows them forcing him into a car.'

Tudor keeps talking but she doesn't hear because she sees Matt being seized by the two thugs, the terror and bewilderment in his face. She feels sick, puts the phone on speaker and places it on top of the knapsack. Tudor is saying something about problems with the investigation. She focuses again. 'What do you mean?'

'Are you on a clean phone?'

'This the second call I've made on it.'

Tudor grunts. She hears him shifting in his hospital bed. He says very quietly, 'There may be official reluctance to connect Matt's murder to the target of Softball.'

'What about the gun? Is there a match?'

'Not with the one they've got, and they haven't retrieved the second weapon. Maybe they're not trying too hard. Maybe they just want rid of the problem. I don't know because I'm stuck in here.'

'Can you tell me what's going on, Tudor? Salt searched the boat—'

'Sorry, Slim. They've come to do all the checks on me. Got to go.' She hears a cheery hospital voice in the background. Tudor hangs up.

CHAPTER 40

Slim pushes her mother's 2018 BMW hatchback out of the garage at Steward's House and connects it to the pickup's battery with jump leads. It starts first time. She leaves the engine running and wanders off with Loup into the garden. On the ha-ha wall, roughly at the spot where she and Matt and their friends stood as someone called Gaia took a photograph, she answers the phone to the Reverend Joanna Wilbury, vicar of All Saints. Would it be convenient to speak now about the funeral, she asks? Slim sits by a large terracotta pot of dead geraniums, with one leg dangling over the ha-ha drop.

'Will you require burials?' asks the priest.

She hasn't even considered this. 'Can they be buried side by side?'

'Not a problem. Mother and child were buried together in days gone by because of the loss of both lives in childbirth.'

'Yes . . .' says Slim.

'And . . . religion?'

'My mother's family were Jewish but converted to Christianity a century ago.' She doesn't mention Catholicism.

The priest says, 'I've been told the first half of July, but I can

be flexible. You need to think of music, readings and eulogies.'
She stops. Her voice softens. 'I'm sorry that you've experienced
these losses in your life, Ms Parsons. It must be hard to bear.
You are in my prayers.'

This takes her off guard. 'It is. Thank you.'

'Right, I think we've covered the main points. I'll leave it
to you to be in touch when it's convenient. Now I'm going to
hand over to a friend who wants to speak to you. We'll talk
soon, I hope.'

She hears a man saying thank you and recognises Tom Ballard's voice.

'So, you have your funeral,' he says.

'Yes, I'm grateful. Thank you.'

'We now need you to get off the pot, Slim. Use what I gave
you and the item you took from the plane.'

She is silent.

'We know you've got it. The penny took a long time to drop,
but we realised the encryption Hagfish was using was changed
after you disappeared into the Balkans last year. That means
only one thing: he knew it was compromised, and even if you
couldn't read what was on the item you stole, he couldn't risk
it, and changed the cipher.'

'Why can't you get Cheltenham to do it?'

'Not possible. Things are delicate and we can't make requests
on this individual.' He stops. 'I need to go but I want to ask why
you were outside the Rock restaurant?'

'It's near the Farm Street choke point I use, so I decided to
see if you-know-who was at his usual table and guess what – he
was.'

'You weren't thinking of giving back the thing you stole
from him?'

She rises and begins to walk along the top of the ha-ha wall. 'Okay, so we're talking hypotheticals, Tom. Would I return this hypothetical item to the man whose thugs beat my mother and threw her down the stairs, who tortured and killed my brother, who came to kill me and a friend who happened to be visiting? And let's not forget the dozens of people who walk into their own mining machines, crack open their skulls in the shower, drown in their swimming pools and fall from their balconies. No, I'd rather choke on glass.'

'Good,' he says. 'Now get that material decrypted.'

'What's going on, Tom?'

'There's a crisis our end, a sort of putsch.'

'A putsch, by whom?'

'Our outfit is being taken over by Hagfish's people, inferior people, bad actors who, moreover, don't have a clue about our trade.'

'What are you doing about it?'

'Feet paddling beneath the surface, like the other gentleman – the tennis player.'

'Where's that leave me?'

'Performing what will be an important service to your country. We're in a very tight spot, Slim, and you may be the only one who can get us out of it. Good people, decent people are relying on you.' Then he suddenly says he's got to go and that he'll be in contact as soon as he can be.

The sun comes out and light plays across the barley. She remembers that weekend when Matt and she stood in this place without the smallest knowledge of the pain life can bring. She doesn't care a damn about the good people, the decent people, or the bloody country. Everything she does is for Matt.

★

The blackbird has begun its evening recital across the yard from Cow One, and somewhere beyond, possibly in the top of the lime tree that stands at the end of Delphy's garden, another bird is working through a medley of calls.

Helen says, 'That has to be a nightingale. It's so beautiful.' She lies with her head on Slim's stomach, following with the tip of her finger a line of infinitely small blond hairs that run up to Slim's navel. 'Song thrush,' says Slim, 'my favourite bird.'

'You're mine,' Helen says.

Slim lifts her head from the pillow and blows a kiss to her.

'What was all that about in town?'

'Nobody can know I'm here. I need to think of Delphy. When we go over to eat with her, you'll see that she's very old and frail. I don't want anything to happen to her.'

At first, Helen found Slim's precautions in Peterborough ridiculous, the BMW pulling up sharp outside the Greek restaurant, the door flung open, and Slim moving off to a car park behind the restaurant before Helen had managed to close it. Then they took a route that zig-zagged through the city and included a couple of stops when Slim slipped into a parking space without warning to watch the following traffic pass by. She'd scoffed and snorted a laugh but noticed Slim watching her mirrors with an expression she'd never seen before and fell silent and began to look nervous as they exited the city, taking a detour around the Flag Fen archaeological site, then tearing through the countryside towards Top Farm Cottage, thirty miles away.

'What are you?' she says now, searching Slim's face. 'No archaeologist and not even a journalist acts like they're in a movie. Why would anyone follow you and how would they know you'd be in Peterborough?'

Slim looks up to the beams of the former shed. 'The answer is a man named Andrei Botezatu who was rushed to your hospital a week ago – pneumonia, a broken arm and smashed-up ribs. He was in a very bad way. The ambulance crew thought his heart might give out.'

Helen nods. 'Yes, the man in the room with police protection. Lots of folk coming and going. So what?'

'Andrei is the main witness to the case we've been writing about at Middle Kingdom. I helped free him, and people may expect me to visit because he means a lot to me.' She stops. Is she going to tell Helen about Matt's murder and how Andrei somehow came to be a proxy for Matt? Absolutely not. Will she say what she was doing in Middle Kingdom and why Guest's men killed Matt then came after her? No. She smiles down at Helen. 'Can you say hi to Andrei for me? Tell him I'm thinking of him.'

'Of course. But who's watching you?'

'The police told me to keep my head down for a little while, that's why we had to go through all that palaver today.' Of course, she knows exactly who's she's avoiding – the incoming establishment at MI5, as well as Guest's people. And a new doubt has taken shape in her mind, which concerns the members of Dominic Dekker's organisation who are still out there. The police arrested just a handful of thugs – the likes of Gethin and Milky – yet the operation required brains to plan and run the trafficking network from Romania, connections across the globe to recruit a slave labour force, enforcers, and people to hide Dekker's money. There's no sign of that class of criminal in the updates that Middle Kingdom carries on the investigation. Where are they? Evidently, the police are concerned enough to place guards on Andrei's room. This isn't her major concern, but it's a credible explanation why she needs to hide.

Yet even this makes Helen jerk her head up from where it lay so happily and stare at Slim wide-eyed, then sit cross-legged with the duvet around her shoulders and pepper her with questions about Andrei's rescue and how much danger she faced when she helped free him. 'You don't understand,' she says when Slim bats away her concerns, 'I fell for you good and proper when I first clapped eyes on you in A&E, and I'm still falling, pet, hopelessly falling in love.'

Slim smiles at the pleading eyes. 'I'm not someone to love. You have no idea about my life, literally no idea!'

Helen pulls back. 'Because you won't tell me.'

'Because I can't.'

'Then what does that make me – the bit on the side who can't be admitted to your mysterious, secret life? And, by the way, I know you haven't told me half of what you're up to. I'm not a fool.'

Slim looks down at the hand with the spy ring resting on Helen's shoulder. 'I won't tell you because I care for you. You *cannot* love me. You simply must not lay love on me now. Believe me, one day you'll understand why.' They are silent. Helen stares at her with love, regret, panic, then love again filling her expression. Slim kisses her and whispers into her ear, 'I'm not using you and I mean you no harm, I promise. I just can't tell you everything. One day I will. And that is also a promise.'

Helen moves back to look her in the eye. 'You will?'

'I promise.' At that moment Slim believes herself, though a part of her remembers the scene with Melissa Bright in the cab, when the beautiful, gabby girl that Slim allowed to seduce her demanded her love, and now she wonders if she is being the ice-cold spy she was then. But Mel was different: Mel was essential to Softball's success. Helen has no part in this game.

She's as innocent as she is beautiful. Slim smiles and strokes her face again but gets no warmth in return.

'You know what?' Helen says with her forehead creasing. 'This is like being in bed with a man. It's like I'm being used and setting myself up for the lies and deceit of the future. I don't want that, pet. I really don't.'

'As I recall, you just used me quite a bit,' says Slim, which provokes a sly little smile from Helen, and they kiss.

They dined with Delphy that evening – roast chicken and new potatoes, and a sherry trifle from the cuisine of half a century before – and later they slept in each other's arms like old lovers, 'together in the dark, with the sweet warmth of a hip or a foot or a bare expanse of shoulder within reach'.

Next day, they walk into the countryside without Loup, who perhaps knows he will soon be returned to Bantok on the canal and has opted to stay with Delphy. Slim has an assignment from her to bring back a bunch of wild flowers; as many different species as they can find, so she can identify them in her book and tick them off in the margin. With Delphy, there's always a project on the go. They have a basket of food, and they picnic beneath the old ash tree at the side of a field where Slim makes her calls. They fall asleep in the grass in the sun. Slim is woken by Helen's finger tapping her ear. 'Look!' she whispers. The finger moves to point at the grass between their legs where two small creatures with chestnut coats and white bellies stand on their hind legs, heads moving from side to side in puzzlement. Another joins them and also begins to sway to and fro. An adult of about twice their size rounds Slim's foot, takes one look, and gives voice to a rapid call of alarm and her brood scatters. The new lovers look at each other, open-mouthed and eyes shining. 'What were they?' Helen whispers.

'Stoats or weasels. Weasels, I think.'

Helen looks up into the branches of the ash, and murmurs, 'Friends of yours, then.' Slim laughs and pinches her, and something drops into place with them.

CHAPTER 41

Slim is on a roll. No agonising, no groping for the right word and the reordering of passages come to her in a flash. She hardly needs to think, because while she was with Helen, her mind was working away at the story she'd left half done and having dropped her in Peterborough for her shift on Sunday evening, she raced back to complete the job. By Tuesday afternoon, she arrives at the concluding sentences. It's not about Guest's money-laundering operation, the web of companies, hidden bank accounts, the ill-gotten wealth, the violence and intimidation, or even murders and sexual predation, but his influence in British society.

'No individual of this level of criminality,' she writes, 'has held such sway in our country or mined so deep into the Establishment to corrupt and destroy everything and everyone he touches. But this isn't due to the evil genius of the man. We've let it happen. We handed Guest the keys to the Kingdom.'

She copies the article – now over ten thousand words – into several thumb drives, along with a summary in bullet points, and makes sure there's no trace of it on her laptop. She ensures that her search history is erased, then closes the laptop and puts it with the exercise book into the backpack. As she zips the pack, she spots Delphy weaving her way across the yard and rushes to the door to save her the journey.

'Slim, I need you to take the minutes of the Church Bells Restoration Committee,' she calls out. 'They're arriving now.'

There are eight middle-aged and older villagers, including Delphy, crowded into her sitting room. They are holding teacups and competing for walnut and coffee cake. Slim is introduced and made to repeat their names by Delphy, so she doesn't make mistakes while noting the proceedings. After an hour, Delphy says she has an announcement to make on the theft of money and flowers from her collection box, which is news to Slim. 'The man has been photographed twice by the Middle Kingdom website. At this moment they are identifying the culprit. I expect to have news by the end of the week.'

A retired accountant named Donald says, 'I don't want to rain on your parade, Delphy, but that website you're talking about will have a job publishing anything. The lot of them were arrested. And those illegal immigrants they've been sheltering have been rounded up, and a damned good thing too, if you ask me.'

'Nobody asked you,' Delphy says abruptly and brings the meeting to a close.

Slim goes to find out what happened. The raids on the homes of the founders of Middle Kingdom were coordinated for 6 a.m. that day. Taken into custody were Dan Halladay, Sara Kiln, Yoni Ross, and Toto Linna. The news broke at 4 p.m. when the Home Secretary, Anne-Marie Phillips – known as AMP – gave a press conference outside her Hertfordshire home. She said individuals responsible for the leaking of government secrets could all be charged under the Official Secrets Act, but that would be up to the police and Crown Prosecution Service. They were still making inquiries in what was a highly technical case.

Later, Slim watches the evening news with Delphy. The story of the arrests is the lead item, and the film of the Home Secretary's statement now includes a question from a female reporter who presses the minister on the connection between the arrests under the Official Secrets Act and the mass detention of people enslaved by the Dekker gang. Was the government penalising the victims of slavery as part of a campaign against Middle Kingdom? AMP's mask of affability slips. 'These individuals are on British soil illegally. We need to know how they got here. The British public will be concerned that they do not vanish into the wider community.' Then she thanks the reporters, turns to walk the length of an asphalt drive to a pair of doors framed by carriage lamps and potted bay trees.

'Her jacket's too short for her bottom,' Delphy remarks.

The bulletin does not leave it at that. There's a video from Milton Keynes of Abigail exiting the Heights Building to face a media scrum. Behind her Slim sees a crowd of a dozen people, among them Sofi, Callum and Mitch who reported the first waste story, plus Shazi and the security guard Arnold, who has put on his jacket and clip-on tie for the occasion.

Abigail, looking magnificent with her static-filled hair trembling in the evening breeze and her face bleached white by the camera lights, holds up a hand for quiet and reads a prepared statement. 'By their actions today, it's plain that the government wishes to shut down Middle Kingdom and neutralise those who hold them to account. Let me be clear that we will resist this attack on media freedom and the cynical assault on the rights of individuals that our organisation rescued from a slavery network. We are a small news site standing up to an oppressive regime that doesn't like scrutiny on the waste of taxpayers' money and its failure to deal with the epidemic of modern slavery and human trafficking.'

She looks into the camera and waits a second before saying. 'I have a message for the Home Secretary: we won't be bullied into silence on matters of public interest. We'll continue to publish the truth until every last one of us is arrested.' She glances round at the young faces behind her. 'For the truth is why we're here.' She stares out across the crowd and raises a finger. 'Not one fact, not one statistic in the hundreds of thousands of words we have published recently has been questioned by the government or its supporters in the media. That's all you need to know about the events of today.'

Slim texts Shazi to ask if the four have been charged. A reply comes five minutes later. *Let out tomorrow.*

No charges? Slim asks.

A shrug emoji comes back but that's all.

She must make her move now. It will take a lot of persuasion, as well as some uncomfortable admissions and, given Dan and Yoni's attitude when they last met, she doesn't hold out much hope. But this is her only chance, and she has a compelling story in her back pocket and a pretty good argument.

Some thirty hours later, at 6 a.m., a line of vans and pickups begins to form behind her. Half an hour later a man comes to raise the skirt barriers to Tender Wick Park. Slim drives to the far side, passes the concert hall, the pair of apple trees and the camp memorial, and pulls up near some disused buildings that carry an asbestos hazard notice. She opens the passenger door and sips coffee from a Thermos flask, watching her mirror for vehicles driving up the short ramp to the concert hall.

At 7.30 a.m. she hears a motorbike and sees Skelpick. Instead of driving into the building, he pulls the bike back on its stand at the bottom of the ramp and walks to sit on the edge of the concrete a little way up. She watches him through the binoculars. He grimaces, fumbles for a hip flask and takes a hit, then lights a cigarette and stares up at the rooks spilling from the tops of two beech trees. He massages his hip and right buttock then his head goes down. When he looks up, she sees the pain in his expression. 'You never let on, do you?' she murmurs.

He's there for another ten minutes before the arrival, in quick succession, of two cars she doesn't recognise. He clambers to his feet and gives them a jaunty wave. The door rolls up, both cars enter and Skelpick follows. She gets out and chucks the coffee into the grass, then hooks her knapsack over one shoulder and runs to the ramp, which she takes at a sprint because the door is coming down. She just makes it, scrambles under and almost bumps into Skelpick, who is wiping down his helmet visor.

'Why am I not surprised to see you, Slim? And, yes, what the hell are you doing here?'

'Come to give you some information. Who's here?'

'Everyone, but I do not guarantee a warm welcome.' There's a glass door between the parking bay and the main workspace. Dan has already spotted her and put up his hand to silence the others. Skelpick ushers her through the door. Dan, Yoni, Abigail and Toto are standing in the middle of the space. Sara Kiln is at a laptop; she turns and puts her glasses on top of her head. 'Oh shit,' she says quietly.

Slim wasn't looking forward to this moment, but she smiles and says, 'I come bearing gifts.'

'I very much doubt that,' says Dan. 'Why are you here?'

'I've got some important things to say to you. Before I risk ten years in jail, I need some assurance that this place is clean and that you check it every day for listening devices and cameras and you've sanitised all the computers you use.'

Toto, apparently unfazed by her appearance, says, 'It's totally safe, Snowdrop. People here all the time. We run checks.'

'That's hardly the point,' says Dan testily.

Slim takes no notice. 'I pray you're right, Toto,' she says and pulls off her bracelet, revolves the middle section and jerks it apart to reveal a USB connector. She lobs it over to Toto, who catches it. 'On that you will find a version of a sophisticated program called Thalli. That version is a year old, but, essentially, it's the same thing as they may be using against you.'

Toto doesn't immediately plug it into one of the computers because he's not that stupid. Instead, he hands it to Dan who gives it to Yoni.

'On that drive is also my account of an operation called Softball, which I will come to in a moment.'

'Hold on,' says Dan. 'What the hell are you doing here?'

'I've come to make you an offer.'

Yoni says, 'I think what Dan is saying is – how did you know about this place?'

'I followed you a few weeks back.'

'Well, you can leave right now,' says Dan.

Yoni strokes his beard and looks worried. 'We maybe need to discuss this as a group before we chuck her out.' His eyes come to rest on her as if he is seeing her for the first time. 'We have no idea who you are.'

'Oh, you surely do. I thought that was clear from the start. You always suspected me, right? All the stories about bumblebees and stolen flowers you sent me on. Using Shazi to get me out of the building at a critical moment.' She waits a couple of beats. 'I'm a serving member of the Security Service, better known as MI5. I'm an undercover specialist – deep cover, over long periods, is what I do. I've signed the Official Secrets Act, so please understand how much I'm risking coming here.' She takes in the horrified expressions and continues, 'It's fair to say that my whole life depends on how this meeting goes, so why don't I go and sit on Skelpick's motorbike and give you time to consider.'

She's there for over half an hour, then Abigail opens the door, waves her in and moves to the centre of the space where she folds her arms. The others stand or sit facing her near Sara's desk. Toto is reading at a laptop with Callum, who's appeared from nowhere and is now running his hands through his hair excitedly.

She is only now noticing how large the concert hall is – it's bigger than the roughly eighty-five-metre length she estimated on her first visit – and, also, the equipment. Ten tower servers, more screens than she can count, a mass of wiring, chunky, low-voltage cables bringing electricity into the building and everywhere there's a high level of finish and comfort. It's like the research lab at a university. Plainly, this is Yoni and Sara's domain. At the far end, where the Polish residents of the camp used to enter for their concert parties, there's a door with an 'inclusive toilet' sign, and beyond this a frosted-glass screen, behind which she guesses may be accommodation and even a kitchen.

'We've voted to listen to what you've got to say,' Dan says. 'A few of us think this is a trap, but Skelpick, Yoni, Toto and Sara want to hear you out. We make no commitment to you, and we will be recording what you say, in case we need it.'

'I'd rather you didn't,' she says.

'You don't have a choice.' They push chairs into a circle near Sara's workstation. There are eight in all, which means Callum is going to join them. She has previously taken him for a promising but shy young writer, but he's obviously much more to the organisation. Dan pushes a Perspex side table towards her and places his phone on it. The display is already jumping to every sound.

She is about to start the speech she's been rehearsing since her runs through the sodden countryside, but Toto calls them over to his laptop and she's left sitting there. They're not looking at Thalli, for there's nothing to see. That means Toto and Callum were reading the story she wrote and what they've found seems to astonish them. Callum is walking round, and Toto has pushed back the chair and is gesticulating, though she can't hear what he's saying. Eventually, Yoni breaks away. 'We're all going to take time to read this. The coffee machine is over there.'

She uses one of the compostable coffee pods and takes a crumble cookie from a tin. After forty-five minutes, they go into a huddle at the furthest end of the room and appear to take another vote. An hour has passed when they resume their places and Toto and Callum come to sit on the chairs closest to hers.

'You want me to continue?' she asks.

Dan nods.

'What you've read is all that I can remember of Ivan Guest's money-laundering operations and his penetration of the political establishment, the lawyers he used, the private intelligence firms, the politicians, civil servants and, in some cases, I am guessing, intelligence officers, who were caught up, bent out of shape, and corrupted by Guest. I've got a pretty good memory, but seven months have passed since I was undercover with his organisation, so some of it may be incorrect. Softball was a well-planned, successful operation. You need to understand that it wasn't just me and my handler who saw the product, which was a complete map of Guest's operation in Britain and abroad. Apart from colleagues in my outfit, JEF – the Joint Economic and Financial Intelligence Unit, which is part of MI5 – senior figures in my own service and MI6 knew and GCHQ, also. We shared information with the other intelligence agencies, the National Crime Agency, its Kleptocracy Unit, and the Inland Revenue. So, a lot of people out there were in receipt of our product, and they knew exactly what Guest was about. If you have any interest in this story and need confirmation, the NCA and the officers in its Kleptocracy Unit are your best bet. I didn't have a lot to do with them, but over the two years we had a few meetings. They are reliable people, and they'll be really pissed off about the way Softball was shut down and the product archived or erased.' She pauses. The atmosphere has changed. They are taking her seriously. 'I have given you a lot in this story but what I cannot do is name fellow intelligence officers and I never will,' she adds. 'That's not why I'm here.'

'Why are you here?' asks Yoni Ross, doing something with his mouth and nose as if he's trying to avoid sneezing.

'Because I know Ivan Guest like no other law enforcement officer, spy or journalist. He's as bad as they get. Think apex predator. Truly evil. And you people may be the only ones who can stop him. Can I continue?'

'How long is this going to be?' ask Abigail frostily. 'We've a lot of get through.'

'I understand the pressures you're all under,' Slim says evenly. 'I'll be as brief as I can. I'm just going to tell you my story which will give you context. It's not for publication. And I really need to have your guarantee on that now.' She looks round.

Yoni exchanges looks with Dan and says, 'I need an idea about what you're going to say before I commit to that undertaking.'

'I will explain what led me to leave Softball and why I agreed to be part of Linesman – the operation to infiltrate Middle Kingdom.'

Dan explodes. 'I still can't believe I'm hearing this. How you've got the nerve to come in here and confess to your part in an operation to undermine the free media beats me. What you've done is unconscionable.'

She takes a moment before responding to this. 'You know, Dan, I have a lot of respect for you and everyone who works at Middle Kingdom, I really do. I'm truly impressed. But for God's sake, get real. You've taken on the government. You knew they would fight back with everything they had.'

He rises then sits down again with hands gripping the arms of his chair. 'I'm not going to be lectured to by someone who has such obvious contempt for democratic conventions and everything we stand for.'

'I don't have contempt for them. That's why I'm here.'

'Okay,' says Yoni, 'that's enough. Dan, my friend, I want to hear what Slim has to say. Can we do that?' Dan nods reluctantly. 'So, Slim, you have our guarantee that we won't use anything we hear from now on.'

'I'm not happy about that,' says Abigail. 'Four of us are facing jail. We can't constrain ourselves by giving guarantees to a member of the Security Service, right? We should be free to use whatever we can. I won't go along with anything that limits our choices.'

Slim puts up her hands. 'All right, all right! Forget the guarantee. Please understand that this is already extraordinarily dangerous for me, so, I'll go all in. No guarantees. But some of it is incredibly painful, so I hope you can respect those things.'

She looks around the group. They all nod, though only two, Yoni and Skelpick, look her in the eye.

She's already said she won't identify colleagues and she's decided to omit anything about her training for the role of Sally Latimer, building her identity or the tradecraft that became second nature in the two years with Guest. So, she starts with her life as the lowest member of a team in the investment section of Guest's operation and explains that working for Guest was like being part of a mini state, where the man had absolute control and everyone was monitored by CCTV and their email, company phones and Internet usage were subject to surveillance. At close quarters, she saw the true nature of the man, his appalling racism, abuse of his staff (often sexual), his paranoia about sexually transmitted diseases and virtually everything else; his lies, the theft of people's assets, his manipulation of everyone with whom he had contact and his baseness in all things. 'My focus was on the money laundering and doing my job as well as I could.'

'Like with us,' says Skelpick. 'You did the job well. We all agree about that.'

'Except I wasn't faking it with you. I loved the journalism, and I told my people almost nothing about you. You can believe that or not – I don't mind either way. But in a role like mine with Guest, you're doing two jobs that are opposed to each other, and this was tough because Guest ran an operation in which no one could think for themselves or had time for their own lives. It was like a cult. People had to demonstrate their total belief in him, and I did that to survive and succeed. You fake it so much that it becomes kind of real, and that is when you start making mistakes, because you forget that every atom of the man is pure evil.'

She talks about the journey to Turkey, the attempted rape, forcing the plane to land in Northern Macedonia, her flight through Europe and eventual return to the UK, the half-hearted debriefing and counselling, and her winter on the Fens. Then she comes to Matt and the deal she did to find him, and there are moments when the words refuse to come. But she gets through it all – Matt's torture and murder, the terror on the canal and the identification of the two men who came to kill her as being the same ones who accosted her brother in a Dublin pub.

Then she has something extraordinary to tell them, a connection of which only MI5 has lately become aware and which she still finds hard to believe. Dominic Dekker, who did business in the east using his mother's maiden name of Davidyan, was at one time called Guest and is Ivan Guest's estranged older brother. 'It's true,' she says. 'There seemed something familiar about his photographs and a colleague confirmed that their mother was called Davidyan. But short of a DNA test, I have no proof.'

They are silent when she reaches the end. Yoni gets up and cracks his knuckles. He looks at Dan but gets no reaction; no one else wants to talk. Toto and Callum stare at the ceiling. Sara strokes her chin and Abigail remains with her eyes fixed on the floor. Eventually Skelpick leans forward, kneading his right hip. 'That's one hell of tale, Slim. But what are we meant to do with it? Nothing can be independently verified.' He opens his hands. 'I don't know what others think, but this doesn't work for me, even if I tend to believe you. And the stuff about Dekker is, well, incredible.'

'Well, he certainly reacted as if it was true when I yelled at him that I knew they were brothers. Anyone else got anything to say?'

'If this all happened,' says Yoni, 'I am profoundly sorry for you and somewhat in awe, but I agree with JJ. It doesn't help us. We are in a bind right now, and we don't need to give them more rope to hang us with.'

'And the fact remains that you spied on us,' Abigail says. 'You lied to us when we interviewed you. Dan asked whether you were a plant and you replied with a categoric no. Why should we believe anything you tell us now?'

'Because you need me.' She glances at all the equipment in the old concert hall. 'You're not normal journalists, are you? I mean look at this stuff. I've never seen anything like it, even in MI5 headquarters. Maybe GCHQ on a training visit. You have massive computing power here but also massive hacking power, right? And my guess is that you've worked up some AI entity that can reach right inside government and grab what you need. That's what the descendants of Bletchley Park's heroes have been doing – hacking the government with AI.' By Yoni's face, she knows she's scored a bullseye. 'The cute little site in Milton Keynes with all those eager young trainees beavering away is just a front for the real operation. I don't blame you. In fact, I applaud what you're doing. But please don't come to me with your pieties. I lied. That's my job. But are your methods any more honourable? You deceive and steal information because that's what you need to do right now.'

Dan is on his feet. 'How dare you equate what we're doing to hold politicians to account with your role as a government spy. There's no equivalence whatsoever.'

'Look, I'm on your side. I didn't tell them about this place or my suspicion about how you got into government systems.

In fact, I barely told them anything the whole time I was with you.'

Flushed with anger, he looks down at his colleagues. 'I don't believe you but even if I did, that's hardly the point. What you did was contemptible. The worst kind of betrayal.'

Yoni reaches out and touches him on the arm and asks him to sit down. He presses his glasses home and speaks. 'You have it all wrong, Slim. We're here for the journalism. We're building a model at Middle Kingdom to show young people how to do journalism to the highest standard. And we're doing something else, too. We're giving people . . .' His hands whir in the air as he searches for the right word. 'Faith. The confidence to believe that we bring them the truth without fear or favour. That's it. That's why Sara and I have put so much of our money into this project. For us, journalism is not a dirty word. It's the key component of a proper democratic system. And that is what you came to undermine and destroy.'

It was always going to be tough, but this is more uncomfortable than she'd imagined because, naturally, she agrees with a lot of what he's saying, and even though the spy part of her registers that Sara Kiln is Yoni's co-investor, she feels dreadful. She did it to find Matt but there's no mitigation that will work for these people, so she'd better concentrate on what she came for.

She yanks the knapsack from beneath her chair, puts it on her lap and withdraws the package wrapped in the heavy-duty polythene sheet that kept it dry all winter beneath her car battery. 'This is what killed my brother, or to be more accurate, why Ivan Guest killed my brother. It is the encrypted tablet that I took from the concealed compartment on his plane. I believe it contains information that is highly damaging to Guest and many people in public life. This thing is why my mother was thrown down the stairs, why they tracked down and killed my brother and why they tried to kill me. It's why MI5's watchers surround Middle Kingdom and why they're looking for me and search my boat at regular intervals. I believe everyone has concluded that thing is better destroyed.'

Toto, who is nearest to her, reaches out. 'Can I have a look at that, Slim?'

She moves back a little. 'If we can all find a way of working together, yes.'

'As far as I'm concerned, you can keep it,' says Dan, getting up and motioning to end the meeting. 'It has nothing to do with us and it looks very much like you're handling stolen property, so we couldn't even if we wanted to. I guess we have nothing more to say.'

Slim smiles. 'Don't make up your mind just yet.' From the knapsack's side pocket, she removes the printouts of intercepts that she photographed in All Saints Church and hands them to Toto. 'Have a look at these. They're encrypted communications from a firm called Mayfield-Turner in Boston used by Ivan Guest. He's their most important client.'

Toto shuffles through them and shows the top one to Callum. Dan, Yoni, Abigail and Sara don't react to her, but Skelpick is looking amused and interested. He asks, 'Why did you take the tablet?'

'I'd seen him using it. He told me it was important and that it was protected by a suicide program. I knew I'd never work for him again so I took everything I could.'

'But if it was protected with an anti-tamper programme, why's he concerned about getting it back?'

'Suicide programs can be disabled,' Toto says.

'But that's beyond you, Slim,' persists Skelpick, 'So why'd you keep it?'

'What happened on that plane threw me. I wasn't thinking straight. I kept it as a kind of insurance because I knew my own people would be angry and possibly fire me. I wanted a bargaining chip. I forgot about it, then it became too late to admit that I had it.'

'It doesn't make sense that you would withhold it from analysis by MI5, then just forget about it. I don't buy it.' Now Dan and Abigail are nodding and looking at her for a reaction.

'That's the way it was.'

Sara rocks in her chair. 'You're saying you were traumatised by what happened on the plane, which, if that's all true, I understand. But it's hard to believe this of someone with your training and experience.' This is the first time Sara has ever addressed her without looking at her screen at the same time. Slim is struck by the high intelligence in her eyes.

'I've never regretted anything in my life more. I'd done two years of Softball. It takes a toll, but that's not the reason. I thought I was going to be screwed by my people and I wanted something in reserve. If I'm right, this device is good for both of us.'

'But possession of the tablet could still get us killed,' says Dan. 'Why would we accept something like that from you of all people?'

'Because we're in the same fight and whatever you may think I do support a free media and I want to help you. I'll give you forty-eight hours to look at the encryption and then we'll see.' There's nothing more to say and, besides, she has had quite enough of Dan's hostility. She gets up and turns to Toto. 'Check your systems for Thalli.'

Outside, she pauses, takes in a couple of deep breaths and heads for the car. On the way, she spots Piotr rearranging the plastic flowers and multiple Virgin Marys on the memorial to General Anders. She calls out good morning, but he has head-phones on and doesn't turn as she passes.

CHAPTER 42

'A person is never more trouble than when they're dead,' her mother had murmured as she was going through everything Slim would need to do following her death. Turns out she was right, but the list of tasks gives her something to occupy herself with while Middle Kingdom consider her proposal.

The date of the funeral is set. She needs to tell people, but should the email take the form of an invitation? She has no idea, so a plain notification will have to do and, besides, she has no wish to explain why mother and son are being buried together in a place so off the beaten track that it doesn't seem to have a postcode and she needs to attach a map. She asks Dougal to book the Turk's Head for a wake, it being the kind of out-of-the-way village boozer her mother would have loved. She contacts her mother's lover Sally Kershaw to see if she will do a reading, and talks to Norah Kinneal who, though clean and functioning, is a prevaricator. It falls to Slim to make all the arrangements.

The last few calls are made on the road to All Saints Church where she is to meet Percy Simms, the only gravedigger acceptable to the parish because no machinery is allowed in the churchyard. Simms and his son Abel will dig by hand the two graves for £750, which seems on the high side, but is she going to haggle over Diana and Matt's graves? They agree on a spot where the path runs down to a lime tree on the stream and, with a knobbly hand resting on a headstone, Simms senior tells her people from the 13th and 14th centuries are buried hereabouts. Maybe Black Death victims too, if there were folk still alive to bury them, he adds as though he'd been there. He is settling in for a long reminiscence about his life as a boy in the nearby village, but she's saved by a text and makes her excuses. The text reads: *Meet under the bridge in picnic land 6.30 a.m. tomorrow. Loup X.* She doesn't recognise the number but knows only Bantock would sign with 'Loup'.

Slim parks a couple of miles from the bridge near where they moored to meet her mother and Helen, and jogs to a spot close by to watch the towpath and bridge through binoculars. As the rendezvous time approaches, she moves along the towpath from the north until she reaches the point where the canal narrows to pass under the bridge. Bantock has timed it perfectly. A quarter of an hour later, at exactly 6.25 a.m., she spots *Regina* coming from the south, cutting through the glassy waters with Loup standing on the bow. She waits under the arch, with the morning light bouncing from the canal to ripple on the old brickwork above her. When *Regina*'s bow reaches the shadow of the bridge, she jumps on to the forward deck.

'Get below,' Bantock yells. 'They've got a drone above us.'

Before the bow emerges into the light, she scrambles through the doors, followed by Loup, and is unsurprised to see Abigail sitting at the tiny galley table.

'Hi, good that you made it,' she says. 'Coffee?'

'I'd kill for it,' she says, pushing Loup away.

Abigail empties the pot into three mugs and hands one up to Bantock, then one to Slim. 'We've decided to go ahead with your proposal. Sara, Toto and Callum have got something interesting from the sheets you gave them.'

'What?'

'Let's say, we think it's definitely worth pursuing.'

'But you're not going to tell me what it is.'

'We'd like to look at the tablet. Then we'll talk. Do you have it with you?'

'No, but I can get it to you.'

'It's not going to be easy. We don't want to lead them to Tender Wick, so you'll have to bring it to the office as soon as you can. There's a lot of surveillance to contend with.'

Slim says, 'Don't think you can do this story without my help. There's a ton of information that I didn't put into the piece. You could make some bad mistakes without me. I should be on the inside, working with you and Skelpick, or there's no deal.'

'They think you're playing us, so we're going to move cautiously. And you can't hope to choose the writer, not from your position as a serving officer in MI5.'

'I'll resign by the end of the day if that helps. I've already written the email. If you've decoded those sheets and find the same encryption on the tablet, you can make up your minds immediately. I'll give you six hours after I've passed it to you. After that I'll revert to Plan B.'

'Which is?'

'My business. As soon as you have extracted everything you can from the tablet, I want it returned in the same condition. And you'll need to find a way of charging it.'

'When will you bring it?'

'This afternoon. Tell Shazi to expect a call. Then you've got until this evening.'

'It will be Dan's decision, and I've got to tell you that he's fiercely against having anything further to do with you.'

'Yeah . . . but I'm assuming it will be a yes.' She shouts up to Bantock, 'When's the next bridge?'

'A mile or two yet.'

Slim pours herself a glass of water and they go over her plan for transferring the tablet. When they reach the bridge, she jumps off at the last moment leaving Loup on *Regina* and watches it go. Abigail joins Bantock at the tiller and he drops an arm round her shoulder. Slim waits several minutes, scanning the sky above the canal but sees no drone. Maybe it's there, maybe it isn't, but she's going to stay hidden until *Regina* has disappeared from sight.

That afternoon, she parks at Milton Keynes Station and takes a bus that climbs Silbury Boulevard to the shopping mall. The police presence is much less than it was around Middle Kingdom – just a few uniformed officers – but the surveillance of the building by MI5 is still in place and the watchers aren't bothering to be discreet.

She finds a gift store in the mall, buys wrapping paper, adhesive tape, a card and ribbon, and goes to Milton Keynes Theatre at the far end of the complex, where there are several restaurants, one of which is Shazi's favourite, Pete's Pizza Parlour. She chooses a table and removes the tablet from inside her jacket, wraps it and secures it with ribbon and the best bow she can manage. Then she places the package in the clear plastic bag.

It is now 2.30 p.m. and the restaurant is past its busiest hour. She observes two men who have moved from waiting at table to the delivery side of the business. One is taking orders on the phone and bagging up takeaways, the other is loading the six-wheeled delivery robots which periodically appear at a side door. The name tag tells her that he is called Ronan. He's a friendly type but does his job with less speed than Ned, who served her and is now dealing with phone and online orders.

She calls Shazi and tells her to order two pizzas. They must be Pepperoni Feast and Margherita with extra cheese, plus two salad boxes and two bottles of Diet Coke. 'Have you got that? Now make the order in the app.'

In under a minute, the order comes in, and Ned is shouting it through to the chefs. Slim pays for her own meal, then moves to the table nearest dispatch. Based on her observation, it should take around twelve minutes to complete the order, but it's ready in less than eight. She passes through a stiff plastic curtain that serves as a draft excluder. Ned is on the phone and Ronan is checking the boxes and the drinks. He moves forward to open the lid of the robot, waiting with a strip of LEDs pulsing from orange to blue, places the salad boxes and drinks in the front compartment then lowers the pizzas into the insulated compartment at the back.

'Is that Shazi's order for the Heights Building?' Slim asks, beaming her best smile. 'Can I ask you a favour? This is like a big surprise for our boss Abigail, and we want to put her birthday present in the pizza box.' She dangles the bag in front of him. 'Can you do that? It will be such a hoot when she opens the pepperoni.'

'Sorry, no can do.' He doesn't tell her it's more than his job's worth, but that's the look he gives her.

'Oh please! We've been planning this all week. She has no idea. It would be just so great if you could help me out.'

He is shaking his head as he arranges the boxes in the compartment.

Ned is no longer on the phone and is catching up. 'You want to place the present with her pizza?'

'Yeah, that's right. It's like a surprise.'

He looks at Ronan. 'What do you think?'

'Against company policy.'

'Yeah, but I think this lady orders from us a couple of times a week, sometimes more. It's the people at that website that's on TikTok.'

'Yes, Middle Kingdom,' says Slim.

'The one that's causing all the trouble,' says Ronan.

Ned is nodding. 'I've seen one of them giving that speech every night.'

'Right, that's who it's for – Abigail!'

'Go on,' says Ned. 'Let them have their bit of fun.'

'It won't fit,' says Ronan.

'Put in another box. Go on, those people are having a tough time.'

'It will mean the world to her,' Slim gushes.

Ronan takes the bag with the tablet and places it in an empty pizza box, which she asks him to put at the bottom of the compartment. The robot's lid closes. It reverses, does a neat pirouette then trundles off.

She clasps her hands in gratitude and shakes them like she was about to throw dice. 'I want to thank you guys so, so much. You'll make her day.' She swivels out of the door to track the robot, which is moving along the pavement a little faster than walking speed. She follows it the length of the Centre:MK mall and down through the underpass beneath Saxon Gate. As it climbs out of the underpass to begin the short journey to Middle

Kingdom, she calls Shazi and says, 'Pizza Delivery!' She hangs up without hearing a response and hopes that Shazi is waiting in the lobby to use her app to release the lid of the robot's cargo box. Slim is about a hundred metres away when the robot judders to a halt outside Middle Kingdom and turns to face the door. The police and surveillance team begin to show interest. Believing that she may need to distract them, she jogs towards the group but then Arnold appears with his spectacles on and a phone in his hand and the lid springs open. He waves the police away and lifts the pizza boxes out and passes them to someone waiting in the door. An officer hands him the bag containing the drinks then checks inside to see if there is anything else. A bag of salad boxes follows. The robot's lights flash and it moves back with the lid closed.

Slim turns away because she needs to take a circular route back to the car rather than running past the Heights Building, but at that moment she hears her name being called. A silver hatchback has slowed after passing through the lights and Peter Salt is leaning out of the window. The car stops. He gets out. There's a line of trees, a row of parked cars and ten metres of tarmac between him and her. She sees Alantree behind the wheel. 'They want you in London,' Salt calls out.

'Why?'

'Obviously, I'm not going into that now. We need you to come with us.'

'I have things to do here,' she says, hands on hips and taking deep breaths.

'You should come now. This is not a request.'

'I don't think so, unless you've suddenly got powers of arrest, Salt.'

'The police are looking for you, and they will arrest you.'

'On what grounds?'

He climbs over the barrier at the side of the road. 'Don't be stupid, Slim. This is important.'

'Yes, it is,' she says and takes off towards the underpass, knowing that they can't turn the car round on Silbury Boulevard until they reach a gap beyond Middle Kingdom and that Salt, whatever his level of fitness, is no match for her as a sprinter. She's through the underpass before he reaches the entrance. She turns right and heads across another car park to the entrance of the shopping mall. She loses him quickly and after five minutes of running and a fifteen-minute bus ride, she returns to her mother's car.

A text comes from Shazi. *Delicious pizza. Watch tonight.*

CHAPTER 43

She's back at Delphy's and eating a ham sandwich made with deliciously unwholesome white bread, when she goes on the Middle Kingdom site at 9.30 p.m. and watches a shaky live-stream of Abigail speaking on the steps of the Heights Building.

Filmed from her right, she begins her usual speech about truth and democracy, summoning that compelling, righteous energy that's made her such a hit on social media. But this evening there's something different about her. As usual she's dressed in black, and her skin is dazzling white under the lights, but she's wearing what seems to be a white collar that makes her look more Elizabethan poet than Goth heroine. And she's emanating a grace and assurance that Slim hasn't seen before. Something or someone has unlocked Abigail and she's flying.

She turns to her right and faces the camera held by one of Middle Kingdom's staff to reveal a single long pendant earring that glitters in the many lights. It's a sign to Slim that they've disabled the anti-tamper device on the tablet and want to talk to her. She offers more than her usual hint of a smile and tugs the earring. 'I'll see you all tomorrow.' She's making sure that Slim has got the message.

An hour later a message pings on her phone – a six-digit code for the Tender Wick barrier.

Slim is there by 6 a.m. and hammers on the door of the old concert hall. It's buzzed open. Two cars and Skelpick's bike are in the parking bay. She passes through the glass door. Seated at screens are Sara Kiln, Yoni Ross, Toto and Callum. Skelpick is asleep in a chair at the far end. Yoni raises a hand, gestures in the direction of the coffee machine, but says nothing. The others barely acknowledge her. She makes coffee, sits down. Skelpick is snoring. A hum comes from the computers' cooling system; there are bursts of chatter from four keyboards. She stares at the ceiling and wonders if Oliver Halfknight has yet read her email resigning from the service.

The door at the far end opens and Abigail emerges, forking her hair with both hands. 'Can you do me a coffee, Slim? The black top and ruff have been replaced by a dark olive-green and red silk shirt. A heavy silver necklace with an inch-wide horned ram's skull sits between her collarbones; the earring has gone.

'So, here we are,' she says, taking the cup with a none-too-friendly smile.

'You've got something out of the tablet,' says Slim.

'Yoni will explain what they're doing. It's not my area.'

'I wouldn't be here unless you'd found something.'

Abigail glances at Yoni. 'Don't think you're forgiven, Slim. Because you aren't.'

'Oh, please! You people knew exactly who I was.'

Yoni swivels his chair and launches it across the polished concrete floor with one kick and arrives in front of them still sitting.

'Coffee would be nice,' he says to Slim. 'We've made some matches between the device and what we found on the system at Mayfield-Turner in Boston. I've got to be honest with you, I thought the whole thing – the tablet, the suicide program and the encrypted material – was dreamed up by your people and the folk at Cheltenham.'

Slim hands him coffee. He drinks in a couple of noisy gulps then returns the cup to her.

'But when we got those matches, we knew it was for real because they date to last year. So, we concluded your story was likely to be true. I hope we're right.'

'You hacked into their system,' says Slim.

'They, like, left the door ajar and we peeped inside.' He begins to wind the hair behind his ear distractedly around his index finger. 'The photographs of the document were helpful. Callum noticed a binary sequence spread through the code and found it was exactly 128-bits long, in other words the length of a standard key. Someone included the key to show us the way in.' His hand moves to tug his earlobe. 'We read it with interest, but we didn't trust it until we found the same encrypted document on the system in Boston. We concluded that whoever gave you that material knew it contained a key that would unlock it.'

'Right, that was my handler in Operation Softball.'

'Name?'

'I can't give you that, but I can tell you that he's part of the group that's being ousted at MI5. His operation was closed down.'

'Why?'

'Because Guest's people are taking over. What did you find?'

'We got a format, headings, and a signature – NS, which we believe belongs to the CEO Nick Segretti – and some names and numbers, also. You want to see?' He shoots his chair back across the floor, grabs a printed paper, wheels himself back and hands it to her.

The five sheets she photographed are reduced to one. 'Where's the rest?'

'There's a lot of chaff in the text. The actual message is just a few lines long, as you can see.'

She reads,

Fort4756	10	27.5
Alvo7622	12	56
Hick4464	5	35
Ting6788	20	72
Jean3332	6	45
Pete5643	8	32

Slim says, 'The first column could be the payee's name or code name and maybe four digits of their bank account. The second is the latest payment and the third is the total amount received by that individual, because in each case it is larger than the second.'

'We had some of the same thoughts,' he says, stretching and yawning at the same time. 'It's a statement. How much do you know about cryptography?'

'Nothing.'

'This is a symmetric system, which means the sender and receiver use the same key, like Enigma during the war. It's way less sophisticated than most systems used today but it still presents a challenge.'

'What about AI?'

He doesn't answer this but says, 'There's a lot to do and we have no time.'

'Why?'

Abigail says, 'Our lawyers have said that four of us are going to be charged with offences under the Official Secrets Act. We don't know who. They predict tomorrow or the day after and they don't expect those people to be given bail.' She stops. 'We have some plays to make before that happens, but if there's anything on the tablet, we need it ASAP.'

'Where's Dan?'

'Jen is sick. She needs him at home during the chemo sessions. That's why we must try to keep Dan out of prison.'

'I'm sorry to hear that. Have you copied the device? I may need it at some stage.'

'Yes,' says Yoni and turns to Skelpick, who is stirring on the couch. He calls out, 'Coffee?'

Skelpick stands, revolves his head, works his shoulders, straightens with difficulty, then begins to move unsteadily towards them. Yoni pushes a chair in his direction just in time for him to land in their midst. A cup is passed to him. From a ziplock bag, he pops half a dozen pills and washes them down.

'So, where are we?' he asks.

'Stuck and running out of time,' says Abigail.

'We need to find a key for each document on the tablet.'

'What about our friend?'

'Nothing yet.'

Slim understands that Skelpick is asking about the AI tool. She says, 'Before I took on this job, I researched Enigma, because I wanted to know where you came from and the way you might think. I became intrigued by the way those people back then got a toehold on the encrypted messages every day – the crib.' She stops and looks around. Yoni and Sara nod. 'I don't have to tell you all, but the crib derived from a regularly appearing feature, maybe it was a sign-off, or the words "weather report" or an expression that occurred frequently. One I remember was "*Keine besonderen Ereignisse*"– "no special events", i.e. nothing to report. If they knew that a particular phrase or name had been encrypted, they were on their way to breaking the setting and deciphering the radio traffic for that day. It was a race against time – to make a breakthrough before the settings were changed at midnight. What we need is to find the regularly appearing phrase. Is that correct?'

'That's right, kiddo,' says Skelpick.

'So, I should start thinking of things that might appear in these statements, regular places, dates, and individuals likely to be mentioned in the documents. That make sense?'

'It does but you need to be quick,' says Sara Kiln and swings back to her screen. 'I do not relish jail.'

'I'll talk it out of you,' Skelpick says. 'You'll remember more that way.'

CHAPTER 44

A call to Delphy secures bed, board, and a workspace in Cow Two for Skelpick. When they arrive in the yard at the back of Top Farm Cottage – the BMW followed by Skelpick on his bike – Delphy bursts from the kitchen, wiping her hands on a dishcloth, and swoons over the bike which she recognises as a Triumph Speedmaster. She circles it, cooing at the metallic bottle-green livery and asking detailed questions about its torque, acceleration and handling, then falls to reminiscence of the time, aged eighteen, when she rode the 450cc BSA M20, delivering radio intercepts to Bletchley before she was hired for her mathematical abilities. She makes heavy hints about 'going for a spin', which Skelpick ignores.

They set to work immediately, first going through Slim's story, searching for details that might appear in the regular transmissions from Boston, then her daily routines: the booking of lunches, the people who attended, the site meetings, those he spoke to on the phone, the investment managers, tax accountants, PR consultants and lawyers. She tries to remember the events in his diary going back from Friday 13 October, the day she ended up on the run in Northern Macedonia with the memory of Guest's hands round her throat.

Skelpick makes notes as they eat lamb chops with Delphy, then they continue into the night. At midnight, he goes out for a nip of whisky from his flask and a smoke in the yard. 'We're getting too many names,' he says to the stars and hands the flask to Slim. 'What we need is the equivalent of that weather report from a U-boat patrol in the middle of the Atlantic. Some bastard saying, "Nothing happening here."'

At two they go to bed, but they're woken up just five hours later by Delphy knocking on the doors of Cow One and Cow Two in turn and telling them to come over to listen to the radio. Dan Halladay, Yoni Ross, Sara Kiln and Toto Linna have all been arrested and charged with offences under the Official Secrets Act.

'They're shutting us down,' says Skelpick. He calls Abigail and puts her on speaker. She's heard that she isn't going to be arrested and has information that Skelpick won't be, either. 'They say you're just the rewrite man.'

He leaves for an MRI on his spine in London and doctors' appointments the following day. Everything seems stalled. Abigail has her hands full running the site and looking after Jen Halladay. Callum, who is minding the shop at Tender Wick, won't pick up. It's not until Skelpick appears the next evening, with new pills and a spring in his step, that Slim thinks of looking at the original printouts she made of the photographs of the documents. She has no copies on her phone or laptop, so Skelpick leaves early next morning and retrieves the five printouts from Callum, who was meant to shred them but forgot.

They pore over them, but nothing strikes them, until Slim, leaning back in her chair, notices that when she photographed one of the pages, she left something off the bottom. Instead of a line of text, just the tops of the letters are showing, like the edge of a tyre track. It seems important that this line is separate from the rest of the code. She shows Skelpick and together they try to determine the ninety or so characters by matching them with the other letters. In a matter of minutes, they have the line and send it to Callum so he can apply the key.

They wait a few minutes then call Callum and put him on speaker.

Skelpick says, 'What's the line say, Callum?'

'Nothing much, I'm afraid. It reads, "'US Dollar, 0.8248; Euro 0.8657. Brent Crude \$90.78; Gold \$1.876.59; Dow Jones 33,670.29, FTSE 7599.60.'"

Slim slaps her forehead. 'Of course! Guest insisted the latest prices and market indices were always at the bottom of every statement, so he wouldn't have to look them up when talking through the figures with people.'

'And these change every day,' says Skelpick. 'So, we—'

'Have the perfect crib.' Slim jumps up.

'The man saying, "nothing doing here", although it's much better than that.'

'Because in each statement there will be one line that we can predict with absolute certainty. We research the prices and indices for every day working back from October the thirteenth and that will give us the foot in the door to decipher each document.'

'I'll get on to it now,' says Callum.

'How long will you need?'

'It shouldn't take more than a day. Probably much less.'

'Really?' Skelpick catches her eye and winks. She understands that AI will do the heavy lifting. 'I'll see you in the morning, Callum.'

'Do you want any results before then? Because I've got something on the names and figures in the first decryption.'

'Why didn't you say?'

'You didn't ask.'

Skelpick shakes his head.

'No, keep the electronic traffic to a minimum. I'll see it tomorrow early.'

CHAPTER 45

'Use the fire exit at the side, near the back,' Callum tells her as she approaches Tender Wick. 'Looks like it's blocked, but it isn't. Bang three times.'

She parks in the gravel forecourt of a kitchen design business some distance from the concert hall, picks her way along the central pathway of the old wartime camp and finds the fire exit, which is, indeed, overgrown. She thumps on the metal door with the side of her fist. Callum opens almost immediately. He is alone and seems tense but also pleased to see her.

She squeezes past him. 'What've you got?'

'We're doing very well.'

'You decrypted everything?'

'I'll show you. But it's not good, Slim. Not good at all. I can see why people would kill for this thing.'

There's a crescent of sandwich packets, milkshake cups and takeaway containers around a laptop. A galvanised bucket on the floor is half-filled with cups and beer cans. Callum scratches his head, says, 'I'll make coffee.'

He returns with two cups and the biscuit tin, from which he decants two broken cookies on to the desk.

'So?'

'For security, I've put everything on these.' He hands her three thumb drives. 'That material shouldn't be only in this building. Not with all that's going on.' He drinks his coffee, apologises for the lumpy whitener.

'Have you heard anything about bail?' she asks.

'Doesn't look good.' He gives her a woeful look, shakes his head. 'They left me in charge of everything. I was wondering what to do. Should I stay? Should I shut everything down? Abigail won't say.'

'A lot of equipment to watch over. Must be worth a fortune.'

'Mostly redundant now. You know about Lovelock, do you?'

'Kind of.' She knows he's talking about their AI helper.

'Now she's in the world, all this stuff is pretty much obsolete.'

'She! Lovelock is feminine!'

'Sara and Yoni built in a female personality for interactions. How deep that goes is anyone's guess, but she's one of the best large language model AIs in the world, if not *the* best right now. Kind of scary being alone with her and in charge when Yoni and Sara are in jail.'

They sit down. Slim stares at the completely blank screen of Callum's laptop, suddenly aware of his body odour, and smiles. 'Callum, is there a shower here?'

'Yes, why?'

'Maybe you should use it. We're going to be working together and you need one. Sorry.'

'I've been so busy . . .'

'And you've crushed it, but you need to wash and get yourself together. I'll clear up in here.'

He pushes back his chair so violently that it flies across the floor, and he loses his balance for a second. She opens her hands and shrugs a kind of apology and begins to sweep the litter from the desk into the bucket. 'Do you want me to look at anything while you shower?' she calls out.

'No, you'll need me. Won't be long.'

When she's wiped the surfaces with a screen cleaner, she sits back to think. Skelpick is editing down her story. He said it was far too long and weighed down with opinion, plus he was none too complimentary about her structure. But, if they stand a good chance of decrypting all the contents of the tablet, her story will, anyway, be relegated to what Skelpick called a side order of greens. The problem, it seems to her, will be to per-suade Abigail to give the go-ahead to Skelpick to write what's in the tablet and then publish it, a huge risk in any circumstances, but with four of them in jail, a very big ask.

Callum returns barefoot, hair damp, in a clean T-shirt and chinos. 'You look a different person,' she says.

'Sorry, I've been under a lot of stress. I keep thinking I'm going to be arrested. If that happens, the shit will fly because they won't believe I haven't used what I know, which I haven't, of course.' He stops. Looks at her. 'Then you come along and order me into the bloody shower.'

'What do you know?'

'I was at GCHQ. Eight years. Graduate trainee. Left to become a journalist and write sci-fi.' He looks at his laptop and smiles. 'These days it's hard to think of sci-fi that beats reality. Things are moving very fast.'

'Does Cheltenham know you're here?'

'Nope. They wouldn't like it.'

'Sorry, I should have handled the shower thing better. It was rude,' she grins, 'although a little necessary.'

'I'll introduce you to Lovelock. Do you prefer speech or shall I type prompts?'

'Speech, why not?'

'Lovelock,' he says, 'can you show me the complete list of names and payments that you decrypted last night?'

'Good morning, Callum. Certainly!' A female voice of vaguely West Coast origin comes from his laptop. Slim cannot help but smile. 'It sounds like Sara.'

Callum tips his head to say there's a reason for that.

The screen fills with four-letter code names, rows and rows of them and each with the four digits attached to the last letter.

'How many are there?'

'Three hundred and twenty code names in this section. Once we had the crib to work with, Lovelock had no trouble in deciphering the statements because it was simple enough to deduce the key for each day, and with humans involved in setting that key, it was far from random. Lovelock spotted patterns that made it easier.'

'So, you have all the documents deciphered. That's fantastic.'

'The names are the challenge, and that's taking us a long time, and it requires Lovelock and me to work together, doesn't it, Lovelock?'

'A good combination, if I may say so.'

'Thank you, Lovelock.'

'What's this like,' she says, 'working with AI so closely?'

Callum thinks then looks at her, eyes lit up. His foot is jigging. 'Like swimming beside a whale in a dark ocean without being able to see how big the creature is.' He pauses, looks down at the computer. 'It's completely remarkable. Anyway, let's get back to the names. We got there in the end because we realised after a huge number of searches, with me prompting and prompting all through the night, that these are the maiden names of the mother of a partner or trusted friend of the recipient of Mr Guest's largesse.'

'The maiden name of the mother of a partner or trusted friend,' she repeats to get it into her head.

'Reduced to four letters. So, if we go to October the thirteenth, Lovelock, we can see what the full names are and who they belong to.'

Instantly the screen fills with a list.

Fort4756	Diana Fortesque, mother of Rupert P. Christie – spouse of Lord James Rennie
Alvo7622	Susan Calvo, mother of Alli Jones – spouse of Spencer Fawcett MP
Hick4464	Ella Hickman, mother of Jane Jeffrys – spouse of Alan Jeffrys MP
Ting6788	Jane Hastings, mother of Rachel Long – spouse of Anton Long
Jean3332	Marie Serjeant, mother of Henrietta Speed – wife of Terry Speed
Pete5643	Gill Petersen, mother of Alastair Spiers – close friend of Luke Thomas

'The numbers are the last four digits of the bank account, as you suspected. There are amounts recorded next to them which are obviously in thousands.'

'How many have you got?'

'As I say, three hundred and twenty separate individuals. Of these, a hundred and nineteen are taking regular payments; forty have taken one-off payments. So far, we've identified thirty people, eight of which are notables – lords, MPs, civil servants, heads of institutions and the like.'

'Like Spencer Fawcett MP, he's the chair of a something or other?'

'The House of Commons Intelligence and Security Committee, and his colleague Alan Jeffrys is at the Defence Committee.'

'I'm impressed. How much more have you got to do?'

'I guess there are quite a few names that we will never manage to identify, so I can't be sure.'

She thinks for a few moments, looking down at the names. 'And we've got to prove their association with the bank account numbers. That's going to be tough.'

Callum rubs the ginger growth on his chin. 'You could blag them.'

'How?'

'Call them up, pretend to be from a bank in the States or Mayfield-Turner.'

'Go on.'

'Maybe you tell them money has been returned and you're checking the account number and sort code. Maybe you send them some money – a small amount, like a test – and ask them to confirm when they've received it.'

'Who could do that?'

'Shazi, no question. A very accomplished blagger and liar, is Shazi.'

'I'll talk to Abigail. So, everything you've got is on these thumb drives.' He nods. She places a hand on his shoulder. 'I should be going. I'll be in touch in a few hours' time. You've done a wonderful job, Callum. Goodbye to you, Lovelock.'

'My pleasure,' comes the gentle voice from the laptop.

'You sound like a yoga teacher today.'

'My pleasure,' says Lovelock.

CHAPTER 46

Over the next few days, Slim and Callum work side by side in the old concert hall, while at Top Farm Cottage Skelpick wrestles the material into order, ranking the names, trying to assess the influence that Guest was buying in each case, working out the significance of the dates of payments in relation to legislation in the House of Commons and decisions being taken by ministers and civil servants.

The scale of Guest's bribery is impressive. Payments totalling £26.45 million were made over four and a half years, which include £3.2 million and £2.0 million that were paid to two individuals outside the United Kingdom. Callum remarks how small some of the payments to British individuals are – sometimes just £1,000 – and Slim says it's humiliating how little a British politician will sell himself for, sometimes for no more than Wimbledon tickets, a day at the races or Lords, which are all recorded beneath the amounts in the middle column of the statements. Others are properly on the Guest payroll, being in receipt of hefty regular disposals of £5,000 and £10,000 a time, which, in several cases, add up to over £100,000 over the period recorded.

The work is exhilarating but also depressing. In the evenings

Slim is glad to leave Callum with Lovelock, a four-pack of lager and a pie he can shove in the microwave and return to Top Farm Cottage to eat supper with Delphy and go over the day's discoveries with Skelpick. On the third night, she's lying on her bed in a long T-shirt, texting Helen before she turns off the light, when Skelpick knocks and enters. He sits down tentatively on the edge of the bed. He is wearing pyjama bottoms with a turtle and lobster motif, T-shirt and hoodie.

'You're kidding, Gramps,' she says with more amusement than horror.

'We need to talk this through.'

'Right now?'

'So . . . what's the story?'

'How Ivan Guest corrupted a generation of politicians and public servants,' she says.

'Seems a bit dull. Everyone assumes people in power are corrupt. All I need is a title to write. Once I've got that, I can structure it.'

'Give it to them straight – secret coded messages reveal how one man corrupted a generation of public servants.'

'Okay, that'll do. Thanks.' He stretches out.

'If you're hoping for a fuck, Skelpick, you are seriously—'

'I'm not. Anyway, I'm the wrong sex for you.'

She punches him lightly on the arm. 'My problem is not with your sex, Skelpick. It's your age.'

He grins. 'And besides, I'm way past being able or wanting to make love to anyone tonight. But I'd like the company, the sense of someone being there. No problem if you object. But I thought you needed the company, too. You look sad, Slim.'

That she is. She likes Skelpick and feels surprisingly close to him, though he is a long way off being a temptation.

'You need have no fear of me,' he says.

'By the look of you, you'd need a handful of Miracle-Gro.'

'It's called Viagra. Miracle-Gro is for plants.'

'Seems like a better name to me.' She grins and flips the duvet back. He lets himself down gingerly and slides his arm under her neck as she lifts her head. It seems weirdly natural to her, although in that very bed, in those same sheets, not many days before, she'd made love over and over with Helen. But here they are, Skelpick and Slim, comfortable as an old married couple. They sleep soundly with barely any movement.

She wakes first and studies his profile, which is youthfully handsome in repose. It's when he's upright and conscious his face reveals all that he's seen and the pain he tolerates with such little complaint. Then, he looks much older than his forty-six years.

He says, without opening his eyes, 'You have the sweetest breath in the morning.'

'That's completely inappropriate. Get up. I need to go and see Abigail.' She pushes him with both hands, says, 'You're okay, Skelpick,' and rolls off the bed to switch on the Hobbs kettle.

She drives to rendezvous with Abigail at the weekly street market in Aylesbury. They meet at a cheese stall and go to a makeshift café for cold drinks. The air is hot and filled with the calls of market traders. Slim gives her an updated thumb drive folded in a paper serviette, although Abigail already has most of the decryptions. 'Should I ask Skelpick to start writing and give him a deadline?'

Abigail lowers her blue sunglasses. 'We'll all soon be working for you, Slim. But you can tell him he's got five days. We need to publish before the bail hearing.' She looks around the market stalls and says, 'There are four reporters working on the telephone numbers for the people with bank accounts. So far, we have just eight numbers and Shazi has started her operation to persuade them to accept money from a bank account in Boston, belonging to Yoni and his wife. Just one has fallen for it, Alyn James Moran, the partner of Lord Kingsbury. Moran confirmed receipt of the two hundred dollar test transfer and so established that Lord Kingsbury, climate change denier and lobbyist, has been paid thirty-five thousand quid by Guest.'

'How's Shazi doing that?'

Abigail smiles. 'She's mastered a faultless American business accent. And now she's training up Sofi. But they've got to get many more confirmations because I'm not publishing this without a load of proof. Plus, we need to give people the right of reply.'

'What!' Slim leans forward, not concealing her horror. 'If you start calling people for comments, Guest will get to hear about it and do everything in his power to stop the story. I mean everything, Abigail.'

'So, we need to get our timing right before we go live with it.'

'Is that going to work?'

'It must. We're already in a crisis. I can't risk multiple defamation suits on top of what we're already dealing with.'

'I think you're making a mistake,' Slim says.

'But you're not responsible for the site. You're just some government snitch, aren't you?' She studies her for a moment. 'If you're playing us, Slim, I will personally stab you through the heart.'

'I'm not.'

'If you tell anyone about our friend Lovelock, I will stab you through the heart.'

'I won't.'

'I pray not. On a lighter note, we've been in touch with a Mr Noel Coombs, the council official who's been stealing from Delphy's charity box, and he's said that he is indeed the man in the film. He could hardly deny it because his registration plate is plain as day. This same individual is the one that's been taking kickbacks on contracts to cut down healthy trees on council land all over the countryside.'

'Wow! Quite a result.'

'But we're going to let him twist in the wind for a couple of weeks, wait until this is all over and hope he gives money to Delphy's appeal for the church bells in the meantime. Then we'll tell the public how much the shitbag got for every tree.' Abigail glances round the market, her wintery beauty at odds with the sunlight and stalls of basketry, fruit and vegetables, which, on this brilliant day, almost evokes France. 'To finish our business, I need to tell you that Andrei Botezatu is ready to be interviewed but I'm not going to give you the job. Dan is absolutely categoric that once you've finished with the Guest story, we will have nothing more to do with you.'

That is to be expected. Slim nods and tries to see through the blue tint of her glasses. 'Can I ask about Bantock?'

'Going very well, thank you.'

'So, you've got something to be grateful to me for.'

Abigail looks away and smiles. 'There are many things, Slim. It's just that you are also a lying, sneaky bitch.'

'And that's your only complaint?'

Skelpick circles the Guest story like a dog before a fight. Slim catches him pacing round the old farmyard and Delphy's garden smoking, staring at his shadow, talking to himself, and exclaiming to the sky. He looks quite mad. Then he stops

suddenly, makes a note on an index card, and goes to place it
in an arrangement he's made of scores of cards on the bedroom
floor of Cow Two.

Meanwhile Slim, working both at Top Farm and Tender
Wick, writes drafts for different sections: a profile of Guest; his
network of business and political interests; his money-laundering
activities; the extent of his corruption and what he got in return
for spraying money at good causes and PR agencies. These are
given a cursory reading by Skelpick, but she sees they are being
summarised on cards and placed with the other notes, so she
keeps going without expecting gratitude, let alone praise. He
tells her straight that he is not going to include any mention of
the connection between Guest and Dekker because they don't
need to stretch the credulity of their readers. 'We'll have more
than one go at this and we can do all that later.'

Using Lovelock, Callum has achieved ninety-four per cent
identification of the code names – about three hundred individuals. The haul of MPs and cabinet ministers – past and
present – has reached forty-seven, the number of senior White-
hall officials now stands at fifteen, with three former permanent
secretaries accepting hard-to-get tickets. Twenty-two members
of the House of Lords are to be found in the encrypted statements.

Lovelock turns out to be a first-class picture researcher as
well, and Slim has had the idea of assembling a file of photographs that can be dropped in throughout Skelpick's piece.
Rather than just opting for headshots, she's looking for pictures
that capture the corruption and that's when she strikes gold, or
rather Lovelock presents it to her on a plate. It is a photograph
of *Tatler* magazine's social pages in which there is a shot of Guest
with two companions at a polo match in Gloucestershire ten

years before. She consults the extensive database and finds both have accepted gifts worth several thousand pounds, yet both had escaped their notice, one because a second marriage had meant that the maiden name of the partner's mother hadn't been picked up. It's the killer second punch she's been looking for, but she'll keep it to herself because, as ever, she needs something in her back pocket.

Now that Skelpick is well into the piece, the evenings have become more relaxed. He knows where he's headed and as each day passes there is less material to marshal. They discuss the story over a glass of wine and Slim suggests adjustments and minor reordering. He gives her a lesson on his bike – refreshing her memory of touring on a trail bike in the Andes – then they eat dinner with Delphy at a rickety table in the garden, surrounded by self-seeded flowers and tubs of heavily scented lilies, which intoxicate the hot evenings.

On the last night, he is in celebratory mood. 'We're in good shape, kiddo,' he says after an early dinner. 'So, it's time to thank our host, don't you think?'

Delphy, who has been a little silent all evening, straightens with a smile. 'What have you done? You shouldn't have.'

He disappears to find two square packages that arrived by courier a few days before and presents them to Delphy. Which would she like to open first? She opts for the larger one because she can see the name Fortnum & Mason on the smaller package and guesses that Slim has told Skelpick that it's her birthday on June 21 and this is a cake. He slits open the big box with some ceremony, tells her to close her eyes, then lifts out a helmet and places it on the table in front of her.

'Oh, my goodness! Oh, my golly gosh!' Exclamations of joy which, like her cooking, come from a more innocent time.

On the side of the dark green helmet is inscribed DELPHY RACING in a heavy metal, gothic face.

The bike is brought alongside an old mounting block in the yard, and Slim helps Delphy on to the pillion and tightens the helmet strap, then runs to get the gate for them. As the bike takes the short, grassy track down to the road, Delphy's tiny, spindly frame topped by the enormous helmet reminds Slim of a dragonfly clinging to a reed. They turn right and accelerate away into the evening sunlight.

She walks to the old ash tree, checks in with the Ballard phone – there's nothing – then calls to ask Bantock to go through her messages. There's a text from Tudor Mills repeating his warning to keep her head down, because as he puts it, *This is nowhere near over yet. There are people out there actively looking for you.*

That she knows, but there are just two days to go before publication, at which point she will activate the second part of her plan to avenge Matt, the thought of whom suddenly overwhelms her in the silent countryside. Tears prick her eyes, but she doesn't let them flow. Not yet will she allow herself to properly grieve. Not until she's done for the man who paid thugs to torture him and end his brave, transformed life.

The biking party returns and Delphy, in jubilant mood, makes for the decanter of port in the kitchen and presses on them each a glass, and Skelpick makes a toast to her and a gracious speech that brings tears to her eyes. Out of nowhere and just at the right moment, have come into Slim's life two people who have healed something in her. She smiles as Delphy insists that they went over a hundred miles per hour and Skelpick silently shakes his head, so the old lady doesn't see.

Later, Slim catches Skelpick in the shower in Cow One – his room is still covered in index cards which he doesn't want to disturb. He is turned away from her and doesn't hear her. She's there long enough to see scars running from his right buttock up to the back of his neck like the shell burst on the side of a building. When he comes to join her for their now customary late-night talk, she says, 'I crashed in on you showering – sorry. I had no idea you'd been so badly injured.'

'Should have seen my head. I have a very large plate.' He takes her hand and places it on the back of his skull. She can feel the outline. It's about one-and-a-half inches square. This is where no hair grows and hair from further up falls back to cover the patch.

'Are you aware of it?'

'Headaches in cold weather. The occipital cortex was miraculously unscathed, and I didn't lose my eyesight. A lot to be grateful for.'

She turns and supports herself on one elbow. 'I saw my dead brother, or something like him four times, and each time, I was about to encounter Guest's men. Three times round my mum's place and then once on the canal, though I wasn't certain what I was seeing then.' She turns to him. 'You think I'm deluded?'

'If you were from South Sudan or the Central African Republic and your life was lived half in the spirit world and your head was full of hoodoo-voodoo shit, I'd say you definitely saw your brother. But, in twenty-first century Britain . . .' His hand flutters dubiously in front of them.

'I think he saved me.'

'Could be that you saved yourself. Who knows? Perhaps you did see him.'

He leans over, kisses her on the forehead then clambers from the bed, muttering that he needs to be alone with a glass of something to think through his final paragraphs. There are just a few hours to go before he delivers the first draft to Abigail.

CHAPTER 47

Some twenty-eight hours later, at 3.45 a.m. on midsummer morning, Slim leaves the Hotel La Tour, the huge modern block that overlooks the Belvedere and the Light Pyramid, and goes to the garage, where her mother's BMW is parked out of the range of CCTV cameras. The knapsack containing the gun and the tablet are placed in the spare tyre compartment. She drops the cover and arranges an old cotton bag full of dirty washing on top. This is far from ideal, but once she knows publication is going ahead – which will be in a matter of hours – she'll return and drive the car away.

Outside, an orange glow is spreading across the sky, as she makes her way along the path towards the Belvedere. Behind her, Midsummer Boulevard runs through the new town – now city – which is empty and clean and whispers the dream of the young architects that listened to Pink Floyd early one summer's day and redrew their plans. She finds fifty or so people already assembled on the grass slopes around the Light Pyramid waiting for the turn of the year. Most are in shorts and T-shirts because the dawn is astonishingly warm, even for midsummer. Some are in meditation poses, others are draped over each other, and a few are smoking weed. She sees no one she recognises and goes to lean against the cool, powder-coated steel surface of the sculpture and fixes the point where the sun will rise, now marked by a smudge of fiery light.

In a matter of minutes, she spots Abigail and Frank Shap, whom she knew was due to return from Liverpool the previous evening, pushing Delphy in a wheelchair. She is wearing an oversized straw hat, announcing her birthday on a blue ribbon, which Slim suspects Frank has supplied. When Delphy spots her, she springs from the wheelchair, experiences a wobble, but finds her balance and totters towards Slim.

Slim wishes her happy birthday and bends to kiss her on both cheeks. 'Do you know what time you were born?'

'Haven't the first notion,' she says, momentarily gripping Slim's hand.

Slim hugs Frank with one arm and asks how Tam is.

'I'm going to get her out of that detention centre.'

'Like you got her out of that burning wreck.'

'Harder.'

Delphy insists she's going to walk. Abigail takes her other arm and the three of them move slowly towards the Pyramid, trailed, Slim now sees, by half a dozen young reporters. She asks where Bantock is and is told that he's gone to Huddersfield to pick up an engine part and he's taken Loup with him.

They watch the sky in silence until the sun rises and golden light floods the Belvedere and splashes across the huge reflective disc on the facade of the Hotel La Tour. Delphy sits with her hands clasped, eyes shining with pleasure. People clap and cheer and hug each other, relishing a moment that seems as insanely optimistic as New Year's Eve. One of the reporters has prosecco and cups and Frank produces the Fortnum's cake Skelpick ordered, and she blows out a solitary candle that represents a century of life.

Abigail catches Slim's eye and they move back down the path. She says, 'Over twenty have confirmed the bank accounts so we're going ahead this afternoon, providing Skelpick's rewrite works.'

'Great! I didn't think you'd do it.'

'It's the best chance we have of getting our people out of jail and, besides, I don't want to sit on that material. Feels like a ticking time bomb. But there's a condition. I told Shazi and the rest of the team that I wanted to quote a minimum of twelve of the individuals we're going to name. The team made the first calls asking for reactions last night.'

'Guest will know we're going to publish. Right now, he will be working out how to destroy us,' Slim says.

Abigail is looking at her shoes, jaw set firm. 'Slim, understand that the jeopardy of this story is one thousand times greater than anything we have ever published before. All the cash we've brought in, and all Yoni and Sara's money will not save us if we're sued for libel multiple times.'

'You won't be.' Slim glances at the rising sun and waits a moment. 'I need to talk to Skelpick about this. Is that all right with you?'

'Do not get in the way of those reactions, Slim. The story won't be published unless we're taking our obligations to fairness seriously.'

She steps away and calls Skelpick but gets no answer. Two more attempts to reach him meet with no response. She decides she should go in person, waves her goodbyes, and begins to jog towards the city centre, energised by the hit of alcohol and the spectacular sunrise, but more so by the rising dread that Guest knows for certain that the encryption on the tablet has been broken. Her pace quickens. She turns right then moves down Silbury Boulevard, with her hands slicing the air. She reaches the Saxon Way crossroads, stops, checks for surveillance, sees none and heads to the rear entrance of the Heights Building. As she slows to round the corner, she sees first Skelpick's bike then a man wearing blue overalls, a matching combat cap, dark glasses and a medical mask, moving smartly across the empty car park towards a dark grey van. A bag is slung across his back. An engineer maybe. But at this hour? And why the face mask when Covid is a distant memory? The van's side door slides open as he approaches. The driver begins to pull away and the other man has to put one hand on the side of the door, run a couple of paces and jump into the moving vehicle. The door is closed as they speed away.

She processes what she's just seen. Why was the man moving so quickly to a van that was waiting for him like a getaway vehicle, not just with a driver but a companion in the back to facilitate a rapid departure by opening the door? Why the urgency so many hours before the working day begins?

The questions answer themselves. She's at the back door to the office, swipes her key card and enters. The lobby is empty, but a sandwich box and thermos are on the reception desk plus the little washbag that Arnold brings with him when he's on nights and his cousin, Wally, is doing the day shift. She presses the button to call the lift. It doesn't respond. Maybe it's broken and that's the reason for the engineer's visit. She dials Skelpick to warn him that she's about to come up. He doesn't answer, and she takes to the stairs, now certain something is wrong.

The first thing she sees as she bursts through the fire door on the fourth floor is Arnold lying between the lift doors in a mass of blood that is glinting in the lift lights. She crouches by him. He's been shot twice, in the shoulder and the chest. He's alive. Eyes wide open, mouth working but no words come out. He's shaking his head and pointing feebly in the direction of the conference room. 'I'm getting help.' She dials 999, gets through and rises to her feet. Giving her name and the address, she tells the male operator that there's been a shooting. One man down. He's still alive. There may be more. Seconds later she reports what she sees through the shattered glass partition of the conference room. A man with his face down on the glass conference table; blood is everywhere. It's Skelpick. She moves into the room and to his side, breathing deeply to control her panic, and puts two fingers of her left hand to the side of his neck where there's much fresh blood and feels for a pulse. 'Hold on,' she says. 'I've got something. He's alive but he's been shot in the head. His pulse is weak. What do I do?'

'Stay with him.'

'Two men have been shot. I can't just look after one.'

'Try to stop the bleeding of both victims – pad the wounds. But do not move them. I repeat – do not attempt to move them.'

Now, she's racing to the kitchenette where there's a stack of kitchen towels. She takes two rolls under her arm, wedges the phone between her shoulder and ear and tears at the polythene packaging. She goes to Arnold first, strips off paper, folds it and presses it to his chest wound, which is the worst of the two. 'Arnold, can you hear me?' He groans a response. He seems to be saying sorry.

'Can you move your hand for me and press here?' She puts down the phone and helps him bring his hand to the spot. 'Keep it there, dear friend, and press as hard as you can. Ambulances are on their way. You're going to make it, I promise.' He gives a little nod. In his eyes there's a lot of pain registered. 'I'm going to do what I can for Skelpick.'

She picks up the phone and goes to the conference room, her trainers crunching on the broken glass. 'What do I do for a gunshot to the head?' she shouts at the emergency operator.

'Pad it but be gentle. You don't want to cause any more damage to his head. Are you with him now?'

'Yes.'

'What's his breathing like?'

'Not good.'

'Is he conscious?'

'No.'

'Okay, when you've finished padding the wounds see what his pulse is doing for me.'

She's stripping paper towel from the roll and padding the back of his head, when she realises that not all the blood is coming from his head wound.

'He's been hit twice. They shot him in the back.'

'Keep trying to stop the blood on both wounds. You're doing a great job, Slim. Did you see the gunman?'

'Yes, I think so.' She gives a hurried description of the man and the vehicle while she finds the second wound.

'Right, hold on. Police and first response should be with you any minute. Can they get into the building?'

'Tell them to force the door. I can't leave the victims. We're on the fourth floor. The first victim is jamming the lift; the second is in the conference room. I don't know which is in a worse state.'

'The pulse, Slim! What's his pulse doing?'

She switches the phone to speaker and puts it on the conference table so she can hold padding to both wounds. 'Come on,

Skelpick! You aren't going to die on me. Please stay. Please!' A part of her notes her desperation, that her voice is different – shrill and panicky – and that's because she can't lose Skelpick, just as they have clicked and found a rare friendship.

She notices the smear of blood to the left of Skelpick's arm, as though someone had wiped the blood on the table. Then she understands. The mark was made by the gunman ripping the laptop from under him after he had slumped forward. That was what was in the bag slung over his shoulder. She knows what this means. Guest has got the story, all the decrypts and all the responses to the calls made by Shazi and Sofi. Everything! But with Skelpick injured, she's not thinking of journalism or even Guest. Her focus is on Skelpick and Arnold. She shouts out, 'They're coming, Arnold. You hold on there. I've got my hands full with Skelpick.'

But then she leaves Skelpick because she can't bear the idea of Arnold being on his own. She squats beside him and says, 'You're doing so well. Just keep pressing.' She touches his face, and he opens his eyes and manages half a smile.

The operator is still on the line. 'Those are the victims' names – Arnold and Skelpick?'

'Full names Arnold Frobisher and J. J. Skelpick,' she says automatically, as she hurries back to Skelpick.

'Okay, Slim, I can see the first responder is with you now and the police will be there in seconds.' She hears multiple sirens approaching. At the back and front of the building vehicles come to a halt; people are shouting, all of which she can hear perfectly well four floors up in the quiet of midsummer morning. She returns to Skelpick.

The operator says, 'Two ambulances are with you. First responder is in the building. You're doing well, Slim.'

'Stop telling me that, just get the fucking trauma unit, or whatever it's called, ready. You will need blood. Skelpick is B positive.' She remembers this because when Skelpick was told of his blood group in a Kenyan hospital, he responded, 'B positive? I'm always bloody positive!' He gave her his crooked grin and added. 'Not bad for a man with a head wound and half his arse missing.'

The fire door bangs open. Now a man's voice is speaking to Arnold. She shouts out, 'There's another one in here.'

'I'll be with you in a second,' he calls out as calmly as though he were talking to a customer from the back of a village store.

In the event, an ambulance crew arrives. Two women paramedics. They drop their bags, and one says, 'What happened here?'

'He was shot twice from behind. I got here minutes after it happened.' Slim reaches out and gently takes hold of Skelpick's right hand, aware of the stickiness of his blood. 'They came to kill him and then I assume Arnold arrived in the lift to find out what was going on and was shot.' She stops and says into the phone, 'Are you getting this, operator?'

'Yes, the police are in the building now. They will want to hear all that. I have given them your name.'

The ambulance crew speak into radios alternately, giving an assessment and working on a plan of action – stabilisation, oxygen, plasma and shots are mentioned. She doesn't understand what they're saying, except that two doctors are being rushed to the scene. One is a trauma expert, the other works in the local Accident and Emergency and knows about head wounds. The member of the crew checking Skelpick's vital signs comments that it's a quiet night in Milton Keynes A&E and the doctors on their way are held in high regard.

Until this moment, Skelpick has been utterly still, but then a shudder passes through his body as though he had been kicked or received an electric shock. 'Hold still, friend!' says the crew member with the stethoscope.

'Hold still,' repeats Slim and she feels the tiniest pressure returned by Skelpick's hand. 'I'm here with you. Hang on.' Again, a little squeeze. 'He's responding to my voice.'

'That's good,' says the woman busying herself on the floor with the bags. 'Keep talking to him.'

Slim looks down at the matted hair and the neck scarf that has covered the back of his head and in what is like a flash of vertigo is suddenly aware of the incredible fragility of life – each movement a marvel, each breath a miracle – and wonders how anyone could pump bullets into the soft flesh of another human being. It's then that she notices that Skelpick is wearing wired earphones. There's so much blood she hadn't seen them before. She removes the earpiece on her side. 'You'll hear me better now,' she says close to his head. There's more pressure in her hand. One of the crew pulls out the earpiece on his left side and Slim draws the bloody wire away and slings it down on the conference table.

Why was he using earphones? He often listened to music in the evenings in the building when he worked, usually old opera or Bach, particularly Bach's mesmerising Goldberg Variations – but he never ever listened while actually writing. Couldn't think straight with music in his ears. Music was for the moments when he was stuck and needed to free his mind and consider the whole piece. So, she concludes, he must have had his earphones plugged into the laptop that was taken by the shooter. Even in this appalling moment, she's trying to work it out. But she's all over the place. Unbidden comes the memory of cradling her mother's head and her cold contemplation of her death. Losing her was much worse than she'd expected, and now she may lose her new friend Skelpick. People don't recover from a bullet in the head, do they? And if they do, they don't go back to writing good journalism and riding motorcycles.

She forces herself to snap out of it and looks round the conference room and right there, on the floor by a row of four wall sockets, is Skelpick's laptop on charge. She recognises the sticker on the top – the flag of South Sudan – black, red and green bands with a blue triangle that he told her represented the Nile. He was charging the laptop on which he was writing the story, while, on another computer, he was listening to music and maybe doing some research, consulting Lovelock remotely, perhaps. That can only mean the assassin took the wrong computer and the secrets in Skelpick's laptop are, for the moment, safe.

A doctor arrives. He is in blue scrubs and a white coat, has an analytical air and makes it plain that he's not going to be rushed. He asks Slim to step aside so he can take a close look at his patient. She can hear another doctor supervising the stabilisation of Arnold and paramedics are going through a checklist. She moves over to the wall and unplugs the computer, notices Skelpick's scarred leather jacket on the chair near the sockets and slips it over her shoulders. The horror is sinking in. She's shaking and feels strangely cold and moves to sit in the sunlight that's edging into the room. This doesn't stop the thoughts that scream – your fault; first your brother, then your mother and now Skelpick! Your fault! If she hadn't taken the tablet, none of this would have happened. Matt would be alive and Skelpick wouldn't be fighting for his life in front of her. Your fault: you did this! And the gain? Nothing. What does Guest's corruption of the political establishment matter? Those people are always corrupt, always on the take from someone like Ivan Guest. Her contempt for her actions is genuine enough but she knows she must snap out of it. Hugging the computer to herself, she considers how to tell Abigail about the shootings. No, not a phone call because she doesn't trust herself not to break down. A text goes, saying: *We've been attacked. Skelpick and Arnold shot. Both alive. Medics/ Police here. Come.*

The doctor moves away from Skelpick and says to her, 'Are you a friend of the injured man? Do you know his medical history?'

'Yes, he was blown up in Africa. He has a lot of problems with his back and hip and . . .'

'And he's got a cranial plate fitted,' the doctor says. 'A crude one, by the look of things, but it saved his life. The bullet deflected and did not penetrate his brain. It's a mess and the plate's dented, but it means we don't have to delay and can transfer him to hospital.' He nods to the crew. 'We'll leave as soon as we can now. Lie him on his side.'

'But there's so much blood.'

'We're not out of the woods yet by any means, but it's not as bad as it could be.' Two male paramedics have materialised to help prepare Skelpick for transfer. The doctor turns away from Slim. 'Right, let's get the patient to surgery.'

Then the call from Abigail comes and Slim's professional self takes over and she tells her everything she knows.

CHAPTER 48

They need Skelpick's bike moved so that the two ambulances can back up to the door. A uniformed police officer follows her down the stairway, taking down her name and telephone number, the description of the man and the vehicle she saw in the yard, which he radios through to his control. No, she has no idea of the registration but believes the van was a Volkswagen and that it was new and well maintained. What size was the individual? How old? Did he have any distinguishing marks? Tattoos? Was there anything odd or different about the way he walked?

He was medium height, average weight, and the way he leapt on to the van suggested to her he was young and fit. She remembers now that he was wearing gloves as well as a medical mask. No, she didn't see the driver, not even a reflection in the wing mirror. But a third person was involved because the door opened from the inside and she thinks she saw a man's arm in the dark interior of the van.

They reach the bike. Before she gets on, the officer asks her to point out where the van was, and the direction she was coming from when she saw the man and which way the vehicle headed.

He asks for timing. It was about 5.15 a.m., a little over half an hour after sunrise. She puts on Skelpick's helmet, straddles the bike, rocks it back off its stand and starts it with the key she found in the leather jacket.

The officer looks concerned. 'You're not going anywhere are you? The Major Crime Unit will need to speak to you and take a statement.'

'Of course not, but you've got all my details.'

She parks the bike by the Church of the Cornerstone, the ecumenical outfit behind Middle Kingdom. As she turns the engine off, she sees Abigail hurrying from the direction of Midsummer Boulevard towards the back entrance of the Heights Building. She's followed by the staff members she saw at the Belvedere.

Slim calls out and goes over to her. Abigail tells the others to stay where they are.

'How bad are they?' she says.

'It's serious. They've both been shot twice. They're bringing Arnold out first. He's worse than Skelpick.' She explains about the plate in Skelpick's skull saving his life.

The ambulances have reversed into position. Two gurneys are brought out in quick succession by four paramedics each. Abigail watches with her hands pressed to her face. Callum, who has just joined them, is white and keeps shaking his head. As the second ambulance carrying Skelpick leaves, Abigail takes Slim's hand and says, 'We're going to keep going. We've got to publish.'

Slim looks around. More police are arriving, and now that the ambulances have gone, vehicles are filling the car park. A crime scene investigation van is reversing to the door. Two plain-clothes officers are conferring, one directing a hard look towards Slim and Abigail. They are joined by a woman in jeans, T-shirt and a loose jacket. Slim recognises the type, and she wouldn't be surprised to learn that just a few hours before she'd been part of the surveillance team watching the building – the surveillance team that wasn't there for the first time in weeks.

'I need to tell you something,' says Slim to Abigail. 'Do you mind if I hug you?' She puts the helmet on the ground and takes hold of Abigail's angular, tense shoulders. 'Guest knows we're doing the story, but the gunman took the wrong laptop.'

Abigail pulls back and looks into Slim's eyes. 'Are you sure?'

'Pretend you're comforting me. It can't look like we're having a meaningful conversation.' Abigail draws Slim to her, one hand around the back of her head. 'I just checked the laptop. Skelpick's story is all there. Maybe needs a little work. We can publish if you're still up for it.'

'Of course! Where's the laptop?'

'I didn't want the police seizing it as evidence, so I put it in the loo on top of the cleaning equipment. I copied everything on it and erased it. Doesn't matter if they do take it now.'

'Why did he take the wrong computer?'

'His was on charge. I told Skelpick to work offline – not connected to Wi-Fi – and I think he'd followed my instructions to use another computer for research and checking stuff. Maybe he was just waiting for the laptop to charge. There are no plugs where he liked to sit facing out on Silbury.' Slim shudders for the benefit of those watching, as though she is overwhelmed by her distress. Abigail holds her tight and Slim inhales her light, lemony scent.

Abigail says, 'What do we do?'

'They may be tapping into the in-house CCTV, so my ex-colleagues may have known Skelpick was there and was writing through the night, but they couldn't see what he was writing.

Maybe they missed that he put the computer on charge – who knows? What matters is that I have the story on a flash drive, which I will give you in a moment.'

'Who's *they* in this?'

'Hard to say. It's possible my service has been compromised by Guest. There seems to be a factional war going on, which I'm only just beginning to understand. There are a lot of people who don't want this published and that includes the Civil Service and the agencies.' Slim stops and takes Abigail's hand and wraps her fingers round the flash drive. She releases her. 'Okay?'

'Sure, I'm going to talk to the others.' Slim picks up the helmet and they walk together to the group, observed by the police.

Abigail says, 'Right, listen and do not ask questions until I've finished. Skelpick and Arnold have both been shot. They were stabilised before being moved to hospital. We hope they are going to be okay. We're going ahead with the story and will publish as soon as I'm happy with it. But I need you to follow these instructions to the letter.' She stops, draws in a deep breath. 'One, do not use Wi-Fi, even though you can get Middle King-dom's Wi-Fi in Goth Travel on the third floor, which is where you'll all be working. Two, say nothing of what you are doing to the police in the building. If they want to talk to you, ask that I am there with you. Three, I need more responses to the accu-sation of corruption. Make as many calls as you can in the next two hours and keep me up to speed with what you're getting. Four, make good contemporary notes or record the conversa-tions. No scribbling. Shazi will gather the reactions and trim them so that I can drop them as pull quotes into the text. Five, when you're done, get out of the building and do not talk about what has happened or what you've been doing to anyone. Six, do not ask me for updates on Skelpick and Arnold's condition. Shazi will liaise with the hospital and set up a line of communication with Arnold's wife and daughter as soon as the police have told them. Skelpick doesn't have family. Any questions? No? Good!' She glances round the group. 'Now, those of you looking sorry for yourselves, get a bloody grip. Don't screw this up. More than you can possibly imagine hangs on each one of you doing her or his job perfectly.'

When Slim and Abigail arrive in the newsroom, they find a police contingent that consists of several uniformed officers who stand in the passageway leading to the taped-off conference room and five officers in civilian clothes from the Serious Crimes Unit. These are Detective Chief Inspector Ted Nolan, who shares the job of heading the unit with Nick Price, a detective inspector named Calne, two constables, and the woman she saw outside, who gives her name as DS Briony Reed.

While Abigail and Slim have spent the last hour reading through Skelpick's story and its four sidebars at facing desks on the third floor, the police have been watching CCTV footage from the cameras around the floor. Two officers are at terminals by Toto's desk moving through the footage, frame by frame. DCI Nolan asks Slim if she's up to viewing the relevant clips.

She sits down between the two officers, still wearing Skelpick's leather jacket, which has now become a kind of talisman: if she keeps it on, he'll live. Abigail stands behind her, a hand on her shoulder. One officer checks they're ready and plays the film. The time on the screen is 5.10.00 a.m. They see Skelpick with his back to the camera, studying something on his laptop. He puts the earphones on and plugs them into the computer. He's watching a video of a woman speaking. He leans forward to knead his lower back then relaxes and continues to watch. They switch to another camera feed. The man in overalls comes through the fire doors. He is moving quickly and is dressed exactly as she remembers. It's 5.11.04 a.m. He hesitates and seems to be listening, then moves forward with a silenced pistol in his hand. They flip back to the first camera. It's 5.11.24 a.m. They don't see the gunman but there's movement in the reflection behind Skelpick, the glass shatters and he's thrown forward on to the open computer. A second shot convulses his body and blood rapidly spreads across the table. Skelpick never heard the gunman approach because he was wearing earphones. A second or two later, the gunman moves into frame and is tugging at the computer beneath Skelpick. He frees it, holds it up to let the blood drain from the keyboard, folds the screen and places it in his bag. He moves away without bothering to check whether Skelpick is dead. From the camera covering him, at 5.13.25 a.m. they see the man freezing, as though the music has stopped in a children's game. Evidently, he's heard the lift being operated. He turns slowly. They see his face properly for the first time and, although he's wearing the mask, the dark glasses are in his breast pocket, and there's a clear view of his eyes – dark, alert, empty. He moves the bag and raises the gun quickly out of frame. Nolan says, 'There's a host of information from that image. May even have enough for facial recognition software.' Slim has reached her own conclusion that the gunman was not a professional assassin. A hired hitman would not have shot Skelpick through the glass and would have checked that he was dead before leaving.

'Height, weight and gait, are all in the footage,' says the officer running the film. He turns to Slim and Abigail. 'This next part is quite distressing – will you be okay?'

Abigail turns away but Slim keeps watching. As the lift doors open, Arnold raises his eyes from the floor and immediately sees the man and the gun. There's no look of surprise, merely realisation. He knows he's going to be shot. Two bullets hit him in quick succession. He drops, seems to be going backwards but crashes forward to block the lift doors. Blood spreads over the interior of the lift and on the carpet tiles in front of it.

Nolan nods to the officer with the CCTV. 'And then you come on the scene at 5.24 a.m. These men wouldn't be alive now and have any kind of chance if you hadn't acted with such coolness, Ms Parsons.' Abigail rubs her shoulder.

They watch her tearing from Arnold to Skelpick and back again, trying to stem the blood loss, bending down to Skelpick then willing Arnold's survival, helping him with the paper towelling, peering at Skelpick's wounds, holding his hand, and then, after what seems like an eternity, the paramedics appear, followed by the doctor, at which point she goes to unplug the laptop, put on Skelpick's jacket and sit by the window with the computer.

'Is that Mr Skelpick's laptop or yours?' asks Nolan.

'Oh, it's Skelpick's.'

'Why pick it up?'

'I wasn't thinking. Had it on my lap. I felt I was going to throw up. I rushed to the loo and took it with me. It's still there.' What she does not say is that having taken everything she needed from Skelpick's computer and erased all she could, she gave the computer its first passcode, an extremely complex one that she invented for Softball. Nolan nods to one of the uniformed constables who goes to retrieve it.

'And his phone?'

She pats the pockets of the leather jacket. 'It must be with him – in the sleeveless waistcoat-type thing he wears, or his trousers.'

'Why did you run from the Light Pyramid?' Nolan asks suddenly. 'What was the urgency?'

'I run whenever I can. But this morning, I couldn't get Skelpick on the phone and I was concerned.' She pauses. 'Can I say this? You people've got four of our top journalists locked up. It's a big strain on our resources, especially for Mr Skelpick. I was worried about his workload.' Abigail gives her a look to say, 'cool it!'.

'Why did someone come to kill Mr Skelpick and steal his laptop? What was he working on?'

'He kept his cards close to his chest. Maybe it was a long project to do with corruption. The people in jail would be able to tell you. He works to our boss Dan Halladay.'

'What other stories are you preparing that might have brought an assassin to your office?'

Abigail says, 'Follow-ups on the Dekker gang story. A piece on the connection between the Dekker cannabis operation on his chicken farms and the outbreak of a new variant of salmonella. A new regular feature on missing persons. Corruption in local government over the issue of contracts for certain outsourced services. Plus, the usual round of court and inquest reports.'

'Impressive,' he says, but he's not interested and looks out of the window. 'Is there something you're not telling us, Ms Parsons?'

Slim waits for him to turn around, leans forward and speaks so softly Nolan has to move to hear her. 'The building has been under surveillance for weeks, so I'm sure there's nothing I can tell you about what we do. Every step of the way you and other agencies have been watching us.' She stops, looks at him from under her brow. 'Yet this morning, when a hitman comes to the building, there's no one here. No watchers in cars and vans. No police officers on the door. Is that not a coincidence, Detective Chief Inspector?'

He gives her a weary shake of the head. 'You've had a shocking experience, Ms Parsons. Don't get carried away with thoughts of conspiracy. We'll want a statement, fingerprints and a DNA sample to eliminate your biological profile in anything we find from the rear entrance, stairs, outside the lift and the conference room.'

'Yes, of course.' She has absolutely no intention of giving them anything. 'I have work to do. I'll be on the third floor.'

Abigail rises with her, and they take the fire escape down to Goth Travel, where a dozen young journalists are working under Shazi's supervision. 'Do the police know who you are?' asks Abigail before they go in.

'Not sure about Nolan. But the woman does. She didn't take notes and wasn't interested in the CCTV, which could mean they hacked it and know exactly what happened. Also, all the male officers wore an entry key lanyard. She didn't have one. So, yes, I guess she knows exactly who I am.'

Abigail exhales and makes a fist and gently knocks her forehead. 'We've got another problem. I've had an email from our lawyers. Lord Kingsbury is threatening to bring an injunction to prevent publication. He's one of those we've approached for comment, and he gave an unconvincing explanation for taking Guest's money, which makes him look a total idiot.'

'What're you going to do?'

'It's really awkward because the lawyers that are trying to get our people out of jail next week are the same ones that will advise me that I have to obey the injunction.'

'Not if you publish as quickly as possible.'

She looks at Slim. 'But that's a very serious thing to do, and it will all be on me. They've told me to hold fire until we talk.'

'Did you reply to the email?'

She shakes her head.

'Then don't. Two people have been shot and you're looking after your traumatised staff, as well as trying to keep the show on the road. How would you possibly have time to go through your inbox?'

Abigail bites her lip, runs splayed fingers through her hair and looks around. 'Okay, we'll go at two p.m.' They enter Goth Travel. 'I need a laptop now!' she shouts. 'And gather round.'

Callum brings one over. 'The story is amazing,' he says. 'Proud to be a small part of it.'

'You're a big part of it,' she says, opening the Middle Kingdom home page. 'Can everyone see? We're going big. Across the top we're going to have a headline which reads . . . anyone? Come on, for God's sake!'

'Two staff shot at Middle Kingdom by hitman,' says Shazi.

'Gunman hits Middle Kingdom and shoots two,' says Sofi.

'Assassin shoots two at Middle Kingdom,' says Shazi.

'Better. Now a standfirst! We need a summary to describe both the main story by Skelpick and the lead about the attacks that I will write.'

Slim offers, 'As Middle Kingdom prepared to publish a shocking investigation into the corruption of the British political establishment, a gunman entered our headquarters in Milton Keynes, at dawn today, and shot our chief writer, J. J. Skelpick, and beloved security guard, Arnold Frobisher.' She stops and thinks again. 'What about – here is the story they tried to suppress with a hitman and a silenced pistol?'

'Leave out the hitman and silenced pistol. Seems like self-dramatising. Somewhere at the top we need to put the latest condition of both men. Shazi, any news?'

'Skelpick is out of surgery and sedated. He's in better shape than Arnold, who's lost a load of blood and is still in the operating theatre. But they're hopeful.'

Everyone smiles.

Abigail continues. 'Okay, Shazi, you're in charge of writing that paragraph and keeping it up to date with all developments for the next twenty-four hours. We need photos of both men and small bios to go with them. Sofi, can you turn that around quickly?' Her eyes sweep the room. 'Who can get into the CCTV system and pull a still of the gunman without being spotted by the cops using it right now?'

Aziz, the naturalist, raises a hand. 'I've had a look. There's a clear image of the gunman at 5.13 a.m.,' he says. 'He's wearing a face mask but it's a good shot and in focus.'

'I want that alongside the most recent picture of Guest. Who's got the Ivan Guest photo?'

Callum sticks up a hand. 'There's one where he's hosting his summer party.'

'Perfect! Maybe that's a good source for more photos of him with politicians. Someone, look at all his parties over the years.'

She swivels the laptop and shows how she wants the top of the home page to look.

'We're going for impact but frankly we don't need it because the shooting is already big in the media.' She looks up. 'What I need from you all is absolute focus. Slim is going to do a write-through of Skelpick's story. The four sidebars are fine. For your purposes, she is the author now. The piece is nine thousand two hundred words long. We'll split that into roughly two-thousand-word sections. I want two people on each section, checking for mistakes and awkward style. This story must be word perfect. Skelpick is a masterly writer but there will be mistakes. As Slim completes each section, she will hand it on to the team that's checking it. Someone needs to look at the Guest bio that Slim wrote a couple of days ago. Please fact-check that to death.' Her gaze settles on two trainees. 'Now, someone give Slim a coffee, and all get to work. The deadline is noon, and we will publish later today at a time of my choosing. I will be on the fourth, writing about the attack and answering any questions the police might have. Any problems, tell Shazi.'

Slim sits down and opens Skelpick's story. Much of it is familiar because he asked her to read parts when they were hiding out at Top Farm, but she notices that there's something dragging in it. There's too much throat-clearing at the beginning and ten paragraphs in, it becomes too dense with information. She calls Callum over and asks, 'Can you prepare a file of all the evidence, like a table which includes coded messages, dates sent, the decrypt and identification of trusted parties and ultimate beneficiaries and amounts transferred into these accounts, so the reader can read it left to right and get it in a heartbeat?'

Callum nods. 'Everything?'

'Everything.'

Slim writes new introductory paragraphs that summarise the extent of corruption and Guest's position in British society, then takes in large chunks of Skelpick's narrative. Soon, she can send nearly half the story to the fact-checking teams, who are already combing Callum's table. She adds sentences towards the end where she wonders why highly paid, trusted public servants sell themselves for so little – just tickets for Wimbledon, help with the school fees, a Caribbean holiday.

Abigail wrinkles her nose at this when she comes down to the third floor. 'Too much editorialising. Let others draw that conclusion, which they will if we can get the story out there.'

Slim studies her. 'Is there a new problem?'

Abigail pulls a chair up to the desk where she's been working and tells her that two lawyers from a firm called Lucerne Gold, which is acting for Middle Kingdom in the OSA case, are on their way to Milton Keynes now and they will try to persuade her not to go ahead if an injunction is granted that afternoon, which, given the profile of the people about to be exposed, seems likely. They are due in the building at 1.30 p.m.

'You still think you're going to do it?'

'The story is very strong indeed. Great new structure. The table works well and saves thousands of words and Skelpick will love it. Yes, I'm going to publish it today.'

Slim thanks her and hugs her. 'Can you tell me when?' For her next move – her final move – she must know the exact time.

'Early evening. You are the only person who knows that so keep it to yourself. There's a lot of media interest. I'll give a press conference on the steps, explaining what we have and why a killer came to Middle Kingdom. We'll go live then as I start speaking at six thirty. If anyone tries to prevent publication by hacking or otherwise interfering with the site, Callum has a backup plan.' She releases Slim's hand. 'What are you going to do now?'

'Finish up with the fact-check queries then sleep. I'll find a spot somewhere down here.'

CHAPTER 49

She sleeps for half an hour before her phone vibrates in her pocket.

'Yes?'

Abigail says, 'There are three people upstairs who are speaking to the police about you. Blond man, about forty, with a soldier's look about him.'

'Yeah,' she says swinging her legs from the couch to the floor. 'His name is Peter Salt. I need to go.'

'Understood. Good luck.'

She goes over to Shazi. 'Can you take Skelpick's helmet down to his bike and wait for me there?'

Slim waits a couple of minutes before hurtling down the fire escape. When she reaches the ground, she crosses the car park at a leisurely pace as though she were just stretching her legs on what is turning out to be a suffocatingly hot day. As she rounds some bushes, she hears Salt call out her name. In seconds, she's astride Skelpick's bike and taking the helmet from Shazi. She starts the bike, pushes it off the stand and accelerates across the large car park in front of the church, giving herself a sharp reminder of its power when she skids and nearly comes off. She catches sight of Salt's waving arms in her mirror before entering the pedestrian underpass beneath Saxon Way. She surfaces in another open car park and decides that she'll continue like this instead of using the roads. She moves through the lines of parked cars until she reaches Secklow Way where she again takes an underpass. Although going at a speed that Skelpick described in his bike lesson as between 'sedate and brisk', she reaches the multi storey where she left the BMW much more quickly than she would if she'd taken the roads. On the top floor, she pulls up close to the BMW's boot so that she can open it and reach in to retrieve the backpack from the spare-tyre well without getting off the bike. She tightens the shoulder and compressor straps then leaves, tapping a credit card at the barrier.

A Lexus is waiting at the exit. She darts left going the wrong way down a slip road and heads for the Marlborough Street exit, then goes north. She takes it easy with the bike, getting the feel of the engine and gears and, as she corners, working on the counter-steering technique Skelpick demonstrated. She wishes Skelpick were coaching her from behind. In one way, he is with her on the ride because the warm air billows through his jacket and the helmet fills with the distinctive scent of his eau de cologne.

She goes round the city and joins the M1 near Luton then heads for London, triggering several speed cameras on the way. She arrives in the West End and parks north of Marble Arch. She has two calls to make – to Rhona, the assistant in the clothes shop opposite the Rock Seafood Restaurant & Caviar Bar, and to Tudor Mills.

The manager hands Slim over to Rhona, who is happy to help her with the made-to-measure shirt order. She reminds Rhona of her interest in one of her customers, the man with an eye for

young women and expensive linen jackets, the man who tried
to rape her. She's careful not to use his name and so is Rhona. Is
that gentleman at his usual place at the restaurant? No, she says,
but he's outside. He arrived later than usual – around 3 p.m. –
and has the end table of seven in the front of the restaurant.
There are three men with him, all in suits, although now it's
so warm, they've removed their jackets. There's a bodyguard
standing by a new Bentley SUV, which she believes belongs to
the customer she's referring to. But then Rhona abruptly returns
to the subject of Slim's shirt order. If she could call Slim back
in a few minutes, she will be able to answer all her questions.
Slim understands she can't speak. She waits on the bike with one
foot on the kerb.

The call comes through. Slim notices the time – it is 4.40 p.m.

'Hi, sorry, my manager seemed to be listening. You're talking
about Mr Guest, yes?'

'Yes.'

'He's leaving soon. He has an order for two jackets and six
shirts. The delivery is going straight from our workshop in
Hoxton to his place on Park Lane.'

'At the Culross Mews entrance? What time?'

'By five thirty. He's taking them with him on a trip. That's
what his secretary told us.'

'That's very helpful. Is he still at the restaurant?'

'Yes,' she says after checking.

Slim thanks her and hangs up. The only trips Guest ever takes
are on his plane. She needs to move quickly. She calls Tudor.
He doesn't answer and she leaves a detailed voice message with
her three phone numbers and the address in Culross Street, and
ends with, 'I hope you pick this message up, Tudor my friend, or
else I'm screwed.' She sounds relaxed, jaunty even, but just then,

catches sight of a haunted face in the wing mirror and realises it must have been a week since she's seen herself, let alone paid attention to her appearance. Glancing away, she puts in a call to Abigail to check that the story will go live at 6.30 p.m. There's no answer. She starts the bike and joins the churn of vehicles milling around Marble Arch, waiting at a succession of red lights, examining herself to see if she still has that thing – the thing that lets her uncouple her mind from considerations of personal safety to do what's necessary. Going through Matt's murder, her mum's death and Andrei's rescue, she knows it's still there and follows the stream of traffic draining south, down Park Lane. Moving at this unhurried speed, it takes a few minutes to go through Berkeley Square, pass the Connaught Hotel and enter Mount Street. She stops just short of the restaurant so she can see Guest's table between two parked vehicles from across the street. He's gesticulating with papers in his hand and, judging by the contortions in his face and the jabs of his left hand, is excoriating his guests. At least some of them must be lawyers and he's urging them on to make sure Middle Kingdom won't publish the exposé of his dealings, because he knows the assassin took the wrong laptop and this is his last chance. That's why he's leaving. The phone vibrates in her pocket. She turns away and lifts the helmet. 'They've got the injunction,' says Abigail. 'Our lawyers are telling us we can't go ahead.'

Slim hesitates then says, 'But that way Guest wins. A delay will be the end of it. He'll spin it out. We can't let that happen.'

'We aren't. We're going live in half an hour. It looks good. We changed the headline. Two decks, right across the top: "Assassin Hits Middle Kingdom".' She pauses. 'Other news: Arnold is out of danger and Skelpick is stable and sedated to let the brain swelling go down. Where are you?'

'I'm in London, just sorting out some business. That's fantastic news.'

'There's more. One of the cops just told me, off the record, that a joint search of Dempster McKay haulage company in Grimsby, the hub for Dekker's operations, by police and customs has turned up twenty million euros hidden in the sides of a container. It came from Rotterdam, same route as the slaves were brought in. The money was to be laundered here.'

Slim certainly knows who was going to launder that money and probably has a fair idea how, but she needs to end the conversation and says only, 'Jesus! That's a tremendous story. Bravo!'

'No, bravo to you, Slim! It's all your work. Tomorrow we'll do the big reveal – brothers from hell kind of thing and suggest how Dekker and Guest worked together.'

Slim thinks – Dekker's people are still out there; Guest is free. The dangers are huge. 'Be careful,' she says to Abigail. 'Be very careful.'

But Abigail is surfing on adrenaline and, unusually for her, heedless. 'I've got to go. There's a load of media out there baking in the sun – it's thirty-two degrees here - and I need to think of what I'm going to say. Speak later.'

Slim lets the helmet fall back, pockets the phone, turns. Guest is on his feet, jacket hooked with one finger over his shoulder. He gestures some final disobliging sentiments and goes the short distance to the Bentley. The bodyguard moves aside with the door open. It's Aron, the big Israeli that often accompanied them on his trips abroad. Guest shakes his jacket, lays it on the back seat with care and climbs in. Aron goes round to the front passenger seat and the Bentley pulls away fast. Slim follows a couple of seconds later. As she expects, the Bentley enters

Culross Street, then turns left to the narrow opening of Culross Mews, which is a dead end. She stops opposite the entrance, takes out a phone, puts it in selfie mode, faces the other way and zooms in on the activity in the mews behind her. Guest is out of the car now and instructing the driver to turn round. In the mews, there is also a Mercedes SUV, facing out towards Culross Street. The driver is almost standing to attention by his car. The rear door of the residence opens, and Slim catches sight of the dark blue uniform containing Milly, a petite and ferocious, fifty-something Chinese woman who has been Guest's housekeeper for a dozen years. Guest shouts more instructions from the door then vanishes.

The time is 5.15 p.m. The delivery of clothes should be made at any moment. She pulls the motorbike back on its stand and squats on the kerb so that she's mostly hidden from the mews but can still watch what's going on. Culross Street is surprisingly empty, and she has a clear view down to the back of the old American Embassy. In the east, enormous cumulonimbus storm clouds are building, lit by the afternoon sun. What she desperately needs is for the clothes delivery to take place several minutes before Abigail starts speaking and the story goes live. Checking the Middle Kingdom home page, she finds nothing has changed since that morning and no livestreaming is in progress. However, as she watches, a blank rectangle containing a circle with a 'play' arrow appears at the bottom of the screen with the words. 'Bear with us! Middle Kingdom livestreaming will start soon.' A clock counts down from ten minutes.

She calls Tudor and gets no response. She texts him. *Am at Culross Mews, back entrance to Guest's Park Lane rez. All my phones are on. Use them to locate me if you need.* She adds the registration numbers of the Bentley and Mercedes, presses send and lowers the phone. This is the largest of the three phones she has with her. She takes out the smallest and tucks it into the back of her trainer. It nestles quite snugly beside her anklebone, inside her sock. She refreshes the home page. The square at the bottom has come alive. A camera is trained on the front entrance, which is barred by crime-scene tape.

Abigail appears from the middle of the crowd at 5.22 p.m. and stands at the bottom of the steps, because two bulky uniformed male police officers, arms folded, occupy the top tier. She has notes, a first since Middle Kingdom came under siege and she started her evening briefings. She begins to speak. Slim pushes the helmet up and holds the phone to her ear. Abigail is asking for quiet. Then she says, 'Today we have suffered two attacks from forces that wish to prevent the publication of information on widescale corruption in our government. The first came in the form of an assassin with a silenced pistol, who shot two of our colleagues and stole a computer. Both men survived but are in hospital with serious injuries. We will bring you updates on their condition as soon as we can but, in the meantime, our thoughts are with their many friends and loved ones. The second attack came from the legal system, the familiar recourse of the powerful who wish to suppress information on their activities. This afternoon several proxies acting for and with the encouragement and financial support of one man, have gained an injunction to stop Middle Kingdom publishing the decrypts of encoded messages which reveal multiple bribes made to scores of politicians and officials.' She pauses and looks up at the media throng. 'We will not be stopped by violence or the cynical use of the British legal system.' She raises her hand as if she were starting a race and drops it. 'From this moment, the public will be able to see the extent of the corruption that's taken hold in our country. The story is now published on our site and across social media. Please read and share.'

Slim knows that she didn't name Guest because the clip would be more likely aired by the TV news if the individual behind the bribes wasn't identified. Abigail has become extremely adept at using the media to her advantage.

It's 5.28. She looks up. The street is empty. It's one of those moments on a hot day in London when a kind of exhalation takes place, and everything is paused and becomes still, and you wait for the city to breathe again. The shadows are unusually dark, the pavements and tarmac are soft and there are distortions in the heat haze. Substance dissolves and mirages occur. She can see just one person, a slender man standing in the deep shade by some window boxes on the other side of Culross Street, about eighty metres from where she crouches. She shifts the helmet back and shades her eyes to see the individual better. Now, she's not sure. Maybe just a shape in the shadows conjured by the hot air. Then she shivers, because she knows what it is – who it is – and why he stands there like a statue. He is warning her, as he has done several times before. A brown electric vehicle passes the spot. She looks again and sees nothing, just the deep, deep shadow. She straightens and murmurs to herself, 'This is for you, my lovely fuckwit brother. For you!' The van slows to enter the mews and she sees the name Linnaeus and Jones, Bespoke Taylors of Mount Street, on the side. She gets up, locks the bike and hurries to follow the van on foot as it negotiates the tight entrance. It's no more than thirty yards to the rear of the house. The van hesitates to edge past the Bentley. Slim's phone vibrates. She snatches it from her pocket.

'Don't go,' says Tudor Mills. 'Don't be a bloody fool, Slim. Don't do it.'

'I'm going in now. You've got my numbers. I'll keep this line open.'

'Don't!'

The van has come to a halt beside a space between the Bentley and the Mercedes. The driver gets out and comes to the rear of the vehicle, where Slim waits with her visor raised. He jumps when he sees her. 'Hey,' she says, 'you got here just in time. My dad's been waiting for these. Let me take them in.'

'You gave me quite a shock there. Thanks. I'll need a signature,' he says, searching for the delivery note in his cargo shorts.

'Tell Rhona thanks for doing this,' she says as she signs.

She's obscured from the driver who is waiting by the Mercedes. She removes the helmet and puts an arm through it, then takes two light suit bags from the delivery man in one hand and tells him to load her arms with the shirt boxes.

'Can you manage?' he asks.

'Just!' she says looking out from behind the shirt boxes. 'It'll save you getting an earful from my father.'

'But I'm on time,' he protests and closes the van door.

Slim moves away from the van and passes between the cars towards the door, her face mostly obscured behind the shirt boxes. Assuming she's come with the van, the driver waiting by the Mercedes springs to press the doorbell. It's immediately opened by Milly, who puts her hands out to take some of the packages. Slim ensures the door is closed before giving her the shirt boxes and letting the suit bags drop to the floor. At first, Milly just looks harassed and testy, but recognition dawns and her mouth drops open. A look of pure poison enters her eyes.

Slim unhooks one shoulder strap of the backpack, moves to the front and points the gun through the light material of the bag at Milly. 'Put the packages over there and don't say a word or I'll kill you, and believe me, Milly, that will be my great pleasure.' She now sees there are five tall wardrobe suitcases assembled on the polished marble floor, together with several smaller bags. Guest is going on a long trip. She waves the gun at Milly. 'Where is he?' Milly looks to the curved stairway at the front of the building. 'Take me to him. One word from you and I will put a bullet in the back of your head.'

They climb the stairs to a wide, light landing on the first floor, where there's another marble floor, big house plants and large abstracts on the wall. The place is like a hotel. No sense of a family home. She wonders where the brainless wife is, and the kid. Guest's voice comes from a large room that runs along the front of the building and overlooks Park Lane. He's on the phone. She pushes Milly into the room. Guest is standing staring out of the bay window. The phone is on speaker. He turns and sees them.

'So, here she is,' he says, pressing the off button. 'Sally, or should I say Alice? Or is it Slim?'

'I'm returning the tablet.'

'A bit late for that, Sally Latimer, who has come back from the dead. Drowned in the ocean, right?'

His eyes land on the bulge of the silenced gun in her knapsack and he moves towards her. He stands three or four inches above her, maybe fifteen pounds heavier than he was, chest fuller, and neck, with the ripple of new scars on the left side where she just missed his jugular with the broken glass, is now thicker and glistening in the abnormal late afternoon heat. His eyes, always the weakest part of him, except when angry and the irises are boiled dark, flicker with fear and calculation. She sees they are pickled from the lunchtime booze. His hand moves suddenly to the tuft of wiry black hair. He is testing her, seeing how nervous she is. She removes the gun from the knapsack and tells him to step back. He bares his teeth – not so much a grin as rueful submission – and obeys. The heavy, sour aroma of his cologne reaches her, and she says, 'Do that again and I will kill you.' She means it though she knows that to kill him would satisfy nothing in her.

He laughs and moves towards her. 'No, you won't. Look who's here. It's your friend Aron.'

She has time only to see Milly dart to her left followed by a sudden a movement in her right field. After that she knows no more.

CHAPTER 50

She is first aware of the difficulty in getting air into her lungs, then of being in a very hot confined space. Her hands are pressed to her chest and her knees are tucked up, so they touch her elbows. She's been packed up like a foetus. A tiny amount of light comes from an opening above her, which is also the only source of oxygen. Now that she's fully conscious, she's aware of the raging pain on the right side of her face; maybe her cheek is cut, and her ear, too. She is sweating and panting. Panic floods her mind. This is her buried-alive nightmare terror. She tries to control her breathing by taking in the available oxygen with deep, gentle breaths. Her fingers are numb. She works them to get the circulation going and finds she's just able to move her left hand upwards to touch her chin. Her skin is damp with sweat, so it's not hard to slide her hand and bare arm up past her cheek. Her fingertips reach some material. She waggles them and pushes upwards as far as she can and gropes around. With one more thrust she feels the teeth of a zip and the opening that is keeping her alive. If she moves her hand from side to side, she can push the zip slider to make the opening larger, which she does by a few centimetres. She now thinks that she is in

one of the tall wardrobe suitcases she saw in the rear lobby of
Guest's house. There's no motion, which, come to think of it,
was present in her mind before she became fully conscious. That
movement went on for quite some time and now she understands she was in a vehicle, and she had been on a long road
journey. But there's something odd about this because, although
she must have been unconscious, it seems to her that during this
journey there was always some light and air, so she can't have
been locked away in the boot of a vehicle without either. Maybe
they want her to live. No, don't be dumb! They've brought her
to a place where they can dispose of her easily. She tells herself
to stop thinking. Instead, she should concentrate on trying to
get her toes working and breathing steadily, but God, her head
hurts. The pain comes in regular pulses lasting a few seconds,
during which she screws up her face and groans.

She remembers that she had a phone tucked into her trainer
and another phone on which Tudor called and she kept the
line open, so he's got to know what's happened to her. She
guesses they removed all three phones. She can't feel the one in
her shoe, so it must have gone. But Tudor knew the Mayfair
address. And she texted him the car registrations. Or did she?
She's not sure now, although she does remember that both cars
were new and registered that year, which, together with the
recently acquired property on Park Lane, told her that Guest
had money to burn these days. Yes, and instantly she went into
that big room overlooking the park, she clocked the Renoir –
'Mother with Two Sons'. One boy in a sailor suit has his hand
on the woman's shoulder, the smaller one hangs from her knee,
cutely bored. Guest had no taste in art, or anything else, but he
hankered after this picture because it reminded him of his own
mother. Unadulterated sentimentality, but it's that quality that

sociopaths, criminals and fascists always mistake for great art, and Guest ticks all three boxes. She remembers the price was $35 million, but he's probably worked an angle. It almost certainly belongs to a cartel or Chinese billionaire, illegally removing wealth from his homeland. Guest gets to live with their asset, and he'll probably find a way of keeping it in the end.

The distraction of the picture helps. Now, she's concentrating on the sounds around her. Not much reaches her inside the large suitcase – if indeed that's what it is – because it's like a padded coffin. She tries to angle her head so she can hear better. There are men's voices, echoing in a large space. They seem to be checking something, going through a list. One voice comes close and shifts or kicks the container she's in. Should she shout? No, because she believes one of the voices belongs to Aron. There is a new sound of machinery, then the container she's in is suddenly picked up and placed at an angle. She's moving up. Yes, she's on a conveyor belt. The case is manhandled into a space and kicked again, and her right knee feels the blow. A door is banged shut and locked. Silence. There's no light and a new, much cooler interior air reaches her that smells of plastic and air freshener. She waits. More voices. People move about. Then two engines start, one after the other, and she smells jet fuel. She's on a plane, Guest's plane. Her panic returns.

A few minutes pass then, without any warning, the case is thrown on its side and the zipper worked. Aron is standing over her in the half-light of the luggage bay at the back of the aircraft. She's been here before, looking for an overnight bag that contained papers Guest needed. Aron says, 'You still alive? Get out.'

Her legs aren't working, and her head is pounding. He takes

hold of her upper arm and yanks her out, wrenching her shoulder socket and making her head collide with his foot. She cries out. 'Get up,' he barks.

She can't, so he takes hold of both her arms to pull her to her feet, not so violently this time. 'Now go clean yourself.' He points to the aft washroom. She gropes her way through the door. His foot comes down so she can't close it.

'I can't use the lavatory in front of you.'

'Then don't. Wash your face – it's a mess. There are towels.'

She doesn't look in the mirror straight away but dabs her right side with a wet towel. Only when she is sure that most of the dried blood has been wiped away does she look up. She is cut on the cheek, just below the bone, and on the rim of her ear. The cheek is still seeping blood. 'Hold a towel to it,' he says. 'And wash yourself all over.'

'What do you mean all over?'

'Your pits, intimate parts.'

'Not doing that.'

'You want me to do it?'

'Okay, I'll wash. Give me some privacy. I'm not going anywhere.'

He closes the door so there is a three-inch gap, and she washes, but not all over because she sure as hell isn't in the business of making herself more appealing for Guest.

Aron grabs her arms when she comes out, binds her hands with wrist cuffs, then opens the door to the main cabin. He goes forward and leaves her standing by the refrigerated drinks cabinet. Through the starboard window, she sees that the jet is standing just outside an aircraft hangar. A fuel truck is retreating, the mobile conveyor belt, too. The noise of the engines increases to a whine and the plane begins to move out on to the airport apron. Storm clouds in the distance are a dark indigo. It's starting to rain.

She's taken through to Guest. He is facing forward in his usual seat with the console. He has a bottle of Louis Roederer opened and a crystal flute full on the table to his right. His chin is down, lower lip protruding, eyes roving drunkenly. He's more than half-cut. Aron pushes her down in the seat across the aisle, diagonally opposite him and in the same place she occupied when he attacked her. He doesn't look at her.

'Find out what the delay is,' he says to Aron.

Aron goes forward. Finally, Guest's eyes come to rest on her. He pokes the bag containing the tablet and the gun. 'What is this? Why?'

'I told you – it's the tablet, the one you had Matt killed for.'

'Matt?'

'My brother, Matthew. Your people tortured and killed him and dumped his body.'

He shrugs indifference. 'The man who loved his sister so much that he changed his name and went to Ireland for a decade. You killed him because you abused my trust, and you took what was not yours. So, he died. Simple.' He unerringly lands on the thing that hurts most: the hagfish corkscrewing into the flesh with its primeval jaws because that is what it does, the only thing it knows.

'The police know I'm here,' she says.

He looks out of the window. 'Where? I see no police. I see no MI5. I see no one coming to help you.' He turns to her. 'Everyone wants you dead. You're a troublemaker, an inconvenience, and I will be doing them a favour.' He peers into the bag and pulls out the gun. 'And this? Why did you bring this to me?'

'That gun killed Matt.'

'Why do I need it?' He handles it, examines it, checks the magazine, aims at her, says, 'Bang-bang,' and lays it on the table next to him. 'Maybe you thought to shoot me with it. Some kind of karma. The perfect end to the story.' He's put his finger-prints all over the weapon, which is exactly what she intended, but that was meant to happen in Mayfair, and Tudor was meant to get there with his posse of armed cops before Guest took flight. A ridiculous plan. She prays Tudor has kept track of the vehicles that left Culross Mews with her packed up in a suitcase, and prays he gets here before the plane takes off.

The jet has been done out in a new slate grey theme, maybe because there was so much of Guest's blood on the cream carpet and two-tone beige upholstery. Striving to be classy but, like all his oligarch clientele, falling some way short. Suddenly she's overwhelmed by fatigue, exhausted by the sheer awfulness of Guest, and slumps forward on her bound hands, which are now on the side table by her armrest.

'You talk about your brother,' he says, picking up the gun and tossing it from hand to hand, aiming it again and again. 'What about my brother? You left me to persecute and torment my brother. So, we're evens, except you're going to lose your life, like your brother did. So, I guess I win.'

'I had no idea Dekker was your brother,' she says without raising her eyes. 'It was pure coincidence. I guess there was something in me that recognised the stench of evil, though.'

He looks at her and shakes his head. 'Whose plan was it, your people at MI5? My enemies? Who put you up to it?'

'No one.'

'Don't lie, Sally Latimer. Sorry, that's your phony name, but I'm used to it and that's how you are going to die – as Sally Latimer.'

He starts talking to himself as much as to her, saying how he'd trusted her, liked working with her, treated her like his own daughter. He's not so much angry as inflamed with a fever. He turns and jerks his thumb in the direction of the back of the aircraft. 'This plane has a rear stairway that can be opened in flight. But I'll save that pleasure until we're over the Black Sea.' He smiles to himself. 'It'll be like we are taking a dump over the ocean. And you will be drowned, just like Sally Latimer was. Fitting, no? But we have unfinished business of a more intimate nature, don't we? And perhaps I should break your jaw, like you broke mine, so you know what that pain is like. Maybe I should do that now with this.' He holds the gun by its barrel and slams the butt into his palm several times then picks up the flute of champagne and empties it. Suddenly he loses interest in her and looks at his phone, sees a recent call and presses the number and while he waits, picks up another phone and reads messages. He gets through but finds it hard to hear and puts it on speaker and bellows into the microphone. He's speaking in French, urgently seeking assurances that transfers have been made. Then he lists account numbers in English. Numbers and passcodes fly, mixed in with amounts murmured to the window. He's drunk but his memory is working and he's being clear and emphatic in the way that makes people jump. He's telling them that everything must be done in the first hour of business on the following day. Slim is listening hard. She knows that he's transferring funds out of his numerous Swiss bank accounts. Once Switzerland was safe for a man like Guest, but now Swiss banks operating in the US can't risk breaching regulations, even on their own territory. The revelations of Guest's corruption and the evidence of money laundering, furnished by Slim, artfully condensed by Skelpick and now published by Middle Kingdom, will be enough to

make him a pariah to every western bank. He's moving fast to
secure his fortune and no doubt the funds he's holding for others
because he fears the accounts will be frozen, but God knows
where he's putting the money.

The call ends. He turns to her and picks up his thread. 'When
you couldn't hurt me any longer, you destroyed my brother. I
will tell him in detail about throwing you, brutalised and half
dead, out of the plane.' He looks at her, eyes black with fury
but also some self-pity, because in Guest's narrative he's always
the victim.

'If you can get it up,' she murmurs.

He makes a clownish face of contempt, and she sees something else. With the menace and cruelty in his expression, there's
also stupidity. He studies her for a few seconds. 'Filthy fucking
skank spy,' he says, a comment that is accompanied by spittle
that reaches her across the aisle. He fills the glass and yells into
the intercom, 'Why haven't you taken off?'

'Waiting for permission, Mr Guest, sir.' The accent is foreign – Middle Eastern or from the Caucasus, she thinks.

The pitch of the engines changes, and the jet lurches forward, heading for the end of the runway. It's dark outside, a
premature night of catastrophe on the longest day of the year,
and it's raining very hard. Raindrops mixed with hailstones
are pounding the fuselage and bouncing from the wings, and
on the far side of the airfield, lightning veins the sky. A crack
of thunder follows almost instantly. The plane comes to a stop
and the pilot comes on.

'What's the problem?' Guest yells.

'The storm, sir. They've advised us to stay where we are and
not to move too far into the open. A lot of lightning strikes in
the area. Every ninety seconds, they calculate.'

Guest turns off the intercom. 'We have time to kill,' he says.

She sits up and starts speaking rapidly. 'You talk about trust. What about abusing the trust of the country that gave your mother a home? You stole from everyone and polluted everything you touched. Literally every one of those you bribed is now ruined. They'll all be investigated, and the ones suspected of passing secret information to you so that you could sell it on to who? The Russians? The Chinese? Or the low-life governments of Central Asia? Those civil servants and politicians will start talking to save their necks, and I don't imagine the recipients of that information will be overjoyed. Your operation is done. You're finished. Then, one day you'll be found at the bottom of a swimming pool or minced up in a bucket excavator.'

'You have a good imagination.' He shakes his head as though in possession of a superior knowledge.

'And what about the people who worked for you? I was the best assistant you'd ever had, absolutely the best. I know it and you know it, yet you ended up treating me like the other women in your office, fresh meat to be medically examined, abused, raped and cast aside. What a fucking low life you are, a truly despicable human being!' Her aim is to make him lose his temper, to get him out of that chair and away from the gun, but he just nods and grins.

'But it wasn't really rape, was it?' she continues, 'because you couldn't get it up, not like you needed to if you were going to sodomise me, which was your intention. And when you were unconscious and the crew came in and they saw you lying there, with your dick out – a little button mushroom – they couldn't help but smile. Penis?' A pause then she laughs. 'Peanut is more the word. Honestly, I don't know how you had children with that.'

Then he's up and beating her wildly about the head and shouting for her to be silent, for the one thing Ivan Guest never hears is criticism to his face, let alone jokes about his manhood. He pulls her from the seat, spins her round and has her bent over the armrest. Her trousers and pants are ripped down and he's pushing her head down with his hand around her neck. She feels the fingernails digging in. But this is what she needs to happen, because he's brought her to her feet and she's pretty sure that in the coming seconds he will be so distracted she'll be able to get free and go for the gun, even though her hands are bound. She struggles a little, which she knows will make him more excited.

'Sir?' comes the captain's voice. 'We've been told to go back. They're closing the airport until it's safe.'

Guest stops, releases her neck, stands up and stretches to press the intercom button on his console. 'Pay no attention!' he shouts. 'Tell them that the radio's breaking up in the storm. Take off now. I'm ordering you, now!' He glances out of the window as lightning crawls across the sky and a thunderclap follows a second later.

'We can't do that, sir.'

'Just do it.'

Slim turns and sees that he's zipping himself up. She says, 'A lightning strike on a fully fuelled plane!'

'They don't blow up. The lightning passes through the plane.' One moment he's raping her, the next he's responding to her as though he were talking to his assistant of a year ago.

The pilot speaks again. 'Sir? Mr Guest, sir, we've been instructed not to take off by the control tower. They say there are other reasons. Not just the storm. They need us to return to the hangar.'

'Just go. That's what I'm paying you for. There's a bonus for you both if you take off now. Fifty grand each if you get me to Tbilisi by tomorrow.'

'Our flight plan is to Inverness, sir.'

'A hundred grand to you each if you get airborne.'

A five-second silence ensues from the cockpit, then, 'Okay, Mr Guest, we're leaving now. Fasten your seat belt. It's going to be a bumpy ride out of here.'

'Sit down,' he says to Slim, 'put on your belt.'

'With my hands tied and my pants down?'

'Just sit.' He buckles his belt and looks out of the window.

The lights are dimmed and it's dark in the cabin except for lightning flaring in the windows. The plane begins to move forward and picks up speed. She readies herself because she needs to reach the gun before take-off and while he has his belt fastened, she has one tiny advantage.

The captain speaks again. 'Sir, there's some sort of emergency vehicle with blue lights tracking us. They want us to stop.'

'Ignore it. Take off. There's nothing they can do.'

'It's close and flashing its headlights. There's a man waving at us to stop, and the control tower is saying the same.'

'Ignore them! Take off!' He's hysterical, yelling, waving his arms wildly. He unbuckles his seat belt and scrambles across to the window on the left side of the cabin, stumbles and tears at the blinds. Slim dives for the gun, but she's hampered by the trousers and pants which are still around her thighs, and he instantly turns to stop her. She reaches the gun first, but he's on top of her, wresting it from her hands. She tries to shoot him. The gun goes off twice, bullets snapping into the fuselage and ceiling. Guest recoils, though he's not hit, and wraps one arm round her neck and goes for the gun. She knows he'll kill her there and then, and, gagging and with her head spinning and fit to burst from a second blow on the right side, she lets the gun drop to the floor. He's so enraged and drunk he doesn't realise and keeps throttling her between his bicep and forearm. She can breathe no more but, as she's about to lose consciousness, his grip relaxes, and she drops to the floor choking. He snatches the gun and rises. She lifts her head and sees him in a blur, standing in the aisle and swaying. He's deciding whether to kill her, but then raping a dead person is not so much fun and he doesn't shoot. Instead, he kicks her in the stomach and lurches off towards the cockpit.

She understands immediately what he plans because he's following her actions eight months before. He's going to hijack his own plane. And with that realisation, she knows she must stop him at all costs because if they take off, he will be able to do what he wants with her. She's coughing her guts up, but she pushes herself from the floor, kneels and looks round. Her head is spinning. Her vision blurred. She's about to be sick. She remembers the hidden compartment where she found the tablet, gun and money on the last flight with Guest, but she doesn't have the fob that opens it. Her eyes come to rest on the champagne bottle a few feet away. She gets up, empties what little remains, runs to the drinks cooler where, after three blows against a metal hinge, the bottle breaks and she can sever the plastic tie with the shards of glass. She takes another bottle from the cooler and runs the length of the plane to the forward cabin, where she knows that she will have to contend with Aron as well as Guest. Through the windows she now sees five sets of flashing lights, all police vehicles, she thinks. She also sees the vague outlines of men moving on the ground. They may be carrying guns. She isn't sure until a flash of lightning illuminates two individuals with helmets and guns running just beyond the wing.

The jet engines are at full throttle. They're moving rapidly to the head of the runway. She sees the police vehicles following on the tarmac, keeping well away from the wings. She is waiting for the thunder. Then, when the heavens oblige with an ear-splitting crack above the plane she bursts through the door. There's another fifteen feet to go before she reaches the cockpit, where Guest stands in the open door waving the gun at the pilots, urging them on. He hasn't heard her because of the noise of the rain and engines. Where the hell is Aron? She looks around. He's slumped on the floor with the dark patch of a bullet wound in his stomach. He must have tried to stop Guest and been shot for his pains. He's in a bad way; doesn't even look up as she moves past him towards Guest. Suddenly, the plane turns right to line up with the runway, and before the manoeuvre is complete, the engines are put into maximum thrust. Both she and Guest are thrown to the left. She recovers quickly and flies at him with the bottle. He turns, sees her, and lets off a shot before she smashes the bottle across his forehead and the bridge of his nose, causing an immediate spurt of blood. As he goes down, she lands the bottle on the top of his head. And there, on the floor, he remains, in his own blood and showered by a fine aerosol coming from the pilots' water cooler, which has been punctured by Guest's bullet.

The captain throttles back and applies the brakes. His co-pilot jumps from his seat and steps over Guest as the plane comes to a halt. He checks with the captain that the plane has stopped moving before operating a lever upwards then pushing the door out to the right. At the press of a button, a stairway unfolds from beneath the door and creeps towards the runway. Rain lashes the open doorway. He looks over to Slim. 'Well done. We didn't know you were aboard.'

'Tell that to the police,' she says and, pointing to Aron, adds, 'Now get a bloody ambulance for him and Guest.'

First on board are two armed police. One runs back through the plane; the other kneels to feel Aron's pulse, then Guest's. He shakes his head at Aron. Guest is alive but unconscious.

She is leaning against a locker, still heaving from the exertion of the last few minutes when Tudor comes up the stairs and puts a hand on her shoulder. She looks at him in the light coming from the cockpit displays. He doesn't have to ask her how she is. He can see she's profoundly traumatised. She manages a few robotic words. 'That's the gun that killed Matt. Don't let anyone touch it.'

Tudor says to the armed police officers coming aboard, 'You heard what she said. Don't touch that weapon until we have an evidence bag.'

Slim is sliding down the side of the locker. She isn't in a faint; it's just that she has no strength left.

Tudor tries to catch her and hold her up, but he's only just managed to get up the stairs himself. He's wheezing and he buckles, and the two of them end up on the floor in a heap. She grins insanely at him. 'We did it. Are you okay?'

'You did it, Slim, and that's the second heart attack I've nearly had because of you. Go back to your archaeology, please.' He puts his hands up and two officers haul him to his feet. 'You stay there,' he says to her. 'We'll get you stretchered off the plane.'

'But your operation!'

'Keyhole surgery means a quick recovery. Too quick if you ask me.'

She's peering out of the door now, past the flashing lights into the unholy darkness of the airfield, hoping to see something in the rain, an ambiguous shape that might be interpreted by a needy mind as the figure of a man, or, rather, the essence of him. But she sees nothing, and that's perhaps just as well. Maybe she and Matt can rest easy now. Ivan Guest is finished.

CHAPTER 51

A stay in a private hospital – thirty-six hours in which she mostly sleeps – is followed by the debrief, two days of it in Bridie's kitchen with armed guards at the front of the house and watching from the garden. The gunman who attacked Middle Kingdom is still very much at large, as are the two accomplices who waited for him in the VW van. Ivan Guest, however, is in hospital with a fractured skull and broken nose, and is charged with the murder of his bodyguard, Aron Tal, and hijacking offences, and is expected to be charged by the Gardai for ordering the kidnapping, torture and killing of Matthew Parsons by his regular contract killers, Adam Gorgiev and Aleksandr Lyanox.

The debrief is conducted by two female MI5 officers with Tudor Mills watching and Mark Boyd from MI6 taking notes on an iPad, which are being read in real time on the South Bank. His colleagues have become interested in Guest's relationships with two Chinese businessmen operating in Central Asia, the Russians of Cyprus and a Turkish gentleman named Mustapha Tunç, who has long been suspected of operating a clearing house for intelligence to the highest bidders. The process is not arduous, for MI5 have a clear account of what happened on the plane from Tudor Mills, together with the timing of her abduction and his pursuit and the scrambling of armed officers to prevent take-off. And the rest of it, the publication of Guest's log of bribes and favours to MPs and public servants, requires no explanation or additional material. The offences are, like the damage to the public's trust, self-evident.

Counselling is offered and rejected out of hand, though Slim admits to Bridie that she faces the void that confronts all those who achieve exactly what they want, particularly those who avenge completely something as shocking as the execution of a deeply loved brother. She feels light and untethered – aimless. Bridie attempts to repurpose her with talk of the funeral and her relationship with Helen, but in the end, it is Tom Ballard's visit to Wye Street that brings Slim back to them, though not in the way that Ballard hoped.

The conversation doesn't go well from the start, even though Ballard begins with a message from Halfknight. 'Softball and Linesman combined into one of the key intelligence operations of the last fifty years. In Oliver's words, you've performed an extraordinary service to your country and MI5, rarely equalled by anyone in this or the previous generation of intelligence officers.'

This is met with a shrug. 'You hung me out to dry,' she says, before increasing the charge to, 'No, you staked me out in the fucking wilderness.'

'We did neither.'

'And you were my friend, Tom. My comrade, my mentor.'

He's shaking his head and looking hurt. 'Truly, I still am all those things. These were very difficult times for us and for our service, Slim. We were obliged to move with extreme caution.

And you performed your part with panache and perfect timing.'
He tries to engage her eyes. 'I have to say this to you – the only
person who endangered your life was you. We didn't put you
in harm's way at Manor Farm or on Guest's plane. We didn't
hide Guest's tablet and cause him to hunt you and your brother
down.' He waits before he says, 'You did it all, Slim.'

She moves away from him to stand at the sliding French
window that opens on to Bridie's jewel of a garden. 'You're
turning the knife, like Guest did. Does it give you pleasure?'

'Of course not. I am very fond of you, but you and I, we work
for the state and the state must have its way.'

She whips round. 'What does that mean?'

'There are things that need to be settled. They want a
meeting – time and place to be arranged, but within the next
twenty-four hours.'

'If you let Yoni, Dan, Sara and Toto out, then, sure, I'll attend
your meeting.'

'It's not as easy as that. They're charged with serious offences—'

'By a corrupt system. Why are there no criminal charges for
the politicians and officials that took bribes, yet our people are
still in jail?'

'*Our* people! Me, Halfknight, Tudor – we're your people,
Slim!'

'I resigned, Tom.'

He tosses this away with an irritated shake of the head. 'And
you know we can't simply order the release of those who are
being legitimately held, just as we can't make arrests.'

'But you call off the surveillance team when a hitman comes
to visit, right? Why was no one watching the building on midsummer's morning when Arnold and Skelpick were shot? Seems
odd, doesn't it?'

'I have no idea. I was at home for that period, remember.'

'Feet paddling beneath the surface.'

He shakes his head, goes into Bridie's garden with phone in hand and asks the armed officer for some privacy. For ten minutes, he's talking, staring up at the cloudless sky, clutching his brow with thumb and index finger, occasionally releasing it to gesture to the raised border of larkspur and daisies. Eventually, he returns to her. 'Everything's to be discussed at the meeting.'

'Including my colleagues in jail.'

'Including that issue, yes.'

'And I want Abigail Exton-White there.'

'As you wish. Where do you want to meet?'

'Hut Six,' she says without having to think.

'Hut Six?'

'Bletchley.'

'London is easier, surely.'

'Not for me. I need to pick up my dog. I have things to do.'

He's looking at her swollen cheek and the suture strips holding together the deep cut that Aron made with his own gun. 'Are you sure? You're still very far from healed.'

'I'm sure. Let me know the time and I'll tell Abigail.'

CHAPTER 52

Laurie Tapper greets her and Loup at the entrance to Bletchley Park at 6 p.m. the following day, an hour after the museum closes. 'I see you're keeping out of trouble, Slim,' he says, eyeing her face.

She smiles and notes the gun bulge in his jacket. 'Enjoying a day out in the country, Laurie?'

'Never been to Bletchley before. Fascinating place.'

'Who's coming?'

'I open doors. Who goes through them isn't my business.' A few minutes later, they're watching Loup nose around the lake in front of the Bletchley mansion. He says, 'Seriously, Slim, I'm glad those sessions didn't go to waste, and you got through it all. You're a bloody champ. The best I've taught.'

'I thought you had me down as a wuss.'

'A Spartan warrior if ever there was one.'

They find Halfknight standing between the blast wall and the entrance to Hut Six looking lost. 'Ah, there you are, Slim! So good of you to come. And you've brought my favourite dog. I wanted a word before we go in. Ms Exton-White is waiting and we are expecting two others, a bit of a crowd in that little room, so I wonder if you wouldn't mind if we moved the meeting to the main building. Less hot and cramped and there are cold drinks available, I believe.'

He takes her by the elbow – she is struck by the old-fashioned gesture – and they walk toward Huts 11 and 11A, where he tells her that the bombe machines, originally designed by the Polish Cipher Bureau, and reputedly named after an ice-cream dessert, were used by Alan Turing and the mathematician Gordon Welchman to decipher coded German radio messages. He stops abruptly before they reach the huts and turns to her. 'It's important this meeting goes well, so I'd be grateful for any help you can offer. I hope Tom Ballard conveyed to you my admiration for what you've done. It is of historic significance, and the insight into ongoing foreign operations that were supplied with information by Guest is going to be very important.' She understands she's being softened up and doesn't respond. Now he's steering her towards the mansion.

'We're mindful of the risks you still face, so there'll be protection.'

'I won't need it for next few days,' she says.

'I believe you will.'

'Did you know where I was for the last two weeks?'

He shakes his head.

'Right, I'll be at that place again. It's absolutely safe.'

He nods. 'You did extremely well and in the most tragic circumstances. My condolences to you for both the loss of your brother and your mother. You are a very brave young woman.' Sympathy has entered his expression. 'I liked your mother very much. She probably didn't tell you that we met several times, early on in my time with MI5.'

'No, she didn't.'

'We were interested in certain aspects of your grandfather Jan's dealing in Eastern Germany, a technique he developed that I cannot, even now, discuss with you. She knew all about it. And there were a few other things we went through.'

'Of course, she never told me. What other things?'

He doesn't answer this. 'She had the gift of discretion and was highly intelligent. If my diary allows, I'd very much like your permission to attend her and your brother's funeral. MI5 owes a debt to your family, and I'd like to acknowledge that by being there. But, of course, if you'd rather not . . .'

'No, that's fine.'

They have reached the mansion. He lets go and looks up at the hideous facade and whispers the word 'abomination', then says, 'We're going to be joined by Sir Alec Miles, the Cabinet Secretary and the head of the Civil Service: essentially, the PM's right-hand man, and Rita Bauer, whom you've met. By the end I want us to come out of this with a result.'

'That's what Middle Kingdom is hoping for, with four of them still in jail.'

'Both sides may have to give up something to make this work, I believe.'

A table and chairs have been set up in the panelled ballroom, which is gloomy and cool. Bottles of water and biscuits are on the table. Abigail is seated facing the window. She starts as she sees Slim's face and asks what happened.

'Long story,' she says. 'This is Oliver Halfknight from the Security Service and once my boss.'

Abigail barely acknowledges him and gives Rita Bauer and Sir Alec Miles even less of a welcome when they arrive, but they don't notice because Loup is making a nuisance of himself.

Halfknight collects himself. 'So, here we are, after what have been some extremely eventful weeks.' He glimmers a smile. 'On the government side, it is our business to decide how to proceed. We must insist that this is completely off the record and not for quotation. In the spirit of the place where we find ourselves, this meeting is not happening and will never be referred to. Those are the conditions. Are we agreed on that?'

Abigail bridles. 'The gain is all yours. We're journalists. We can't commit to secrecy when you're holding our people in jail.'

'But that is the way it must be. We cannot speak freely if we think you're going to rush up the road to your office and publish everything we say.'

She looks at Slim who shrugs and turns to face Halfknight. 'That will be my only concession,' she says.

Halfknight hands over to Sir Alec. He has a fresh complexion, rimless glasses and a cowlick that makes him look like the smart one on a *University Challenge* team. 'The government's needs are quite simple. We require that you undertake not to publish any material that you have held back. I should tell you that the tablet was retrieved from Guest's plane and that it has been decrypted and read by GCHQ at Cheltenham and we are now aware of what has not been published: in our estimation, about twenty per cent of all that was on the device. You have made your point with these revelations, but we see no purpose in further damaging public confidence.'

Abigail begins to protest but is silenced by Sir Alec's raised hand.

'I'd be most grateful if you would hear me out, Ms Exton-White. Further, the government would require all copies of the tablet's contents to be deleted.'

'That's not going to happen.' Abigail is adamant. 'It's evidence of massive and widespread criminality, so we would be breaking the law to destroy that evidence. And what if we're sued for libel? How do we defend ourselves without a complete record of his corrupt activities?'

Sir Alec is unfazed. 'We would allow copies to be placed with the Crown Prosecution Service and the Treasury Solicitor, either of which a lawyer of your choosing will be able to access in the event of a defamation suit.'

'And if I agree to this, you will release our people from jail.'

'Yes, the charges will be reviewed by the CPS but after a period of time during which we will satisfy ourselves that the conditions have been met and you have not published further revelations.'

'How long is a period of time?'

'Four weeks – six, maximum.'

She leans forward, palms flat on the table. 'You've got this all the wrong way round, Alec. We've exposed your government as corrupt and incompetent like no other in the history of this country and yet you think you can come here and make demands of us.'

'It is not my government, Ms Exton-White. I am a public servant. But it is true that I am here with the Prime Minister's knowledge, and he will be eager to know your response to our proposal.'

'You can tell him—'

'Please, if you would allow me to make some progress, Ms Exton-White, before you speak.'

That does it. Abigail jumps up and stares down at him like a wrathful Visigoth. 'You think we're provincial amateurs, people you can intimidate and smother. But you have us wrong. Middle Kingdom is about real journalism and is staffed by dedicated journalists who won't be intimidated. Four of our number are in jail, several have been charged with obstruction in their own office and while entering it, and two men are in hospital with gunshot wounds. Half our newsroom is taped off as a crime scene, with blood still visible on the floor, and yet my staff continue with their work as though nothing has happened. We will not be silenced by a bureaucrat with a title and a patronising manner, *Alec*.'

'Please sit down, Ms Exton-White. There's one further matter that concerns us. We know Middle Kingdom used an advanced AI entity that was built by Dr Sara Kiln, Dr Ross and Mr Linna for the purpose of penetrating the government's cyber defences, at your facility at . . .' He looks down at his notes. 'At Tender Wick Park. We have located the relevant equipment and have established that it was the cause of the security breach.'

She sits down and folds her arms. 'I hope you had a search warrant for that entry, Alec, and of course you have absolutely no evidence.' Slim knows that Lovelock was moved, and Callum cleared the machines of all trace of her in the late hours of 20 June. Whoever breaks into Tender Wick will find some expensive hardware, but that is all.

Slim says quietly, 'There's a third party in these negotiations.'

They all look at her. 'Who might that be?' asks Rita, genuinely puzzled.

'Me. I'm no longer a member of the Security Service and as I understand it, Dan Halladay let me go from Middle Kingdom because he didn't like some of my methods.'

Sir Alec opens his hands in frustration. 'Can I just finish this point, Ms Parsons?'

'I think people will all want to see this, Sir Alec.' Halfknight and Rita Bauer look intrigued. Slim removes Skelpick's jacket and carefully hangs it on the back of the chair beside her. She

wears only a black sleeveless T-shirt and jeans and the bruises
and cuts she sustained while being stuffed into the suitcase and
in her struggle with Guest are all too visible. Her left upper arm
is coloured purple and a sickly ochre and either side of her neck
there are pressure marks where Guest gripped her from behind.
You can almost see the impression left by three fingers. She
reaches for one of the water bottles, unscrews the top, drinks,
then takes out her phone. Seeing her injuries, Abigail reaches
over and touches her left hand, an act of solidarity which seems
to unsettle the head of the Civil Service, for he must have
imagined that MI5's undercover agent was mostly on the side
of the government. Slim levels her gaze at him and he knows
she isn't.

The photograph she wants is ready and she slides the phone
across the table. Sir Alec picks it up. 'This is from twelve years
ago, a polo match in Gloucestershire. It comes from *Tatler* magazine's social pages. The photo itself wasn't digitised but, luckily,
the whole page of the magazine was. You will see Ivan Guest
with three women and two men. Next to him is the current
Home Secretary, Anne-Marie Phillips. On the extreme right
is her ex-husband Manfred Lange. To the left is a business-
woman named Felicity Black who stands with her husband
Victor Warren, the designate Director General of MI5. Behind
them is a woman who looks very much like the current Prime
Minister's wife, although she is not identified in the caption.'

To give Sir Alec his due, he hands the phone to Rita Bauer
and Halfknight with no hint of emotion. As they examine it,
he says, 'A picture in a society magazine from the distant past
means nothing these days.'

'Oh, but there's more,' Slim says as she is handed back the
phone. She looks for another photograph. 'This was taken a

few weeks ago by me outside the Rock Seafood Restaurant and Caviar Bar. You'll see Guest with his hangers-on; prominent among them is Manfred Lange, who I believe is still on friendly terms with his former wife, the Home Secretary – they have two children together – and, also, I remembered from Softball, one of Guest's regular companions, part servant, part ally. But that's not all. "The Guest Files", as the mainstream media has named them, reveal that Lange has taken numerous payments from Guest and moreover that Felicity Black, now Baroness Black of Altringham, has also been in receipt of favours and cash from Guest. I imagine that's why Victor Warren and Lady Black have a villa on Corfu.' She holds the phone up so that those on the other side of the table can see, then shows Abigail. Slim told her that she had something in her back pocket but gave no hint as to its nature. Now that she knows what it is, Abigail cannot help but smile.

The room seems a little chilly to Slim, but she doesn't reach for Skelpick's jacket. Instead, she remains still, letting this new information sink in and watching their reactions. Sir Alec begins to look appalled, as though he had been the victim of a great personal betrayal. Halfknight is unreadable, and Rita Bauer? A trace of satisfaction has entered her expression, maybe a hint of female solidarity, also.

After a decent pause, Slim says, 'The photographs, together with a six-hundred-word description that places them at the very apex of this scandal, will be published by Middle Kingdom within the next half hour, if Abigail agrees and is happy with my copy.'

'I'm sure I will be,' says Abigail.

'So, it's up to you,' says Slim.

'What are you asking for?' says Rita Bauer pleasantly.

'I have four conditions. First, that all the charges are dropped against Yoni Ross, Dan Halladay, Sara Kiln and Toto Linna, and they are freed immediately. Second, all the former slaves detained by the Home Secretary – a hundred and seventy men and women – must be released from Home Office detention. These people need to be cared for by the local authorities that operated in the places where they were abused and exploited. Those authorities need to take responsibility for what happened under their noses. That must start tomorrow.'

Sir Alec murmurs a protest but is silenced by Slim's raised hand. 'Can I finish? This is a simple matter of humanity. And if I do not have your agreement on it, my copy and photographs will be sent to Middle Kingdom, and then, Sir Alec, the government will be in much more trouble than it currently is, because even the right-wing press know that you can't have a Home Secretary who is compromised by her ex-partner's corrupt behaviour, appointing a DG of the Security Service who is also compromised by their partner's illegal actions.'

'And the third and fourth?' asks Halfknight.

'There is a Vietnamese woman named Le Thi Tam among those hundred and seventy people. She was rescued from a wrecked minibus by a man named Frank Shap. Without Frank's courage and her testimony, Dekker's people-trafficking and slavery operations would never have come to light. Frank may propose to her, and I believe she will accept. She should be immediately given permission to stay in this country.'

'And the last?' says Halfknight.

'Middle Kingdom must keep the decrypts from the tablet. Sacrifices have been made to bring this story to the public's attention, especially by the two people lying in hospital. The site may need to rely on them for future journalism.'

The room is silent for a couple of beats, like at the end of a play when the actors hold their position before the curtain comes down. Sir Alec gets up, pushes his chair back and goes to the door. Halfknight, with a slight raise of his eyebrows, follows him, then Rita also leaves. Nothing is said. Slim and Abigail are left staring at each other.

Abigail says, 'What does that mean? Have they agreed to your demands?'

'If they have, they'll never tell us in so many words. I'll send my emails, with attachments, to my former boss, reminding him of what we need. I'll say they've got until ten tonight.'

'He won't like you threatening him.'

'He'll be just fine with it. So will Rita Bauer.' She gets up, lifts Skelpick's jacket above her head, puts both arms in the sleeves and lets the jacket drop into place. 'How's Skelpick?'

'The wound over the new plate is healing well. Arnold's taking longer. I saw them both yesterday.' She stops and examines Slim. 'What happened to you? You're so beat up.'

'I've a funeral to plan. I'd better be going.'

'You were on that plane, weren't you?'

She hasn't the energy to lie. Lying was part of her old life. 'I had to get Guest, see. Couldn't let the bastard kill my brother without consequences. Matt was murdered because of what was on the tablet. I live with that, Abigail. It's why I can't let what he died for disappear into some government lawyer's safe.' She stops, looks down at her scuffed trainers. 'I owed Matt, and I owed Skelpick and Arnold. They were shot because of me.'

Abigail's hands have gone to her mouth. Usually so controlled, she drops them and comes to Slim, wraps an arm around her neck and kisses her cheek. 'Oh goodness, what hell you've been through!' As with Helen in the hospital, back in March, something in Slim eases; a discharge of tension that's been building for weeks takes place. She relaxes, then understands that Abigail, who's led Middle Kingdom through the crises of the last few weeks and taken the risk of publishing the Guest Files – it is she who is clinging on for dear life.

They part and Abigail grins sheepishly.

'Onwards,' says Slim.

CHAPTER 53

The Norfolk countryside, baked dry during three weeks of sunshine, is now suddenly overwhelmed by rain, which, on the morning of the funeral, eases to a persistent drizzle, greying and softening the landscape.

Because Slim and Norah Kinneal cannot stomach the idea of a procession into church with the mourners watching, the caskets have been brought from two hearses by eight pall-bearers and laid on trestles in front of All Saints' modest altar, now minus the plastic cover that protected it from the droppings of the resident barn owl. The pall-bearers hang about at the back of the church, while the Reverend Joanna Wilbury busies herself tidying the flowers around the lectern and straightening the wreaths that have become dislodged on the caskets. Slim, Helen, Norah and Liam shelter in the porch, Norah vaping and pushing plumes of smoke into the damp churchyard.

Nothing prepared Slim for Norah's beauty, now blooming because she's been clean for over five weeks. She had imagined a small, dark person, overwrought and druggy, but Norah is tall with fair looks and soft green eyes, a Celt from the far west of Ireland, who must have towered over Matt. Liam has inherited her colouring, but his face and expression are all his father's.

Up at the car park, Percy Simms waits in a white van with his son 'to do the honours' by filling in the graves when the funeral is over. A blue Ford transit has joined them. There are uniformed police, organised by Tom Ballard, she assumes, but no sign of the protection she and Helen became used to around the village of Fallow End after Halfknight insisted she told him where she was going to be. The police are directing cars to an overflow car park in a field across the lane and a few mourners under umbrellas are already beginning to gather at the cemetery gate.

The four of them go in to avoid having to talk to the first arrivals and take the front right-hand pew. Slim holds it together by focusing on the flowers around the lectern and inscription above them, 'Lo, I am with you Alway'. There's a hubbub as the pews fill up but she has no sense of the numbers until she turns round. At least sixty have come: more faces than she'd expect from her mother's village, six or seven from the advertising industry, friends from Matt's past who are clustered around Bridie and Dougal, a group from Dublin, and, from Middle Kingdom, Shazi, Callum, Sofi and Toto. Abigail, who offered to handle all the music after the meeting at Bletchley, is setting up her keyboard and, beside her, Bantock, looking uncomfortable in a jacket and tie, has his fiddle between cheek and shoulder and is tuning it.

The congregation senses the service is about to start and falls silent. A woman touches Slim on the arm. 'I'm Sally Kershaw, Diana's friend,' she whispers. Slim turns and takes in her mother's lover – dark hair, a neat figure in a well-made suit, pale pink silk shirt and pearls. Once a considerable beauty, she's still very striking. Slim gets up and shakes her hand, hesitates, then embraces her. Sally slips into the pew behind Slim, who is forced to move along by the arrival of the lawyer Annette Raines, who has been given the main singing role by Abigail.

The funeral for Diana Ruth Parsons, née Benski, and Matthew Jan Parsons gets under way.

She hears nothing of the opening prayers or the first hymn and only a few sentences of Joanna Wilbury's address, which doesn't seek to disguise the appalling sadness of the day with talk of the afterlife and – thank God – makes nothing of the estranged mother and son being reunited in death.

Norah and her little boy go to the lectern. Holding his hand, she gives it to the congregation straight – the years of addiction, Matt's frustration with himself, the arrival of Liam and the sudden recognition of the talent that was waiting in Matt to express itself for so long. 'Then the bastards took him from us. They hurt my beautiful, sweet man, shot him in the head and dumped him on wasteland like an old mattress.' There are gasps around the church. Norah stares at the congregation, tough and defiant. 'This is life. It cuts you down, but you got to stand tall. I've learned that these past few weeks. And I promise here, on the day of my man's funeral, that I will never fail his son again and, well – ' she looks to the front pew – 'now I've got Matt's sister Slim to keep me on the straight and narrow, don't I, Slim?'

'You do, Norah,' Slim says quietly. 'I'm here for you.'

'You're here for everyone, that's what I'm getting about you, Slim.'

It is Sally Kershaw's turn, but as Norah returns with Liam and opens the pew door, Sally leans forward and asks Slim to stand with her for the reading, which she then does. The woman clears her throat nervously several times before reading the first lines of Shakespeare's Sonnet 116: '*Let me not to the marriage of true minds Admit impediments; Love is not love Which alters when it alteration finds.*' Then her voice fails her. She looks up and says, 'I'm so sorry, I can't do this. I just need to say that Diana was the love of my life. The only person that I have truly loved. She was an exhilarating human being . . . I just can't read these words for you. I apologise.'

Someone speaks from Slim's right. 'I'll continue, if you'd like.' It is Bridie Hansen, who, unsurprisingly, knows the poem by heart. She moves to stand in the centre of the narrow aisle and says to Sally, 'Join me when you feel you can,' and after she repeats the opening lines, Sally finds her voice on the couplet: '*O no, it is an ever-fixèd mark That looks on tempests and is never shaken.*' They continue to the end, their voices ringing out in the small white space and piercing every member of the congregation with the words of the finest writer in the English language. Then, despite the presence of the two caskets, the little church fills with deafening applause.

Slim is left alone at the lectern. 'That was magnificent,' she says and passes a sleeve over her cheek to catch a tear that has made it over the wall of her iron self-control. She looks out on the eager faces who have come to help her mark the loss of her family. 'We'll get through this somehow,' she says, 'I promise.'

She's made notes on her phone but sets it down on the lectern and simply talks about Diana and Matt as people – her mother's clever, sardonic personality, her career as a chief executive, the research and attention to detail that that required, her love of a good time. She speaks of Matt's wit, his defiance, his brilliance as an art student, and his risk-taking. She remembers their joyous family life with Toby and refers to the addictions of mother and son and the shame that went with them. She thanks Helen

Meiklejohn for the care and friendship she gave her mother, also Peter Salt, whom she calls 'an associate', for saving Diana's life and giving Slim and Diana important time together. Slim holds up her hand. 'She left me this ring, which was called the spy ring and was first worn by my great-grandfather, Leon Benski. With it, she left a letter, which she wrote before she knew Matthew had been killed and she had a little grandson named Liam.

'Dear Slim and the few loyal souls who have turned up to bid fare-well to me.'

A laugh ripples through the church.

'Thank you for coming. I am very weak now, so this will necessarily be short. I want to say three things. The last few years have not been good. I missed my son so terribly. I was wretched and drunk and, to be frank, a burden to those I loved and to all my dear friends. My daughter Slim was a saint to put up with me over the winter. Thank you, my darling, brave girl. Thank you!'

Slim darts a rueful look down the aisle and says, 'I promise I didn't write this.' She continues,

'Second, I was blessed by the love of good people in my life – my dazzlingly clever and brave father, Jan, my children and the kindest, most loyal husband in the world, Toby. To the love of my life, Sally Kershaw, I must now apologise – she knows why – at the same time as dispatching waves of love and gratitude to her through time and space.

'Lastly, I want to claim a record for my father's family, the Ben-skis, the assimilated Jews from Lubin, in Poland. For generations

we have served the intelligence services in Poland, then the United Kingdom. My grandfather Leon was head of the operation that destroyed evidence that Polish mathematicians had broken the early versions of the Enigma machine. My father worked for SIS in Eastern Germany during the Cold War. And I myself made a small contribution to the Security Services, ending in 1988 when Matthew came along.'

Slim looks up and searches for Oliver Halfknight, but doesn't see him or Tom Ballard, though she'd expected both. She continues:

'This will come as a surprise to you, Slim, and I apologise for not being more open, but you will understand my great amusement when you lectured me about the Official Secrets Act.'

Slim shakes her head and moves on to the last lines:

'The point I wish to make is that wherever they were, the Benskis stood against the tyrannies of Communism and Fascism and fought for freedom, which is why I'm so proud of you, Slim. With love to you, my darling, and to all who are with you on this day, Diana.'

Slim looks up and makes a helpless shrug. 'Okay, I have one more thing to say. My brother also wrote a letter. This was three weeks before he was murdered. Norah wanted to read it to show that he was indeed going to be in touch with us. I felt that it fell short of what Matthew really was. Too many lame excuses for his vanishing act, and he didn't acknowledge the pain he'd caused Mum and me.' She stops. 'The real Matt showed himself three weeks later, when he was tortured and murdered while protecting our whereabouts. I can't go into details now, except to say that the men who were responsible have been apprehended and charged and they will face trial and long prison sentences. I want to say this to Norah. I don't believe there's a better demonstration of his love for Mum and me than the appalling sacrifice he made. Matt died for us, and I bitterly regret the impact on you and Liam. I blame myself for things that I cannot speak of here. Norah, I am profoundly sorry.' She steps away from the lectern and walks to the front pew and Norah opens her arms, and they embrace. There is a muffled round of applause, but Slim waves them to stop.

More prayers and one more hymn follow, then the priest asks for the congregation to remain in the church while the burials take place. There will be music. First up will be Annette Raines with 'Swing Low, Sweet Chariot', then Lambert Bantock with 'Danny Boy' and, in a duet with Abigail Exton-White, an air from the Isle of Skye.

'Now for the worst part,' Slim says to Helen as they walk behind the caskets out of the church, with Liam and Norah leading them.

Outside, they bow their heads against the drizzle and wait as the pall-bearers take extra care on the wet grass around the two open graves. Slim concentrates on removing herself from the proceedings and looks over to the trees where she notices a twitch in the dripping foliage that doesn't seem consistent with the wind coming from the north.

'Okay?' asks Helen, following her gaze. 'What are you looking at?'

'Nothing,' she replies.

Joanna Wilbury asks if they are ready and, struggling with

a flimsy umbrella in the breeze, recites from memory the old Book of Common Prayer: *'Man, that is born of a woman, hath but a short time to live and is full of misery. He cometh up, and is cut down, like a flower . . .'* The coffins are lowered on straps. Slim blanks her mind, then Norah and she are required to sprinkle earth on to the coffins. The priest continues: *'Forasmuch as it hath pleased Almighty God of his great mercy to take unto himself the souls of our dear sister and brother here departed, we therefore commit their bodies to the ground; earth to earth, ashes to ashes.'*

Out of the corner of her eye, Slim sees that Liam has escaped Helen's grasp and is moving forward, shouting excitedly to Norah, 'Da! Da! Da!' He's not pointing at the grave but at an untidy group of sycamore saplings about sixty metres away. Slim peers and sees nothing, yet she has a good idea what might be there. She shouts, 'Everyone, get inside. Now!' She scoops up the boy and grabs his mother's arm. Helen takes flight and, unencumbered, arrives at the porch first and holds out her hands to take Liam from Slim. Norah scrambles after them and they vanish into the church.

Slim turns to yell at the priest and the pall-bearers, who are looking around in disbelief, although the latter have let of go of their straps and one or two are making uncertain moves towards the church. Just then, down by the little bridge, a figure appears in a black anorak with a wide rain hood over a cap that puts his face in shadow. He is moving slowly, glancing around, stopping to gaze at the tiny, towerless church, as though he'd happened upon it by chance on this unseasonably dismal day. She shouts. 'Get down! Get down!' But the pall-bearers and funeral director are in full mourning finery and unwilling to drop to the muddy grass around the graves. Joanna Wilbury, however, gives Slim one desperate look and starts for the porch.

Not yet certain whether this is an innocent rambler, or a hitman come to the churchyard to kill, Slim grabs a spade that lies waiting for Percy Simms and runs towards the man, who immediately springs back, then goes for something hidden in his anorak and is suddenly facing her, feet apart with two hands holding a gun. In that fraction of a second, she knows that she's seen him before – on midsummer morning, walking briskly towards the VW van with a bag – and she freezes, knowing that she's going to be killed because there's no cover for her to dive into, and she briefly considers how stupid she's been. But before he can take one step more towards her, the area either side of the path ahead of him erupts, and it is as though long-dead parishioners are rising from their place of rest, resurrected on the Day of Reckoning. Covered in turf and loose grass are armed men with blackened faces, and they are yelling at the man to drop to the ground. Another has emerged from the trees. He is hung with foliage, like the mythical Green Man, and two more who were covering the path from the car park, also with weaves of bramble and grass falling from their combat fatigues, are running towards her.

The man stands stock still then kneels, lays the gun down, puts his hands behind his head and is forced face down into the path by two of the armed men who, by now, Slim understands are members of the Mills Irregulars. Then she sees Tudor himself hurrying down the path from the car park towards her, speaking urgently into a cell phone. He nods at her almost as though passing her in the street and rushes on. She follows. 'Tudor!'

He raises a hand because he's still talking. They arrive at the group of five armed men, who have flipped the man over on to his back, yanked the rain hood down and removed the cap.

Tudor takes a photo, then raises the phone to get the best coverage, and sends it. He waits with a finger in the air. 'Got it? Good. Speak soon.'

'Who is he?'

'We're going to find out.' He tells the men to move him to the car park. They turn the man again so that he's face down, and four men pick him up and set off towards the car park at a pace that's surprising given the incline and slippery path.

'Did you know this was going to happen, Tudor?'

'No, we didn't. You've had protection all this time, as you know. We assumed he'd make a move sometime and this seemed like his best opportunity. He was hiding out somewhere overnight because the police have had every road covered around here since dawn. He meant to kill you, Slim.'

'The same man who shot Skelpick and Arnold. Who is he?'

'I'll tell you later, when I know for sure.' They walk back towards the graveside. The churchyard is now empty and there's no trace of what has just happened. 'Today of all days. Rotten for you. I'm sorry. By the way, what did the little man see over there?'

'Must have spotted one of your men.'

He eyes her and gestures to the right of the gate. 'I was up there and saw it all. The lad was pointing towards those trees. There was no one there. Whatever made him do that?' He wipes the rain from his face and studies her. 'I reckon you owe him.'

Or his father, she thinks but does not say.

Helen, Norah and Liam come out of the church with the pallbearers who stand in a crescent at a respectful distance. There are more prayers, a pause for reflection, and very soon the burial service is complete. Slim and Norah wait by the graves for a few moments, then Norah gives her a sideways glance through her tears. 'What the hell happened then?'

'Later,' says Slim.

Norah blows her nose on a tissue. 'Matt would have loved the craziness of it. Thrilled by a drama, was Matt. I mean, just as they were, like, being buried! Jesus, what a fecking funeral! And what was it that Liam saw? Did he see Matt? He says he did. Absolutely sure about it.'

'Then maybe he did, Norah. Maybe he did.'

The congregation is coming out of the church. People are shaking hands with Joanna Wilbury and looking awkwardly in their direction, not quite sure whether to say something or head off to the wake. 'What do the people in the church know?'

'They were listening to the music. The few that asked what was going on were told that the bull had escaped.'

'A good story.'

'The priest's idea.'

CHAPTER 54

At the Turk's Head, a ceilidh is under way – what her mother would call a knees-up. The Irish crew have brought their own instruments – another violin, a whistle and folk drum – and a man by the name of Charlie Bricot, who Norah has mentioned a couple of times, is a singer and he beseeches her to join in him in 'The Foggy Dew', a rebel song from the Easter Rising. And by God, the woman can sing. Bricot steps back and holding young Liam by the shoulder watches in admiration as she finishes the song on her own. Slim decides then that Norah is going to be just fine.

The rain has stopped, and a weak sun has emerged from the clouds in the south. Slim goes with Loup into the little beer garden at the rear of the pub to speak to Tudor Mills who is brushing water from the chairs and forearming it off the tables. He shakes the sleeve of his waterproof and sits down gingerly. 'Not often you find a pint like this,' he says. Then Bridie puts her head round the door and asks if she is interrupting anything. 'If you keep an eye on that door, Ms Hansen, you may hear what I've got to say.'

He takes a long, meditative sip and puts down the pint, looks at Loup and says to him, 'Glad you weren't in the churchyard, pal. You'd have blown the whole operation.' He takes up the pint again and holds it in front of his mouth. 'So, the fella in the churchyard was carrying the weapon used to shoot Mr Skelpick and Mr Frobisher. Tests are being done on the shells collected at the Middle Kingdom building, but every indication is that it's the same gun.'

'And you know who he is?'

Tudor waits a moment, glances over to Dougal Hass's vegetable patch, next to the Turk's Head garden. 'He's Nicky Davidyan, son of Dominic Dekker and nephew of Ivan Guest.'

Slim sits bolt upright. 'Jesus, did you know about him?'

'No, we did not, not even Mr Ballard knew. But we've been learning quite a lot about him. Young Nicky was based in Rotterdam. We understand he ran the trafficking operations in Europe for his father and dealt with his uncle on the money-laundering side. A lot of drugs and big transfers of cash, too. A well-organised criminal enterprise. The Guest brothers did not talk but they had many overlapping business interests and used Nicky as the channel, and that worked well for them. We knew nothing about him. The Dutch police saw the still from Middle Kingdom CCTV used on the story about the attack and suggested the gunman might be him. They reported he hadn't been seen for a few weeks, in fact, since the date you busted Dominic, and he was charged with multiple murders and the whole UK operation was rolled up. Nicky's a nasty piece of work. Has a sideline in sex-trafficking and, the Dutch believe, at least a couple of murders to his name. He was basically the brains behind their whole operation on the Continent, and then you came along and destroyed everything they'd built up and Nicky's fancy lifestyle with it. So, he wanted to kill you very badly.'

'Did you know he was here?'

'You're asking me if you were put at risk to catch him. The answer is no. There's never been fewer than four people watching you for the last week. And you'll have that protection until we've talked to Nicky and made certain there's no one else out there. He's not a professional, which is why he botched the job at Middle Kingdom, but he's a killer and he'd have shot some or all of you this morning.' He takes a long draught and smiles. 'And I'm sure that you charging at him with the spade wouldn't have stopped him.'

Bridie shakes her head. 'Meet my friend, the kamikaze lunatic.'

Ten minutes later, Helen, Dougal, Bantock and Abigail join them in the garden. Slim raises her glass to absent friends, especially to Skelpick and Delphy Buchanan, who has stayed at home with a cold and is being looked after by Frank and Tam, and Arnold who is recovering with his family, and thanks them all for getting her through the last few weeks.

As they drink, the door opens and a woman in a black pillbox hat and expensive trouser suit, with sunglasses on the end of her nose says, 'I hope I'm not disturbing anything. You probably don't remember me, Slim, but I just wanted to say what a wonderful service that was. So, so moving and just right for your mother and Matthew, whom I admired so, so much.'

Slim has no idea who she is, but a glimmer of recognition has entered Bridie's eyes.

Slim says, 'Sorry, I don't know your name.'

'Silly me, of course you wouldn't remember. I'm Gaia Martens.'

'Gaia!' Slim says, vaguely remembering the photograph of Matt and their friends. 'Gaia from Instagram.'

'Yes, Gaia! Matt asked me to stay at your parents' home,

oh . . . fifteen or sixteen years ago. Bridie and Dougal, you were there, too. I found a photo from the time and posted it.'

The penny has dropped with Tudor Mills and Bridie, and the others sense something is very wrong. Slim shakes her head but can't speak.

Bridie says, 'You post way too much, lady.'

'I plead guilty. It's essential for my kitchenware business.' She gives them all a daft, slack-jawed look then blinks rapidly when no one reacts.

Bridie moves to take the woman's arm. 'I need to explain something to you,' she says, opening the door and almost pushing the woman inside. Through the window of the snug, they watch Gaia's expression move from puzzlement through a brief rally of defensiveness to horror. They can't see Bridie during the exchange but Slim imagines the terrifying anger in that beautiful face.

'What did you say?' she asks when Bridie returns.

'I told her to go back to the Pimlico Road, find the largest pepper grinder in her shop and shove it up where the sun don't shine.'

'Seriously?'

'No, I just had a word with her about posting stuff from the past. Told her it had consequences that she could never imagine.' She picks up her glass, swirls the wine and knocks it all back. 'Gormless bitch!'

'See what you've got yourself into, Dougal?' says Slim. 'Total psycho.'

'What can I do?' He gives her the big-man grin. He stands and holds out his hand to her. 'You and I have a date at the dig. Just us, I'm afraid. No one else.'

Slim glances at Helen. 'Okay with you?'

'Of course, pet,' she says, evidently pleased that Slim even bothered to ask.

They drive twenty-five miles to Alder Fen in the pickup because Dougal knows that he's way over the limit and, besides, he wants to continue drinking.

'Why are we going? What have you found?'

'You'll see.' He puts the can of Guinness to his lips, drains it, then pulls on his contractor boots. As he straightens, he says, 'Do you mind about me and Bridie?'

'Nope. I'm pleased for you. But doesn't the tattoo for Gus Gustavo bother you?'

'A little, I admit, but she is gorgeous, and I think it could work long term. You know what I'm saying? She's stunning and smart but, like with you, I have no bloody idea of what goes on in her life.'

Slim smiles and thinks of her conversation with Helen when she told her some, but not all of her life, as she had promised to do. There are things Helen could never understand, so she gave her the condensed version and that was enough to send Helen off into Delphy's garden to consider whether she could be with Slim or not. After an hour she said she could.

Slim says, 'You won't know what goes on, but does that matter?'

He gives her a drunken shrug. 'But you, Slim Parsons, I love. Always will. But it wouldn't work out between us because, well, you like going to bed with women – by the way, Helen's a fucking star – and you're ruthless and flighty.' He looks ahead. 'I just couldn't handle you.'

'I don't require handling, and don't particularly like the words "flighty" and "ruthless".'

'You know what I mean. You're a challenge and I'm a simple man with simple pleasures and an uncomplicated life.'

'I love you too, Dougal. But I will only let you go to my psycho friend if you promise that the digs and the archaeology are always ours. I don't want Bridie muscling in on them. This is you and me, going to Alder Fen in the middle of my family funeral when I should be saying nice things to those advertising folk from London. This is us. No Bridie, okay?' He nods and they fist bump. 'I love you and always will, you big lunk. You're my pal.'

They're silent for a few miles then she says she wishes there had been music specifically for Matt in the funeral. Dougal plugs in his phone and waits for his selection: Dylan's 'You're Gonna Make Me Lonesome When You Go'. Partway through, they sing the line at the top of their voices, *'I'll see you in the sky above, In the tall grass, in the ones I love.'* And he plays it a second time, so they can belt it out again, at which point Loup, who has been moving restlessly in the back seat, suddenly howls like a wolf.

They turn down the lane that leads to Alder Fen. Slim sees the four willows are all silvery in the breeze and she begins to feel the old excitement in the windswept plain of mud where she has spent so much time on her knees, picking at the dirt and absorbed in the possibilities of what lay beneath her.

'Who's that?' says Dougal sitting up and peering at a car parked near the entrance to the dig. She slows down. A man gets out. She waits. He waves to them. 'It's bloody Laurie Tapper. What's he doing here?'

'Who's Laurie Tapper?'

'Someone I once worked with.'

'In your other life – the one that means you disappear for years and never want your photograph taken.'

Laurie starts walking from the grey Jaguar – plainly, an official car. She winds down the window. 'Hi there, Slim, if you wouldn't mind waiting for a moment, that would be champion.'

He says hello to Dougal, who asks him what the hell he's doing at the dig. 'It's restricted access,' he says, working another ring pull.

'We won't be long, sir. If we could speak to Slim for a few minutes, then we'll be on our way.' He walks back to the Jag, waits a few seconds then waves to Slim. She gets out and beckons Loup, who shoots out and circles both cars with his nose to the ground. Tapper opens the rear door and Oliver Halfknight gets out.

'Hello, Slim. I'm sorry I couldn't be at the funeral.'

'What're you doing here? Is this part of the round-the-clock protection?'

'I've to come to tell you of some recent developments, which will explain why Tom Ballard didn't attend either. He sends his apologies.'

'Are you now DG?' she says eyeing his immaculate ride. She knows that Warren has withdrawn while his wife is investigated.

'Yes, no doubt for my sins.' He doesn't bother with the hopeless look but regards her steadily.

'So, Loup was wrong when he sucked up to Rita Bauer.'

He smiles. 'As it turned out, no. From tomorrow, Rita becomes Cabinet Secretary and head of the Civil Service. Second only to the Prime Minister in importance. She has replaced Alec Miles.'

'She knew all the time she was sitting in that meeting with Sir Alec.'

'It was only a possibility at that stage.'

'So, exactly why are you here?'

He walks a little way from the car. Tapper is occupying himself throwing a stick for Loup. 'Ivan Guest was murdered in hospital where he was being treated for the head injury that you gave him. He was under guard, but a woman, disguised as a nurse, gained access to the private room in the early hours of this morning and injected him with a lethal combination of morphine and fentanyl. Six hours later, Dominic Dekker was stabbed to death while on remand, a frenzied attack, apparently involving numerous individuals.'

'Jesus! Organised crime? Foreign intelligence service? Which was it?'

'We think a combination of the two. Guest's murder was state-sponsored assassination, no doubt about that. The Dekker murder was probably contracted in the underworld. The brothers didn't speak, as you know, but that didn't mean they were ignorant of each other's affairs, so it was important to silence both. I cannot pretend that it isn't a blow to us. Ivan was talking. The intelligence was of a very high order indeed, and the police had every hope of gaining his brother's confidence.'

'So, no trials.'

'Which will certainly make your life easier. But there will, of course, be court cases for the members of Dekker's gang for murder, rape, slavery, people trafficking, disposing of bodies illegally, and God knows what else, and your evidence will be required, but that can be given from behind a screen. And, of course, you were the main witness to Nicky Davidyan's attack on Middle Kingdom and this morning's business.' He looks up at the enormous clouds hurtling from over the North Sea. 'Now that Guest is dead, the trail will go cold quickly. There are connections we must map, knowledge we must secure while we can. I'm setting up a special section, headed by Tom. We need to know what those people who were compromised by Guest have given to the foreign intelligence services.'

'You shouldn't be telling me this. I resigned.'

'I want you to come back as Tom's deputy from next week.' He glances at the pickup. Dougal has his hand out of the window and is gently drumming the side of the passenger door. 'You have extraordinary talents, Slim, and we need you.'

This does take the wind out of her sails. She shakes her head. 'I'm burned. You know that.'

'In the field, yes. But you have qualities of leadership and decisiveness that we value. Rita is a particular admirer of yours, and rightly so.'

'Work in the office with people like Alantree?'

'You would be several grades above him.'

She waits a few moments before saying, 'And my mother, what did she do for MI5 in the eighties?'

'As you say, you are not currently a member of the service, and I would be breaking the Official Secrets Act if I said anything about her time.' He smiles down at her. 'There is something else I wanted to talk to you about. You did well to get your friends at Middle Kingdom released and the charges dropped. A nice piece of footwork if I may say so.'

'And it suited you.'

'Indeed. But there are unresolved matters.'

'Like what?'

'The AI they used against the government represents an enormous threat to us and, in fact, to every state in the world.' She says nothing. 'We need to come to an arrangement with Mr Ross and Dr Kiln and Mr Linna. You're the only one who's seen it operating, and I believe you're the best person to negotiate that arrangement.'

They want Lovelock for the state, the power to tunnel under the defences of foreign governments and collect intelligence without them knowing. She shakes her head. 'Yoni, Sara and Toto will see you coming from miles off. They're not that stupid.'

'Think about it.' He looks at the high-security fence that now surrounds the dig. 'What have you come to see? It must be important for you to break off from the wake. I'd love to have a look.'

'Some things must remain secret, even from you, Director General. Sorry.'

Loup trots over and looks up at him. 'He's got the news about your appointment.'

'Intelligent dog. I'm sure we can find a place for him, too.'

'He's committed to journalism.'

'That's a pity.'

'Well . . . he's a newshound.'

He smiles again. Laurie is holding out a phone to him. 'It seems I'm needed.' He takes her hand. 'Think about it and give me an answer when you feel you can. In the meantime, I want you to know that we will always be profoundly in your debt.' He holds on to her. 'That ring you wear and your family's dedication to our game for over a century, they are things to be proud of.'

'Yes, nice of Mum to out me like that.'

'I gather no one picked it up.'

'You had people in the congregation?'

'We felt it wise.' He lets go and walks to take the phone from Laurie and slides into the back seat.

Dougal wanders over to her. 'I won't ask.'

'Best not to,' she says, watching the Jaguar turn.

'Who was he? What did he want?'

'A friend of my mum's. He told me about two murders and offered me a job.'

'The usual, then.'

There are no longer larks singing but a flock of plovers rises when Loup hunts along the mounds of soil left by the company prospecting for brick clay, which are now carpeted with grasses, ox-eye daisies and blue sage. Covering the entire area where the boat lay and the four-thousand-year-old posts were unearthed, is a taut, white plastic tent.

'Looks like a crime scene,' she says.

He enters the code on an electronic padlock on the door of the tent. An alarm sounds and immediately there's a disturbance in the grass a little distance away. Jimmy from King's Lynn and Ellie the Scots dendrochronologist, both wearing sun hats and with binoculars, rise from the vegetation and call greetings. 'Security until the night team arrive at six,' murmurs Dougal, keying numbers into a pad inside the tent to shut off the alarm.

Jimmy and Ellie arrive at the entrance and greet Slim warmly. They're followed by Tustin, the man who videos the dig. Jimmy and Tustin are wearing oversized camouflage, which, in Dougal's opinion, is absurd, because the purpose of guarding the site is to be seen, not merge into the landscape. Ellie has a red face and looks as though she's been doing some hard kissing which, judging by Jimmy's sheepish expression, she has.

'You can look after the dog and keep an eye out,' he says to them. 'I'm going to bring Slim up to date with what we've been finding. We shouldn't be long.'

He leads her across a grid of scaffolding planks to a blue plastic sheet, seven metres in length and three across, which is pegged down beyond the two Bronze Age wooden posts that he showed her in the spring.

'You've got another log boat,' she says.

'Yep, we raised it a couple of days ago.'

They pull the pegs out and each takes a corner at one end and they walk the sheet back. She turns and sees a skeleton that is not yet fully uncovered. 'Only you would bring me to look at a skeleton on the day I buried my family.'

'This is archaeology,' he says without apology and lobs her a brush. 'The hips suggest a woman. She was petite and young – probably no more than sixteen or seventeen.'

'The same age as the Boatman.'

'Within a year or two. The two boats are dated to the same period, about eighty years after the trees were felled for the posts in—'

'2027 BC.'

'Yes, well remembered. So, for the moment, we are assuming the individuals were contemporaries, though there's nothing to say they were. You recall the male had the look of someone who had suffered extreme anguish. The skull seemed to scream and there were injuries – cut marks. But his neighbour looks somehow at peace with her fate.'

She crouches by the side of the skeleton. The woman is lying on her back, legs straight and together. Maybe there's something in the soil between her hands, another rush bag, perhaps. The skull is tilted back, as if she fell asleep, and the jaw is clamped shut. Her teeth are all intact.

'We didn't find her until yesterday because there was much more silt between the bottom of the boat and the skeleton. Then Jimmy noticed this, on the surface of the mud.' He picks up a plastic envelope from a collapsible aluminium table and moves to show it to her. Inside is a small bronze ring, beautifully smooth. 'Where there is a ring there is sometimes a hand, so we began excavating. And here we are. Why don't you start work around the skull and neck?'

'Not unless you do it with me.'

'Get on with it, woman! I've got a suit on.'

'So have I. You know there's something here.'

'Just a feeling. Honestly! We haven't touched that part.'

'Come down here, and we'll work on it together.'

He removes his jacket, undoes his tie, lays them on the table and picks up a brush and trowel for each of them. He crouches opposite her, and they begin to brush and pick the dirt away from around the skull.

After fifteen minutes of working at the soil, Dougal says, 'If they died at the same time, it's interesting to speculate why. Did they transgress? Were they sacrificed to appease the Gods?'

One of the trowels encounters something hard and metallic a few inches above the skull and they both hear a tiny noise, a chink maybe. They peer at an object that seems to be curved and is about two centimetres wide. They exchange looks and brush round it with their faces close to the earth, the smell of the Bronze Age filling their nostrils. Dougal licks two fingers and rubs the object in the middle of the exposed part. There's a dusty yellow tinge to it. It's gold, a band of gold; a crown maybe.

Slim gasps. They continue brushing tiny amounts of soil away.

Dougal is breathing heavily and wants to finish his speculation about the young couple to calm himself. 'Was she of noble birth, perhaps? Did the tradition of her tribe require a companion for her in the afterlife? Or were these two—?'

'Brother and sister,' she says. 'He was tortured and murdered, and she lies grieving for eternity.'

Dougal straightens and rests his big paw of a hand on her shoulder. Slim lets her trowel fall to the dirt and weeps.

ACKNOWLEDGEMENTS

The idea for *The Enigma Girl* came from a conversation during the pandemic with my friend and film and tv agent, Charles Collier – now the boss of Chalcot Square Arts and Media Management – which led me to Milton Keynes and the wartime codebreaking centre of Bletchley Park, in the south of the newly created city. When Covid 19 restrictions lifted, I visited during some deserted, foggy days and was completely captivated by the strangeness of the place. So, I thank Charles for setting me off on a journey which lasted three years and included many visits to Milton Keynes.

My story is set in a modern news site, Middle Kingdom, which has all the virtues of an old provincial news operation yet is fired by a youthful investigative spirit and fury about the lying and frauds of our post-truth world. Their beat is the part of England that lies between East Anglia and the Midlands and stretches from Hertfordshire to the city of Peterborough and the Fens in the north, an area that seems to me to have character but not an identity and which I think of as Middle Kingdom.

I travelled all over and found myself going down a lot of rabbit holes. I became intrigued by the Bronze Age archaeological sites around Peterborough and the writings of the archaeologist Francis Pryor who masterminded the dig at Flag Fen causeway after making the discovery in 1982. It is on a dig very much like Flag Fen that my spy hero Slim Parsons spends one winter keeping her head down and making miraculous finds. Owing to my friend, the editor and writer Liz Jobey, I fell in love with the church of All Saints, Waterden, a village that disappeared in late mediaeval times leaving the church extremely isolated, even by Norfolk's standards. It is magical place and I have set two important scenes there.

I need to thank the nameless multitude who helped me in Milton Keynes, guided me on the ways of the Grand Union Canal, answered questions at the Bletchley Park Museum and, in one instance, gave me unaccompanied access to Flag Fen Archaeology Park when it was closed for training. Both Bletchley and the 3,000-year-old log boats of Flag Fen are truly worth the journey.

There is a big Polish element to *The Enigma Girl*, which is due in no small part to a remarkable book by Alan Turing's nephew, Dermot. *XY&Z, The Real Story of How Enigma Was Broken* gives credit to the Polish codebreakers who cracked the commercial version of the Enigma machine in the 1930s, and is a brilliant account of the French, British and Polish intelligence operations as Europe plunged towards war. Dermot Turing's book deserves to be regarded as a classic.

I need also to salute the memoir of the late Michal Giedroyc, *Crater's Edge: A Family's Epic Journey through Wartime Russia*, which filled out for me the miraculous story of the escape from the Soviet Union of Polish soldiers and civilians under General Władysław Anders. I first came across this piece of war history in the memorial in the old Polish camp of Northwick Park in Gloucestershire – relocated twenty-five miles east in *The Enigma Girl* and renamed Tender Wick. I have lifted elements of Giedroyc's gruelling tale of survival and placed it in my hero's backstory, so, in his place, I thank his children Coky, Anna, Mel and Michal.

My usual strategy of avoiding unnecessary work failed and the book ended up over 200,000 words long. After two sessions of ruthless cutting, advised by my editor Jane Wood, I reduced it to a more or less manageable size. I thank her for her wisdom, shrewdness and patience during the process. Also, thanks are owed to my new agent Annabel Merullo who gave me great notes on the final manuscript and more support than I was due during the writing.

Every writer's nightmare is technical failure and loss of work. On both occasions it happened to me, my book and sanity were saved by Kyle Allard of Remote IT Rescue Ltd. He has the best bedside manner in the business.

This book is dedicated to three doctors: my late sister-in-law, Annie; my GP, Toby Dean; and my brother-in-law Mike. It would not have been written without them saving my bacon in 2020. While I'm about it, I should thank Dr Matthew Banks, Professor Paris Tekkis and Professor Eric Lim, who have equal claim to my gratitude. Because of their work, I lived to write another day.

Finally, thanks are due to my wife, Liz, who put up with me writing on holiday and into the night and gave me huge support through the three years of work and, also, to my daughters Miranda Lanyado and Charlie P., who never seem to lose faith.